The Secret Diary of
Hendrik Groen

The
Secret Diary of
Hendrik Groen

HENDRIK GROEN

Translated by
Hester Velmans

GRAND CENTRAL
PUBLISHING

NEW YORK   BOSTON

Copyright © 2014 by Hendrik Groen en Meulenhoff Boekerij b.v., Amsterdam
Translation copyright © 2016 by Hester Velmans

Cover copyright © 2017 by Hachette Book Group, Inc.

Grand Central Publishing
Hachette Book Group
1290 Avenue of the Americas, New York, NY 10104
grandcentralpublishing.com
twitter.com/grandcentralpub

First published in the Netherlands as *Attempts to Make Something of Life. The Secret Diary of Hendrik Groen, 83¼ Years Old* by Meulenhoff 2014. First published in Great Britain by Michael Joseph 2016.
First U.S. Edition: July 2017

Grand Central Publishing is a division of Hachette Book Group, Inc. The Grand Central Publishing name and logo is a trademark of Hachette Book Group, Inc.

The publisher is not responsible for websites (or their content) that are not owned by the publisher.

The Hachette Speakers Bureau provides a wide range of authors for speaking events. To find out more, go to www.hachettespeakersbureau.com or call (866) 376-6591.

Library of Congress Cataloging-in-Publication Data has been applied for.

ISBNs: 978-1-4555-4217-8 (hardcover), 978-1-4555-4214-7 (ebook)

Printed in the United States of America

LSC-C

10 9 8 7 6 5 4 3 2 1

Tuesday, January 1, 2013

Another year, and I still don't like old people. Their walker shuffle, their unreasonable impatience, their endless complaints, their tea and cookies, their bellyaching.

Me? I am eighty-three years old.

Wednesday, January 2

Great clouds of icing sugar were spilled a moment ago. Mrs. Smit had put the plate of apple tartlets on a chair because she wanted to wipe down the table with a cloth.

Along comes Mrs. Voorthuizen, who inadvertently parks her enormous bottom right on top of the pastries.

It wasn't until Mrs. Smit began looking for the dish, to put it back, that someone came up with the idea of checking underneath Mrs. Voorthuizen. When she stood up she had three tartlets stuck to her flowery behind.

"The apples match the pattern on your dress perfectly," Evert remarked. I almost choked to death laughing.

This brilliant start to the new year should have given rise

to all-around hilarity, but instead led to forty-five minutes of carping about whose fault it was. I was glared at darkly from all sides, on account of having found it funny, apparently. And what did I do? I mumbled I was sorry.

Instead of laughing even harder, I found myself groveling for forgiveness.

For I, Hendrikus Gerardus Groen, am ever the civil, ingratiating, courteous, polite, and helpful guy. Not because I really am all those things, but because I don't have the balls to act differently. I rarely say what I want to say. I tend to choose the path of least confrontation. My specialty: wanting to please everybody. My parents showed foresight in naming me Hendrik: you can't get any blander than that.

I'll wind up spiraling into depression, I thought. That's when I made the decision to give the world a little taste of the real Hendrik Groen. I hereby declare that in this diary I am going to give the world an uncensored exposé: a year in the life of the inmates of a care home in North Amsterdam.

I may die before the year's out, true; that's beyond my control. In that circumstance I will ask my friend Evert Duiker to read a few pages from this diary at my funeral. I'll be laid out, neatly laundered and pressed, in the small chapel of the Horizon Crematorium, waiting for Evert's croaky voice to break the uncomfortable silence and read some choice passages to the bewildered mourners.

I do worry about one thing: what if Evert should die before me?

It wouldn't be fair, considering that I have even more infirmities and funny lumps and bumps than he does. You ought to be able to count on your best friend. I'll have to have a word with him about it.

Thursday, January 3

Evert was keen but wouldn't guarantee he'd live longer than me. He also had a few reservations. The first was that after reading publicly from my diary he'd probably have to look for another place to live. The second consideration was the state of his dentures, caused by a careless jab of the pool cue by Mr. Vermeteren. Since he has a cataract in his right eye, Vermeteren needs some assistance with his aim. Evert, ever prepared to help, was standing behind him giving directions, his nose lined up with the cue. "A little to the left and a bit deeper..." and before he could finish Vermeteren had rammed the back of his cue right through Evert's snappers. *Score!*

Now Evert looks like a little kid waiting for a visit from the tooth fairy. People have a hard time understanding him because of the lisp. He'll have to have those teeth fixed before reading at my funeral. But that's not going to happen any time soon; the denture repairman, it seems, is out of action. Two hundred thousand a year, an assistant who's a real looker, three trips to Hawaii every year, and still his nerves are shot; how is it possible? Maybe years of having to deal with ancient dentures so food-encrusted that they're crawling with maggots have sent him over the edge. So to speak.

The New Year's doughnuts they're serving in the Conversation Lounge downstairs can only have come from the thrift shop. Yesterday morning I took one to be polite and spent a good twenty minutes trying to get it down; as a final resort I had to pretend my shoelace had come undone so that I could duck under the table and stuff the last piece down my sock.

No wonder they had hardly been touched. Normally anything that's free around here is gone in the blink of an eye.

In the Conversation Lounge, coffee is usually served at 10:30. If the coffee hasn't arrived by 10:32, the first residents start glancing pointedly at their watches. As if they had something better to do. The same goes for tea, which is supposed to be brought in at 3:15 in the afternoon.

One of the most exciting moments of the day: what kind of cookies will we have with our tea and coffee today? Both yesterday and the day before it was the elderly doughnuts. Because of course "we" wouldn't dream of throwing food away. We'd rather choke to death on it.

Friday, January 4

Yesterday I took a walk to the flower shop to buy some potted bulbs. So that I can tell myself a week from now, when the hyacinths start to bloom, that I've made it to another spring.

Most of the rooms in this retirement home keep their Christmas decorations on display until April. Next to an ancient sansevieria and a primula whose days are numbered. "Be a shame to throw it out."

If Nature's role is to bring cheer to a person's life, it certainly doesn't do the job in the room of a Dutch old-age pensioner. There the condition of the houseplant is usually an accurate reflection of the state of mind of the human entrusted with its care: both just waiting for the sad end. Since they have nothing else to do, or are a bit forgetful, the old biddies water their plants at least three times a day. In the long run not even a sansevieria can survive that.

Mrs. Visser has invited me in for a cup of tea tomorrow afternoon. I should have declined, if only because of how she smells, but I said I would love to stop by for a minute. There goes my afternoon. What a stupid wimp I am. On the spur of the moment I couldn't think of a good excuse, so I'll have to endure the mindless jabbering and the dry sponge cake. How she manages to turn the moistest of cakes into dusty cardboard is beyond me. You need three cups of tea per slice to wash it down. Tomorrow I will take a bold stand and turn down the second helping. Start a new life.

A new life in scrupulously polished shoes. I spent half the morning on them. The shoes themselves were done relatively quickly. Trying to scrub the shoe polish out of my shirtsleeves took much longer. But they're nice and shiny now. The shoes, I mean. The sleeves I just rolled up in the end. I couldn't get them clean.

It's bound to raise some eyebrows. "How *do* you always manage to get your sleeves so grubby, Mr. Groen?"

Life in here consists of either *never* or *always*. One day the food is "*never* served on time and *always* too hot," and the next, "*always* too early and *never* hot enough."

On occasion I have ventured to remind people of their

previous, rather contradictory statements, but they don't have much use for logic here. "Ah, Mr. Groen, you *do* have a lot to say for yourself, don't you!"

Saturday, January 5

A kerfuffle again last night at dinner: Indonesian fried rice on the menu. Most of the old folk in here are of the potato-and-cabbage-hash persuasion: none of that fancy foreign fare for them. Even back in the mid-sixties, when spaghetti was first introduced to the Netherlands, they'd said no thanks. Spaghetti simply didn't fit into the week's menu: endive Monday, cauliflower and cream of wheat Tuesday, mince Wednesday, beans Thursday, fish Friday, soup and bread Saturday, and the Sunday roast. If they really threw all caution to the wind and had hamburgers on Tuesday, it made a real mess of the rest of the week.

Foreign grub just isn't our thing. We're usually shown the menu a week ahead, so that we may choose from three different options, but sometimes there's a slip-up. Yesterday, for some unknown reason, there was nothing but Indonesian fried rice. Something about a delivery mix-up. It wasn't the cook's fault—naturally.

The choice therefore was fried rice or fried rice. People on restricted diets were given bread.

A tidal wave of indignation. Mrs. Hoogstraten van Dam, who insists on being addressed by her full name, just picked at the bits of fried egg; van Gelder doesn't eat rice but scoffed down an entire jar of pickles, and fat old

Bakker demanded that they bring him some gravy for his rice.

My friend Evert, who sometimes joins us for dinner when he gets sick of his own culinary prowess, offered his unsuspecting dinner companions a jar of hot sauce. "Would you care for some ketchup with your rice?"

He was the picture of innocence as Mrs. De Prijker proceeded to spit her dentures into the relish. She was helped out of the room, coughing and sputtering, upon which Evert picked up her teeth and started passing them around like Cinderella's slipper, to see if anyone wanted to try them on. When the facilities manager reprimanded him, he was all bewildered indignation. He even threatened to go to the food inspector to report that he had "found" a set of dentures in the relish.

Before dinner I had tea with Mrs. Visser. Her conversation is even more tepid than her tea. Told her the doctor had said I shouldn't have any cake. But why? she asked. I said it was my blood sugar, it's on the high side, somewhere between twenty and twenty-five. I blurted it out without thinking, but she decided it was very sensible of me. She pressed three slices of cake on me when I left, in case my blood sugar went down again. Those slices have found a home in the fish tank on the third floor.

Sunday, January 6

My "dribbling" keeps getting worse. White underpants are excellent for highlighting yellow stains. Yellow underpants would be a lot better. I'm mortified at the thought of the laundry ladies handling my soiled garments. I have therefore taken to scrubbing the worst stains by hand before sending the washing out. Call it a *pre*-prewash. If I didn't send out anything to be laundered it would arouse suspicion. "You *have* been changing your underwear, haven't you, Mr. Groen?" the fat lady from housekeeping would probably ask. What I'd like to reply is, "No, fat lady from housekeeping, this pair is caked so firmly onto the old buttocks that I think I'll just keep wearing them for the rest of my days."

It has been a trying day: the body creaks in all its joints. There's nothing that will stop the decline. At best you have the occasional day when you're not bothered as much by this ache or that, but genuine improvement is not in the cards, ever. Hair isn't suddenly going to start growing back. (Not on the pate, at least; it readily sprouts from the nose and ears.) The arteries aren't going to clear themselves out. The bumps and lumps won't go away, and the leaky nether parts aren't going to stop dripping. A one-way ticket to the grave, that's what it is. You never grow younger, not by a day, nor an hour, not even a minute.

Look at me whining and moaning like an old geezer. If that's where I'm headed, I might as well go and sit in the Conversation Lounge downstairs. Complaining is pastime number one down there. I don't think a half hour goes by without somebody bringing up their aches and pains.

I do believe I'm in a rather somber mood. You're supposed to enjoy your sunset years, but it damn well isn't always easy.

Time for a little stroll. It's Sunday afternoon for Pete's

sake. Then a smidgen of Mozart and a large snifter of brandy. Perhaps I'll stop by Evert's too, his thick-headedness can be very therapeutic.

Monday, January 7

It appears that an investigation was launched yesterday into the sudden demise of the fish on the third floor. A considerable amount of cake was found floating in the water.

I suppose it wasn't one of my brightest ideas, tossing Mrs. Visser's sponge cake into the fish tank. If she should ever hear that the fish died from soggy-cake overdose, the evidence will point straight to me. I had better start preparing my defense; I'll swing by Duiker the lawman for some good advice. Evert is an expert in the art of little white lies.

Pets are forbidden in this home, with the exception of fish or birds "as long as they do not exceed three or eight inches in length, respectively," it says in the house regulations. Just in case we wanted to keep sharks or white-tailed eagles.

The policy has caused a great deal of anguish for poor old biddies mercilessly torn from their dogs or cats when they move into the House of the Setting Sun. No matter how calm and sedate, old or lame the animals are, rules are rules: off to the pound. "No, madam, it makes no difference that Rascal is the only creature in the whole wide world that you love; we simply cannot make an exception." "Yes, we understand that all your cat ever does is sleep on the windowsill, but if we were to allow one cat, then someone else would want to bring in three Great Danes that sleep on the windowsill, wouldn't they? Or maybe a purple crocodile."

Mrs. Brinkman holds the record; she managed to hide an old dachshund under the sink for weeks before it was discovered. Someone must have ratted on her. To have lived through the war, as we all did, and still be so heartless as to turn in a mangy old dog! And instead of tarring and feathering the traitorous collaborator, it was the poor little dog the director deported to the pound! Where it spent the next two days howling pitifully before dying of a broken heart. And where was the SPCA when we needed it?

The director thought it best to keep Mrs. Brinkman in the dark about this turn of events. When Mrs. Brinkman finally managed to catch the right streetcar to take her to the pound, her dog was already six feet under. She asked if her dog could be exhumed and laid to rest beside her when her own time comes. She was informed that "it's against the rules."

Tomorrow I have to go to the doctor.

Tuesday, January 8

There was a notice on the board by the elevator.

A quantity of cake crumbs was found in the fish tank on the third floor. The fish in the tank have died as a result of ingesting the cake. Anyone who is able to shed some light on this incident is kindly requested to report to Mrs. De Roos,

floor manager, as soon as possible. Anonymity honored upon
request.

I went to see Mrs. De Roos at eleven. What marvelous irony for someone like her to be named after a rose! Even "Mrs. Stinging Nettle" would give her too much credit.

It would make sense if truly ugly people were extra nice, to compensate, but in this case the opposite is true: this one's a solid wall of cantankerousness.

But to resume.

I told her I might be able to provide some explanation about the cake incident. She was immediately all ears. I explained that I had been reluctant to refuse Mrs. Visser's homemade sponge cake and had left a plate of it on the table in the third-floor pantry, fully confident that some resident would appreciate the offering from an unknown donor. To my regret I realized that the cake had somehow ended up in the aquarium and that my blue plate had disappeared.

De Roos heard me out with undisguised incredulity. Why hadn't I eaten the cake myself? Why the third floor? Was there anyone who could corroborate my story?

I asked her to keep it confidential. She said she would see what she could do.

She then began wondering how Mrs. Visser could have baked the cake herself in the first place. Cooking or baking in one's room is strictly forbidden. I hastened to add that I wasn't sure that it was homemade, but it was too late: the cake mystery was out of the box. I'll lose Mrs. Visser's friendship; not a big tragedy in itself, but the distrust and suspicion in our unit, already rife, will be whipped up for weeks, and there will be no end to the gossip.

I went to the doctor's office today. He was off sick. If he hasn't recovered by Monday, they'll dig up a substitute. If it's an emergency, the doctor of a rival nursing home will see us. Some in here would rather die than let "that quack from Twilight House" have a look at their wrinkled carcass. Others prefer to call in the air ambulance for every little fart. Speaking for myself, it doesn't make any difference which doctor ends up telling me there's nothing much that can be done.

Wednesday, January 9

I have to say I was a bit off my game yesterday because of the dead-fish business. I came down with a bad case of the runs from all the tea I'd had at Mrs. Visser's, combined with my nerves. Spent half the morning on the toilet with some old reading material I'd borrowed from the Conversation Lounge.

Quite a mouthful that, "Conversation Lounge," but it doesn't do justice to what really goes on there. The "GGG Suite" would be more accurate. In which the three Gs stand for *Gossip*, *Grousing*, and *Gibberish*. A full day's work for some.

Evert stopped by briefly to fill me in on the latest through the door to the bathroom stall: everyone now suspects everyone else, seeing a potential fish assassin in every co-inmate. My absence has aroused suspicion. I've asked

Evert if he would quietly spread word of my diarrhea, as an alibi of sorts. I wasn't up to much except leaving the bathroom stall door ajar as well as the door out to the hallway, in order to air the place out. I can usually stand my own smell but this time I was making myself nauseous. Both literally and metaphorically, for what a calculating piece of chickenshit am I—in this case a rather fitting image.

Speaking of fresh air, I really need to get out for a bit. After a whole day of dry toast and Imodium, I think I might risk venturing outside again. To go and look for the celandine, which—so say both the newspaper and the nature calendar of the Phenological Observation Network (another mouthful!)—is the first true sign of spring. If besides the celandine I were to find some coltsfoot, cow parsley, or wood violets as well, I'd know that spring had truly sprung. Pity I haven't the faintest idea what those plants are supposed to look like.

Nature is six weeks ahead of herself. But—bad news for the migratory birds that have made the decision to stay put this year—there's a cold spell on the way.

Thursday, January 10

The care home has a lovely garden. But for some inexplicable reason it is locked. In winter no one is allowed in. For our own good, presumably. Management knows what's best for us inmates.

So if you want some fresh air at this time of year, you have to make do with a stroll around the neighborhood. Ugly sixties apartments. Dismal garbage dumps masquerading as strips of grass. You would think that at night the street cleaners roll through the area strewing litter instead of sweeping it up. One has to wade through a sea of cans, empty potato chip bags, and old newspapers. The people who used to live here have almost all traded their apartments for a modern row house in Purmerend or Almere. The only ones left are those who can't afford to do so. Turkish, Moroccan, and West Indian families have moved into the vacated buildings. It makes for quite a jolly melting pot.

My range these days is about a quarter of a mile each way, with a pause on a bench at the halfway mark. I can't manage much more than that. The world is shrinking. Starting from here, I can take one of four possible half-mile round trips.

Evert has just been to see me. He is getting enormous pleasure from the kerfuffle surrounding the fish massacre, and has a plan to turn it up a notch. He wants to mount a second offensive, this time with pink fondant petit fours. He thinks the color will have a more dramatic effect on the water. Yesterday he took the bus to a supermarket a few miles down the road especially to obtain a supply. If he had bought them here, in the home's mini-market, they would be bound to remember his purchase. The cakes are now stashed in his cupboard. I asked if he thought they were safe there. "It's a free country; a person can hide as many petit fours in his own home as he wants, can't he?" he said.

Saturday, January 12

The home's director, Mrs. Stelwagen—I'll have much more to say about her later, in all probability—has announced an energy-saving measure: the thermostats in the residents' rooms are not to be set above seventy-three degrees. If the oldies are cold, they should simply wear their coats, is the message. There is an Indonesian lady who likes to have her thermostat at eighty-one degrees. There are bowls of water set out all over her room to increase the humidity. Her tropical plants are thriving. There hasn't yet been a decree stipulating the maximum size for houseplants, but I suspect Stelwagen is working on it.

Mrs. Stelwagen is always friendly, ready with a willing ear and an encouraging word for everyone, but concealed beneath that veneer of sympathy is an unhealthy dose of self-importance and power lust. She is forty-two years old and has been in charge for a year and a half now but is always on the lookout for an opportunity to kick or ass-kiss her way up the ladder, depending on whom she is dealing with. I've been watching her for a year or so.

I also have a most valuable informant: her secretary, Mrs. Appelboom. Anja Appelboom was the secretary of the last director, Mr. Lemaire, for twenty-three years, until the latest merger, when Lemaire was forced into early retirement. Anja has two years to go before she gets her pension, and since a new office manager was appointed over her head, she's determined not to let Stelwagen get the better of her again. Anja still has access to all the meeting minutes and confidential documents. A few years ago she lived next door to me and saved me from the homeless shelter by arranging for me to come here. More on that some other day perhaps.

I often have a coffee with Anja in her office on Thursday mornings. That's when Stelwagen and the office manager are off to their meeting with the unit managers and the district manager. Promotion to district manager is the next leap Stelwagen is hoping for.

Having coffee is a chance for us to gossip. "Can you keep a secret?" she'll often ask before launching into a blow-by-blow of Stelwagen's latest machinations. We've collected quite a dossier on her.

Sunday, January 13

Last night Evert tossed six pink fondant petit fours into the fish tank on the second floor. The goldfish gorged themselves silly. Their corpses are floating up there among the cake crumbs. All hell has broken loose.

Evert simply excused himself during after-dinner coffee, announcing he was going to the bathroom, then climbed the stairs, peering around to make sure no one saw him, and chucked the cakes he'd been hiding under his jacket into the water. He deposited the plastic wrapper neatly in the wastepaper basket—not such a bright way to dispose of the evidence, I suppose, but luckily the janitor has already been around to empty the trash containers.

The fish tank is tucked away in a rather dark corner, so no one noticed anything last night. The operation wasn't without risk; if he'd been nabbed, he'd have been obliged to call in the moving van. Perhaps somewhere deep down he doesn't care if he gets caught, even though whenever he's in a tight spot he'll lie through his teeth, and rant and rave, swearing he had nothing to do with it. That's how the game is played, he says. His philosophy: the only point of being alive is to kill time as pleasantly as possible. The trick is not to take anything too seriously. I envy him. But I'm a fast learner.

I myself was rather on edge yesterday, because Evert had told me about the attack beforehand so that I could prepare a foolproof alibi for myself. It wasn't easy. I had to hang about in the Conversation Lounge until finally a couple who live on my floor stood up to go upstairs. "I'll walk with you, for some company," I said. Mr. and Mrs. Jacobs did give me a rather funny look.

The alarm was sounded just after nine this morning. Mrs. Brandsma, on her way to church, caught sight of the fish floating belly-up. They tried to keep it quiet at first, apparently, but Brandsma had already blabbed about it to everyone she encountered on her way to find the duty nurse. My next-door neighbor has just knocked on my door: "You won't believe what I just heard..."

I'm looking forward to all the chin-wagging when I go down for coffee.

Monday, January 14

Another pet catastrophe: Mrs. Schreuder accidentally vacuumed up her canary while she was cleaning its cage. When after several desperate minutes she finally managed to control her shaking hands enough to get the vacuum cleaner open, there wasn't much left of her perky little birdie. She should have turned off the machine immediately, of course. Her little Pete was still alive at first, but gave up the ghost a few minutes later. Schreuder is inconsolable and racked with guilt.

The only victim support from the staff was the advice to throw out the cage as soon as possible.

Everyone in here has strong views on the subject of cake crumbs in fish tanks. But ask them what they think of the war in Syria and they'll stare at you as if you'd just asked them to explain the theory of relativity. A handful of fish floating belly-up are a thousand times worse than a busload of women and children blown to smithereens in some far-off country.

But let's not be hypocritical: I am enjoying the fish scandal immensely, I cannot pretend otherwise. The outrage that has overtaken the entire population here is remarkable. I'm about to go back down to the Conversation Lounge for some more juicy fish talk.

Winter has arrived. Not a flake of snow on the ground, but yesterday I saw the first old man stepping outside with wool socks pulled on over his shoes. To guard against slipping.

Tuesday, January 15

Here it is, the first snowfall of the year. Which means nobody ventures outside, and everyone's stocking up on provisions. In our little shop downstairs there's not a packet of cookies or bar of chocolate to be had anymore. The war, you know.

It's lucky for today's young people that we are just about the only ones left who've lived through the war; soon they won't have to put up with any more old-fogeys' tales about tulip-bulb soup and having to walk seven hours for a bunch of carrots.

The final count is seven dead fish.

Yesterday the police were called in. The two young constables hadn't a clue how to go about solving the case. None of the bright efficiency you see on TV from these two. First they inspected every nook and cranny of the aquarium. As if they thought there might still be one left in there in need of resuscitation.

"Yeah, they're dead all right," said the one.

"The cake's what did them in, probably," said the other.

Stelwagen had ordered the dead fish to be left in the tank as evidence. Maybe she'd been expecting a forensic pathologist. Who knows?

In any case, the officers just seemed eager to get out of there as soon as they decently could. The director was insisting on a thorough investigation, but the younger cop told her that it would entail lodging a criminal complaint.

Couldn't she do that right now? No, she'd have to make an appointment at the station, either in person or via the website.

Fine, but what were they supposed to do with the dead fish? The constable suggested the garbage can. "But don't leave them in there too long. Or you could flush them down the toilet." Then the gentlemen turned on their heels and vacated the premises. "'Night, ma'am." Mrs.

Stelwagen was appalled. "Outrageous! It's simply outrageous! Is this any way to treat the taxpayer?"

It was a pleasure to witness the woman's helpless tantrum. Apparently her power has no reach outside the four walls of this institution.

Wednesday, January 16

Evert dropped by. To avoid the Conversation Lounge, we went for a little shuffle through the snow: walk for five, rest for five. We are faced with the inevitable: rollator, mobility scooter, or the Canta LX microcar. Such sexy options.

A week ago, in front of the secondary school around the corner, a boy of sixteen or seventeen showed off a tomato-red Canta he must have "borrowed" from his grandmother. He used the little car to tote the prettiest girls' schoolbags, with the pretty girls themselves following on their bikes. I haven't ever seen a youngster driving a mobility scooter for fun, or pushing a rollator. That is why my preference is for a nicely pimped-out Canta. Even if that throws me in with all the other pathetically bad drivers at the wheel of one of those tin cans.

A Canta plowed full steam ahead into a candy store the other day, coming to a stop in a deluge of licorice and assorted jelly beans, with two fat ladies' horrified faces smashed against the windshield. Their little dog had gotten stuck under the brake pedal. Truth is better than fiction.

Here the topic of almost every conversation is either the snow or the great fish caper. The old biddies keep coming up with the most fanciful conspiracy theories, and some aren't shy about making unsubstantiated accusations. For example, close to the time of the murder, two residents saw Mrs. Aaltje in the hallway where the fish tank is located...

The fact that her room is on that hallway, and that, being three floors up, she can hardly be expected to climb in through the window, did not deter anyone. Poor Aaltje, a timid little mouse who can't weigh more than ninety pounds and doesn't dare look you in the eye, has never harmed fish nor fly.

After the cops' visit, the director called a meeting "to allay fears a bit." She informed us that every room on the second floor had been thoroughly searched "for form's sake." As if the perpetrator's room would be revealed by the presence of cake crumbs galore. No one piped up to ask if management had the right to inspect the rooms. I didn't either; didn't have the nerve.

However, over coffee there was plenty of whispered innuendo about rooms on other floors that could stand a thorough inspection as well. Accompanied by vehement nods: "Oh, yes!"

Thursday, January 17

I've been reading back through my diary entries. Perhaps they're a bit gloomy so far. I assure you that there are some decent people in here too!

My friend Evert, of course. He lives independently just around the corner in the retirement apartment building, with his dog—an old, friendly, very intelligent, lazy mutt named Mohammed. Whenever Evert's gout acts up, I'm the one who walks the dog. Walking the dog doesn't entail very much, owing to my limited range, but then Mo's range is even more limited than mine. One loop around the building, that's it. A trickle against ten tree trunks, and once a day a turd deposited on the grass, which I have to whisk away in a little plastic bag since I am being spied on from dozens of windows. If I were to leave a poop in the spot where it was expelled, there would be a scramble to be the first to report me.

Then there's Edward. A man of few words. He is hard to understand because of his stroke, but he chooses his nearly unintelligible words carefully. Whenever he does attempt to say something, you know that repeating "Excuse me?" several times will be worth it. What he economizes on words, he expends on shrewd observation.

Grietje: a real dear, friendly and sympathetic without fawning.

Graeme, the last of this group for now, seems insecure and introverted but always tells it to you straight, without riling you.

These are the men and women I don't mind sitting with over a cup of tea. It's more or less a given, really, because something as simple as whether to sit down next to someone or not follows strict unwritten rules. We all have our prescribed places: at the lunch table, at bingo, in Moving to Music class, in the Meditation Room. If you want to be hated, just try sitting down in someone else's spot and not moving when one of these doddering old babies comes up to you, pouting, and says, "That's where *I* sit." ("Well, if I may venture to say so, you seem to be *stand-*

ing at the moment. Right in front of my nose.") That is if you haven't already been warned, as you're limping to an empty chair, "That's where Mrs. So-and-so sits!" Upon which everyone always apologizes and shuffles on. When what you really should do is sit down. And say, pointing to the other empty chairs, "She'll sit over there today, or she can just take a hike."

Friday, January 18

Over the past three days management has issued a travel restriction; after all, who wants to risk a broken hip? It doesn't improve the mood around here. Not that the residents tend to go out much even when it isn't slippery; but still, most take a daily stroll to the shopping center, the mailbox, or the park. And the greater the prohibition, the greater the need. The old biddies are sitting by the window today staring at the snow that just will not melt, complaining about the council that keeps the roads ploughed but leaves the pavement and bicycle paths awash in brown sludge. They do have a point.

The staff have swept the front steps so that we can make our way unhampered from the front door to the bus stop. But the agonizing uncertainty about what might await you at the other end, when you get off the minibus, makes most people decide not to risk it. Fear is an ever-present counselor.

The fish tempest-in-a-teapot has died down somewhat. It was only a matter of time before something else came along to distract people. Well here it is: besides the snow, it's the rumor that the council wants to raise the parking rates. The oldies worry that if the meter needs to be fed with one euro more, their children will come less often. If my children were so put off by having to pay one damn euro extra that it made them stay away, I wouldn't want them to visit me at all. When I ventured, very cautiously, to express my opinion on the matter over coffee, I was told that it was easy for me to say, seeing that I don't have any children and never have any visitors in the first place.

There is a grain of truth in that. Almost every name in my address book is crossed out. Two that aren't may or may not still be alive. Another doesn't remember who I am. That leaves only Evert and Anja. Graeme, Edward, and Grietje aren't listed in my address book. Not a very impressive list of friends, is it? The choice is either dying young or enduring an endless string of funerals. I now have just five more funerals to go, max, not counting the ones I go to only out of politeness.

Saturday, January 19

Friday is Feel Good Fitness day. That's when you see the old biddies scurrying down the halls on their way to the "gym" in the most remarkable exercise outfits. The ladies are truly past the point of shame, and it is not a pretty sight. Pink leggings hugging skinny, bony knees or fat, jiggling thighs, form-fitting T-shirts pulled tight across what were once a pair of breasts. The physical decline on proud display. At my age, it is not conducive to feeling good.

The venue: a little-used conference room in which the tables are pushed to the side and the chairs arranged in a circle. The exercise largely takes place sitting down, so as not to dishearten the wheelchair-bound. There's a bit of waving of arms and legs to the beat of some cheerful music. And groaning. And loud proclaiming of ailments preventing the execution of certain moves. "I can't do that with my colostomy."

Then it's time for a game of ball-tossing. Confession: the ball isn't in play all that much. It's the vocal çords that get the most exercise—cheering one another on for the simplest of exploits. Like a mother applauding a toddler who after twenty tries finally manages to catch the ball: "*Yes! You did it! What a clever boy!*"

We're all very good sports, let's just put it that way.

So indeed, yesterday I attended Feel Good Fitness. It was my first time. And also my last. When it was over and the instructor—"Call me Tina"—gushed that I should definitely come again next week, I told her right then and there that once was enough.

"Oh, and why is that?" she asked suspiciously.

"Because with so much female pulchritude about, I can't concentrate on the exercises properly. I stiffen up." I'd blurted it out without thinking. It wasn't until I'd said it that I felt myself getting hot. Much more so than during the fitness class.

Hey, I'm beginning to speak my mind, or nearly! I am improving by leaps and bounds. Thanks to this diary, perhaps.

Tina stood there nonplussed. The sarcasm was clear, but I hadn't laid it on thick enough that she could object, not with all the dolled-up old tarts still standing there. Most of them still consider themselves "quite attractive." Self-knowledge tends to decrease drastically with age. Just as in children it increases year by year.

Sunday, January 20

We pensioners are definitely not bearing the brunt of the economic crisis. According to the calculations of a prominent research institute, a single retiree living off a state pension is going to be two (two!) euros better off per month this year. So the panic Henk Krol and his 50Plus Party set off was for nothing. A majority of the residents voted for him in last year's election.

People with generous private pensions and those who have taken early retirement are getting a bit less, but they have more to start with. Anyway, there are no early retirees in here.

It's astonishing how frugal the residents are. Even people living on the state pension are able to squirrel away quite a bit, though God only knows why they bother.

Last year some residents of another nursing home won the jackpot in the lottery. The fuss associated with having all those millions wound up making a good number of them thoroughly miserable.

I am seeing to it that I'll be deep in the red when I die.

With the help of the Virgin Mary calendar that I won at bingo in December, I have calculated that from the shortest day, December 21, until today, a month later, the sun has risen just eleven minutes earlier and set thirty-seven minutes later. Curious, isn't it?

I've been a bit constipated lately, you see, and the Virgin Mary calendar hangs in the bathroom. It has passages from the Bible but also recipes, quotations, and jokes. Tomorrow, January 21, is the day of St. Agnes, virgin and martyr. She died in 304. Just so you know.

There was a fuss in the paper again about a mentally handicapped boy who was found chained to the wall in his care home. The reason wasn't given; he probably gets violent. There are people in the dementia unit here who can hardly throw a punch or even stand up, but they too lie there trussed up like escape artists who've forgotten the trick to breaking free. You are welcome to come and have a look, paparazzi.

Monday, January 21

My daughter would have been fifty-six today. I try to imagine what she would have looked like. I can't see beyond the image of a four-year-old, dripping wet, slack in a neighbor's arms. I watched them approach in seconds that were without end.

Not until fifteen or twenty years later did a whole day go by when I didn't think about it.

No one is going out: snowstorm!

More gloom and doom: Evert has diabetes.

Actually, he's had it for a while. Evert doesn't follow the doctor's orders all that carefully, and the doctor's assistant took it upon herself to rub it in.

"Certainly, Mr. Duiker, if you insist on drinking *and* eating the wrong things *and* smoking, there's not much I can do for you, is there?"

"Those are the only pleasures left in life, sweetheart."

"I am not your sweetheart."

"Nor are you my doctor, Madam Assistant."

Even so, he's a bit worried, Evert. He used to frequent his local bar, where he was friendly with a fat patron who also had diabetes. The man would down twenty-five pints on a normal night. Afterward he'd have a few shots of whiskey at home.

One fine day Evert's friend's toe turned black. The toe had to be amputated. Then other toes. Then a foot, then the leg below the knee. Everything that turned black got sawn off in the hospital. He was a regular customer there. He was a very friendly guy who simply couldn't stop drinking or smoking. For a while he was still propped up at the bar on an artificial leg, but then he wound up in a wheelchair and could no longer get to the bar. Two months later he was dead.

Evert's nightmare: to start turning black at the extremities and wind up at the mercy of doctors and nurses.

Tomorrow I'll write about something cheerful again.

Yet another to-do about the price of parking. The ever-cantankerous Mr. Kuiper has submitted a proposal to the Residents' Association to introduce paid *indoor* parking.

Practically no one in here walks with a cane. The residents like to push one of those rollator things instead, with handbrake and a shopping basket. If you get tired you can rest your weary behind on it. Some tootle about on mobility scooters, even indoors. Those machines take up quite a bit of room. They also seem to be getting bigger. They're a status symbol.

Management is worried about traffic jams and has asked that the rollators and scooters be used indoors as little as possible. That got the hobblers terribly upset. But when Kuiper proposed following the City of Amsterdam's example to solve the parking problem by making people pay, all hell broke out. I do think that Kuiper has a few screws loose.

This home was built in the late sixties, when children started having such busy lives that they couldn't have their aged parents move in with them anymore. Or they simply didn't feel like having their parents live in, and I'd be the last to be much surprised by that. Be that as it may, about forty years ago homes for the aged began to sprout from the ground like mushrooms. And so nice and spacious too! Rooms measuring 250 square feet, bath alcove and kitchenette included. A married couple was granted another 85 square feet for a bedroom. Over the past twenty years there's been some half-assed remodeling, but the space is still far too small. They never took into account the armada of rolling equipment. The elevators aren't big enough for more than two scooters or four rollators at a time. And then it takes a good fifteen minutes before they've all maneuvered themselves in or out. Impatiently ramming into people's legs. Standing right in front of the door when people are still trying to get out. The solution Stelwagen came up with was to commandeer one of the elevators for the staff. Which made the line for the other elevators even longer, of course. You now have to leave even earlier in order to reach your destination on time. They ought to start giving traffic reports. I used to take the stairs, but am no longer able to, so these days you'll often find me standing in the line.

If a fire ever breaks out in here, the entire population will be cremated. Only the staff will be able to make it outside in time.

Wednesday, January 23

I casually asked the doctor about the availability of the pill that cures all ailments. He pretended he didn't understand. "Such a cure-all doesn't exist, I'm afraid." I didn't have the nerve to ask again.

He did find my list of complaints impressive, however: the dribble, pains in my legs, dizziness, bumps, eczema. But he couldn't do much about any of it. A little placating with a pill here and an ointment there. He even discovered a new one: high blood pressure. I didn't have that before. So now I have pills for that as well.

Our oldest resident has passed away. Mrs. De Gans. For

many years as senile as a goldfish, she had to be tied to her chair so she wouldn't slide off, but still—hooray!—she reached the grand old age of ninety-eight. Just old enough to have lived through World War I.

Three months ago the local alderman brought her a cake on her birthday because she was the district's oldest citizen. They propped her up at a table for the photographer of the local paper, but in a moment of inattention she plopped head-first into the whipped-cream cake. It made a great photo op. Sadly, the director refused to allow it to be printed in the paper. The alderman, who is so fond of seeing his own face in the newspaper, ordered a fresh cake to be rushed in, but by that time Mrs. De Gans had already conked out and could not be woken up.

So now she is past ever being awakened again. Not that it makes a great difference.

I don't think I'll go to the funeral. I'm finding them hard to take these days.

Thursday, January 24

The atmosphere in the home is not improving. There's been snow on the ground for over a week, and a fierce east wind, so everybody stays indoors, sulking at being cooped up. Short daily walks and an errand or two are the activities life normally revolves around in here. Without those, there's even more time to keep tabs on each other. The day has to get filled with *something*.

Yesterday, wanting a breath of fresh air, I went and sat down on the bench by the front door. I hadn't been there more than a few minutes when the receptionist told me I wasn't supposed to sit there. A shivering old geezer next to the entrance is not good for business. "You can look out the window, can't you?"

I muttered, "Just wanted to stick my nose out for some fresh air."

"Your nose is purple, Mr. Groen, and runny."

Mr. Hoogdalen has been driving a mobility scooter for a few months. Three days ago his son, who owns a garage, took it home, and he returned it this morning. All pimped out. Spoilers, extra-wide tires, GPS, sound system with speakers, horn, and the cherry on the top, an airbag. All quite unnecessary but no less brilliant for that. Hoogdalen, proud as a peacock, drove his Lamborghini-scooter round and round the home. Of course there were snide remarks but fortunately also some compliments. That's what it's about, isn't it? Keep living and doing what you love.

This morning there was an obituary for Ellen Blazer, the talk show producer, in the newspaper. I wonder how many obituaries the newspapers keep in reserve, just in case. If I called the newspaper, would they tell me? Or, to be more specific, could Nelson Mandela, for example, have requested to see his own obituary ahead of time and been allowed to make some changes?

Friday, January 25

I did manage to go quite a distance today before fate intervened. A motorbike nearly ran me off the pavement, and the next instant I found myself lying flat on my back.

"Just act as if nothing were the matter" is the knee-jerk reaction when that sort of thing happens, and that reflex still seems to be in perfect working order. I picked myself up, slapped the snow from my coat and looked around to see if anyone had seen me fall. Fortunately no one had, and I could trundle back to the home, no harm done. When I greeted the orderly he stared at me in surprise. "What's happened to you?"

"Oh, nothing. I just slipped."

"Nothing? You're covered in blood!"

I felt the spot on my skull he was pointing at, and indeed, it was rather sticky. A nurse was sent for, who immediately started nattering about stitches, so, long story short, I and my bloody head sat in the ER for an hour and a half and now I have a white turban on my head and am keeping to my room as much as possible to avoid the finger-wagging.

"Doesn't it hurt?" That's how it usually begins, but sooner or later comes the follow-up: "You really shouldn't go out when it's so slippery." There's your biggest headache, right there.

"That white bonnet is most becoming on you." Evert stopped by to rub a bit more salt in the wound. If there's ever a shortage of rubbing salt, Evert has plenty in his personal stash.

To pay him back I crushed him at chess. Usually I aim for a fairly equitable endgame, with a win for one and then for the other, but this time, to his consternation, he was checkmated in fifteen minutes.

"That blow to the head seems to have done you some good," he remarked. "It's done wonders for your chess game, anyway."

I said that I hoped it would also do wonders for my pool game tomorrow.

"Ah, but your memory's shot, Henk, because pool is three days from now."

He was right. Strange that I'd gotten it wrong.

Saturday, January 26

The last Saturday of the month: bingo night. Geriatric gambling addicts competing for a box of cherry-liqueur chocolates. The head of the Residents' Association takes it upon himself to call out the numbers. Don't even think of opening your mouth while he's at it. Whenever the number forty-four is called, Miss Slothouwer always says, "Hunger Winter" and the entire room looks up, perturbed.

Not long ago a group of residents wanted bingo moved to Wednesday nights because Saturdays are for family visits—which is hogwash actually. The real motivation was probably whatever program was on TV on Saturdays. The Wednesday night choir promptly objected and proposed Monday night, which was quashed by the pool club. The pool club thought Friday night was a better option. That met with stiff resistance from the Feel Good Fitness people, who were too tuckered out from their afternoon exercises to face the exertion of a game of bingo in the evening.

When three meetings of the Residents' Association

were still unable to come to an agreement, our own King Solomon, Mrs. Stelwagen, decided that everything should stay as it was for now. Relations within the committee have suffered as a result. The knives are out.

Bullying, at school or on the web, is a popular topic in the press nowadays, but you seldom hear about intimidation in homes for the aged. Respectable senior citizens can't possibly be bullies! How wrong they are. Just hang around here for a day and you'll know. We have real experts at it here. The Misses Slothouwer, spinster sisters, are a greatly feared duo. This morning the first Miss Slothouwer twisted the top of the salt shaker loose before her sister passed it to their favorite victim, Mrs. De Leeuw, who promptly dumped the entire contents, top and all, onto her fried egg. Mrs. De Leeuw gazed in bewilderment from her egg to the empty shaker and then at her neighbor. "It's got nothing to do with me. It's your own fault. You're so clumsy of late," Slothouwer snapped at her, her sister nodding in agreement. I've no idea why they do it. Mrs. De Leeuw, unlike the lion that is her namesake, is a timid little thing. She's always apologizing for whatever's gone wrong around her, just to be on the safe side. It would take someone committing suicide, and leaving a note clearly laying out the reason, to make people take notice of the bullying that goes on in here.

Sunday, January 27

I tried, but did not make it to the end of bingo night. When a fight broke out over who was the winner of the fifth prize, a liver sausage from ALDI, I pleaded a migraine and went back to my room. A migraine is a handy ailment, because it's always accepted as a fair excuse. When I first arrived, when no one knew me yet, I happened to mention my fictional migraines, and have had frequent occasion to make use of them since. Squinting a bit and rubbing my forehead will do it. Some concerned soul will always ask if I have a migraine coming on. Then I have to "have a little lie-down." No questions asked, and that's that.

I've just come from the Meditation Room. I sometimes pop in there on a Sunday for the ecumenical service. One Sunday it's a vicar leading the service; the next it's a priest. They fit in well, since they're both almost as old as the congregation. The vicar is a jokester. He takes God with a grain of salt. The priest is old-school, preaching hellfire and damnation. It doesn't make a hell of a difference, actually, since they are both fiendishly hard to understand.

With death on the horizon, I'd say that a healthy proportion of the inmates here cling tightly to their faith.

After the service there's always raisin bread and coffee.

Yesterday there was a great hoopla over the rise in the individual contribution to the cost of residential care. It had been in the newspaper: pensioners are to be charged an "income adjustment supplement" of 8 percent on top of the means-tested 4 percent. There was great outrage over this news. But when Graeme asked who among us was in fact rich enough to be required to pay it, only Mrs. Bregman put up her hand. She thought we were talking about the Residents' Association fee.

The occupants here are mostly piss-poor, with at most a modest pension here or there.

It was funny that even the 50Plus Party in Parliament had agreed to the rise in the individual levy. Henk Krol's explanation: "We had only just taken our seats in the House and saw that everyone else was voting for it, even the Socialists. We were bamboozled, basically." I read the quote aloud to the group. Some were of the opinion that the other parties really ought to have warned Henk beforehand.

Monday, January 28

At coffee hour this morning I congratulated Mr. Hoogdalen on his extraordinarily fine scooter. He showed me all the upgrades. The only thing he wasn't able to demonstrate was the airbag.

He wants to start a scooter club: the Antelopes. He admitted he'd stolen the name from somewhere. I told him that I might be in the market for a Canta Cabrio, but that I was still thinking about it. He for his part was willing to consider allowing Cantas into the club.

At first I was inclined to find a polite way to wriggle out of it, but his club has suddenly begun to sound rather appealing. It might be fun to be a tour organizer. I can just picture a long line of mobility scooters slowly *putt-putt*ing across an unending flat landscape. With a senior landing in a ditch every now and then.

Two years ago, there was an accident in Genemuiden involving a Canta. (I like to save interesting items that I cut out of the newspaper.) Both people on board were killed. But note this: they were aged ninety-six and ninety-seven, respectively! Ploughed head-on into another car. Perhaps their doctor had refused to give them the euthanasia pill; who can say?. You survive two world wars and you meet your Waterloo in a flimsy tin can that lands on its head on a verge near Genemuiden. One hundred and ninety-three years between the two of them. Not bad, really. It didn't say if they were married. Maybe she was his mistress, like Ted Kennedy at Chappaquiddick. That would just be too perfect.

Speaking of newspaper clippings: Friday's item: the escape of fifteen thousand crocodiles. (Can one have two colons in a single sentence?)

Tuesday, January 29

At 6:45 yesterday evening, almost all of the inmates were gathered around the flat-screen television in the Conversation Lounge. What was Beatrix going to say in her annual Queen's Speech? And there it was: she is abdicating. Apart from that announcement her short speech was rather a letdown, to tell the truth. Mrs. Groenteman, who's a bit daft, wondered if the queen would now be put in a nursing home.

The room of the recently deceased Mrs. De Gans has been hurriedly emptied so that it can be rented out as of the first of the month, this Friday. Business is business; money is money. Poor Gansie's only daughter was given three days to remove her mother's things and store them some-where or donate the lot to the Salvation Army. Otherwise she'd have had to come up with another month's rent. She called someone who advertised in the Yellow Pages that he paid good money for household contents. Upon casting a glance at the deceased's effects, he promptly turned around and left. "That's not worth my while even loading into the van." Tactful guy.

Granted: Mrs. De Gans had neither money nor taste.

In the end the daughter selected a few keepsakes and donated the rest to the thrift shop.

She'd begged Mrs. Stelwagen for three more days, to no avail. "I'm *so* sorry, such a shame, I *wish* that I could tell you something different, but I simply *have to* follow man-agement's rules," Stelwagen must have sanctimoniously told her. Will have to ask Anja if I am right. If the home itself has to take care of clearing out the room, they send the bereaved next of kin a bill for €580 or more, even if the job took less than an hour.

If she knew of this, Mrs. De Gans would be rolling over in her grave. The grave she hasn't even been buried in yet. Yesterday afternoon there was an opportunity to say good-bye to her—the last viewing day, so to speak. It's the harsh law of the dotage jungle: either view or be viewed. She's being laid to rest this afternoon.

Wednesday, January 30

I had better not air my republican sympathies right now. This is not the time to shout *Down with the king!* I don't really mind Beatrix, but I do think it's time for her to take a step back. She ought to devote more time to her painting and less time to her hairdresser. That stiff hairdo has irked me for years. I shouldn't let it aggravate me, but I can't help it. There are at least thirty pictures of Bea on the front page of *de Volkskrant*. Not a single hair out of place in any one of them.

The queen is greatly revered in here. The magazine *Royalty* has pride of place on the coffee table, with *Hello!* and *Women's Own*. Evert once tried to slip in a copy of *Playboy* as an experiment. Within an hour it was gone! All the magazines have a big black stamp with the name of the institution on them, so that nobody will have the nerve to remove them from the common rooms. That *Playboy* wasn't stamped.

A few residents have already put their names down for the minibus to Dam Square on April 30 for the inauguration. They don't want to miss out on the royal festivities.

I'm going to look in on Evert in a few minutes. He's had another attack of gout, and so I have to let out his dog, Mo. According to Evert, you can tell Mo's intelligent from the way he growls whenever Stelwagen is in the neighborhood. She ignored the growling once and went to pet him; he bit her hand, or rather, he just missed and nipped her dress instead. An expensive dress, it was. Ever since then the relationship between the director and Evert is rather icy, to put it mildly.

There's a sign on the door: RESPECT THE GROWL.

Last night when I went to fetch the dog I found Evert nodding off in his chair. When he has gout he doesn't drink, but takes loads of pills instead. As soon as the attack is over it's back to the other way around.

Meanwhile I'm looking after both dog and master. Mo is grateful and Evert mumbles that it isn't necessary. He hates being pitied, so everyone had better stay out of his way. He'd like to see them put up a NO WHINING sign in big neon letters over the front door. He tolerates me. I do a little shopping, pop a frozen dinner into the microwave for him and then leave. When he's recovered he always has a gift for me: a big bunch of tulips, half a kilo of smoked eel, a pin-up calendar.

Thursday, January 31

The royal-family experts have been asleep at the switch: nobody gave us advance warning that there was to be an abdication. After two days of a Queen Beatrix deluge in the newspapers, on the radio, on TV, and at the table, I'm beginning to wish for some kind of honest-to-goodness disaster for a bit of balance.

Beatrix's actual birthday, which is today, is always humbly celebrated in here with a round of cream cakes. Not the orange ones, I hasten to say; those are only available on the official Queen's Day, on April 30. Some of the residents also like to deck the place out in flags. Small flags for the table, since a big flag hanging on the wall is, naturally, out of the question. The rules are clear on this point: no holes in the wall. Every room comes equipped with four picture hooks in preassigned spots, and you just have to manage with those.

Mr. Ellroy tried to hang his moose head from one of those little picture hooks. It crashed onto his sideboard, smashing his tea set to smithereens. They wouldn't give him a bigger hook, no matter how he begged and pleaded—he's very attached to his moose. "If we start allowing it, Christ knows where it will end," the head of Buildings and Grounds told him. That's the argument that ends all arguments in this place. As if the residents would suddenly rise up as one and begin nailing all kinds of stuffed trophies to the walls if they let Ellroy have a more substantial hook for his moose. The head is now balanced on a chair. Ellroy can't really use it as a coat rack anymore; he does like to toss his hat onto it. He usually misses. Bending down to pick it up from the floor costs him a great deal of effort, but time and again the challenge of the antlers beckons. Nice guy, only he's as deaf as a post. Which is a shame, because I'm sure he's someone you could have a nice chat with otherwise.

Friday, February 1

I just had an unannounced visit from the social worker. Lucky for her I'm almost always home. It was quite a surprise.

I made her a cup of coffee and inquired to what I owed this pleasure. She began by beating about the bush. Was I still enjoying life? Was I feeling at all down?

She sat there charmingly hemming and hawing. She's quite young and inexperienced at her job but was endearingly trying to do her best.

I asked what had prompted this interest.

"Oh, it doesn't really matter."

"Well, miss, if it doesn't really matter, you can tell me, surely."

And then she came out with it. The doctor had sent her over. Probably because I had casually asked about that euthanasia pill. He'd made this poor dear come and check on me to make sure I wasn't about to jump off the roof.

I assured her that I had no plans in the near future to commit suicide. The word startled her a bit: "Oh, sir, that isn't what I meant."

"I know what you meant. Everything's A-OK. And tell the doc that I would appreciate it if he took care of his problems himself. Another cup?"

No, she had to go.

Yesterday I paid a visit to Anja, my informant in the boss's office, and she gave me a copy of Mrs. Stelwagen's report on the fish murders. I am not fingered as a suspect. Evert isn't either. She is convinced the culprit is one of the staff—an attempt to undermine her position, she thinks. She is going to install surveillance cameras in the hallways. I wonder if that's legal.

Saturday, February 2

"STOP THE ROT, KEEP MOVING." That was the banner headline of a newspaper article, with the subheading: "Scientists all over the world are seeking the root causes of the problems of aging, and their solution." Wow, scientists, right on time, aren't you? For us it's far too late. But come on over, there's plenty of research material staggering about in here.

Biologically speaking, you become superfluous on your fortieth birthday or thereabouts, since the children are born by then and approaching self-sufficiency. That is when slowly but surely the rot starts to set in, with hair loss and reading glasses. On a cellular level too things start going wrong. You have more and more errors of division and multiplication. A slowing metabolism leads to a weaker nervous system, which also makes the mind begin to weaken. (I'm giving a rough summary of the article.)

They don't know very much yet, but one thing is clear: *Use it or lose it.* You have to keep both body and mind active, especially the prefrontal cortex, the part of the brain that controls functions such as planning, initiative, and flexibility. Well, we may presume that the management of this place doesn't care much about the prefrontal cortex. Neither money nor trouble is spared to keep the oldies docile, passive, and lethargic, camouflaged by bingo, pool, and "Feel Good Fitness."

Let me not, however, place the blame squarely on the staff. The inmates are only too willing to let themselves be coddled and patronized. And let's be honest, I do understand the temptation sometimes. There are days when I don't mind being a bit of a lazybones myself.

I am going to keep moving for a bit. Let's see how far I get. The head bandage from my fall has come off, so I'll be spared the snide comments.

The 50Plus Party stands at nine seats in some polls. In six years there will be more voters over the age of fifty than under. Seemingly from nowhere all kinds of political parties are getting wise to this. They have discovered the disgruntled senior citizen. We have become interesting, all of a sudden. Not that in here there is much political awareness. "They're robbing us blind" is about the most complex opinion you ever hear aired over coffee.

The new resident who has moved into the late Mrs. De Gans's room—Eefje Brand—seems a pleasant sort. A breath of fresh air compared to the average matron shuffling along our hallways. Not that she doesn't shuffle, but at least she does it with style.

I had a nice chat with her, and she told me it wasn't really her choice to move here. But she was determined "not to let them nail me into my coffin," at least "not yet."

"And anyway, maybe I'll have myself cremated, I haven't decided yet."

I said I wasn't sure yet either, and that neither choice was very appealing to me, six feet under or up the chimney, and she agreed.

"There aren't too many alternatives. Perhaps one could have oneself dropped into the sea from the air. We could ask that Argentinian death-flight pilot."

"I don't think the man's out of prison yet," I said.

I don't believe I have exchanged this sort of banter with anyone since I've been in here. Even my chats with Evert are of a different order. The other inmates talk almost exclusively about the weather, the food, or their ailments.

Well, the weather is fine, the food is passable, and with the help of a handful of pills the aches and pains aren't troubling me very much today. In short: life is good.

Monday, February 4

I read in the newspaper that someone ran over seventy moorhens when his car went into a skid. A moorhen massacre. It must have been a dreadful sight. All those feathers and beaks, all that blood. Either they were huddled together in a tight pack, or it was a monster skid. Moorhens are usually unapproachably skittish. Anyway, I do have to ask myself: did the reporter make an exact tally of the bodies? And what about the injured ones? I can't imagine that every bird died on the spot. There must have been some that were still flapping about. Ugh... It's starting to make my stomach turn, all these persnickety questions I'm coming up with.

Evert often drops in on a Sunday afternoon for a chat and "a glass of something or other." Evert isn't fussy: wine, gin, brandy, whiskey, it really makes no difference to him. I have seen him put away an entire bottle of eggnog with a little demitasse spoon when we were at Mrs. Tankink's. That was all she had to offer. After two little glasses, he switched to a soup bowl and asked for a bigger spoon. As if it were custard. Tankink pretended it was the most normal thing in the world at the time but dined on it for weeks afterward whenever Evert was out of earshot.

Sunday afternoon is for many of the residents the time when they receive visitors.

"Oh, has it been five weeks since we last went to see Mom and Dad? We had better swing by Sunday afternoon." And then they'll come for a cup of tea, and grin and bear it for the next two hours.

Hendrik, be honest: there's a touch of envy here, because you never have any visitors yourself. Except Evert, but you can't really call that a visit.

Tuesday, February 5

There is a great buzz about plans for a euthanasia clinic. Specially conceived for people with an uncooperative doctor. The Netherlands' Right to Die Society came up with the idea. That's a society that must have a rather serious member turnover.

Two years ago Right to Die NL gathered forty thousand signatures in three days in order to force Parliament to take up the question of assisted suicide for people in their seventies and older.

Forty thousand signatures means that Parliament has to do something about the senior who considers his life largely over and who wishes to end it with some dignity. To stop him from going out and buying a bottle of meth and setting himself ablaze in his little room because nobody will help him. That very thing has actually happened, according to Right to Die NL.

The society's opponents suggest making old people's lives much jollier instead, to see if we can be persuaded to stick around. An interesting challenge, I'd say. Let's offer our nursing home as the test case. Bring on the fun!

And in case that doesn't work, why not build a nice clinic for people who would like to step out of life discreetly, with expert guidance? Not too far from here, please, if possible.

Now for something more cheerful, Groen. Think springtime.

I've spotted some snowdrops and even a smattering of premature daffodils. The flowers are a bit confused: first a warm December, then almost three weeks of snow and ice, next back up to fifty degrees, and now hail and snow. Come on, flowers, don't be flustered! I'm in the mood for a glorious spring.

Wednesday, February 6

Financial news is also on the agenda at the coffee table. The SNS bank is in trouble, and the residents who once entrusted their hard-earned nest eggs to it have emptied their accounts. Or rather, had their son or daughter do it for them, because modern banking gives people like us the willies. The cash machine alone is quite an adventure. Having to look over your shoulder to make sure you're not about to be robbed, at the same time peering at the screen in order to punch in the four numbers of the pin code correctly with your trembling fingers, while also pressing your body against the machine to shield the code from prying eyes... It's a complicated maneuver that often goes wrong. That's when one thinks with nostalgia of the good old pay envelope.

There are quite a number of widows in here who before the death of their husbands had never so much as signed a check. All they had was their weekly housekeeping money. When someone dies it's not unusual for an old sock stuffed with cash to come to light.

Next we had a discussion about *Dancing on Ice*. Is there anything more deadly? I was pleased to see that I have an ally in my newest friend: Eefje Brand. It makes for a bond. In an attempt to involve her in the conversation, someone asked her what she thought of it.

"My doctor says I'm not allowed to watch it," she said. Eyebrows were raised all around. I got up the nerve to remark that she had a remarkably sensible doctor. Then Eefje brought up the subject of the weather. The others were left gaping.

When I got up to fetch my newspaper from the little shop, I offered to pick up a TV guide for her, since she has trouble walking. When I asked her which one she'd like, she said I could choose, which I took as a vote of confidence.

"Don't you always read the same one, then?" asked Mr. Gompert in surprise.

No, she tended to buy this magazine one week, and the next week another.

"But surely that makes it hard to find what you're looking for?" said Gompert with eyes popping out of his skull. He simply could not get his head around such chaos.

"Oh no, all I have to do is look it up. Monday usually comes after Sunday, you see, and then Tuesday is next, then Wednesday, and so on."

Eefje Brand, you are not going to make very many

friends in here; however, as far as friends go, I highly recommend myself.

Thursday, February 7

Evert wouldn't mind making Mrs. Brand's acquaintance and suggested that I invite her and him for tea. He promised he would even drink the damn tea this once. I don't know...They might not hit it off. Evert is rough and rude, and Eefje strikes me as delicate and refined. I'm not keen on being caught in the middle, I'll end up with whiplash. But it does have a nice ring to it: Evert and Eefje. Perhaps we'll be the Three Musketeers of this retirement home.

"Our" chairman of the board has been in the news again. He is being forced to do some restructuring: he's giving fifteen hundred home-care workers the axe. A few years ago he received a bonus of €60,000 on top of his €220,000 salary because he had managed *not* to let the company go belly-up. It would seem to me that that's just part of his job. I don't know of many directors who are hired to make the business go bankrupt.

One of the economies this fellow came up with was to slash the apprentice caregivers' salaries. They're now being paid just five thousand euros a year for emptying bedpans and washing shriveled genitals; that is a fifty-sixth of what the boss, sitting in an office that recently had a forty-thousand-euro facelift, has deposited into his own bank account. Woe to the man who thinks he is worth fifty-six times more than the woman who lovingly performs the dirty work.

Friday, February 8

Unrest in our rest home. There was a note on the bulletin board announcing that residents can apply to their doctors for a bracelet saying DO NOT RESUSCITATE. The note was not signed. At coffee hour many of the residents expressed outrage over this far-from-subtle pitch.

"They would like to be rid of us."

"We cost too much."

Fat Mr. Bakker was amenable to being revived by a girl, but was adamant he would not want a man to give him mouth-to-mouth. "I'd rather die." Was there a special bracelet for that?

After the coffee hour the note was gone. No one had any idea who had removed it.

I hope the bracelet isn't too conspicuous, otherwise we'll never hear the end of it. I will ask my doctor about it.

I have invited Eefje and Evert for tea tomorrow afternoon. A proper English tea, triangular sandwiches with the crusts cut off, and chocolates, biscuits, and cake. And something with cream. I'll have to sort out what else goes into high tea. There's a Brit living on the fifth floor, only he's got a foreign surname. He may know only about Pakistani tea customs, but I am still going to go and ask him.

In the hallway I bumped into the sweet young social worker my doctor had sent over to stop me from committing euthanasia. "See, still alive!" I told her, with a broad wink. She had to laugh. She's all right, that one. I can't think when I last winked at anyone. It must have been at my daughter.

Saturday, February 9

I'm actually a little nervous about the visit this afternoon. I keep telling myself to act normally, but in the meantime I've tidied my room, scrubbed the floor, ironed my shirt twice, and bought four kinds of cookies. And I'll have to pop back to the store shortly for something other than English Breakfast tea. I am not following the advice of the friendly Pakistani gentleman. He solemnly presented me with a heavy book about tea customs all over the world. In Urdu.

In Tibet the ninety-ninth protester has gone and immolated himself. There ought to be a special celebration marking the hundredth one. It has also been trendy for some time in the Arab world to express your displeasure that way. It must be said: you do get people to pay attention, even if just for a short while.

I seriously disapprove of the way things are run around here too, but setting myself on fire would be going a bit too far. I do know some other people I wouldn't mind setting fire to, though, to get people's attention.

According to *de Volkskrant*, the Netherlands and the Scandinavian countries have the best elderly care in the world. I mentioned this casually to some of my fellow inmates over coffee. To say that they were convinced would be an overstatement. Either they didn't believe it, or they decided it didn't matter.

"If even here we're pinching pennies to eke out our pensions, what must it be like in other parts of the world?" they wondered, concerned.

The fact that there are perhaps half a billion old people who have never even heard of such a thing as an old-age pension seemed highly unlikely to most of them.

Sunday, February 10

It wasn't a total disaster, the tea. But to claim that I was a relaxed, witty, and intelligent host is not the whole truth either.

Eefje was the first to arrive. I gave her a "house tour" and she kindly characterized it as "cozy." That covers many bases.

Then, with a great deal of noise, Evert barged in. He has my spare key and refuses to use the bell. He walked into the room with a broad grin and an overly loud "Yo!" When I asked what kind of tea he'd like, he expressed surprise, since until now I'd never offered him anything but English Breakfast. And when a bit later I casually brought out the assorted cookies, he said he felt like a king; he had never been treated in such royal fashion before.

"Or is all this in honor of this lovely queen?" Accompanied by a broad wink.

I believe I blushed a little. Eefje smiled and said she felt very honored.

We chatted about this, that, and the weather. Then it

was time to ask Eefje discreetly how she likes our institution. She was diplomatically noncommittal.

"I don't like to be too hasty in my judgment, but besides the advantages, of course, there are a few 'areas for improvement,' to put it in modern-day business parlance."

"Such as?" Evert wanted to know.

"I am still in the process of reviewing it. Perhaps we could devote another tea to the subject in the near future."

"Or something stronger perhaps."

What Evert was asking for was gin—a red flag, or at least an orange one, because alcohol doesn't exactly bring out the restrained subtlety in him.

But again Eefje resolved it elegantly. "Right, perhaps something stronger. I might ask you two to come to my place for a glass of brandy next time. But I'm not promising anything," she added, smiling.

"Or gin instead?"

Evert doesn't need drink to be unsubtle.

"I don't know why, Evert, but I have the feeling that when it comes to alcohol, with you it's quantity over quality. And my guess is that with Henk it's the exact opposite."

"Eefje, I'll have to invite you more often," I said with a grin at both guests.

Half an hour later she said goodbye. Another point in her favor: she doesn't overstay her welcome.

Evert compensated amply for her absence. Two hours and five glasses of gin later I kicked him out.

The minutes of the Residents' Association are pinned to the bulletin board. *"The association will henceforth provide cocktail nuts and pretzel sticks on bingo night."*

The pretzel sticks will probably be set out on the tables in drinking glasses. That will provoke at least one person to say, "Gee, remember when you'd have glasses filled with cigarettes like that, on birthdays and other occasions?" "Ah, yes. One glass of filtered cigarettes, one of unfiltered." If that little exchange doesn't take place, I'll eat my cigar. Or, at least, the cigar band. Ah yes, in the old days, when everything was so much better, we used to save those.

"The Residents' Association's fee will be raised ten cents." I did read it right: ten whole cents.

The biannual outing has been postponed until the organizing committee can agree on where to go. Ever since they were unable to find a new evening for bingo night, the members have been deeply divided on every issue. They'll try to choose a destination and a date again at the next meeting. If they don't succeed, the committee will schedule a new election in order to break the impasse.

James Onedin is dead. He is fondly remembered from the seventies British TV series *The Onedin Line.* One or two old ladies wiped away a tear. Such whiskers! Such boldness! And then, forty years ago, they would have glanced at the guy next to them on the couch and decided that, sadly, he would just have to do.

The elderly may take pleasure in the fact that they are drawing a great deal of interest of late. Not only in the Netherlands, in Germany too. There was quite a bit of hoopla about the book *Mother, When Will You Finally Die?* by Martina Rosenberg. She spent years caring for her demented parents. The fact that some German offspring dump their invalid parents in much cheaper nursing homes in the Ukraine, Slovakia, or even Thailand was widely reported in the papers. Our neighbors to the east have the *Elternunterhalt*, or compulsory parent support, to deal with. If between Mom and Dad's pensions and the piggy bank there isn't enough to pay for the nursing home, the children have to pay up: parent alimony. With a little bad luck, you could find yourself having to pay both child support and parent support.

In our own old-age home, however, the alarming cutbacks in elderly care aren't felt that painfully. Most of the residents have their state pension and a small additional one from their work. If you hoard your pennies, you'll even have some left over. And they are ever so thrifty in here! The main expenditures are on cookies, chocolates, the hairdresser, and the private minibus. Almost no one goes on holiday. Nobody still has a car. I rarely see expensive furniture or clothing. Eating in a restaurant is a waste of money and taxis are the ultimate extravagance. Old people like to deprive themselves.

Meanwhile the average age of the nursing home resident keeps going up. People are living independently longer, and are therefore older when they enter the home. At eighty-three I am one of the youngest.

Once you are here, there is no way out; nobody ever goes back to living in an apartment. They don't throw you out for being penniless either. Sure, the children complain! They're furious that Mom or Dad is obliged to spend *their* inheritance down to the last cent. The longer the parent stays alive, the less is left over. If it were up to me, I would tell them, dear child, it's not my problem.

Poverty among the elderly is much less severe than people think. According to the latest research, just 2.6 percent of those over sixty-five are poor. Sixty-three percent even say they're managing to get by quite well.

The people making the fuss about seniors' being robbed blind are the younger elements of 50Plus, which now has thirteen seats in Parliament. That's Henk Krol and his buddies, who are still in their prime and still have plenty of time ahead of them to enjoy their generous pensions. To have the cut-off at fifty makes no sense. Fifty is the wealthiest and most powerful age group in the Netherlands. Sixty-five, or soon sixty-seven, would be a better starting point. And even then there's an enormous difference between someone who is just retiring and the extremely aged population in here. I would argue for the formation of a 67Plus, a 77Plus and an 87Plus; 97Plus probably wouldn't have enough members to make the electoral threshold.

Wednesday, February 13

The pope has knocked the horsemeat scandal off the top spot of coffee table conversation topics. Everyone thought it was sensible of the holy father to decide to take his retirement. As for the possibility of a black pope, opinions were mixed. Mr. Schut didn't like the idea. He thought Berlusconi would make a better candidate.

Fortunately there were enough of us who had no objection in principle to a black pope; the only objections had to do with the need for a pope at all. Ours was originally a Catholic institution, but with a smattering of other denominations. Tensions between Catholics, Calvinists, and Protestants are never very far below the surface. The pope is a divisive figure to begin with.

Rough sketch of a typical day: Part 1

I get up at around half past eight. Then I walk to the minimarket for two fresh rolls. While having my breakfast I peruse *de Volkskrant*, which has become quite ugly lately. Then I write here in my secret diary for a bit. This takes about an hour. Next I go downstairs for coffee hour, and after I've finished my coffee I have a cigarette. After the coughing fit, at about half past eleven, I take my exercise by going for a stroll around the home or outside. I normally start off in Evert's direction, but lately I often find myself trying to bump into Eefje by accident. I have the feeling she doesn't mind coming face-to-face with me. Seeing that neither of us seems to mind giving chance a bit of a leg up, we'll often sit down together for a second cup of coffee.

I have invited her to a lunchtime concert at the town hall. She accepted the invitation with pleasure but remarked that stairs are a big problem for her.

At one o'clock I have my lunch in the restaurant downstairs, and Evert frequently stops in for a sandwich. If you want to eat in the dining room, you have to let them know a week ahead. That's when you receive a form to fill out. You have to tell them whether you are planning to have lunch and/or dinner for the next seven days, and what you would like to eat. At night you're given a choice of three main courses, two appetizers, and two desserts. You just mark the little boxes with an X. Your name is on the form, as are all your dietary restrictions.

Evert always fills in all seven sandwich boxes, whether he intends to show up for lunch or not. My spy in the office informs me the head cook has complained to the director about the waste of sandwiches for all the times Evert does not show up, but Mrs. Stelwagen couldn't find anything against it in the rules and regulations.

Thursday, February 14

Early this morning Evert slipped a Valentine's Day card under Eefje's door. He came to tell me about it at eight o'clock. He smelled of alcohol and clearly had not yet showered.

"Now you know, and you can pretend it's from you. It's a card with two swans on the front. Very romantic. I'm going back to bed now. 'Night, Henkie."

I was left speechless.

When I went to the corner store yesterday to buy a new scrub brush, there was a young lady of about eighteen behind the till. When I went to pay, I started fumbling around for my money; I couldn't find my wallet at first.

The checkout girl looked annoyed and was going to help the lady behind me, but the lady said, "No, this gentleman was first," and turning to me, she continued, "Take your time."

I finally managed to pull out a ten-euro note.

"There you are."

" . . ."

She slapped the change down on the counter.

"Thanks."

She didn't even deign to look at me.

There are people who despise anything old, gray, or slow. This bratty shopgirl was one of those. It's hard to steel oneself against a total lack of respect.

Mrs. Van Diemen hopes that the new pope, when elected, will in good time come to Amsterdam for Willem-Alexander's coronation. She really wants it to be a Dutch pope. Mrs. Van Diemen is well on her way to the locked ward.

Friday, February 15

Evert received a note from Eefje: "Thanks ever so much for the lovely card. I happened to see you push it under the door. I should like us to become better acquainted."

Evert was quite perplexed. Until I started laughing; I couldn't help it. Hoisted with his own petard. Then he hurled a banana at my head. It hit his only flower vase, leaving a big crack.

"I suppose I'll have to go and buy you a bunch of tulips this afternoon," I teased him. I couldn't help it.

It's driving everyone in here nuts, this never-ending snow!

I stopped by Anja's office to see if there was any more gossip about our director, who was away on important business. Her clothing allowance has been raised by two thousand euros per year. Sorry, not raised but "inflation-indexed."

Here in the home they have a great deal of respect for Stelwagen. For bigwigs in general, really.

I myself prefer to see bigwigs taken down a peg.

A few years ago three of the most powerful men in the world were in the news at once: Boris Yeltsin was too plastered to get off an airplane, Pope John Paul couldn't even get out a "Thank you for the flowers" without nodding off, and Bill Clinton had stuck his cigar into an intern's privates. That's no way to light a cigar, naturally, but what's far worse is that he couldn't stop his unorthodox smoking method from making headlines. And while I'm at it: at the UN Security Council, the Indian foreign minister accidentally read from a speech his Portuguese colleague had left on the podium. He never noticed it was the wrong speech. It took five minutes for a fellow countryman to get his attention.

I only mean to say that we had better take those in authority with a grain of salt.

"I taste horse!" fat Mr. Bakker yelled across the dining room. Upon which almost everyone who had ordered the meatballs was suddenly able to detect the taste of horsemeat. The cook was summoned: "No, that's impossible. The meat came from the wholesale butcher's, as always."

"So? What does that prove? The wholesale butcher can grind horsemeat and mix it in with the beef, can't he? I taste horse, that's final. I am not mad!" Bakker seethed.

Now, the problem is that Bakker *is* mad and a very unpleasant madman besides.

The head of housekeeping was brought in too, but she could sputter until she was blue in the face, nothing helped soothe the disgruntled crowd. Finally all the meatballs were traded in for fish and chips. Most people thought there was little chance of there being any horsemeat in that.

The mince has been ground with pigs' eyes and cows' udders for years, never a word, and now all of a sudden there's a stink over a smidgen of horsemeat!

Downstairs in the common room the radio is always on from ten till twelve. We are treated to the broadcast for hospital patients. No one knows why. Most residents don't mind the Dutch repertoire that's played for the invalids' pleasure: lots of torch songs and rollicking polkas.

One Easter morning a year ago, someone had the gumption to turn the dial to a classical music station: you should have seen the inmates clapping along to the strains of the St. Matthew Passion.

I am trying to train myself to ignore the background music. The trick is not to sit too close to the speakers. The hospital broadcast ends at noon. The relative peace and quiet is a delight to listen to.

Sunday, February 17

The concept of days of the week vanishes in a place where no one goes off to work and every day is the same as every other day. The staff work, of course, but they too do the same thing day after day.

The only day that's different is Sunday—three-quarters of the residents go to church in the morning, and the children and grandchildren come to visit in the afternoon. It's the only contact with the outside world some of the inmates have. And even if the visitors sometimes radiate boredom, it still counts: receiving lots of visitors gives you status around here. Unpleasant Mr. Pot spends the first half of the week jawing on about who came last time, and the second half of the week about who will come next time. He has eleven children. Pot is the kind of man who waits at the crosswalk until there's a car coming, and only then steps out into the road.

I never have visitors. I usually spend my Sunday afternoon watching videos. I am quite up to date cinematically. My room has a fairly decent-sized flat-screen. When it isn't on I hide it behind an imitation-Chinese screen. Sometimes I'll go and watch something at Evert's, but he mostly prefers thrillers and action films, which are not my favorite. Evert's son very occasionally pays a visit, and the odd granddaughter will sometimes pop in. Whether Eefje has any visitors, I don't know.

Rough sketch of a typical day: Part 2

The only people who still sit down for a hot lunch are farmers from East Groningen and residents of homes for the aged. Except us. Don't ask me why we seem to be the exception, but I am glad that we are.

After lunch I often rest my eyes for a quarter of an hour as a prelude to the afternoon's activities. I like to go out, but the truth is that my lack of mobility is making that increasingly difficult. I have trouble walking and my only means of transportation is the minibus operated by Connexxion. That's no picnic, I can tell you. Of course one shouldn't whine about the two euros it costs you for every trip, but Connexxion should really be called Mis-connexxion. They must be trying very hard in order to manage to get so much to go wrong. Let's just say that punctuality and Connexxion have a stormy relationship. Old age and impatience, on the other hand, are on inti-mate terms.

Monday, February 18

Of the five senses, my nose still works best. Which is not always a blessing in here. It smells of old people. I remem-ber thinking my grandpa and grandma's house smelled funny. An indefinable funk mixed with the odor of cigars. Humid clothes kept too long in plastic.

Not all the rooms are that bad. But sometimes before I visit someone I'll stuff cotton wool up my nostrils. Up nice and deep so it isn't noticeable.

The fact that many people here have no sense of smell anymore seems to give them a free pass to fart to their heart's content, and the oral hygiene isn't stellar either. As if offal were the only thing they get to eat here.

I myself am terrified that my dribble is leaving a pee odor wherever I go, so I change my clothes twice a day, douse myself generously with aftershave, down below as well, and suck on a ton of peppermints.

Instead of aftershave I'll sometimes go for a "fragrance." "The new fragrance for the older gentleman." I like to keep up with the times. When I asked at the pharmacy for a scent for an older gentleman they stared at me open-mouthed. Then they tried to stick me with a bottle costing fifty euros.

Many of my fellow residents have never moved past the eau de cologne stage—4711 or Old Spice. The air in here reeks of fifty years ago.

Rough sketch of a typical day: Conclusion

I force myself to go for at least one stroll every day, even in the pouring rain if there's no other option.

In the afternoon I do a lot of reading. Newspapers, magazines, and books. I accept every free trial subscription that comes my way. Not out of thriftiness; more as a kind of sport.

In the late afternoon I'll visit someone for a cup of tea, or, several times a week, I'll go off to Evert's for a glass of wine. Or he'll come over to my room for a cocktail. Evert always arranges for good booze in great quantities. I, however, partake in moderation, or else I'll fall asleep before supper.

After drinks I freshen up and then take myself downstairs for dinner. And despite all the grumbling, I usually find the food quite palatable. I often ask the staff to convey my compliments to the chef.

After dinner, coffee. After coffee, TV. After TV, bed. It isn't particularly adventurous or edifying. I can't claim there's any more to it than that.

Tuesday, February 19

Yesterday afternoon, by pure luck, the rebels' club came into being.

On the third Monday of the month there's often some cultural activity on the schedule, to take place in the recreation room. Usually it's a cringe-worthy exhibition of old people clapping along to someone warbling "Tulips from Amsterdam," but occasionally there's classical music. Everyone shows up, because it's free, isn't it?

Yesterday the Music Association offered a violin, cello, and piano trio. You can normally expect a bunch of uninspired moonlighters who only ever appear before seniors or the mentally handicapped, but this time it was two elegant ladies and one gentleman, about thirty years old, playing with abandon. They were not put off by Mrs. Snijder, who almost choked on a cookie, nor by Mr. Schipper, who slid off his chair and landed sideways in a flower planter. They just paused briefly and calmly resumed playing once the problem was taken care of. (As opposed to the pianist who once kept playing as if nothing were the matter as Mrs. Haringa was being resuscitated. A staff member finally had to shout at him to stop. Even though at that point it no longer made any difference to Haringa.)

After the performance a group of us found ourselves gathered around a table: Evert Duiker (who when all's told prefers Engelbert Humperdinck), Eefje Brand, Edward Schermer, Grietje de Boer, Graeme Gorter, and I, Hendrik Groen. The talk turned to the chronic dearth of distractions. Graeme then suggested that, if there was not enough in the way of diversion within the home, we should seek it on the outside on a more regular basis.

"We'll just have the minibus drive up to the front twice a month to take us somewhere. If all six of us at this table participate, and each comes up with a plan for four outings, then we'll have twenty-four field trips per year. That's something to look forward to, don't you think?"

He was absolutely right, and, at Grietje's suggestion, it was decided to meet in the common room tonight for the inaugural meeting of the Old But Not Dead Club.

I can't wait.

Wednesday, February 20

I had high hopes, and they came true: it was an exciting inaugural session. The laughter was loud, the enthusiasm great, and the alcohol, for us, abundant. Evert had supplied red wine, white wine, and gin.

After a lengthy and lively meeting, the following charter was adopted by unanimous consent.

1. The goal of the club is to increase the enjoyment of advanced age by arranging outings.

2. The outings will set off at 11 a.m. on a Monday, Wednesday, Thursday, or Friday.

3. No whining allowed.

4. The organizer must take into account the various infirmities of the members.

5. The organizer must take into account the limits of the state pension.

6. The organizer will not divulge more information about the trip beforehand than is strictly necessary.

7. Outside of points 2 to 6, anything goes.

8. This club is closed. No new members until further notice.

If necessary, Eefje will put her laptop at the disposal of the person charged with choosing a destination, and she will shortly give a Googling for Beginners course so that everyone can learn how to search for information. Graeme will take on the first outing, followed by Eefje, Grietje, me, Evert, and Edward. You could see everyone feverishly beginning to plot and scheme.

Opinions are divided on whether it was fate or coincidence, but be that as it may, it was an extraordinarily happy combination of circumstances that this particular group of six people just happened to be gathered around one table on Monday afternoon. They are all jolly nice, intelligent and, most important: not a whiner among them.

As if it were a teenagers' party that got out of hand! We'd stayed downstairs until about 11 p.m., and we may have been laughing just a bit too boisterously—at most. Nonetheless the following notice appeared on the board yesterday afternoon:

In response to several complaints about the noise, the management has decided that from Monday to Friday the Conversation Lounge will close at 10:30 p.m., in order to guarantee an undisturbed night's rest for all. Furthermore, residents are reminded to abide by the agreed two-drinks-per-person maximum.

I was never asked by anyone to agree to a two-drink maximum. Prohibition looms, and Evert has promptly declared that he will take on the Al Capone role and organize the bootleg operation. The Old But Not Dead Club is riled, up in arms, and extremely motivated. It wasn't cops, tear gas, or Twitter; a note on a bulletin board was enough. Thanks very much, management.

Edward Schermer surprised all of us by coming out of his shell. Normally he doesn't say much because he is hard to understand on account of the stroke. But just now, at teatime, in front of quite a gathering of residents downstairs, he stood up and in a loud, slurred voice demanded to know who had complained about the noise.

The room immediately went quiet.

Then Edward explained, vociferously and with great difficulty—which is what made it so impressive—that he was sorry the plaintiffs had not come to him first, or to one of the others who had been up late the night before.

Still nobody said a word.

"We may assume, then, that it was not anyone who is here now," he deduced, sitting down again.

Eefje looked around the circle with a benevolent smile. "It is indeed a pity that we don't have the guts to raise these issues amongst ourselves, like adults." With that she fixed a lengthy and pointed gaze at Mrs. Surmann, who grew quite agitated.

"I didn't do it," she volunteered.

"Do what?"

"Complain."

"Well, that's lucky then, isn't it?" Eefje accompanied this with a most beatific smile.

She must have seen or heard something. I don't know if I should ask her about it or not.

Friday, February 22

Asteroid strikes, spontaneously combusting solar panels, horsemeat lasagna, the return of Berlusconi: any of these disasters could happen while we're still alive. The real terror that has gripped the home for the last two days, however, is of being put out on the street if you're not disabled enough. The announcement that 800 of the 2,000 nursing homes in the Netherlands will have to close their doors by the year 2020 is causing great concern. People who are only "mildly symptomatic" will just have to manage on their own. Several housemates have immediately begun embellishing their own infirmities, just in case, so that seven years from now they'll be allowed to stay put. Dear people, let me reassure you: in seven years' time everyone here will either be dead or terminally disabled! That's what I wanted to yell at them.

Old people and their completely irrational fears...

And, if you're unwilling to sit and wait quietly until you get kicked out of your room, why not apply to 50Plus to be trained as a politician? They are looking for candidates for local and provincial councils, and the national or European parliaments; 50Plus seems to keep going up in the polls. It should provide plenty of entertainment, watching all those doddering political novices being allowed to weigh in on this, that, and the other.

My doctor is a strange fellow. When I asked him how he thought I was overall, he asked, "What would you like me to tell you?"

"Well, I should like you to tell me that I'm fit as a fiddle, but perhaps a bit more realistically: how long do I have left, approximately?"

"You could hang on for years if everything goes well, but it could also be over for you by the next quarter."

Who uses the phrase *the next quarter* in this context? No one except Dr. Oomes. Not only that: it made him laugh heartily too.

When I said that he hadn't offered a very clear answer, he laughed again. And since he seemed to be in such a good mood, I plucked up the courage to ask him if he'd been the one to send the social worker around to ask about my suicide plans. He even seemed to find that funny too.

"Indeed, I thought, 'There's no harm in checking it out.' Lovely girl, isn't she?" And in the same breath: "Well, until next time." A minute later I found myself standing outside again, nonplussed and none the wiser.

It's an old lesson, but one that I've had to learn all over again: before going to the doctor, always jot down all your questions, and be sure to go over the list with him item by item.

Saturday, February 23

The old rebels' club is meeting at Eefje's for a Google lesson tonight. The halls are already abuzz. Mrs. Baken has been fishing for an invite: "How nice, I've *always* wanted to learn how to google." But there's a strict door policy, and Baken does not qualify. She is suspected of having told on Mrs. Brinkman for keeping her old dachshund under the sink. Everyone is innocent until proven guilty, but if there's the slightest doubt, you're out.

I have asked Eefje if she knew who had complained about the noise on Tuesday. She said she had overheard Mrs. Surmann tell her neighbor that she'd lodged a complaint with management.

"We can't be one hundred percent certain, since we don't know what her complaint was about, but there is definitely reason to suspect her."

Yesterday, Cook received a request for horse steak to be added to the menu. "Preferably a milk-fed foal, and please, nothing force-fed," read the anonymous note. At least, that was the rumor. And that rumor led to yet another lively debate at the dinner table about which animals one should eat and which should be eschewed. Evert wondered if a monkey sandwich might be an option. That took up another quarter of an hour.

I'm going up to bed for a while. I'm feeling exhausted, don't ask me why, and I want to be fit for tonight.

Sunday, February 24

There was plenty of cursing as people drew open their curtains this morning: more snow. Cursing of a mild caliber, I assure you, along the lines of "Darn it all." But it's true that we are fed up with winter. We'd really appreciate some warming sun for our old bones. Not too warm, naturally; no hotter than seventy-two degrees or thereabouts. It's a narrow window.

While I wasn't looking, Henk Krol the Savior jumped up to *twenty-four* seats in the polls! 50Plus will be seeing to it that the Netherlands' seniors aren't ripped off any further.

"They have it in for us because there's nothing we can do about it. We can't go on strike or anything. We've got no one to stick up for us." "Victim" is the role meant for the sad old coot. It's lucky not everyone joins in the chorus of wailing.

The female residents think Henk's attractive. Certainly, he's often seen wearing a lovely scarf. He could just squeak by, age-wise, as the ideal son-in-law, if it weren't for the fact that he's gay.

We had a very pleasant Google evening last night. Evert pronounces it "joogling" and now several of the other inmates are under the impression that we are learning to juggle. Someone asked when we'd be putting on a show. Graeme: "When we have the balls."

Excellent refreshments and pleasant company. Eefje the charming hostess; Evert, always the loudmouth but this time not *too* loud, drank in moderation; Edward, who doesn't say much, but when he does it's worth listening to; Graeme, ruminative, still rather bashful; and finally Grietje, the evening's revelation on account of her remarkable computer know-how, brought to light in all modesty. In consultation with Eefje, Grietje graciously took command, and we spent over two hours practicing, searching for information using examples suggested by the others. In coming up with examples, no one divulged his or her plans for eventual outings. Evert wanted to find out about Amsterdam's bungee-jumping possibilities. Edward said he wasn't coming, because bungee jumping was *sooo* 2012. It's a shame no one else heard him say it.

Monday, February 25

Mrs. Stelwagen has asked Eefje to come to her office on Wednesday. Eefje seems quite unconcerned. Perhaps she's just a cool customer, or perhaps she doesn't want to make a big song and dance about it. I myself would be rather a wreck if I received an invitation of that sort. I can't imagine that Stelwagen just wants to ask her how she likes it here. Our director is a crafty sort; gracious on the outside, but power-hungry to the nth degree. Always so sympathetic—"Deeply sorry...but it's the rules." Usually her own rules. She finds it convenient to hide behind them. And if necessary, a new rule will suddenly pop up "in the residents' best interests." She is clever enough to see to it there is no outright abuse. Minor infractions are hushed up or the blame pinned on others. Protected by the board of directors, her throne is secure; a temporary throne she'll trade for a bigger model as soon as she gets the chance, I'm telling you.

She's always impeccably dressed, and is invariably friendly, calm, and polite. She hears and controls everything. She has faithful accomplices. Some are known to us, but there must be some working undercover.

She's running a suffocating regime on the QT. Every personal initiative, anything that falls outside the norm, is shot down with a smile.

I asked Eefje if she would like me to go with her.

"What for?" she said.

"Well, she's a tough customer. She destroys people with a sweet smile."

"We'll see. Thanks for the warning. I'll keep it in mind."

Tuesday, February 26

Evert was wondering if it wasn't time for another covert action along the lines of the cake in the fish tank. He wouldn't mind having another lark. "This joint could use a good shake-up." I couldn't really disagree but am afraid that this sort of stunt really only goes after the superficial symptoms.

The real problem is insoluble.

The way I see it, growing old follows the same trajectory as a baby developing into an adult, only the other way around. You go from physical independence to becoming more and more dependent on others. An artificial hip, a bypass, a pill here or there—all it does is paper over the cracks. If death takes too long to come, you end up as a sputtering old toddler in a diaper and with a runny nose. The voyage out, from zero to eighteen, is wonderful, challenging, exciting: you are about to make your own way in life. Around the age of forty you're strong, healthy, and powerful. In the prime of life. Sadly, you usually don't come to that realization until the descent has already begun, as, slowly and noiselessly, your horizons shrink and life becomes emptier. Until your daily goals and ambitions are whittled down to a cup of tea and a cookie—the old-folks' version of the baby's rattle.

Forgive me please. I'm just rambling on.

Whereas in fact I have just taken a few important steps toward going down having a blast. With new friends and wild plans. Whoopee!

Wednesday, February 27

I'm writing this a bit later than usual because I was waiting to hear how Eefje's audience with Stelwagen had gone. We had a cup of coffee together beforehand, and when she left, I wished her luck. She returned fifteen minutes later. There was something sternly resolute about her, but don't ask me what made me think that. Her eyes, perhaps.

"Compliments on your perceptive prognosis, Henk. It didn't miss the mark."

She told me that Mrs. Stelwagen had started off by inquiring how she was and then almost casually mentioned that it wasn't customary in "our home" to receive guests late at night.

"Do you mean me?" Eefje had asked in response.

"It's nothing personal, but in view of the need for peace and quiet, we don't like to have people wandering the hallways after ten o'clock or so."

"I've never noticed any excessive noise, myself."

"Other people have."

"That's a shame. But what does this have to do with me, anyway?"

"I heard that you entertained some guests a few days ago."

"Yes, I did. Very calm and civilized people. I asked my neighbors the next day if they had been bothered by it, but they had not. Fortunately."

This was great. I gave Eefje a high five. The first high five of my life, actually; where that came from, I have no idea.

Stelwagen had seemed a bit put out, but when she said goodbye to Eefje she was all smiles, as if there were no tension between them at all.

"This isn't over, Hendrik," said Eefje. "I feel it in my bones."

We took a little stroll through the garden. There's a

touch of spring in the air. The snowdrops are poking their heads up through the plastic litter and rusting tins.

We're feeling combative. At least I think I can speak for her as well.

Thursday, February 28

I picked up a brochure downstairs, about mobility scooters. I must broaden my range, otherwise I'll wind up being Old But Not Dead's weakest link.

Graeme has announced that the first outing will take place on Thursday, March 14. We'll assemble at one o'clock in the entrance hall.

I've been racking my brain about fun day trips. I haven't come up with anything besides the Rijksmuseum, and that's certainly not going to win any prizes for originality. Besides which, that museum seems to be closed more often than it is open. But no need to panic, I have six weeks to think of something more exciting.

Eefje played me a bit of her double CD *Top 100 Bird Songs*. At number six was the garden warbler (never heard it nor heard *of* it); at number five, the wren; at number four, robin redbreast (I always thought that ticking call was the only sound they made); at number three the song thrush; number two was the nightingale (with a great reputation in poetry and song) . . . and the gold medal goes to the blackbird, finally a bird whose whistle I recognize. And then there are ninety-four more whistling blowhards to go. To each her own.

After ten birds, Eefje could tell my attention was waning.

"Aren't you just fascinated?" she asked wickedly.

I blushed. "Oh, I am."

"If I may be so bold, I don't believe you, Hendrik."

"Well, you're right, I'm sorry, but birds only really interest me when they've been roasted. And at that point they're generally no longer singing." It made her laugh, luckily.

What about the bulb gardens at Keukenhof, would that be something worthwhile? Chances are someone else has thought of it. But six weeks from now would be the perfect time of year for it.

Friday, March 1

Mr. Kuiper found a newspaper article in a file in the library and pinned it on the bulletin board: "DOCTORS IN FAVOR OF REMOVING KIDNEYS FROM TERMINAL PATIENTS WHILE STILL ALIVE."

Mrs. Brandsma immediately canceled the date for her surgery. "Just leave that fibroid right where it is, I won't have them helping themselves to whatever they like in there. After all, we're all terminal in here!" she cried, and she does have a point. The average age in here, I believe, is eighty-nine, so when you say "terminal," you're talking about a high probability. The reason for removing organs from patients that aren't dead yet is that they are fresher. I don't know if you can call ours fresh, exactly. The average age of the kidneys in here is, of course, also eighty-nine. I'm not sure how the expiration dates of internal organs work.

It's a bit grim, really, that article. You'd better not hope for a medical miracle: say you survive a terminal heart attack against the odds, and then it turns out they've removed both your kidneys!

Mobility scooters aren't as straightforward as you'd think. They come in all shapes and sizes. You have to decide how tight a turning circle you want, for example, which is important to know if you want to be able to turn it around in your own room.

The range. How far do you want to be able to go?

Three wheels or four. How tippy is it, can it capsize?

Also of some importance: how fast do you want it to go?

And finally, the most important factor for a Dutchman: what does a thing like that cost?

I'll have a word with Mr. Hoogdalen shortly. He's very knowledgeable. And a nice fellow too.

Saturday, March 2

The woman from Breda who escaped from prison by digging a tunnel with a spoon has yet to be caught. It's great to know that such things can still happen in real life. What if an inmate were to escape from this institution the same way? Now *that* would be brilliant. Just for the symbolism, naturally, since he or she could also just walk out the front door. The hard part comes afterward, since most of the inmates here have nowhere to go. Their children would certainly have no part in it.

"Hello, son, I've come to live with you."

"Sorry, Dad, but that's just not convenient right now."

The fugitive senior doesn't have many options other than a hotel on the Veluwe. Then, once the money's all gone, it's back to the old-age home or the Salvation Army, with your tail between your legs.

Incidentally, here in the Netherlands there are thirteen thousand people "missing" from prison. That's quite a number. The police aren't very good at finding them, apparently.

The old noggin is failing. Senility-light is gradually turning into senility-moderate. I was trying to recall the top ten bird songs but couldn't get past the first four.

What surprises me is that some people can't remember a shopping list with three items on it but are able to sing along to ten thousand songs on the radio. Or at least hum them. All those tunes stored away intact! Music and memory; they must be linked somehow. They ought to set German vocabulary lists or the first law of thermodynamics to music. Or write a musical based on the important dates of Dutch history.

Sunday, March 3

Yesterday a rack from Kring, the pharmacy, appeared downstairs in the lobby, with some fifty different information leaflets. Allow me to give just a sample of the uplifting topics: hemorrhoids, diarrhea, eczema, head lice, incontinence, boils, constipation, athlete's foot, worms, and warts.

Every ailment under the sun neatly arranged in alphabetical order. And without regard for the audience in here, because I also noticed leaflets on acne and postnatal care, matters of no great concern to us.

As if there weren't enough talk in this place about aches and infirmities.

All right, to be perfectly honest, I did slip the incontinence leaflet as unobtrusively as I could into my breast pocket. It seems that I am in good company: there are about a million other Dutch dribblers. Which means enough urine is collected in our citizens' underpants and diapers to fill an entire swimming pool *every day*. Yippee!

There's a great deal of speculation and fishing about where our first Old But Not Dead outing will take us. Evert wants to set himself up as a bookie so that people can place bets on it.

The excitement is akin to the feeling you had as a kid the night before a school trip. If I remember it right, that is.

Mrs. Schreuder (of the vacuumed canary) was wondering who's in charge now in Vatican City. The old pope has stepped down and the new one hasn't been chosen yet. "We are a church without a shepherd," she declared. "Like a chicken without a head," said one of the Slothouwer sisters, never shy about pushing someone's buttons.

I am trying to picture the conclave: 115 elderly cardinals in one room, not allowed to set a foot outside until they've sent the white smoke wafting up the chimney, and that's easier said than done. During the 1978 conclave, the fireplace didn't draw well, and the room filled up with black smoke.

A huge panic: Mrs. Schaar has escaped from the dementia unit. It seems she convinced a new intern that she was allowed out without an escort. The intern's excuse is that her own IQ is somewhere around 55. Mrs. Schaar graciously swept out the front door. She believes she's nobility. She introduces herself as Lady Schaar. Always on the lookout for her estates. Crazy as a loon, and a diabetic too.

A good portion of the staff were sent out to look for her. Someone asked Stelwagen if the police shouldn't be called in. "No, that's not necessary, there's no reason."

The director is terrified of negative publicity and likes to keep the dirty laundry hidden away.

A short time later the floor manager announced that Mrs. Schaar had been found. Probably a lie to make everyone calm down, because Schaar was nowhere to be seen. Evert put the story to the test by casually telling a nurse that he had seen Lady Schaar standing at the bus stop. Two minutes later a couple of staffers were seen heading for the very same stop. That said it all.

Forty-five minutes later Sister "Compostella," a dear with an unpronounceable Spanish name, came and told us that Mrs. Schaar had been found. "But wasn't she already home safe and sound?" asked Mr. Brentjens. "Yes, but now she really *is*," the nurse said brightly.

Five minutes later the baroness was led in through the

back door. Spackled with mud. She later explained that she had been held up by the hunt on her estate. It turned out that she slipped and fell in the mud in a little park about a mile from here, and was unable to get up again by herself. A man walking his dog found her and alerted the police. The officers who brought her back spent at least twenty minutes in Stelwagen's office. Afterward all residents were urgently requested not to spread any gossip about the incident, for our own good. Stelwagen made a point of stopping by Evert's armchair to tell him Mrs. Schaar had not been on any bus.

"I never said she was, sister. I only saw her standing at the bus stop."

"I am not your sister and I have my doubts about what you saw. I would advise you to be more circumspect in future."

Evert, who calls everyone who works here "sister" or "brother," was ready with a retort: "To be even more circumspect than I already am—impossible, Mrs. Sister!"

Stelwagen hesitated a moment, then turned and walked away.

Later some of the staff went around asking if anyone had noticed if Mr. Duiker had stepped outside at all today. He had. Mr. Evert Duiker isn't an idiot.

Tuesday, March 5

Interesting discussion at teatime yesterday afternoon, sparked by the finding that scientists have managed to connect the brains of two rats separated by a distance of several miles.

The question was: whose brain would you want to have linked to yours if you had the choice? Many of the parents among us chose one of their offspring. I don't think that if it were the other way around, a child would enjoy peeking inside his or her parent's head. Mrs. Brandsma chose Tom Jones. Fat Bakker would like to give Obama a piece of his mind.

I couldn't think of anyone myself. Frightening idea, some outsider poking about inside your head.

Great disappointment for a number of residents: they weren't able to reserve a minibus for the coronation on April 30. The bus company won't put on an extra bus to drive them to the Royal Palace. They are now trying to line up transportation to the banks of the River IJ, in hope of catching a glimpse of the royal couple as they sail past. Mrs. Hoogstraten has already bought herself a pricey pair of binoculars. She has begged God to let her make it to April 30, and to see in the new pope as well. She even asked me to pray for her. Sadly for Mrs. Hoogstraten, God and I agreed long ago to stay out of each other's business.

A bank was robbed by two thieves disguised as old people. Latex masks and all. Wouldn't it be a laugh if the men under those masks were actually elderly?

Wednesday, March 6

The first sunny day of the year is the best. Yesterday afternoon I spent forty-five minutes sitting on the bench at the front entrance. I was the first one there. Not long after, the bench was full. A few envious latecomers paced up and down waiting for us to leave. Tough luck.

As the years mount up, everything else slows down. Walking, eating, talking, thinking. Reading too. It takes me three to four days to get through all the Sunday supplements, if I don't want to fall behind on the daily paper. I finally got around to reading a special section on aging yesterday. It's something I've noticed before: old age seems to be in fashion these days. The babies born right after the war are retiring; a few years from now it will be the hippie generation's turn. The age group that's in power now has discovered one important thing: you have to take good care of yourself. No one needs to spend much time worrying about those so-called senior citizens for another fifteen years at least. These over-fifties don't in any way resemble the over-eighties for whom this home is the penultimate resting place. We are the ones who learned to take good care of *others*, namely our own kids, who are now in the prime of their lives. We're feeling rather neglected by those kids at the moment, actually. Many of my fellow residents wound up in here constrained by circumstance: too old and infirm to continue living independently, and too poor to hire the help they needed. They have had to come to terms with the prospect of living out their sunset years in an old-age home.

After a while, the phrase *old-age home* began making people feel uneasy. It was replaced with *retirement home* and then *assisted-living facility*. The nursing home became a "care center." And in the latest version, it seems I am enrolled in a "market-oriented health-services organization providing individually tailored care." I now understand why health-care costs keep skyrocketing.

Thursday, March 7

I took a head count once: we have 160 seniors living in here, give or take. Connected to this care center is a nursing unit that has about another eighty befuddled or seriously impaired geriatric patients. I can't give you an exact number because there's a constantly revolving door of the living and the dead. I would estimate that when they arrive a person has on average about five years left to live, so if you count the care center and retirement home together, that works out to some fifty deaths a year. If you grow to a very old age in here and remain on your feet, you may have to attend as many as five hundred burials or cremations in the last ten years of your life. A lovely prospect.

This morning I couldn't find my keys anywhere. Turned my entire room, including the bed alcove, upside down, small as it is. Luckily I wasn't in any hurry. I must have searched for an hour without swearing (almost), finally to discover the keys in the fridge. Absent-mindedness. Old people, like children, are always losing things, but they no longer have a mom to tell them where to look.

Friday, March 8

Having broached the subject of death just yesterday, I now discover that death has paid a visit to Feel Good Fitness!

Mrs. De Leeuw announced, "I don't feel so good," and two minutes later she was no longer feeling fit either. She sat slumped in her chair and didn't catch the ball that was thrown at her.

"Pay attention, Mrs. De Leeuw," Tina, the exercise teacher, chided her. Then Mrs. De Leeuw slid off her chair onto the floor.

They tried to resuscitate her; the defibrillator was brought in, but all in vain. The dreadful Slothouwer sisters stood there gaping, fascinated, until someone told them to move out of the way. Later, during coffee, they gave us a blow-by-blow of what they had seen. Given the chance, those Slothouwers would happily be spectators at a public execution.

Mrs. De Leeuw's passing put a bit of a damper on the cheerful mood brought on by several days of springtime weather. Some inmates won't set a foot outside the door if it is at all cold or wet. So in the spring, at the first sign of a bit of sunshine, there's a good deal of rapturous outdoor strolling. The announcement yesterday that we may have snow again in four days led to even greater zeal for taking a constitutional.

I wanted to go for a walk with Eefje, but she wasn't home. So I had to make do with my friend Evert. Upon entering his room I found him snipping at his nose hairs with a pair of nail scissors. I was a bit embarrassed, but Evert kept at it, taking his time, even with me standing there. We weren't allowed to go out until he had finished trimming his ears.

"You never know whom you might bump into," was his explanation.

Saturday, March 9

I am ill. I'll spare you the unappetizing details. I hope to have recovered by Thursday, the day of our first excursion.

Wednesday, March 13

It was touch and go, but I am going to make it. The members of the club were wondering if the outing should be postponed, but it isn't necessary. I am back on my feet.

The doctor came to see me on Monday. He casually let on that it looked a bit like the Mexican flu to him. A few years ago the entire country was in an uproar over that flu, and you couldn't switch on the radio or TV without having to listen to some epidemiologist; yet now that I may actually *have* it, my doctor can't even be bothered to give me a proper diagnosis!

One of the nurses later sternly asked that when I tell the other residents I had the flu I would please leave the word *Mexican* out of it.

"Who told you to say that?"

She couldn't tell me.

It does make you wonder. Could Mrs. De Gans's death a month ago possibly have been due to Mexican flu?

"They" are probably worried about another wave of flu hysteria among us.

Yesterday Evert stopped by with a fruit basket: an empty egg carton sporting three kiwis and three clementines.

Eefje brought me a book: *Five Hundred Poems Everyone*

Should Read. I have vowed to read one a day, in the fervent hope that I am granted another five hundred days.

On my doctor's advice I have made an appointment with a geriatrician. My "potpourri of ailments" was something his "confrère" would be interested in. He pronounced the word *confrère* with a rather plummy accent. He wrote a note to his *confrère* and showed it to me. It said, in essence: "Why don't you see if there's something you can do for this nice old gentleman."

They have an opening for me as early as next week. There may be a monetary consideration: old people have to be seen in a hurry, or they might die before you've even made a cent. Once they're dead the only one who stands to make a profit is the undertaker.

My personal doctor says the geriatrician is a "personable" guy. I can't wait.

Friday, March 15

At 12:55, five minutes early (!), the Connexxion minibus drove up to the front door and our group climbed in. We were a bit giddy. It wasn't even three minutes before the peppermints were offered around. Fifteen minutes later we got out at Central Station, where a water taxi awaited us.

After a few minutes on the water, Evert made a pretense of feeling seasick, quite realistically I must say, and then told us about a man he used to know, a frequent traveler who collected the airsickness bags from all the airlines he'd flown on. Then Evert proceeded to imitate Mr. Bean, who, clueless as to what those bags are for, blows up one that's been used until it bursts in someone's face.

Eefje *tut-tut*ted, and suggested taking a vote on whether to expel Evert from the club. Evert was visibly alarmed, until Eefje started guffawing at his crestfallen expression. I'm not fond of that hee-hawing laugh of hers, but it is the only negative I have found in her thus far.

After tootling along Amsterdam's canals for an hour or so, we arrived at the Hermitage Museum on the Amstel, where we disembarked. A sophisticated fellow who was very knowledgeable about art and seemed to assume we were equally keen to learn about it, gave us a lengthy tour of the place.

Then we stopped for beer, wine, and an order of croquettes in a café along the Amstel. That's where the old-people's minibus came to pick us up just after half past five. The driver, in the habit of driving cranky old geezers to and from the hospital, seemed rather surprised at having to flush a gang of merrymakers out of a pub.

Punctually, at six o'clock on the dot, we sat down at the dining table for a repast of meatballs and endive. The six of us were in high spirits, in contrast to the prevailing mood.

Mrs. Stelwagen, on her way from her office to the exit, raised an eyebrow as we pushed our way past her. I may be wrong, but I do think I detected a measure of disapproval in her eyes.

Graeme was lauded, nearly unintelligibly, by Edward, for raising the bar so high on our very first outing: "Ooh sheh she toh."

"You set the tone." Graeme did the simultaneous interpretation, since he's the one who has the least trouble understanding Edward. A touching exchange.

"Ank oo."

"No, thank *you*."

After that, we all collapsed a bit. By eight o'clock the entire Old But Not Dead Club had gone up to bed, so the gossiping could—presumably—begin.

Saturday, March 16

We seem to have caught the bug. Now there's a plan to start a separate cooking club, alongside Old But Not Dead. The original members except one (Evert), bolstered by the addition of Ria and Antoine Travemundi, like the idea of serving up an elaborate and elegant meal once a month. The Travemundis ran a restaurant for many years; they are passionate about preparing food as well as consuming it, and all too often find themselves getting up from the table disappointed. I am expecting great things of them. My own culinary talents run more to elementary tasks like dicing, slicing, and stirring.

Yesterday we were sitting around the table happily rehashing our first outing, when Ria and Antoine timidly came to ask if they might join us. Of course.

They told us they thought our excursion club was a lovely idea. Not that they expected us to invite them to join, naturally; but would we be interested in forming a group to cook and dine together from time to time? Once a month, for example. The object would be to come up with some very special concoctions.

Just the suggestion brought a gleam to many an eye.

Except Evert's. He came right out and declared he wasn't keen on fancy nosh and hated having anything more complicated to concoct than a fried egg.

The rest of the group ignored him; the remaining five of us liked the idea of "fine cuisine" as proposed by Antoine.

It was decided that Antoine, Ria, and I would ask for a meeting with Stelwagen, to obtain permission to use the kitchen once a month.

I'm getting to be quite busy in my old age!

Sunday, March 17

We have a new pope. According to an unreliable source (the Slothouwer sisters), prayers were said in the Meditation Room this morning for him and for good weather. Some just prayed for good weather. I don't think I should count on those prayers' being heard; I'll keep my winter coat handy a while longer.

As far as the new pope goes: he has my sympathy for now, since when he was cardinal he used to take the bus to work. Or the metro. I imagine he must have had to remove his miter to get off or on. (Actually, some skepticism is in order where dignitaries are concerned: the British politician David Cameron used to ride his bike to his parliamentary job out of concern for the environment, but had his briefcase follow him in the ministerial limousine.)

The folk in here are especially pleased for our Princess Máxima, since this one's an Argentinian pope. They expect that Pope Francis, being a compatriot of hers, will surely attend her husband's coronation.

For those of us that never have any visitors, Sundays are not a particularly joyful prospect. The pleasures that once made the day something to look forward to, such as sleeping late, having a big breakfast, reading the papers, or listening to music, are now the daily routine. The only thing that distinguishes Sunday from any other day for me is that it's the day the *other* inmates receive visitors.

It is true that many of the visitors come with just one goal in mind: to get it over with as quickly as possible. Any interaction with other residents is a waste of time. A curt hello in the hall or common room is about the most one can expect.

Not so very long ago I used to take long walks on Sunday afternoons, but I can't do that anymore.

Monday, March 18

Stelwagen thought it was "just a lovely idea," the cooking club. She said she would take it to the various parties involved and discuss with them our request to use the kitchen once a month. She promised to get back to us shortly. Then we were offered a cup of tea and a cookie. After some chitchat she glanced at her watch. "My, is that the time?" Which means: your time is up.

Sometimes I do wonder: a cooking club, isn't that a bit sissy? But on the other hand, if you can't be bothered to give things that don't immediately interest you a chance, you risk being an old stick-in-the-mud. At least it's something to do.

Three more nights' beauty sleep, and then I'll have made it to another spring. In the coming days I'll do some spring cleaning. Wipe down the fridge, clean out the kitchen cupboards. Switch my winter wardrobe over to summer. Keeping gloves and a heavy sweater out, just in case.

Popped over to Evert's yesterday afternoon. He had invited me in for drinks, but when I got there at four o'clock he already had a healthy head start on me. Half an hour later he dozed off in his chair. I tucked a blanket around him, fed the dog, and took it out for a walk, leaving a note on the dresser among the deceased relatives: "Had a lovely time. And thanks for the hundred euros."

Tuesday, March 19

The geriatrician is a candidate for geriatric care himself: aged well into his sixties and weighing on the high side, at least 250 by my estimation. A cheerful demeanor, which I consider a plus when it comes to physicians. Bad news is far more devastating when it's delivered in a funereal voice.

Not that he had bad news for me, this Dr. Young (*What's in a name!*), not to worry; but it wasn't exactly good news either: a number of organs are either nearing their expiration date or already past it. The joints exhibit disturbing wear and tear, the prostate is beyond repair, the lungs are heavily tarred and working at half strength, and the heart is bad. One boon: the mind is sharp enough to be conscious of the decline. No sign of Alzheimer's, at most a little forgetfulness that's normal in old age.

Well, thank you, doctor.

He gave this summation with a twinkle in his eye, cracking the odd joke, and concluding with the remark that he could empathize, since he suffered from almost as many ailments himself. He roared with laughter as he said it. If he hadn't, that would have been something, wouldn't it? A doctor complaining to a patient about his own health!

He prescribed some new pills and stopped just short of letting me decide for myself how many to take. "Physicians are so good at what they do these days that you hardly ever see anyone who's healthy" is how he ended the consultation. I had to think that one over.

As I was leaving I plucked up the courage to ask if he didn't have any mood-enhancing drugs to give me, some good dope to get through the difficult days. He in turn had to think that one over.

I should have made another appointment right then and there.

Wednesday, March 20

This morning the director informed us (myself and Antoine and Ria Travemundi) that the cooking club project was not going to fly because of labor regulations. "Alas, alas!" she added, sighing. Funny, but I didn't for a moment believe she was sorry.

"What sort of labor regulations?" I asked.

She gave us some complicated explanation about who's

allowed to do what and who isn't. It all came down to the fact that we were not permitted to touch the kitchen appliances. The home would not be insured against accidents. I objected that we had no intention of using the kitchen appliances. All we needed were a few pans and knives.

"Yes, but it isn't that simple."

Even for us to be in the same *room* as those kitchen appliances entails an insurance risk, said Stelwagen.

"Could I have a look at those labor regulations?" I asked as neutrally as possible.

"Don't you believe me, Mr. Groen?"

"Of course I do. I just want to double-check something."

"Double-check what?"

"As any manager today will tell you: to double-check is not to distrust. Isn't that so?"

"I'll see what I can do."

"Thank you."

Ria and Antoine had been sitting there listening, open mouthed; only now did they close their mouths again.

By teatime, they had somewhat recovered. They had always trusted the director in the past, but their faith was now rather shaken. They thought it had been courageous of me to challenge her, and I thought so too.

I later reported our exchange to Eefje, I hope without sounding overly self-satisfied. All she said was, "Well done, Groen!"

The incident did inspire me with a great idea for an Old But Not Dead outing. I have looked up seven different cooking workshops on the Internet in our vicinity. There must be one among them that complies with the labor regulations *and* is willing to accept old people. Afterward we'll announce to anyone who'll listen that we have never had such a safe afternoon, even if we come home with a few sliced-off fingers, noses, or ears.

Thursday, March 21

Hurray! I have made it to another spring!

Now we resolutely set our sights on the next milestone, the first strawberries emerging from the cold ground; then we'll try to make it to the Tour de France, the new herring, the first snowfall, New Year's Eve, and on to the next spring. It's important to set yourself explicit goals.

It is the silly season, which here goes by the name of "cucumber time." Nothing much happening in the world. The subject of the new pope has been milked to death, and, for want of anything else, Syria is back on the front page because a Dutchman was killed over there. And there's still six weeks of coronation drivel to go. (Some 360 ermines gave their lives for Queen Beatrix's coronation robe back in the day, but Prince "Pilsner" Alexander's considerable girth may require as many as six hundred skins. Pamela Anderson, *do* something! Save those poor little creatures!)

Here in the home it's all too often cucumber time. At night you realize that nothing important has happened all day. On the other hand, what's important? For some people, simply being offered an extra cookie with their cup of tea makes their day. Of course it's the way the nurse doles out another cookie that does it, as if you'd just won the national lottery: "Oh, what the hell, it's such a lovely day, let's just go for it, have another one!"

At the other end of the spectrum we have fat Mr. Bakker. His record: one entire Limburg apple crumb cake and half of a second cake, washed down with a single cup of coffee. He didn't offer anyone a bite. When he was done he took the leftover cake back up to his room. Everyone hates him.

I have meanwhile come up with a nice little list of excursion possibilities: a cooking class, a paranormal exhibition, bowling, the windmills of Zaandam, a course in fine chocolate making, a football game at Ajax stadium, or the Keukenhof tulip gardens. I must ask at the next meeting whether we can switch the dates if necessary.

In honor of cucumber time, I give you this from the old newspaper clippings box in the "How Can That Be Possible?" category: some years ago Berlusconi was presented with an award for his human rights' record by none other than . . . Muammar Gaddafi.

Friday, March 22

Yesterday Mrs. Langeveld told me something interesting. She's usually well below my radar, but occasionally she'll startle me by popping up into view. We happened to be sitting next to each other over a cup of coffee. Sparked by the mention that the coffee was lukewarm, she said she suspected that our home isn't high on the list of top care institutions, "or they'd surely have been keen to let everyone know."

I asked what list she was talking about, and she lisped (toothlessly) that there is an annual review of the quality of nursing homes and assisted-living facilities. "And judging from this dishwater coffee, you can be sure that we're somewhere very near the bottom."

She didn't know exactly what kind of review it was. I'm going to look it up on the Internet.

The oldest man in the Netherlands is now Tjeerd Epema, 106. If I were to reach his age, I'd be looking at another twenty-three years in this dump. Not a happy thought. The oldest woman in the world is 122. To match that I'd have to spend another thirty-nine years in here.

It could be worse: in America, Carrie C. White turned 116 before she died, seventy-five of those years in a mental institution. They let her transfer to a normal old-age home when she was 110. Giving her some time to enjoy her freedom.

Saturday, March 23

You type "nursing home review," click on a few links and, *voilà*, there is the list of 350 nursing homes and 1,260 assisted-living facilities. The ranking depends on the rating given to the home by its residents, plus an objective grade for the quality of care. We're in almost thousandth place on both counts! In the overall standings that lands us just above 1,100.

These are the numbers for 2009, so our home may score an even higher number today. Or an even lower one, depending on how you look at it.

Why have I never known of the existence of such a list? Of course I do understand why our director hasn't put it up on the bulletin board. At Hofkamp, in Almelo, it's probably pinned up on every door: that one's in first place.

I am going to ask my friends if they remember how this investigation was conducted at the time. It may be something for us to start disseminating now.

Leaving that aside, the list reveals some arresting facts. The home God's Providence in Herten is in 1,230th place. Apparently they're leaving a bit too much up to Providence.

Also noteworthy: the residents of Angeli Custodes proudly voted their home into second place, but according to the objective assessment it stands at number 702. I wonder if management might have given the residents a little assistance here and there filling in the questionnaires. You can never be too suspicious.

And what is going on with Spathodea Court? The residents there put their home in 1,058th place, while the inspectors have it at a respectable number 4. Should we infer that that's where the Netherlands' grumpiest ingrates live out their sunset years?

Henk-50Plus-Krol has messed it up for himself a bit here. Mr. Bakker: "If he can't even stop his own queer-sex shops from going under, how can the guy run Netherlands Limited?" I'm fascinated by that "Netherlands Limited."

Yesterday I counted how many times I heard, in so many

words, that it's ever so cold for this time of year. Ninety-five.

Sunday, March 24

Eefje has a folder in which she collects articles about elder abuse in assisted-living facilities and nursing homes. Some of those institutions leave their charges wallowing in their own poop more often than not.

After reading all the stories about neglect and intimidation, I am inclined to appreciate our own home a bit more. Which is silly, of course, since things being worse somewhere else doesn't mean things are any better in here. As if it were a reason to be ecstatic that you don't have to lie around for three days in a loaded diaper.

The folder came to light after I asked Eefje if she'd ever heard about this ratings list. She had. We discussed the plusses and minuses of our own home at some length. Conclusion: there's work to be done. Proceeding with caution, we will see what we can achieve.

The Economic Policy Bureau has put forward a plan to weigh the costs of care against the actual health benefits. In the case of old people, there is usually little health benefit to be had; a serious operation may result in another year of just muddling through, if that, and then it's curtains for you anyway. So if you are determined to have yourself patched up no matter what, you had better have quite a bit put away, because you'll have to cough up the money for it yourself. No endless string of surgeries for me, thank you very much, even if I had the money. One less thing to worry about.

Old people tend to doze off at times. Mrs. Bregman gave us a masterly example the other day: she fell asleep at dinner with her spoon in her mouth. The custard came dribbling out.

I can sympathize: having trouble keeping your eyes open in the daytime and sleeping poorly at night. Rather inconvenient. Fortunately the fatigue rarely hits me while I'm eating.

The spoon clattering onto her plate startled Bregman out of her sleep. She looked up, astonished, mopped the custard off her dress, or rather rubbed it in further, and went on with her dinner as if nothing had happened.

Monday, March 25

We never talk about "non-native citizens" or "immigrants" in here, only about "foreigners." Whether they have Dutch citizenship or not makes no difference. Political correctness is a rarity.

The Netherlands is a segregated society: white sticks with white, the Turks stick with the Turks, the poor stick with the poor, the ignorant stick with the ignorant.

In our case there's yet another dividing line: old stick with old.

In our home the residents are largely white, poor, not very highly educated old folks. There are two Indonesian ladies and one Pakistani gentleman, and that's it.

We have little to nothing in common with the rest of the Netherlands, unless you count the aides. We do have a relatively large number of immigrants among the staff.

"Sweet dears, they are—I'm not saying they're not—but I'd still rather have a *Dutch* nurse," is the prevailing attitude. The older we are, the more reactionary. There are quite a few out-and-out racists walking around in here; the comments heard in the common room don't lie.

We don't see teenagers very often either, unless they're more or less forced by their parents to go visit Grandma or Grandpa for once. Dutiful visits and stiff exchanges. Teenagers are embarrassed by old people. Old people don't get it, are hard of hearing, don't even own a computer, are slow, are clueless about fashion and music, and all they have to offer you is a cookie. Worlds apart.

Younger children fare much better. They'll babble away merrily, and haven't yet learned to be embarrassed. Old people and toddlers get along famously.

Evert has opened a betting shop; it's one euro per wager on where we're going on our next outing, which is scheduled for the day after tomorrow. The pot goes to the one who guessed correctly. If no one gets it right, the bank keeps the money. The bank is Evert. The old rogue. No one has thrown in any money yet.

The excitement grows. Eefje remains tight lipped.

Tuesday, March 26

One of the goals of this diary was to emerge as a minor but notorious whistle-blower after I'm gone. That idea has faded into the background a bit.

I do notice that writing is having a therapeutic effect on me: I am feeling more relaxed, and less frustrated. It may have come fifty years too late, but there's no use in crying over spilled milk.

Mrs. Slag has an unpleasant daughter who comes for tea once a month and spends the half hour she is here on a Saturday sourly informing her mother she has already heard whatever her mother is telling her. As if there were any point in spending that measly half hour berating and correcting your mother of nearly ninety. As long as what she says is coherent, we're ahead of the game; for while Mrs. Slag is certainly no genius, at least she still has her ducks in a row.

Wednesday, March 27

I'm sitting here in my Sunday best waiting for the outing to begin. Two more hours.

Childish excitement.

I can't seem to concentrate. I'm just puttering around, dropping things.

I've already had to get out the vacuum twice: once for a piece of toast with chocolate sprinkles that slid off my plate, and another time for the sugar bowl I elbowed off the table. I don't know if there's a superstition for chocolate sprinkles on the floor, but spilled sugar means you should expect visitors. I'm not in the mood for any visitors right now, so I'll just mosey my way downstairs and wait for the minibus to arrive.

Thursday, March 28

Evert couldn't have known how close he was to guessing the destination of our little outing with his betting shop: the casino.

We had to be downstairs at one o'clock, well dressed, and with empty stomachs. That was our assignment, per Eefje. Just before our departure she popped around to tell us to bring along some form of identification.

The Connexxion minibus arrived punctually at one and drove us straight to the Holland Casino on Leidseplein. There we were greeted, with some surprise but great politeness, by a handsome young fellow. "I see that the average age here is more advanced than we are used to; I would therefore expect above-average sagacity from you as well." Elegantly put, coming from such a young whippersnapper.

We swept in, treading on thick carpets like monarchs. We were given a delicious lunch and then they explained the rules of the games to us: roulette, blackjack, and one that's much in vogue nowadays according to our host, Texas hold 'em. With our gray hair we felt a little out of place at the Texas hold 'em tables: almost all the other players seemed to be young punks in baseball caps, hoodies, and cool sunglasses.

A miniature racetrack featuring toy horses on rails lurching to the finish line caused great hilarity. Grietje tossed two euros into the slot, punched in her birth date, and with a great clatter of coins won back her initial investment twenty-four-fold when her horse came in first. She shared her winnings with the rest of us, and we proceeded to turn our full attention to feeding coins into various mystifying machines and playing roulette, since we'd all been given a little purse at the start with a couple of tokens in it.

We had made a deal when we'd arrived that we would pool any winnings we made, and when an hour and a half later we emptied our pockets at the bar, it transpired that there was a total of €286 in the Old But Not Dead pot. Everyone was jubilant, even the people working there. Apparently we were a refreshing change from all the strutting young show-offs and inscrutable Chinese. "A round on the house for the team from Avondrood Hall!" shouted the bartender.

After three whiskeys, Evert wanted to stake the entire €286 pot on the number thirteen, convinced we'd be going home with €10,000 in our pockets. "Thirteen, I feel it in my bones!"

We gave his proposal a Calvinistic thumbs-down.

At five fifteen the manager personally came to inform us that the minibus was out front. There were already two other elderly passengers on the bus; they stared at our rowdy group with undisguised disdain. Graeme handed them each one euro. Which they did grudgingly accept nonetheless.

Once home again, we felt all eyes on us. The place was

simply buzzing with a mixture of envy, admiration, and disgust.

Friday, March 29

The banking crisis has brought back the proverbial old sock. From the comments about the run on the banks in Cyprus, I must conclude that a number of residents have withdrawn their pennies from their bank accounts and stowed them under their mattresses, or some other place burglars are sure to look.

I've been to see Anja, my office mole, to ask her if she can find out how the quality-control survey was handled by the management here.

"With the greatest pleasure, Hendrik." She already had a gleam in her eye.

It would be fantastic if she could dig a few hushed-up reports out of one of Stelwagen's desk drawers.

"But be careful, Anja; don't take any risks," I urged her. To see the dear get punished for her efforts would break my heart. I would blame myself terribly. I told her so.

"It's sweet of you to warn me, Henk, but I am responsible for my own actions. Another cup of coffee?" And then she started humming "I Do What I Do" by Astrid Nijgh.

Good Friday. When I was young we had to observe a moment of silence at three o'clock to think about poor Jesus. If in today's Netherlands a father allowed his son to be nailed to the cross, our forensic psychiatrists would be at a loss as to what to do with the crazy psychopath. They would certainly not allow him to be free on probation, not if there were other children at home as well. He'd be banned from setting foot in any lumberyard.

I'll give God one last chance: if at three o'clock this afternoon I suddenly find myself able to run the 100-yard dash in 12.4 seconds, I will return to the bosom of the Holy Mother Church. It's a promise!

Saturday, March 30

My fastest time in the 100-yard is currently 1 minute 27 seconds. I timed myself yesterday, Good Friday, at three o'clock. I might be a second or so off, it might have been a yard more or less, but it was close.

My one-and-a-half-minute sprint required five minutes on a bench to recover.

God wrought no miracle; at the hour His son gave up the ghost, He did not give me back my erstwhile fleetness of foot. So He can kiss my return to the church goodbye.

God did take Mrs. Schinkel unto Himself at the hour of three yesterday. Schinkel was very devout, so I presume she deliberately chose to breathe her last at the same hour as Jesus. I never had much to do with her, but she did seem a pleasant sort. She is to be buried privately; good, that's one less obligation.

"*Pensionado*" has a nice ring to it; it makes you almost wish you were one of those. But then you'd have to spend the entire winter in Benidorm playing boccie with all the other Dutch *pensionados*. And sleeping in some of the ugliest hotels in the world for two months. They have Dutch barbers over there and Dutch snack bars and plumbers, and lately they've even opened a Dutch hospital. Were I forced to spend the winter on the Costa Blanca every year, I would sign myself up for the Dutch hospital's euthanasia ward.

Yesterday at teatime, Mr. and Mrs. Aupers couldn't stop saying how wonderful it was to winter in Spain. They had just got back last week. The continuing cold snap in the Netherlands helped to make their *pensionado* argument even more persuasive.

If a roving travel agent had walked into the Conversation Lounge at that moment, he'd have sold two hundred trips to Benidorm for next winter.

Which would have given us a nice stretch of peace and quiet here.

I am having the kind of day when you wake up totally shattered, do nothing all day, and go to bed at night exhausted from all the resting you've done. If only I had a few of those magic pills in my medicine cabinet, the kind that give the youth of today the energy to rave for twenty-four hours straight. Doesn't mean I'd suddenly have to know how to rave; being able to trudge around for a few hours without getting exhausted would be good enough for me.

Easter Sunday, March 31

I'm not all that keen on Easter. The crafts club has been decorating eggs, to be consumed today at a so-called festive brunch. The brunch starts at 11 a.m., but most of the residents won't give up their strict mealtime schedule. If they're forced to have both breakfast and lunch at the same time, namely the hour normally reserved for coffee hour, it throws them off for a week. So they take their breakfast at the usual time, then at eleven a cup of coffee and two painted hard-boiled eggs, and an hour later they're back for the midday meal.

The three *R*s apply not only to children, but also to the elderly: Rest, Recreation and Routine. Recreation is optional, but Rest and Routine are the cornerstones of this society.

The traditional Easter *Klaverjas* tournament is tomorrow. With fabulous prizes! I am taking part because no one else will partner with Evert. I won't let the boycott against Evert succeed.

Some of the couples play as if it were a matter of life and death. Evert isn't averse to sticking his nose in or rubbing salt in the wound by commenting on every card that's turned over. Until someone explodes and tells him to shut up. I'm sitting there pretending to be deaf and dumb.

I am quite curious to see if our Easter dinner tonight is any good. To be fair, holiday meals are usually quite palatable. But we have a new cook: everything has been coming to the table more overcooked than ever.

Monday, April 1

The others were fit to be tied. Evert and I won second place yesterday at *Klaverjas*: a pepper-and-salt set. Evert suggested that we take turns keeping the pepper mill or the salt shaker, and then once a week, at coffee time, make an ostentatious exchange, in full view of all the envious *Klaverjas* fanatics. That's taking it a bit far for me.

An Easter surprise attack: three Cantas parked outside our front door had their tires slashed. Excellent topic of conversation, but it's a puzzling act of vandalism.

"It's an attack on the Dutch senior citizen's mobility!" cried Mrs. Quint, queen of silly melodramatics.

The police came. It's the second time they've been called in a few weeks. Another pair of bright lights, these cops: they just stood there and stared. "Yeah, slashed, all right." Then they peered up the street as if hoping to catch sight of someone just fleeing around the corner with a knife in his hands.

No, the officers could not take down a report. The injured parties could file a complaint online if they liked. The officers were sorry to hear that none of the injured parties possessed a computer. Grietje finally offered them her PC. After this impressive show of constabulary competence, the cops retreated. Upon leaving they distributed some victim-support leaflets to anyone who held out their hand. So that was *something* they'd achieved, anyway.

A fear of further attacks has set in. The Canta owners are clamoring to be allowed to park their vehicles next to their beds. There's a great deal of speculation about who's behind this terrorist act. All agree that Muslims are the most likely culprits. It may not be quite as bad as the Twin Towers, but it certainly doesn't deserve being pooh-poohed by the police.

"Here's a perfect reason to send in the drones," Mr. Bakker declared.

Tuesday, April 2

At lunch yesterday Mr. Dickhout read aloud a letter from management stating that residents were henceforth required to pay one euro for every cup of coffee and twenty cents for each cookie consumed. This gave rise to a tempest—nay, a veritable hurricane of indignation. It was an outrage! There was no respect for the elderly anymore. The subject of the war was raised, and then the good old days, when everyone was promised a worry-free old age. "Then I'll just bring my own coffee and cookies!" Gompert shouted, upon which Dickhout pointed out another stipulation in the letter: outside food and drink were no longer permitted in the common areas either. When Gompert grew so incensed that I feared he would explode or at least have a heart attack, Dickhout decided it was enough. "April Fool's," he said drily, offering everyone a cookie from a packet he had brought.

Not everyone was a good sport about Dickhout's jest; I saw many a pursed lip. Some made a show of refusing the cookie by way of protest. Others wondered if in that case they could have a second one.

Gompert was looking quite purple in the face.

I gave the joke an eight out of ten, and the execution a nine. Maybe we should invite Dickhout to apply for membership in the Old But Not Dead Club.

Easter Monday, a big day for visitors. Sunny, forty-three degrees, and wind from the east, force 4; just bearable enough to take Father or Mother out for a little stroll, but not for very long. When they returned to the Conversation Lounge en masse, there weren't enough places to sit. I relinquished my chair and went upstairs. I was the only one with no visitors as far as I could tell, and, being the exception, I felt a bit sorry for myself. Up in my room I decided to open the best bottle I had, and three hours later I came down for dinner just a bit tipsy. I had a couple more glasses of wine and barely made it to dessert. I hope I didn't make a fool of myself.

Wednesday, April 3

It doesn't have to be taken for walks, doesn't smell, and never dies. Its name: Paro.

Japan's birth rate now stands at 1.3. Which means that there are more old people, and proportionately fewer children to visit them. Which is why the Japanese have begun marketing Paro, a robot that looks like a seal, specially created to keep old people company. My advice to the Dutch importer of this robot is to make it look like a waddling, roly-poly little dog that loves biscuits.

Italy's birth rate is also 1.3 children per family. What's happened to the good old days when Catholics used to procreate like rabbits?

A shortage of babies now will mean, relatively speaking, a huge surplus of old folks forty years hence. Luckily I won't be here to see it. Old people are already considered of little social value, but if years from now there are even more of us, I can predict that anyone over seventy will get a nice fat bonus for volunteering to be euthanized.

The world won't be better off with two billion mobility scooters wreaking havoc in the streets.

Investment advice for enterprising twenty-somethings: buy shares in adult diapers.

Last night we had an Old But Not Dead meeting in Graeme's room. With Chablis and appetizers, delivered from the snack bar because deep-frying in the rooms is prohibited. There is nothing better than a piping hot croquette with a cold glass of wine. It was a lovely evening.

We decided that if an excursion has to be postponed for some reason, it will not affect the date of the next outing; but we're allowed to swap dates amongst ourselves.

We have had various requests from people who would like to join our club, but after careful consideration we have decided to keep the number at a maximum of six for now. A manageable number, easy to organize, and we all have time for one another. There were one or two rather good candidates; we're putting them on a waiting list. And the rest, eight or so old bores, we can just give the brush-off.

Thursday, April 4

In Amsterdam there is a home for wealthy seniors: they have bridge instead of bingo, Haydn instead of Humperdinck, filet mignon instead of meatballs.

And… unlimited clean disposables. Long-term health insurance pays for the nursing care, and the residents pay four thousand euros a month for food and lodging. If I were to check in there, I'd have to find a cardboard box to sleep under in three months' time.

There are also homes for aging vegetarians, for ancient artists, for geriatric anthroposophists, and for old homeless people; I believe you're not supposed to call them tramps or bag ladies anymore. I don't know if I would exchange one of those institutions for ours. I don't think whiny vegetarians or anthroposophists would be an improvement on our own bellyachers. I would like to live somewhere without griping, moaning, or groaning. A little cantankerousness is fine, otherwise I too would be excluded.

Actually, I don't believe we have even a single vegetarian living here, let alone any anthroposophists. We do, on the other hand, have some ladies who are adept at needlework, and a few gents who are excellent pool players.

I have asked Anja if she could dig up this home's charter and regulations, and photocopy them for me. Plus any other documents that could be relevant, such as the Arbo labor ordinance, to find out if Mrs. Stelwagen's refusal to allow us to use the kitchen is legitimate. I suspect that our club will run into problems with "Madam Management" again in the future, and it will be useful to have a look into the forest of regulations she hides behind.

I've told Graeme and Eefje about it, and they're willing to help me read through them. Evert wasn't interested, "But if the need should arise for another round of cake crumbs in the fish tank, I'm your man!"

Everyone was still reeling from the news: "FISCAL LAW AFFECTS 65-PLUSSERS." And then on top of that, today: "GOVERNMENT INSTITUTES NEW MASTER PLAN TO TURN DEMENTIA TIDE." Rather a lot to digest around the coffee table.

To begin with the tax issue: it seems that the newly simplified tax law, as it applies to old-age benefits, is hiding a fly in the ointment. I just can't believe that *not one* of the Inland Revenue's thirty thousand employees (that's right, thirty thousand!) had the foresight to work out what the consequences of the new regulations would be for us. Everyone's always surprised: "Oh dear, are poor Gramps and Granny taking yet another hit?" The finance minister "will have to take measures to rectify it of course," as he himself now says. And if you ask us, he should be quick about rectifying it too, at least if it means changing it back to the way it was before. Otherwise we'll all be staring at Krol's indignant protest face forever.

As for the dementia tsunami they're expecting, more on that later. Too much misery to cope with all at once.

And it's still too cold for the time of year; we're desperate for some nice toasty sunshine. After three weeks of this blast from the east, wind force 6, everyone's despondent. Summer's nearly here and "your balls," to quote Evert, "freeze to your bum." I am not one to drone on and on about the weather, but even the most high-minded person is only human; you wind up joining the bellyaching rabble, you can't help yourself. I admit it: I'm turning into an old sad sack.

Saturday, April 6

Old people are forever grunting and groaning. Sometimes it's out of exertion or pain, but more often simply out of habit. I have made a small study of it.

The champion grunter is Mr. Kuiper, not my best friend to start with. Standing up, putting on his coat, picking something up, even if it's just a teacup; everything is accompanied by a groan as if he's being run over by a steamroller.

Once I started noticing, it began irking me more and more. That's wrong. *Don't get annoyed, just wonder at it*, my father used to say. Advice meant for others, since my father got extremely worked up about everything.

This morning I plucked up the courage and asked Kuiper what made him groan so when he sat down.

"Who, me?" he replied, genuinely surprised. For half an hour afterward he didn't make a sound, but then, slowly but surely, the grunting started up again. It was like women's tennis. There used to be very little grunting, as far as I'm aware, but nowadays I have to turn down the sound when watching tennis on TV. They're doing it deliberately. And it's contagious: the men seem to be doing it more and more as well.

Meanwhile it's left me with a problem. I'm starting to loathe Kuiper because I notice every little groan. And it's not just him. Quite a number of the other inmates as well.

And, worst of all, I can sometimes hear myself doing it too. How do I break myself of the habit?

I presented my problem to Evert. He thought answering each grunt with an even louder grunt might help. He tried out his theory a few hours later. The grunters gazed at Evert in surprise and asked him if he was feeling all right.

Sunday, April 7

Mr. Schaft from the dementia unit managed to slip through a door that had been left open and sat down with us in the common room. He showed us his new bracelet, proud as a peacock. He maintained that his mother-in-law had given it to him. It read DO NOT RESUSCITATE.

"Do you know what it means?" asked Eefje kindly.

No, he did not.

I asked if he was certain his mother-in-law had given it to him.

That made him laugh, which brought on such a coughing fit that he almost suffocated. Which attracted the attention of the attendants, who conducted him back to the locked ward, so that we are left not knowing who is distributing those bracelets.

Evert saw a business opportunity there, he told us with a perfectly straight face.

I promptly ordered one from him. That stumped him for a moment.

It was a joke, but then again not really. I think he'll probably try making me one.

Be that as it may, I am going to look into whether bracelets of this kind are legally binding. While I'm at it, I might as well investigate if the advance directive requesting euthanasia in case of mental incompetence is valid, because that seems dicey too. Although it's a subject that almost never comes up. "There's a great taboo on the *e-u*-word," was Graeme's solemn but provocative reaction to the resuscitation bracelet. There was some uneasy shuffling in chairs and long and concentrated stirring of coffee cups. "Suicide isn't something these folks care to talk about," Evert added slyly.

Monday, April 8

Spring: anyone who is able to totter took a walk yesterday. Even if only to the bench by the front door. Four of our residents were sitting there companionably discussing the lovely weather when an elderly gentleman no one had seen before sat down in the last empty space. Mrs. Blokker wasn't spry enough to head him off. She glared at him. "You are sitting on our bench."

"I don't see where it's written that it belongs to you," said the man, unfolding his newspaper.

"We always sit here," Blokker's fellow inmates said, backing her up.

"Well, for the next half hour *I'm* going to be sitting here," said the gentleman, unperturbed.

Mrs. Blokker went off to get help but couldn't find anyone but the orderly. "This bench is the property of this home," the orderly tried telling him.

"This bench is located on a public thoroughfare and therefore belongs to everyone," was the answer.

After reading his paper for half an hour in icy silence, he stood up, bowed, and walked away.

I had to listen to this story four times, in every major and minor key of indignation. It was Sunday's major event.

Excursion number three has been postponed for two days because Grietje is still getting over a light bout of pneumonia. The outing was supposed to be tomorrow and has been moved to Friday.

I was very disappointed. Oh, don't get carried away, Groen! You know perfectly well that the members of our club have seen better days and are prone to get sick. The vote we took not to alter the entire schedule if one outing has to be postponed is already being put to the test.

I have finally come to a decision about the excursion I am organizing: it will be a cooking class. After whittling it down to four chefs I found on the Internet, based on price and distance, I phoned each one at least three times in order to determine whether they had enough patience to deal with old people. My ploy disqualified two of the four. In the end I decided on a cooking school called Know Yer Onions because the name implies a sense of humor. They don't take themselves too seriously, which is the way I like it. There are too many people who consider themselves far too important. And yet not one of us is anything but a grain of sand in the desert, a speck of dust in the universe.

That's a bit over the top, Hendrik.

At last, another famous death to deplore over coffee: Margaret Thatcher. There haven't been very many celebrities falling by the wayside this year, and there aren't many people about whom opinions are as divided as the Iron Lady. Mr. Bakker thought she was a wonderful woman: "At least she stood for something!"

I asked him what she stood for.

"Well, she stood for what she wanted."

Grietje: "And what did she want, exactly?"
Bakker: "Is this some sort of cross-examination?"

Yesterday there was a residents' meeting to inform us of the board's plans to adapt this building to today's needs. No idea what exactly "today's needs" are, but the underlying motivation is usually cost-cutting. All under the banner of good stewardship or increased efficiency.

The director said emphatically, over and over, that nothing was set in stone yet, and that the purpose of this meeting was to ascertain the residents' wishes. The pretense that we have a say in the matter. It only led to greater anxiety. Yet another reason for worrying. Residents started hoarding moving boxes that very afternoon. "Old plants should not be repotted," Mrs. Schaap kept bleating at anyone who would listen. The fact that she compares herself to a plant speaks to a self-knowledge for which I'd never given her credit. She does speak, but other than that she leads a largely vegetative existence.

Personally, I am all for a radical overhaul. The more disruptive the merrier, and the sooner the better. At least a year will go by before they start on any actual demolition work, and you never know if you'll still be around to see it.

What if the paramedics don't notice your DO NOT RESUSCI-TATE bracelet until they've got your ticker going again with a powerful electric shock? What then? Would they have to *de*suscitate you? What would people *think*?

Or: what if the spouse of the person who doesn't want to be resuscitated insists that everything possible be done to keep the patient alive, bracelet or no bracelet?

I woke up this morning with these questions spinning in my head.

Wednesday, April 10

My mole in administration tells me that the inspector's office has given advance notice of a "surprise" visit. Complaints have come in. Alarm bells are going off in the director's office. Elder abuse is a hot topic in the papers. Two nursing home operators are in trouble. One of them has had twenty-seven of its homes slapped with an order for extra oversight. "GRANNY ABUSE!" blared a recent headline. Everyone was shocked, shocked! Maybe "everyone" ought to go and have a look for themselves at these homes, to see what you get with poorly trained, overworked, and underpaid personnel. Add to that the nine administrative layers heaped upon all self-respecting nursing home conglomerates, and you'll see that everything possible has been done to guarantee mishaps. After years of efficiency measures imposed by the boards of directors, the only thing left standing is the quality of their own compensation packages. The caregivers, on the other hand, are allowed two minutes and fifteen seconds to hoist disabled residents onto the toilet and pull their pants up again afterward. Which doesn't leave a great deal of time for bum-wiping.

There, I just felt like having a good gripe.

The other side of the coin is that some of the old people in here are such terrible bores that you wouldn't mind letting them wallow in their own poop a bit longer.

A recent scandal in here: a caregiver who was hit by one of the residents hit back. A little slap, which was not uncalled-for. The so-called victim had been behaving worse than a toddler. Nevertheless: caregiver gets the boot; peace restored.

Thursday, April 11

There are days when nothing much happens. Best just not to write anything.

I could prattle on about the food and the weather, but that's already most of my fellow inmates' favorite way to pass the time. Don't even think of starting a discussion about Nietzsche. Which is fine by me, since I don't know a thing about Nietzsche myself.

Just as long as I have nobody whining at me, I'm content.

The trick, therefore, is to be circumspect about who you end up sitting next to in the Conversation Lounge.

Many of the seats are off-limits: they are reserved for the season-ticket holders, the people who always sit in the same chair and make a huge fuss if someone dares to sit down in "their" spot. As for the allocation of the remaining seats, timing is all. If you get there too early there's no choice to make, and if you're too late, there's no choice left. If you and a couple of your friends go and sit at another table—there are tables galore, after all—you're chided for being unsociable. It may seem innocuous, but people get miffed if you don't join their group. They think you're deliberately avoiding them, as if they were pariahs.

Even though I prefer to sit with Eefje or Edward or Evert, on the rare occasion he ventures to join us, all too often I find myself nodding politely as a lady seated next to me ticks off her laundry list of ailments or gives me a detailed synopsis of the latest installment of *The Traveling Judge* on TV. Then, silently wishing that she be struck dumb, I sit there stoically dunking my cookie into my tea.

We're to report to the front gate tomorrow: the rebels' club deploys at twelve noon.

In the meantime, I have made a reservation for six seniors at Know Yer Onions next Thursday. On talking it over with them, I decided to scrap the appetizer; we'll have just a main course and dessert. Otherwise it would take too long and cost too much. I don't know what we'll be making; it's a surprise for me as well. "If there are any dietary restrictions, I can work around those," said our hostess, "and in case of a picky eater, I don't mind rustling up a meatball or two." That sounded reassuringly flexible.

I have ordered the minibus and canceled our supper in the dining room. Cook did not look happy.

Friday, April 12

It's ridiculous. Mrs. De Roos, floor manager, came at the behest of the director to ask why six residents would be absent for dinner next Thursday. I explained that we would be out that evening.

"Oh," she said.

"Yes, we have a little club that plans distractions from time to time," I explained feebly.

"Do you mean to say we don't plan enough distractions?" De Roos asked.

"Not at all," I hastened to say.

"The people in the kitchen aren't happy if six people decide not to show up for dinner."

"You mean we're only here to please the kitchen staff? I thought they were supposed to be there for us and not the other way around. It's their job. So what the people in the kitchen think doesn't interest me!"

That's what I *wanted* to say, but I didn't dare. Instead I muttered that we had already made the reservation.

"What are you going to do, then, if I may be so bold?"

When I said we were going to a cooking class she was silent.

Then she said, "Aha..." Another pause. "Well, enjoy yourselves, then."

She nodded and left. Probably straight to the director's office to report what I had said.

I'm working myself up into a lather about it, but I can't tell anyone, or I'll give away what I've got planned.

Relax, Groen! Time to go. Don't forget your raincoat.

Saturday, April 13

Yesterday Old But Not Dead paid a visit to one of the Netherlands' largest and most notorious old-age preserves: Keukenhof. Actually, it's not just for old people; it's also for the Germans and Japanese. "Have they got their own country all tidied up again after that tsunami? Is that why the Japanese are over here again with their cameras?" Evert wondered.

Estimated average age of the Keukenhof visitor: over sixty-five.

No senior discounts, therefore; giving discounts would cost the park an arm and a leg. People in wheelchairs are allowed in for free, however. It wasn't exactly advertised, but Grietje happened to know about the policy. So off Evert went to fetch a wheelchair for me, and Graeme got one for Eefje. We thought more than two wheelchairs would look suspicious. We spent the forty euros we saved on the entry fees on coffee and cake. And we took turns letting ourselves be wheeled around.

It's a rather prim, excessively manicured park. But it does have masses and masses of flowers. Lovely flowers, even if they're a bit late this year. The weather was fickle: rain-sun-rain-sun. Indoors-outdoors-in-out. It was nice and warm inside the greenhouses and if you filtered out the hordes of tourists, it was a beautiful spectacle.

But there's a limit, even for flowers. Later, over white wine and appetizers, we asked ourselves: was cultivating the seven hundredth species of tulip really necessary?

Grietje had done a clever job on the organizing. She has a helpful grandson, Stef, who drives a minivan. Stef was willing to take his Grandma and friends out for the day for the cost of the gas. Decent fellow, interested in people and their stories. He seemed to enjoy our company. Made us feel quite pleased with ourselves.

At the end of the day Stef offered to play cab driver for us again in the future. Notwithstanding the fact that we'd been sitting in a traffic jam for an hour. Grietje must have counted on a long return trip, for she pulled out a round of French cheese, smoked salmon toasts, and a bottle of wine from her cooler. I've never enjoyed being stuck in traffic as much as I did yesterday.

The delay meant that we were late for supper. Sighing deeply, the head cook was prepared to heat up some leftovers for us in the microwave. Acting as if she'd had to personally go without in order to save all that food for us.

Sunday, April 14

What you might call a stellar day for our home yesterday: one stroke, one broken hip, and one near-asphyxiation on a butter cookie. The ambulance came and went three times in a single afternoon. This gave rise to so much fodder for conversation over tea and coffee that it was hard to keep up with it all. Even though I wasn't closely acquainted with the victims, it does once again make one brutally aware of the facts: it doesn't require a storm to fell an old tree. A puff of wind, in the guise of a butter cookie, for example, could be fatal. We all ought to live as if every day were our last, but no, we'd rather waste our precious final hours on empty stuff and nonsense.

Mrs. Sitta, seeing the toing and froing of ambulances, asked if bingo would be canceled. "Those of us who are fit shouldn't have to suffer on account of those who are not," she brazenly declared. You'd almost wish that at her next bingo game she would have a stroke, break a hip *and* choke to death on a cookie.

On a happier note: I'm about to go and have a cup of tea with my friend Eefje, and I'm going to invite her to dinner with me tonight. I've reserved a table at a fairly posh restaurant.

Live as if today were your last day.

* * *

Monday, April 15

The dear old girl gladly accepted the invitation. She made herself look nice: a little lipstick and a touch of rouge. I must confess that I showered specially before I went, and changed my clothes. Not an excessive measure, in fact. I really must make a point of asking my geriatrician next time if there's anything that can be done about the leaky part or if I'll just have to resign myself to wearing diapers. Not so long ago I used to think that was when one lost one's last shred of dignity, but I realize that I have now lowered the bar a bit. The frog in the cooking pot, that's me.

Caught the minibus to the restaurant at seven and had an elegant and delicious meal that cost me half a month's pension.

Eefje was thrilled and greatly enjoyed the dinner. She let me treat her only on condition that I wouldn't make a habit of paying for everything. "That's a habit I wouldn't be able to afford anyway," I answered truthfully.

It felt good to throw caution to the wind for once. I'd never thought it would be that easy. It definitely had to do with the person I was with.

Home in a taxi.

On parting, a kiss on both cheeks. I felt myself get all hot and bothered. Jesus, I'm eighty-three years old!

Tuesday, April 16

The royalist frenzy is reaching fever pitch. The Residents' Association has been strenuously debating how it should mark the occasion. The end result is that this year we can look forward to the same store-bought orange Napoleons we always get on Queen's Day; moreover, we can watch full Coronation Day coverage on the big screen in the Conversation Lounge.

The postcoronation cruise on the River IJ will happen practically down the street from the home, but it will be virtually impossible for the likes of us to attend. That unfortunate fact is greatly deplored in here. I don't know the exact details, but I believe you're supposed to get there by twelve noon in order to stand, hemmed in, for the next seven hours, ready for a fleeting glimpse of the new king and queen sailing by.

These past few years they've already put lots of extra safety measures into effect for the annual April 30 queen's birthday celebration. They've divided the city into safety zones 1, 2 and 3. Depending on where you live, you might not be allowed to keep your car even in your own locked garage on Queen's Day. Even mobility scooters are banned. There was a great deal of indignation about that around here, as you might expect.

And in spite of all those security precautions, at the cost of seven hundred thousand euros—not counting the police salaries—you'd *still* find everyone glued to the TV, anxiously waiting for another black Suzuki Swift to come tearing around the corner, like the one that tried to ram into the royal motorcade in 2009, killing eight surprised bystanders.

I wouldn't mind having a look at the security plans for the coronation.

The Slothouwer sisters are quite sure: "*Something's* going to happen. We don't know *what*, but we feel it in our bones."

One of the residents asserts that Kim Jong Un, that pudgy little gnome from North Korea, is capable of sending a rocket our way on April 30. The bombing of the Boston marathon yesterday hasn't exactly calmed the jitters.

So the fun is already rather spoiled in advance by all the worried wimps in here.

I look back with nostalgia on the relaxed royal processions of yore, when no one would even think of checking the five-foot-long orange raisin bread baked by the Orange Society of Woerden for explosives.

I don't know how I'll get through April 30 as a closet republican.

Wednesday, April 17

I'm nervous about tomorrow. Will they like my cooking class?

The gentlemen and ladies are definitely speculating about what I have in store for them; one by one they've come to me fishing for hints. Speaking of fish: we finally have some new fish swimming in the tanks made famous by the great cake assassination caper. A note posted on the wall states that this is the last time the management will be purchasing new fish. Another calamity, and the tanks will be gone for good. You should never say that sort of thing to Evert, our own house anarchist. His eyes promptly started gleaming. I made him solemnly swear he would leave the fish alone. He swore "on my mother's life" that he would. His mother has been dead for twenty-five years.

Now Evert is trying to think of something else. A raid on houseplants doesn't appeal to him very much. The elevator is a possible target...

Tonight on TV, an interview with the future king and queen. I noticed that the best viewing spots downstairs were already reserved. There are slips of paper marked with residents' names on the front-row chairs. Like hotel guests staking out lounge chairs around the swimming pool with their towels at eight in the morning. I think I'll tip Evert off about those reserved seats. That just might be the disruptive deed he's looking for, falling right into his lap.

Some of the ladies will put on their fanciest dresses to watch the interview with Prince Willem-Alexander and Princess Máxima. Out of respect. Their fancy dresses aren't always that fetching. On the whole they're rather old and threadbare. The residents tend to take thriftiness to great lengths. They think it's a waste to buy new clothes, since there's a good chance they'll die before the clothes have seen their day. They'd rather walk around in faded dresses, in stockings with runs, and with gaping holes in their shoes.

I am not wholly guilt-free myself. I don't like spending money on clothes either.

Thursday, April 18

I really liked the blue color of it. Máxima's blouse was the thing that interested me most about the entire interview. A number of my fellow viewers were primarily fascinated by the crown princess's bandaged finger. Had she caught it in a door? Infection? Hangnail?

The royalty experts in the studio afterward had nothing to say about the finger. Lots of pompous blather, on the other hand, dissecting the couple's trite answers.

The Boston marathon attack led Mr. Schipper to change his mind yesterday about going to watch the Amsterdam marathon, even though his grandson is taking part. The incorrigible Evert calculated Schipper's chances of landing his Canta upside down in a ditch to be considerably greater than sustaining an injury at the marathon, and told him he would therefore be well advised to get rid of his vehicle. Evert happened to know someone who was in the market for a second-hand Canta.

I must make the rounds of the other Old But Not Dead members, and tell them to wear something comfortable. Preferably nothing baggy or loose that might catch fire. I'll leave out that last bit.

Friday, April 19

It was a great success. In no small part due to the excellent wine that was generously poured at the end of the meal preparation. The chef was what a chef should be: fat and jolly. But strict, as well. You weren't allowed to make a mess of it, as Evert did butchering an eggplant. At that point Rémi—that was the chef's name—told him to behave. Food is not to be fooled with. You're allowed to have fun, but not make fun *of* it.

With utmost concentration we caramelized, we blanched, we wokked, and we sauced. And then we feasted on the outcome. Rémi declared himself proud of us and treated us to a snifter of brandy with the coffee. The lady with whom I'd made the arrangements came to make sure there were no casualties and then sat and had a glass with us.

All too soon the minibus was tooting its horn at the

door. As it turned out, we'd been at it for five whole hours. On the way home I graciously accepted the ovations, and nobody seemed to have a problem with the cost.

I don't see any of us trying to produce the same meal at home. Graeme seemed to be the only one to remember much of it, but since it was almost impossible to understand what he was saying, it's hard to tell.

As we walked in, Mrs. Stelwagen watched our rowdy entrance with a dour look on her face. Normally she goes home by seven o'clock. The interest shown by the other residents, who had just feasted on stewed endive, must have rankled as well. The more sympathetic among them were eager to know what we'd had to eat; the curmudgeons wanted to know what this extravagance had cost.

Shortly thereafter Stelwagen left without a word.

Saturday, April 20

Mrs. Hoogendijk thought it was an outrage: the newly refurbished Rijksmuseum won't let you in on a mobility scooter. She had been planning to scoot past Rembrandt's *Night Watch* on her Canta, "but that's impossible now, I suppose." The spokesman for the museum pointed out, quite rightly, that a mobility scooter is a vehicle, and not a walking aid. The new displays include quite a number of glass cases and loose objects, he explained. If you were to let old people zoom through there on their mobility scooters, you might as well post an insurance assessor in every gallery, together with a security guard and someone to clean up the mess, since most scooter operators are terrible drivers, worse even than Mr. Magoo.

Yesterday I finally received the results of some tests that were done when I went to see the geriatrician. Good news: no new ailments.

The accompanying note from the doctor: "Take comfort in the fact that there are more ailments you *don't* have than ones you do. I would like to see you again in six months."

To celebrate the fact that I don't have lung cancer, I lit up an extra cigar. "They" prefer that you don't smoke right outside the front door, but I couldn't care less. I don't like the residents' smoking room, where you're forced to breathe in all that second-hand smoke. Most unhealthy. The only place employees are allowed to smoke now is in the bicycle shed.

Sunday, April 21

Last night a hearse drove up to the door. Or rather, drove around to the back door that is reserved for the discreet removal of the dead. Mrs. Tuinman was the lucky one this time. She'd had quite enough of life for a while now, so they tell me. I hardly knew her myself.

There is a whole protocol for the disposal of a deceased resident. Edward once tried to obtain a copy of it, but was told it wasn't "public information." That only made him more curious, of course. I know he's been trying to find another way to get hold of it. He has been trying to tease details from a nurse he's friendly with, but she isn't allowed to talk. I have pinned my hopes on Anja. She laughed when I asked her, and she told me she would do her best.

Openness is in short supply in here. The most commonplace matters are deemed confidential. The cause of death, for instance. The staff are not allowed to give out any information whatsoever about the inmates. Not even if someone has a cold or is visiting his daughter.

Evert has been mailing his letters for a while in black-edged mourning envelopes, without affixing a postage stamp. Because, Evert reasons, not only will the surcharge be waived, out of respect, but you can also count on your letter arriving on time.

Until the day he sent his tax forms in one of those mourning envelopes.

But it could be worse: his brother used to drive a second-hand hearse, complete with a homemade coffin, so that he could park in no-parking zones.

Over coffee Eefje remarked that she would love it if on the eve of the coronation Prince Willem-Alexander announced, "Who needs this? I've changed my mind!"

"Did he say that?" three or four people asked, appalled. Many inmates are hard of hearing, and most are only half listening.

Monday, April 22

Evert was off to the hospital this morning. "They're letting me stay overnight," he casually told me yesterday when he came over to ask me to look after Mo for a couple of days.

137

He wouldn't tell me what was the matter. "Nothing special, a few tests."

"What kind of tests?"

"Henkie, I really don't feel like going over all the medical details with you right now. My leg is giving me trouble, all right? They're going to see if they can do anything about it."

I'm not allowed to call him tonight either. To make sure of it, he didn't give me his room number ("I don't know it exactly"), did not sign up for a telephone in his room, and left his cell phone at home. It couldn't be clearer: do not disturb.

I'm feeling uneasy about this.

Tuesday, April 23

With his master in the hospital, Evert's dog is a bit out of sorts too. As I was putting on his leash to take him out for a walk, he deposited a huge, rather elongated poop on the welcome mat. And then gazed at me with those big, sad, innocent, old-dog eyes. It took me twenty minutes to get the stinky mess out of the coir mat. I left it outside in the end because I couldn't get rid of the smell.

Evert is coming home late this afternoon. He telephoned an hour ago to tell me he'll be able to let Mo out himself tonight. "Yes, all's well. Nothing special to report." I couldn't get more than that out of him.

I recently watched an episode of *Krasse Knarren* on TV, a kind of *Big Brother*, only with a group of geriatric Dutch celebrities interned in a house that's supposed to make them feel younger by reminding them of the good old days. A few days later I happened to catch a program about an old people's choir. Next Saturday there's a film about a rebellion in a nursing home. We're everywhere.

Still, it's not as if these shows were representative of the Dutch elderly. The oldest *Krasse Knarren* participant was sixty-nine. The residents in here are well into their eighties or nineties, for the most part.

Nursing homes have over the past few years seen an unprecedented influx of old coots who are no longer able to live on their own. You need a Condition 3 designation (or something like it) to qualify for immediate admission. Condition 3 means you're no longer capable of boiling an egg, and usually you're on your way to the locked ward. Condition 2 puts you on the waiting list, which can take years. By which time you may not need the home anymore. Those lists tend to sort themselves out.

In the seventies and eighties, happy and healthy couples just turning seventy would move into an old-people's home to enjoy a long, comfortable old age. Now it's mainly old coots who could drop dead at any moment.

Wednesday, April 24

"A day and a half in the hospital and not a drop to drink, or very nearly. I need to fill the tank," Evert said to me. When I looked in on him at half past seven to see how he was, he'd already had a couple. He didn't reveal much, except that he'd had to resort to taking quick nips from a "water" bottle when nobody was looking.

When you're young, you can't wait to grow up. As an adult, until about the age of sixty, you want above all to stay young. But when you're as old as the hills, you've got nothing left to strive for. That is the essence of the emptiness of life in here. There are no more goals. No exams to pass, no career ladders to climb, no children to raise. We are too old, even, to babysit the grandchildren.

In this stimulating environment, it isn't always easy to set yourself a modest goal or two. When I look around I see only passive resignation in people's eyes. They're the eyes of people with nothing to do but go from cup of coffee to cup of tea and back again.

I may have said this before.

Maybe I shouldn't grumble so much.

I should just work harder at making sure that every day is worth living. Or at least every other day. There have to be rest days too, just like the ones in the Tour de France.

Thursday, April 25

Yesterday I took in a lunchtime concert. Rereading my own complaints about the emptiness of our days, I told myself to buck up and *do* something. Classical music is wasted on Evert, Eefje wasn't feeling well, and I wasn't in the mood to look any further for company, so I went by myself to one of the free concerts our municipality offers her citizens, held in the town hall.

Alas, "doing something" is no guarantee of a pleasant afternoon. The music was rather monotonous, and seemed to go on forever, which is why I nodded off until some lady angrily prodded me awake. I'm afraid I may have been snoring. Everyone was staring at me. I was terribly embarrassed. When it was over, and I was trying to slink out as unobtrusively as possible, I could still feel contemptuous eyes on my back.

"Come on, Hendrik, stop moping. Doing nothing is the only way to make sure nothing goes wrong. Stop brooding about a minor mistake. And next time you go, you can just go in a false beard." That was Eefje's advice when I visited her on her sickbed. She had no appetite for the chocolate truffles I brought her. She didn't complain, but explained in a businesslike voice that her intestines often gave her trouble. "When that happens, the only thing to do is to stay in my room."

Tomorrow I am invited, on condition that she's feeling better, to come back for a glass of white wine and chocolate truffles.

Friday, April 26

Between bites of custard pudding, Mr. Dieudonné Titulaer—brilliant name, isn't it? but what an old windbag!—read out a newspaper article reporting that, according to the Anti-Intruder Task Force, there's been a huge increase in the number of old people assaulted in their own homes. Dieudonné rubbed his hands gleefully, as if to gloat about how much better off he was living in this safe refuge and not the dangerous world outside. I noted a big clump of custard dangling from his mustache.

There was also, the task force reported, an increased tendency for roughing up the victims to get them to reveal where they'd hidden their money socks. Because one of the reasons for the increase in robberies was that old people hate to use ATM machines and so keep relatively large amounts of cash in their homes. I myself suspect there's a different reason: old people aren't as ready with the baseball bat to defend their possessions. Thieves have a marked preference for defenseless victims.

The tone was set for the evening's conversation. Fear has been sown, and fear is a seed that falls on fertile soil in here. More than half the inmates are afraid to venture out alone at night. We got to hear a whole litany of stories about purse snatchers, intruders, pickpockets, vacuum-selling conmen, and other scam artists.

I went to see Eefje. We watched a DVD. A romantic comedy, a genre that usually sends me to sleep. But not this time.

Saturday, April 27

Children laugh approximately a hundred times a day. Adults only about fifteen. Somewhere along the line we lose the inclination. Those are statistics from a research study. Old people weren't singled out as a separate category, but from personal observation I would say that a rise in age corresponds to a decrease in laughter. Although it does depend greatly on the individual, of course. I've spent the past several days watching for it, and of the people I see regularly, five haven't smiled for three days straight. There are four ladies, on the other hand, who tend to laugh a lot. They laugh so often, and for so little cause, that once you start noticing, it gets awfully irritating. (Which is why you shouldn't pay attention to it; the minute you decide not to notice, however, it's already too late. You find you can't help noticing.)

The middle bracket consists of a majority that seldom truly laughs but smiles frequently. I tried keeping score for a while, but stopped because it became too distracting. I'd count how many times a group of us laughed, but then I'd have no idea what they'd been talking about, with the result that my companions would ask me if I was feeling all right.

Now I am trying to keep track of how often I laugh myself, but that too is harder than you would think. After one hour of tea drinking and one hour of playing pool with Graeme and Evert, it came to three laughs (out loud) and somewhere between ten and fifteen smiles. Not bad.

It has made me painfully aware, however, that when I, or other people, laugh, it is often for social acceptance. A little laugh here, a smile there, for no other reason than to be polite. As a friendly gesture, or because you're too spineless to reveal you didn't think the joke was funny. Or as a way of avoiding the subject.

Sunday, April 28

When you read in the paper that some Dutch celebrity has died, it's fine if you think, "Wow, was that one still alive?"

For it shows that the person in question had already long ago passed into oblivion. But sometimes it's the other way around, and some decrepit-but-still-breathing former star is dragged back into the spotlight. Painful.

Just before he died, a doddering Ramses Korsakov Shaffy was hauled back on stage to sing, quavering and off-key, "We'll Go On." They showed a drooling Willem Duys sitting in a wheelchair, speechless after his fifth stroke, for his last appearance on TV. Tough guy Rijk de Gooyer, when he'd had a few, used to beat big bruisers to a pulp if he didn't like the look of their face. Near death, he was dragged before the cameras, a helpless, lisping mummy, for a reunion with his old friend Johnny. I'd have expected Rijk to put a bullet in his own head before allowing decrepitude to set in.

Why are those vultures of the TV so keen to put on these demeaning spectacles? Why doesn't anyone tell those "wonderful colleagues" that it's disrespectful and a downright shame to parade former heroes once they're old and helpless?

I turn the TV off every time it happens, but I can't turn off the picture it leaves in my mind.

The date of the coronation approaches. The irritation over the accommodations that have to be made by the populace to that Punch and Judy show is escalating. Mr. Schaft, one of the few inmates who still gets around by bicycle, was furious. Last Tuesday the police confiscated— "stole"—his bike at the ferry crossing, all because a week later some big fat guy with a crown on his head is set to cruise by at a considerable distance. The whole city is being cleaned up, raked, and polished, and then, next week, when the whole circus is over, Amsterdam can just go to hell again as far as they're concerned.

But I can't share my opinion of all this nonsense with my fellow inmates. Not a negative word about the House of Orange.

Monday, April 29

I don't feel well. My head is heavy and dizzy. Could it be something's growing in there?

Methinks I have far too many ailments already to start growing tumors as well.

Friday, May 3

For a staunch republican, it wasn't bad timing to be indisposed on April 30. I barely noticed the hoopla surrounding the coronation. I had a raging headache on the big day, and a tummy bug. So I swallowed a nice cocktail of aspirin and Imodium, and stayed in bed. Evert stuck his head in once, as did Edward, Grietje, and Eefje. I pretended to be asleep.

On the second day, I suspected I must be starting to stink, and I thought I'd take a shower. I slipped and fell in the tub. Managed to drag myself back into bed with a great deal of effort and pain. The immediate impulse is not to want to call for help. It's that mixture of pride and embarrassment that stops you.

In the end a nurse arrived, alerted by my next-door

neighbor, who'd heard a funny thud. The nurse called the house doctor, who diagnosed just a couple of bruised ribs, so it seems I've gotten off relatively easy. A broken hip means at least four months confined to bed before you can even think of attempting to shuffle about leaning on a walker.

Now it only hurts when I breathe. The doctor isn't a stickler about limiting painkillers, fortunately, so I was just downstairs for the first time in three days for a cup of coffee. There were even one or two people who actually seemed happy to see me. That did me a world of good, I tell you.

I'll be taking it easy for a few days. I must be in top form again come Monday, because that's the day of Evert's club outing. He has put up a bottle of brandy as a reward for whoever guesses what we're going to do. I did not win: we are *not* going synchronized swimming.

Saturday, May 4

Mrs. Stelwagen summoned me to her office yesterday. First she asked kindly if my swollen knee had gone down at all. "Actually," I said, "there's nothing wrong with my knee, but my bruised ribs still hurt."

Oh, sorry, she was confusing two different accidents. Our director tries her best to show sympathy, but she's a bit lacking in that department.

What she really wanted was to tell me that she had gone to the board to discuss my request to see the regulations, and that the board felt the regulations were not a public matter, and was therefore unable to grant said request.

"And why *aren't* they public?" I asked.

"The board has no comment."

"And so?"

"So, nothing. I am very sorry that I can't help you. Now will you please excuse me? I have someone else waiting. Enjoy the rest of your day."

I slunk off, disappointed; at least, I hope I gave her that impression. I had decided beforehand to make a fuss on principle if they wouldn't let me see those regulations.

Ria and Antoine Travemundi know many people, and among their acquaintances is a friendly retired lawyer. Antoine had told me about him before my conference with Stelwagen. He said he would give him a call, and then perhaps I could pay him a visit to find out what the law says about board transparency. I don't have to worry about compensating him.

I'll go there shortly.

Sunday, May 5

Liberation Day. In a place filled with so many old people, you would expect to hear some moving or shocking stories about the war on May 4 and 5, wouldn't you? But no, they never mention the war, or else they fall back on the old chestnuts—sugar rations and such.

It is striking how little the folks in here know about one another. That thought occurred to me yesterday during the two-minute silence for the fallen. I looked around and realized I knew next to nothing about how any of them had fared during the Second World War. Not even the people I see most often.

I do know quite a bit of Evert's history. I have known him for twenty years or so. He was a printer by trade, and I met him through my work. Our friendship has endured; we have never looked back. His wife died ten years ago. Two kids he seldom sees. He has neither money nor property and no God either. For years he's been playing the role of reprobate with great conviction. A classic diamond in the rough, salt of the earth.

I have known Anja Appelboom for forty years. She never married. Perhaps she waited too long for Mr. Right. Smart, sweet, and dependable. I think she must be lonely.

Evert and Anja, that's what remains of what was once a tolerably full social life—with a wife, child, and friends.

Until three years ago I lived in a nice row house with a garden. The plan was to die there in peace, when the time came. So much for that.

My wife has suffered from manic depression for forty years. She lost it completely soon after our little girl drowned. She decided to drive to Groningen in the middle of the night because she wanted to climb to the top of the Martini Tower; she gave the car away to a complete stranger, a junkie, and returned to Amsterdam in a taxi. She squandered thousands of guilders. In the end she was nabbed for shoplifting by the police and forcibly sedated by her shrink. Then, after months in an institution, she sank into a deep depression. Finally, still shaky but more or less stabilized by a slew of medications, she was allowed to come home. Until the next manic breakdown, followed by yet another depression. This happened five times in a row. The last time, most of our house went up in flames while I was out running an errand. Now she is locked up for good. After the fire, Anja arranged for me to come and live here.

I visit my wife twice a year. She barely recognizes me but takes my hand and pats it. I have never been angry with her.

The calendar tells me that my last visit was over six months ago.

A life in a nutshell.

Over the past two years the emptiness was slowly but surely growing unbearable, but look...suddenly I have Eefje, I have Graeme, Grietje, Edward, Antoine and Ria. It isn't time to kick the bucket just yet.

Monday, May 6

Last night it occurred to me that the reader might like a bit more background information about this old folks' home, to give you a clearer picture, since the chances that you will end your days in this home or a similar one are slim. So I will henceforth pay some attention to describing the stage set on which our lives are played out, and the daily routine.

In the late sixties, homes for the elderly began sprouting up everywhere. A warehouse type of design was acceptable and cheap. Old people weren't used to a great deal of luxury back then. They had been through the war and were easy to please.

The architect of this home decided to make it a gray concrete affair, seven stories high, each floor composed of two wings separated in the middle by the elevators. The wings consist of long windowless hallways, each lined with eight single rooms or two-room "suites" equipped with kitchenettes. The kitchenette consists of four cupboards, two up and two down, a countertop three feet long, and two gas rings that can be used only to heat water or milk for tea and coffee. If you wanted to boil an egg as well, they might just turn a blind eye. There's a small shower and a toilet. The installation of handrails in places where you could slip and fall and the absence of door saddles show that the builders did give some thought to the target occupants.

Each room or suite has a balcony large enough for a garbage can and a hanging geranium.

At the end of each wing on each floor, there's a conservatory-like area furnished with sofas and chairs. Although hardly anyone ever sits there—most residents prefer the large common room downstairs—it is generally frowned upon for someone from another floor to sit there "for no good reason."

To be continued. I should save my strength. At two o'clock I must take myself in comfortable clothes down to the lobby, where today's group leader, Evert, awaits us for what ought to be a memorable excursion.

Tuesday, May 7

Who'd have thought that Evert, of all people, would treat us to a Tai Chi class? The last thing you'd expect of him.

Luckily our instructor didn't mind us having a laugh, and we made good use of his indulgence. We did, however, try in all seriousness to apply ourselves to the slow-motion fighting poses, although I'm afraid that in the case of a mugging what we learned is unlikely to be of immediate use. Tai Chi is a sport you can practice even with a walker, so it's an ideal form of exercise for the elderly. Bruised ribs, however, are another story. I took it very slow, suffering in silence. The Tai Chi master and his comely assistant taught us the glorious names of the various moves; I've already forgotten most of them, unfortunately.

Graeme crashed to the floor while trying the stork imitation; it cost him some points but did not jeopardize his diploma.

Afterward, in keeping with the theme, we went to the Great Wall for a Chinese meal. Grietje ordered, straight-faced, "number thilty-thlee with white lice." Silly, but good for a laugh. It's lucky Chinese people are so tolerant of old people. Respect for their elders was rammed down their throats with chopsticks from the moment they were born. In Western culture, the old are considered more of a nuisance. There's a case to be made for that too.

Upon being bombarded with compliments on the way home for having organized a superlative day for us, Evert tried not to beam with pride. He even seemed to have caught something in his eye. "All right, all right, that's enough of that."

Since our first outing, seventeen people have asked to be admitted to our club. Sadly for them, Old But Not Dead is not accepting new members for the time being.

This morning a "Harassment Protocol" has appeared on the bulletin board in the common room. It lists seven tips for combating bullying. It is a dated directive; it's from two years ago. The work of a Mr. Jan Romme, director of the National Foundation for the Elderly. As if this were an elementary school for retirees.

Tip number one: a counselor must be brought in. Tip number two: bullying information sessions must be held. And on and on in that vein. Most impressive. A protocol like that will surely put an immediate stop to the bullying in here. Something to be considered for Syria too, perhaps? Or for Afghanistan? People are harassing each other all over the world. A global harassment protocol is what we need. With counselors and information sessions.

Not funny, Groen.

It's true: people in here gossip, humiliate, and ridicule one another as if it were the most normal thing in the world. Nothing childish is foreign to us in these parts. The best thing to do is pretend not to notice. And if that's impossible, if it bothers you, speak up or go and sit somewhere else. Or take a swing at them, as Edward suggested. Something I'd never have expected of him.

It's easy for me to say, since I am rarely the victim. There are a few thoroughly rotten apples you have to keep an eye on. Like four-legged predators, they choose the weakest to prey on, not stopping until they have torn them to pieces, if you let them. The best is when, for want of victims, the bullies wind up turning on one another. There are a few interesting vendettas going on. The Ladies Duits and Schoonderwalt are out for each other's blood as a result of some coffee spilled on an antimacassar three years ago. Until death do them part.

Thursday, May 9

A great comfort to know: once you get here, here is where you'll remain until your final departure for the churchyard or the crematorium.

The papers were full of it again: the cost of seniors' care is going through the roof. The solution is twofold: first, the bar to what constitutes disability is to be raised; and, second, the personal contribution the elderly must pay will be jacked up considerably.

Item 1: According to these new measures, quite a few of the residents shouldn't be here at all. They are far too spry and independent. There was a rumor going around that people in that category would be kicked out to make room for more serious cases. The rumor created quite a stir, and in some quarters resulted in an acute exacerbation of existing ailments. Just as a precaution.

But we can all breathe easy now: management has assured residents in writing that they'll never have to leave, no matter how healthy they are. "Unforeseen circumstances excepted."

It's a shame they had to add that proviso.

Item 2: I have gathered, from hushed conversations over coffee, that some residents who hadn't emptied their bank accounts already, have now done so, hiding their nest egg under the mattress or in an old sock. "Seniors' care should be free; we've worked hard for it all our lives," is the prevailing opinion. The two euros for the minibus is already highway robbery.

A couple of sorry cases confessed in a whisper that their children had already withdrawn everything from their bank accounts without asking, "for safe-keeping." Safe-keeping the inheritance, they mean.

"Every day you're still alive costs me oodles of money," Mrs. Schipper's son teased her. He was just joking. His wife, who has no sense of humor, sat there nodding agreement.

Friday, May 10

There's an initiative called An Outing with Grandma. Children are rounded up to spend a day with some poor granny, no relation to them, who otherwise is sitting home all alone. I gather it could also be a grandpa. A group of middle school children took some of our residents to visit the revamped Madurodam miniature park. At the risk of being accused of being a peevish old curmudgeon, I'd much rather stay home. Visiting Madurodam wouldn't be a barrel of fun under any circumstance, but in the company of eleven- or twelve-year-old know-it-alls I've never seen before in my life, it could be a blistering bore.

Stop being so negative, Groen; it's a lovely idea. Especially if you remember that the children of today seem to think you don't have to bother with old people because social services will take care of them. Many adults think the same.

The newspaper that took the trouble of devoting a column to An Outing with Grandma further reported some disconcerting statistics from the Economic Policy Bureau: the Netherlands has some million and a half solitary old people, of whom over 300,000 are extremely lonely. That's a lot.

But it should be said that some old people do it to themselves. In this house alone there are dozens who are to be avoided like the plague because they are boring, bigoted bellyachers. Forgive me for stating the truth, but that's just the way it is.

Frequently overheard: "At least in here there's someone to talk to." That is indeed the great advantage of this place as opposed to living alone, where only the cat or canary can be relied upon to discuss the weather.

I wonder how many of the residents in here suffer from "extreme" loneliness?

Saturday, May 11

Reading about cute American five-year-olds who on their birthdays are presented with their first pink gun, "My First Rifle," complete with real bullets, made me wonder if in American nursing homes the oldies walk around packing loaded My Last Rifles. With all the Parkinson's about, that would lead to quite a few accidents. I haven't heard of any such mass shootings, but I can't imagine there aren't at least some instances of old geezers shot point-blank by fellow residents protecting their God-given property—a piece of cake, for instance.

One advantage to being surrounded by all those weapons is that you don't have to jump through hoops to obtain that elusive euthanasia pill. As long as you can still move one trigger finger, the solution is waiting for you in a holster.

As in every other year, we never seem to run out of things to say about the wonders of spring—nature running riot. "You can just *see* it growing," you'll hear at least three times a day. Then Evert will say facetiously, "I can just *hear* it growing." Occasionally someone will actually try to listen. Sometimes—rarely—they'll say they can hear it too.

I walk to the park twice a day. With Eefje one time, the next time with Graeme, Edward, or Evert. Eight minutes getting there, fifteen minutes on a bench, eight minutes home. There's no haste, and spring is never boring. Sometimes I'll slosh there in the pouring rain. "What's that old coot think he's *doing*?" I overheard some gangly teenagers say, sheltering in a doorway, thinking out loud just a bit too loudly. I was amused; they just didn't get it.

Sunday, May 12

Although the nursing wing is separate from ours, you do sometimes come across a dementia case in the hallways, accompanied by a nurse or a male attendant. Some residents will scoot back inside their rooms, because they think dementia is contagious. Or maybe it's not, but you never know. Keeping out of the way can't hurt in any case, is the basic attitude. And that goes not only for dementia. Cancer patients, homosexuals, Muslims: they're all best avoided. The older the people are, the more scared they are. At our age, surely, there's nothing left to lose, so why not be fearless?

It's the little things that get you. Or rather, that you don't get. A daily annoyance: packaging. Cans with tabs you can't wedge your finger under, vacuum-sealed LIFT UP HERE corners too small to pull, childproof cleaning products, applesauce lids, impossible to twist open prosecco corks, blister packs: they're all specially designed to make it as difficult as possible for feeble, trembling, old hands to manage.

Today a jar of pickles slipped from my grasp as I was trying in vain to get the lid off. My entire room stank of pickles. Glass everywhere; I found the last piece in my carpet slipper.

Someone ought to bring a class-action lawsuit against the packaging industry for physical damage and mental distress. They have to be doing it on purpose. If they can send people to the moon, surely they ought to be able to come up with an easy twist-off lid. All right, I'll admit it, I'm a bit of an old grumbler today.

Monday, May 13

Evert was rushed to the Emergency Room this morning. He called me from the hospital: could I look after Mo?

Two of Evert's toes had turned black a couple of days ago. When he went to the doctor this morning, the doctor immediately called for an ambulance.

What he was afraid of has come to pass: he is following in the footsteps of that old friend of his who kept having to have bits amputated.

He called me from his bed.

"Why didn't you say something?" I couldn't help asking.

"I'd only have been bombarded with unsolicited advice, which I'd have ignored anyway."

He had a point.

He is to be operated on tomorrow morning, and if everything goes well, he'll wake up with only a couple of toes missing.

After we hung up I took a taxi to the hospital to bring him some necessities: underwear, pajamas, toothbrush.

He was trying to cheer me up, but it should have been the other way around. It only occurred to me afterward, and I felt ashamed.

Evert takes things as they come. He weighed the risks beforehand, accepted them, and went on living his life as if he didn't have diabetes. With gusto and bravado. That was still his attitude, lying there in his hospital bed.

When I returned home I informed the members of our club and the staff. The nurses and attendants were remarkably sympathetic. Most of them do have a soft spot for him, after all. Although there's probably at least one who silently wishes even more amputations on him, preferably his head.

Two of our fellow residents couldn't resist remarking,

triumphantly almost, that they'd warned him, hadn't they?

What a rotten day.

Tuesday, May 14

I have just spoken to Evert. He came to from the anesthesia an hour ago. He was operated on early this morning, and they amputated three toes on his right foot, including the big toe. It will be hard for him to walk, especially at first. He's looking at six weeks' convalescence. He sounded exhausted.

I'll draw up a visiting schedule for those who want to see him.

Now I must go and fill in our club members and some of the staff.

Wednesday, May 15

I visited Evert in the hospital this morning. He already has his usual swagger back. He asked the nurse if he could take the sawn-off toes home, to display them in a jar on the dresser. The nurse gaped at him at first. "I believe your toes have already been disposed of," she said a bit nervously.

Evert: "But they still belong to me, surely! I might just lodge a complaint...Don't worry, love, just kidding!"

They've put him in a ward with two other old men. One of them hacks and coughs constantly, and when he's not spluttering, does nothing but carp and fuss. That's according to Evert, anyway, who didn't look too good, pale and drawn, although well enough to wink broadly at every nurse he saw.

"Just ten days or so, and I'll be strutting about like a rooster behind my walker," he assured me.

I had to solemnly swear that we wouldn't put off our excursions for his sake. He did suggest limiting the next ones to stuffy museum visits, saving the fun ones for later. I promised to propose it at the next meeting.

Evert couldn't say how well the operation had gone. The surgeon should have stopped by yesterday afternoon but had been called away on an emergency. There was no one to take his place, and the nurses knew nothing, or pretended to know nothing. The doctor might come by this afternoon.

Patients don't matter very much in hospitals. It's all about the doctors.

A minor trauma avoided: Anouk has made it into the Eurovision Song Contest finals, thank God. Around here people would have preferred an old-timer like Ronnie Tober to sing for the Netherlands, but fine, whatever they think is best for our country... The general opinion here is that all those corrupt Eastern-bloc countries have turned the Netherlands into a Eurovision dwarf, wherefore the Iron Curtain ought to be drawn shut again as soon as possible. "And don't forget to kick all those worthless Romanian accordion players back behind that curtain where they belong!"—thus the ever-diplomatic Mr. Bakker.

"It costs five hundred and fifty euros a day for me to be in here, and for those few lousy cents I have to eat a breakfast of dry toast at seven in the morning, am given three cups of dishwater coffee a day, the food is cold and the bread tasteless. A five-star tab for a no-star hotel. Well, okay, and a nurse who takes my temperature twice a day." Evert Duiker was already full of bluster as he ate an entire box of sugar-free Jamaican-rum chocolates. The hospital won't let him have any alcohol, so he hoped to get some into his system that way. He had rung me specially to buy him some. Cherry-liqueur chocolates were another option.

"And a bottle of mineral water. By Bols, if you get my drift."

The surgeon had popped in a day and a half after the operation to report it had been a success.

"What do you mean, a success?" asked Evert.

"The infected toes have been amputated."

"I don't consider that such a great success."

"Doing nothing wasn't an option," the doctor said unperturbed and made as if to go.

"What next?"

"If there are no complications you'll be allowed to go home in four days. You do have to make an appointment for a follow-up and for physical therapy. Goodbye." And he was gone. Hadn't even bothered to take off the bandage.

For the time being, my diary has become more of a journal about Evert.

Friday, May 17

Last night there was an impromptu meeting of the Old But Not Dead Club. Principal item on the agenda: Evert's condition. We decided to give him a warm welcome home, probably next Monday or Tuesday. The next excursion will be wheelchair-friendly, according to Edward. This will be the last outing of the first round. The enthusiasm is as high as ever, and we are to embark on the second round following the same sequence. At the end of the meeting we raised our glasses to that, and to Evert's health, and may possibly have overdone it a bit on the drink.

Returning to my room I tripped on the doormat and fell flat on my face over the threshold. I was lucky: the white wine had made me as supple as a garden hose, and I got up again unscathed. However, this morning I did discover a bump on my head. I've thrown out the doormat and will need a day to recover.

Falls are common in here. Sometimes people fall by tripping over a rug, as I did, but often they'll just keel over for no good reason. Or they'll sit down and miss the chair. Mrs. Been, getting up from her chair, grabbed the tea cart for support. Someone had failed to lock the wheels, and the trolley tipped over with a great crash. Down went Mrs. Been in a cascade of cookies, sugar cubes, and creamers. Luckily the Thermoses were tightly closed. A brief silence, and then Mrs. Been, on the floor, began laughing hysterically. Everyone joined in the laughter to be polite, until Mrs. Been's laughter turned to wailing. It was at that point that someone went to fetch the nurse. I wasn't there, but it must have been quite a surreal scene.

Saturday, May 18

My temporary dog-walking job means I now have to take a stroll three times a day. Fortunately Mo walks even more slowly than I do. Actually, it's more of a slow-motion waddle. It would be hard for him to get lost on his saunter around the house, so I could just let him go by himself, but for Mo it's more about the company. If he weren't so old and lazy, he'd jump up on me and wag his tail whenever I come in, no doubt about it. As it is, he slowly hauls himself out of his basket, groaning, gives me a few languid welcome licks, and then goes and stands by the door.

When Evert takes him out, Evert sometimes shouts for Mo by his full name. Not that that's necessary, since Mo is never more than about five feet away. It's only when he spies some Moroccans in the vicinity, or people who look like they might be, that Evert will yell, "*Come,* Mohammed!"—in the hope that one of those Moroccans answers to the same name, which is not unlikely. Once Evert's created enough confusion, he'll make an apologetic gesture, point at the dog, nod politely, and continue on his way.

It does embarrass me, though, to have to scoop up Mo's turds and drop them into a plastic bag. I keep my head down, because I know I'm being spied on from behind many curtains. By the way, I read that someone suggested using DNA testing to trace any unclaimed feces back to the dog, so that its master could be fined. Whether dogs would be required to submit to a cheek swab, or could do so on a voluntary basis, it did not say.

Sunday, May 19

This morning I took Mr. Dickhout's mobility scooter for a test drive (he of the April Fool's joke). He had already offered to let me try it out several times, but I'd said no out of politeness and reserve. I was on my way to go out for a walk when he came riding into the lobby.

"Care to give it a try, Hendrik?"

The insurance regulations say you're not allowed to let anyone else drive your scooter, and officially any new mobility-scooter rider is supposed to have three driving lessons before he can drive off by himself, but Dickhout doesn't like rules and isn't worried about such details. He just spent five minutes giving me a few pointers, told me to have fun, and went to have a coffee.

Taking a deep breath, off I went, *ever* so cautiously. I ended up cruising around for a good half hour, taking bicycle paths and cutting through public gardens. It was early in the morning, Pentecost, so there was hardly anyone about. I kept it in "snail" gear at first, which barely lets you overtake a pedestrian, but a few minutes later, throwing caution to the wind, I switched to "hare." The manufacturer assumes all old people are senile, so a little picture of a snail and a hare is easier for them to understand than, say, gears "1" and "2." The manufacturer may even be right.

I must admit, however, it rides wonderfully. It makes almost no noise, you sit there like a king, you don't get tired, and your legs don't hurt. I am sold! My only complaint: it gave me a cramp in my right hand, because you have to keep squeezing the throttle. So, Mr. Manufacturer: please consider adding cruise control.

I was a bit too confident as I drove into the lobby and just bumped the orderly, who was rolling the linen cart out of the elevator. Nothing serious, but the turning radius is wider than I thought. Luckily I don't like the orderly anyway.

The Capri Pro 3 mobility scooter costs only €399. But I'm in the market for something a little more economical. I'll have to pay for it myself, since I'm still able to walk.

Monday, May 20

A dementia patient yesterday stuck a billiard ball in his mouth, and it couldn't be dislodged by any means. He sat there pitifully emitting high-pitched squeaks as two male nurses tried to pry the ball out with a spoon. After a fruitless fifteen-minute struggle, he was carted off to the Emergency Room. It wasn't as big as an official tournament ball, but when I briefly held one up to my mouth, it did strike me as a very large item to swallow. Quite alarming.

Mr. Kloek was furious because he had to finish his game with only two balls.

Evert is coming home this afternoon. He has asked me to put a nice bottle of very old gin on ice for him. And he said I could buy a little something for myself while I was at it, if I liked. The welcome committee consists of the club members plus Ria and Antoine, who are providing a high tea. Ria asked the director if just this once they could cook a few little dishes in their room, but alas, Mrs. Stelwagen was "so incredibly" sorry, but the board would not allow her to make any exceptions to the rules.

"From now on we just won't ask," Antoine said angrily an hour ago. He set the exhaust fan on high and began preparing a veal ragout.

There are flowers on the table, and Mo will have a nice bow on his collar.

Tuesday, May 21

At two o'clock yesterday afternoon Evert was delivered in a wheelchair to the door of his apartment. An orderly pushed him inside, where the welcome committee awaited him: Eefje, Grietje, Graeme, Antoine, Ria, Edward, and yours truly in a party hat, standing by Evert's garlanded chair. Evert suddenly had to blow his nose loudly.

"Did you catch cold in the hospital?" asked Eefje wickedly.

"Uh, no, in the hospital it was the extreme thirst that got to me, mostly," he said, trying to save face. "I'm parched." His voice sounded shrill.

"So perhaps a nice big glass of milk to start?" said Edward.

"I'd rather have a cocktail, please, if it's all the same to you."

"Let me offer you something tasty to go with it," Antoine said, revealing an elaborate spread of both savory and sweet tidbits. There were also tea and champagne.

It was a most enjoyable afternoon. There was strict

agreement, at Evert's express request, that there would be no mention of illnesses or hospitals.

At four o'clock the patient crashed. Seconds later he was fast asleep with a contented grin on his face, a touching sight. We finished our drinks and then cleaned up. Now let's just hope and pray that Evert doesn't lose any more toes. A welcome home like this is fun only once.

Edward's excursion is scheduled for Tuesday, May 28. With a little bit of luck, Evert will be feeling well enough to participate. I feel a bit sorry for Antoine and Ria. Although they haven't said anything, I sense they would love to join us on our outings. I'm going to do some lobbying on their behalf.

Wednesday, May 22

It isn't easy to keep your chin up sometimes. Today the conversation ranged from those two murdered little boys found in a drainage pipe, through rheumatism, hernias, and wonky hips to, finally, the outdoor temperature's refusing to climb above fifty-two degrees. It's the end of May but all the heaters are still on; the thermostat is set at seventy-three degrees. The older, the colder. And then we have to consider the continual cutbacks in elderly care! People sigh, moan, and deplore their circumstances. The stock market seems to be the only thing that's still going up, in a bizarre reverse measure of how bad things truly are.

I read that they've started a nationwide campaign to

combat the national mood of glumness in the Netherlands. The campaign organizers are hereby cordially invited to stop by our home. Lots of work to be done here. They could start with something simple: one day without mention of illnesses or ailments. Anyone who starts complaining about an ache or pain has to pay ten euros into a kitty. We'll spend the winnings on a fancy champagne dinner.

Antoine has given me his friend the retired lawyer's telephone number. I'll give him a call this afternoon to ask him how to go about getting hold of all the rules and regulations.

"He'll enjoy that," Antoine had said.

I'll ask Eefje to listen in.

Thursday, May 23

Our unit head, Mrs. Gerstadt, has given Mr. Bakker a warning: he has to watch his language. Bakker is slowly losing it. Alzheimer's. Maybe they'll move him over to the "other side" one of these days. It would be no great loss. He was never the most civil customer to start with, but lately he's been getting really crass. He curses and swears without any apparent provocation. When Gerstadt had a word with him for constantly raging on about "goddamned shitheads," he glared at the floor, furious. The moment she was out of earshot he told his table companions, "That effin' bitch struts around as if she had an effin' cucumber up her ass." I couldn't help find it hilarious, but the other five people sitting there were shocked speechless. I wound up hiccuping into my handkerchief. They all glared at me. I wouldn't be at all surprised if as soon as we were finished having coffee, Bakker's words, perhaps somewhat sanitized, were relayed back to Gerstadt.

Evert almost fell out of his wheelchair laughing when I told him about it. I may possibly be a candidate for Alzheimer's myself, since I'm finding crude jokes much funnier now than I once did. I am growing less respectable all the time.

Yesterday afternoon I talked on the phone with the lawyer Antoine recommended. "Just call me Victor" seemed enthusiastic and said filing an appeal based on the Governance Transparency Act would be a piece of cake. He suggested that we meet for further discussion. I had the telephone on Speaker. Eefje nodded.

We made a date for Thursday, May 30 at the Toll House, a nice old-fashioned establishment with tablecloths and pub food.

Evert is doing as well as can be expected under the circumstances.

Friday, May 24

"They do make a molehill out of every bull in a china shop, don't they," said Mrs. Pot upon hearing about the latest poison attack in Syria.

"The Arab Spring is a bit like our own, isn't it? More like autumn than spring," mused her neighbor, dunking her cookie in her tea. Mr. Bakker, with his usual self-restraint, remarked that so long as those Arabs were killing each other, he wasn't going to lose any sleep over it.

Analysts of world events at our coffee table are not known for nuance, and are not deterred by lack of understanding either. The same goes, I must add, for news on a more local level. A flood of indignation swept through the home when the mini-market downstairs was shut yesterday for a funeral. It was simply an outrage to have to go for an entire day without being able to buy cheese crackers or hairspray. You'd think we were in Eastern Europe! For a funeral, shouldn't half a day's closure be more than sufficient?

This shop, whose assortment could easily fit inside three moving boxes, is the same one they lambaste for charging twenty cents more for the toilet cleaner than they do at ALDI.

Last night Eefje invited me in for a glass of wine. Inspired by the Harassment Protocol, we discussed the possibility of drawing up a protocol for making old-age homes more pleasant for their occupants. We are of two minds about it. Is it worth doing? Is something like that wasted on our fellow residents? Are our limited energies not better employed making our own twilight years more agreeable? Or, rather, our twilight days; one never knows. We are leaning toward the latter option, but have decided to give it some more thought. At least it gives us a good reason to meet again soon.

A crematorium crisis: the coffin got stuck halfway in, so the oven door couldn't close properly. The coffin caught fire and the smoke seeped into the chapel. The crematorium had to be evacuated. Anyone who hadn't already been weeping emerged teary eyed. That's what I call a spectacular way to say goodbye.

For myself, I've come up with the idea of having a small CD player hidden inside my coffin that will pipe out my voice shouting: "Hello, hello out there!" (*Knock, knock*) "You're making a mistake. Let me out! I'm still alive . . . Oh, don't worry—just joking. I'm dead as a doornail."

Such a pity I won't be there to enjoy it.

I do have to give some serious thought, however, to my last wishes. Not that I have a lot of them, but there are a few things I *don't* want. And I haven't put anything down on paper yet. It's a chore that one tends to put off as long as possible.

The disadvantaged elderly in Amsterdam will shortly be able to ride the buses and streetcars for free. Disadvantaged we certainly are, only it's a pity almost nobody dares to ride the bus or streetcar these days: "The streetcars are packed with pickpockets and purse snatchers!"

Well, you can protect yourself from pickpockets by tucking your wallet somewhere secure, but there's nothing you can do about insolent bus drivers who drive much too fast. I have to agree with my fellow residents, albeit reluctantly: public transportation and the over-eighties are incompatible. It's far too crowded and too fast and demands physical agility you no longer possess. You hold up the other passengers, and they get impatient. It makes old people anxious and helpless. I've noticed that I am getting more hesitant and uncertain myself, though I hate to admit it. So: thanks a lot, public transportation, but we prefer to take our own dedicated minibus.

Sunday, May 26

The first and only item on the agenda of the ad hoc meeting of the Residents' Association: new mobility-scooter regulations, motivated by a head-on collision between two motorized chairs turning a corner from opposite directions. Considerable chassis damage and one minor scrape. Of course, each claimed it was the other driver's fault.

The Residents' Association wants to ask the management to put up traffic signs and mirrors at the blind corners.

Last week, so the rumor goes, a resident wound up in the hospital. Mrs. Schaap didn't just slip and fall, as reported; she was actually knocked down by a scooter. The driver, who wishes to remain anonymous, had been a bit too intent on his shopping basket. The director is keeping the exact details under her hat. The eyewitnesses must have been told to keep their mouths shut "for the sake of the investigation."

There is barely enough room for two scooters to pass each other in the hallway. Add to that the fact that many of the residents are either short-sighted or stone deaf, if not both, and, as you can imagine, this place can sometimes resemble one big circus attraction. It's a miracle, actually, that there haven't been many more casualties, especially if you take into account the average driver's sluggish reaction time.

And if the drivers would just keep their wits about them, then at a speed of three miles an hour there's not much that can go wrong; but the panic at every encounter with another driver or pedestrian means anything can happen.

I wish the grand marshal of this home much luck and wisdom in trying to come up with a traffic plan.

Monday, May 27

This morning I received a brochure in the mail: "Libid Crystal Shots will make your penis hard as steel. Volcanic ejaculations." I had a good laugh at that one. Could it be Evert's idea of a joke?

I had an uncle who used to mark each birthday with the boast that he could still batter down the church door with his dick. And since I'm going there: another uncle was fond of singing a ditty with the unforgettable refrain, "*Aunt Marie, she had a trough big enough for a horse to stuff.*" They still have, I believe, a call-in show on the radio for listeners trying to track down lost or forgotten songs. You get to sing the lines you remember on the air, and they try to dig up the rest of it for you. Should I...?

I must get a move on: our club outing was moved forward a day. It is today instead of tomorrow, thanks to the stellar weather forecast. It promises to be the first balmy spring day in weeks.

Last night Edward checked with each of us individually to see if we could all make it. No one had a problem. Our calendars are completely blank—today, tomorrow, and the rest of the year. We have all the time in the world. We once complained about being overscheduled; now we're thrilled to pieces if there's something to jot down other than a doctor's appointment.

I have to be down in the lobby in half an hour in comfy outdoor clothing.

Tuesday, May 28

We did not have far to go: a leisurely five-minute stroll took us to our destination—the boccie strip on the green on the south side of our building. That is where the exclusive, first-ever *jeu-de-boules* championship for over-seventy-nines took place. Edward had planned it to a *T*: twelve shiny balls, tape measure, large trophy for the winning team, six comfortable folding chairs, table, tablecloth, a Thermos of coffee and one of tea, apple pie, sandwiches, sunscreen, china, cooler filled with cold drinks, smoked salmon and eel on toast, umbrella for shade, and more. All under a radiant spring sun.

Edward had hired Stef, Grietje's grandson, to take care of the logistics, and together they had loaded everything into his minivan that morning, and after a two-minute ride, unloaded it all again and neatly arranged it on the green.

At noon we came trundling up, Evert leading the way in his wheelchair, amazed at what greeted our eyes. First, coffee and cake, then the drawing of lots, and then the tournament. Three teams of two players each playing a full round. Stef was the umpire.

Halfway through the contest lunch was served, and at the end, for the prize ceremony, champagne. The victors were Graeme and Grietje. A respectable second place for Eefje and Evert, who shouted that without toes his aim was considerably improved, and the bronze for Edward and me. Graeme was taunted for being the Paul Gascoigne of boccie because when he won he did look a bit teary.

The one thing Edward hadn't counted on was that half the care home had gathered toward the end to watch. It was brilliant publicity for our club. Only, we don't want any new members.

At four o'clock everything was loaded back into the minivan and our little group traipsed home again. Dead tired, but happy.

Wednesday, May 29

An eighty-year-old man has managed to climb Mount Everest. I have enough trouble stepping up on the curb. It isn't fair. The previous oldest record holder, Min Bahadur Sherchan, now eighty-one, promptly announced he intends to recapture his record next week. There's also been a one-legged woman who reached the summit. On a prosthetic leg, surely? She can't have got all the way up to 29,029 feet hopping on one leg, can she?

The first climber with no arms has also been spotted up there. It's quite a remarkable convoy that makes its way to the top of Everest nowadays. I am waiting for the first incontinent veiled nun to plant the Polynesian flag up there, and then I'll have a go myself.

I have called my insurance company and it appears that I have to be "approved" in order to qualify for a mobility scooter. I can make an appointment for six weeks from now. I think that I'll just go out and buy one myself. I'll check the consumers' guide to see if they've tested any mobility scooters recently.

There are three categories of buyers. The first, and biggest, group takes the middle road: not the cheapest but certainly not the most expensive product. A second, much smaller, group always goes for the most expensive, and the last group decides on the cheapest version. Unless I have a reason not to, I always go for the cheapest. At least I'll be saving money. Naturally, cheap can cost you in the end, but on the other hand, expensive is bound to cost even more.

Call it coincidence: yesterday there was an article in the paper about an all-terrain scooter, the Action Trackchair, with tank-tread tires. You can drive it across hill and dale, and through heavy snow. Ten thousand euros, there's the rub.

Thursday, May 30

Evert is not doing well. The wound just will not heal. A nurse comes daily to change the dressing, so that's not the problem.

"She's a looker! So I don't mind if she has to keep coming."

He still talks the good talk. But when I picked up the dog this morning (I continue in my role as full-time dog walker) he did not hear me come in and I overheard him say to Mo, "Your master may not be around much longer, Mo, and honestly, I don't know what's to become of you."

I coughed, rather uneasily, to let him know I was there.

"Did you overhear what I was saying, Henkie?"

"Yes."

"What do you think, should I have Mo put to sleep if I die? You can't put an old brute like him in a shelter. You can't do that to the shelter."

"Jumping the gun a bit, aren't you?"

"Well..."

I am prepared to look after Mo, but only as long as Evert's alive. If he dies, his apartment has to be surrendered—without the dog. And dogs are not permitted on my floor.

Friday, May 31

Eefje and I had an appointment yesterday afternoon with the retired lawyer, Victor Vorstenbosch, seventy-one. A sophisticated, self-satisfied fellow who, as he admitted to us in a plummy voice, tends to "get rah-ther bored at home." He was looking forward to rolling up his sleeves again. His former office never called him to consult him anymore, and that did not sit well with him, he didn't mind telling us. He'd like a chance to show them he's still a clever old fox. In short, he was keen. He promised he would this very week contact the administration to request, under the Governance Transparency Act, any document that may have even the faintest relevance. The request will be made under his name. Eefje remarked astutely that our home wasn't a publicly owned institution, and that the law might therefore not be applicable. Yes, she had a point there, Victor admitted. He would take it into consideration in his pursuit of the rules and statutes.

He said we could come back in a few days and review the draft request, which he prefers to keep with him at home; he has lost faith in the trustworthiness of his fellow man over the years. "That nursing home confidentiality clause doesn't carry much weight, and email security is virtually nonexistent."

We seem to have landed in a spy thriller! Let's just hope we can dig up some juicy scandals.

Mr. Schansleh, a friendly fellow who lives on the third floor, was a passionate pigeon fancier before moving here. He couldn't get over it: some Chinese man paid €310,000 for a Belgian prize pigeon. "Unbelievable, just unbelievable!" he kept saying. Edward wondered what would happen if an expensive pigeon like that ever decided to join his gutter-mates on Dam Square. Or if some hunter shot it out of the sky, for a pâté. "Would it taste like three hundred thousand smackers?"

"Well, yes, you have some that vanish without a trace," Schansleh said gloomily. He admitted he had lost dozens of birds over the years.

Bad news.

Yesterday Grietje and I went for a walk. After five minutes we had to sit down for a rest on the bench the council has so kindly provided. The sun was shining. After the usual pleasantries we found ourselves discussing more personal matters. She told me she has started "losing it" quite a bit of late, both literally and figuratively. "I'm good at camouflaging it, but someday I won't be able to do that anymore. It's making me feel very insecure. I'll suddenly find myself standing in the elevator, for example, with no idea how I got there or where I'm going."

I didn't really know what to say. We were silent for a while, then I suggested she might want to go to her doctor to be tested for Alzheimer's. And that any time she felt confused she should seek help from the people she trusted. They would set her right. "You can come and knock on my door whenever you like, Grietje. I'll gladly help you, as much as I can."

Grietje, the epitome of kindness, but always a bit closed and reserved. I was surprised that she was confiding in me. And also rather proud. And sad. In short, it wasn't easy, all those feelings at once.

Evert seems to be doing a bit better. At the physiotherapist's he is giving it his all—which manifests itself mainly in the amount of curses emerging from his mouth while he's doing his exercises. Once, when Evert was about to step on the treadmill, one of the assistants made a show of stuffing cotton wool in her ears in jest. In response Evert plugged his own mouth with a huge wad of the stuff.

Sunday, June 2

I had a bad night thinking about my talk with Grietje. Everything seems to point to Alzheimer's. I asked her this morning if she had mentioned it to anyone else. She has not.

"Not even to your doctor?"

"No, he's an unpleasant man."

"Would you mind if I asked the others for advice?"

She needed some time to think about that.

I did some browsing on the Internet. There are some 250,000 people suffering from dementia in the Netherlands. Alzheimer's is the most common type. Your chance of getting it is one in five. And, rather alarmingly, you live on for another eight years on average.

It isn't something we're unfamiliar with here, of course. There are plenty of folks in here who start losing their marbles as they age. And after those first marbles, they keep losing more. Until all that's left in the old noggin is a jumble of loose ends. If you're lucky it's a happy jumble; if you're unlucky, a frightening or aggressive one. Fortunately we don't have to witness the last stage of disintegration close up; by that time the poor things have been moved to the "other side"—the locked ward. When people start stirring the soup with their hands, or flinging their poop, their departure is imminent.

I don't want to see that happen to Grietje.

Monday, June 3

The board has sent a letter to all the residents saying the care in this and other institutions is to receive a "makeover." When management starts using that word you had better watch out: *makeover* means cutbacks and reorganization.

From the letter: "The makeover will lead to improved quality in the long run."

Yes, yes. The only thing missing was a vow "to put the elderly back in the driver's seat." The company's spin doctor seems to have left a perfectly good piece of malarkey on the table there.

Our prime minister, Mark Rutte, also promised to put the Dutch people back in the driver's seat. Have you noticed anything changing?

Even though no one was able to pull anything concrete from the board's letter, opinions were divided. To some, we were on the road to hell, whereas others read the same words and beheld paradise gleaming on the horizon. Old people run the gamut of human beliefs.

One thing is certain: when all's said and done, the planning and reorganization will inevitably entail a raise for the board of directors.

Tuesday, June 4

I wonder how the first anarchist old-age home in the Netherlands is faring? It's a nursing home by the name of De Hoven, in the hamlet of Onderdendam in Groningen province. Two years ago they decided as an experiment to do away with all rules and regulations. Well, perhaps not *all*. Knowing what the average senior is like, I'm afraid such freedom would mean murder and mayhem. And bingo every day.

The director of De Hoven wanted to see whether her colleagues and the residents would be happier without rules. The "regulation-free care" experiment was to be conducted by scientists from the University of Groningen.

I have looked online but can't find any mention of the outcome.

What made me think of it was a new rule that's just been imposed here: only low-energy light bulbs are to be used in the rooms. The environment, you know.

I went over to our lawyer's house to look at the draft letter requesting that we be allowed to see our institution's rules and regulations. It all sounded very legalistic, so legalistic that I couldn't make heads or tails of it. It did inspire confidence. It was a pity Eefje wasn't with me; she's got a sharper eye. She wasn't feeling well.

Although it was only two o'clock in the afternoon, Victor the lawyer poured me an enormous snifter of very expensive cognac and gave me a cigar, which I cautiously puffed on, coughing and wheezing. Victor is a bit of a caricature of the tweedy gentleman, a role he plays with gusto. Pretense and reality all rolled into one, but in his case the two don't really contradict.

Mrs. Visser set out this afternoon by minibus for the IKEA on the other side of town with two suspect coffee cups in her bag, to ask for her money back—although they're not the actual LYDA jumbo cups that are being recalled because the bottoms tend to fall out, but a different IKEA design. Says Mrs. Visser, "Who's to say these *will* hold scalding-hot water?" It has been almost three hours, and Mrs. Visser still isn't back.

People in here don't like taking risks. If there's a recall on any food item anywhere in the world, every kitchen cupboard is thoroughly excavated for potential samples of the offending can or package. On the other hand, people are not fussy about expiration dates. Throwing food away is a dreadful shame, even if it's covered in mold. "Just scrape it off or scoop it out and it's still perfectly fine to eat!" Which does much to explain the frequency of food-poisoning cases among the elderly. Meanwhile the kitchen has to check the butter every day to make sure its temperature is between forty-one and forty-five degrees.

A new record was set recently: in clearing out a deceased resident's room, they found something in the refrigerator that was seventeen years past the expiration date. The room was spic-and-span otherwise. That's the rumor, at least, for, of course, that sort of thing is never made public.

We have another excursion set for tomorrow. The weather report predicts perfect conditions for the aged: not too warm and not too cold, very little wind and no humidity.

Thursday, June 6

If you happen to see any Amsterdam municipal guards around—I believe they are now called neighborhood-watch officers—you can be fairly sure the coast is clear, for they tend to avoid danger at all costs. So in nice weather you'll find them sunning themselves on the bench by our door. I expect that for the paltry salary they make you can't blame them for avoiding troubled neighborhoods ruled by street gangs. I have never witnessed one of them stopping a motorcycle that's racing along the bike path at fifty miles an hour with the roar of a fighter jet. Municipal guards radiate sad impotence. Their uniform is also always a bit too tight.

It could be worse; some time ago I read that in The Hague the average meter man or maid gives out one parking ticket a day. Apparently they don't work on commission. I wonder what the interviewers are looking for in applicants for the job?

There we go: yesterday we had the first complaints about the warm weather! "It always gets so muggy here in the Netherlands!" according to fat Bakker. Only two days ago he was still complaining about the cold. Sometimes I'd like to kill him.

I am wearing my best and only lightweight suit. I have also unearthed an old-fashioned straw boater. I want to look a bit like Maurice Chevalier. We are to report after lunch for an outing organized by Graeme. He's been saying for days that as long as the weather's nice it can't go wrong.

Friday, June 7

At one o'clock sharp three pedicabs pulled up in front. Driven by three strapping young fellows, so we don't have to feel sorry for them. One of them was a friend of Graeme's son, who had organized our transportation. We were helped on board courteously, and, with many eyes on us, the convoy moved off. I shared a cab with Evert, who immediately launched into "Bicycle Built for Two." Every single lyric and refrain. He sounds like an old crow.

The trip took us through the Waterland region: Zunderdorp, Ransdorp, Uitdam, and Zuiderwoude. Picturesque old villages seemingly untouched by time but, judging from the fancy modern cargo bikes on the driveways, in fact taken over by rich Amsterdam yuppies.

Evert regaled me with stories of the past; from time to time we heard peals of laughter from one of the other pedicabs, or Eefje would demand a bird-watching halt. I recognized the godwit from its picture on the matchbox, but that's as far as my bird expertise goes.

In Zuiderwoude we were driven to a wine shop. The greengrocer is no more; a sommelier has taken his place. A wine tasting was planned for us, with snacks. Tidbits which, according to Evert, were too light for really heavy drinking. In a wine tasting, you're not supposed to swallow but spit; still, there are limits to our compliance. We'll spit when we're sick, but not when we're imbibing. We let the pedicab boys join in the tasting on condition they promised not to drive us into a ditch on the way back.

After an impromptu passing of the hat we bought two

dozen bottles with the proceeds. A good time—I can't think of a better way of putting it—was had by all.

We started the return journey with some more singing, but soon we all nodded off.

We were deposited at the front door, and the drivers were each given a bottle of the wine as a tip. Evert made a show of reluctance to part with the bottles. "*Partir, c'est mourir un peu*" (to leave is to die a little), he said solemnly to a bottle he cradled in his arms. Amid laughter, we then gaily waved goodbye to the drivers.

We always discreetly settle up with the organizer the day after the outing. Expensive? Let's put it this way: an outstanding price-quality ratio.

Saturday, June 8

There's a "DIY Alzheimer's Test." The name is a bit misleading, since the test is designed to find out if someone *else* has Alzheimer's. I did test myself, however, and got a reassuring result: no Alzheimer's.

The reason I'm mentioning this is that I paid close attention to Grietje on our trip. She seemed to be enjoying herself immensely but did occasionally have a dazed look on her face, and sometimes one of surprise. I haven't known her long enough or well enough to administer the Alzheimer's test to her, but she does have symptoms that point in that direction. What she herself told me is not reassuring.

To realize that you are slowly but surely losing your grip on reality... Unlike the frog in a pan of hot water that doesn't realize it's slowly getting cooked, you're painfully aware for a long time of your own deterioration. You find yourself sinking more and more into a deep black hole and spending less and less time crawling out of it, certain you'll only fall in again. Still time enough to see where this leads: ending up like one of all the other befuddled, frightened, or furious old bundles of misery (not counting the few that remain obliviously cheerful), anxiously trying to retrieve what no longer exists. And then confined to bed or listlessly drooling in a wheelchair. Tied to the bed once there's nothing more they can do for you. No dignity left.

Poor Grietje. What can I say to console her?

Sunday, June 9

Mrs. Surmann decided to dry her wet slippers in the microwave. She set the timer for twenty minutes and then went to watch TV. The slippers melted and set off the fire alarm.

I shouldn't be surprised if management used the incident as a pretext to outlaw the use of microwaves.

The same management has sent out a letter announcing that cameras are being installed in the hallways "for our own safety." That's really the last straw. The word *Gestapo* has been muttered. "Has she completely lost her marbles, that Stelwagen woman? *Cameras?* To find out who's been tossing cakes in the fish tank, or whose rollator won't move over for the nurse with the pill trolley?" Graeme was uncharacteristically incensed. He vowed he'd personally trash those cameras. Evert promptly offered to help.

I think Mrs. Stelwagen has overplayed her hand this time.

Most of the inhabitants don't want surveillance cameras in here. Although they do like the other kind of camera. Whenever the local TV station shows up to film a one hundredth birthday, they fall over themselves to get in the picture. Residents who for years have done nothing but mumble are suddenly capable of belting out "Happy Birthday" at the top of their lungs. Ladies who always sit downstairs in the same grubby gray shift are suddenly seen wearing an exuberantly flowered dress and party hat.

Fortunately, the forty-five minutes of showing-off the cameramen filmed last time was cut down to exactly fifty seconds for the broadcast. Everyone was terribly disappointed; some even felt seriously insulted.

Monday, June 10

Yesterday was the kind of day when you doze off four times over the newspaper or in front of the TV, then stay up tossing and turning half the night. I first tried a glass of warm milk and honey, then swallowed two sleeping pills.

According to addiction experts, I am one of the 930,000 Dutch over-fifty-fives who resort to a pill when sleep won't come on its own. It seems old-age homes are teeming with junkies. They're addicted to sleeping pills containing benzodiazepines. Huh? Yes, benzodiazepines. They also help assuage anxiety and fretting. But they come with a dangerous side effect: you might break a hip. In the Netherlands alone they've caused over a thousand broken hips, by the experts' estimate—elderly folks who wake up in the middle of the night in an extra-doddering state, stagger to the bathroom and take a fall. *Crack.*

Tuesday, June 11

Our club meeting yesterday was hosted by Evert. A rather disappointing performance. He burned the appetizers: blackened croquettes and charred chicken nuggets. His exhaust fan is very efficient, so nobody noticed the smell of burning. Elderly noses. The liver sausage was past its use-by date. We had to make do with cheese and of course an overabundance of alcohol.

The clamor to include Ria and Antoine Travemundi, our home's aged culinary whiz kids, grew too loud to ignore. They were immediately and unanimously voted in as probationary members of the Old But Not Dead Club. A delegation consisting of Grietje and Edward was sent to invite them to join us forthwith. They came and were quite moved; they heartily thanked each and every one of us in turn. Antoine had tears in his eyes.

"Isn't it nice we can all still be part of this," said Eefje sardonically. Antoine nodded. Ria laughed a bit awkwardly. Then they went back to their room to raid their fridge for some French cheeses, serrano ham, and smoked salmon, to celebrate their hard-won initiation.

"Ha, that's the only reason we got you to join us!"

We never discuss too many orders of business at once, to give us the excuse to have another meeting. This time the only item on the agenda was to evaluate the first round of excursions. Nothing but praise all around. A veritable flurry of feathers in our caps.

We drew up a fresh list of outings and their proposed dates:

End of June—Ria and Antoine (As probationary members they will be counted as one for now.)
Mid-July—Graeme
End of July—Eefje
Mid-August—Grietje
End of August—Yours truly
Mid-September—Evert
End of September—Edward

Sounds good: we have a lot to look forward to right up until the end of summer.

Wednesday, June 12

Grietje came over for a cup of coffee. Not without a purpose. Having consulted the Internet and her doctor, she now has enough information to know she is definitely on the road to dementia.

"It doesn't make me jump for joy, but there's nothing anyone can do about it. I'm just going to try to keep going as long as possible."

She asked me to help her achieve that goal and was also going to appeal to a number of other people, including the rest of the club. On condition that we be completely honest with her, telling it like it is. No pointless pity. I had to solemnly swear that I'll entrust her to the good care of the medical ward once she becomes a burden or unmanageable. She couldn't suppress an ironic little smile as she said it. She knew that there was nowhere else for her to go, and she had resigned herself to it. But before giving up she was determined to give every ounce of her strength to enjoying life "as a person in her right mind."

I got a lump in my throat and vowed to do everything in my power to support her. She thought that "everything in my power" was a bit over the top but said, "Fine, that's why I asked you."

We discussed what form that support should take, but that isn't an easy thing to work out. We are going to sleep on it for a night or two.

Thursday, June 13

I sometimes detect a faintly hostile attitude from my fellow residents. I know that they often gossip about our little club. "Snooty go-getters," we are. "Ingrates" for turning up our noses at the many diversions that are already offered here.

"Full of themselves, aren't they?" is another one.

For some, disappointment at being left out turns to envy and spite. Envy and spite that have plenty of time to take root in here.

Never underestimate the grudge holders, the schemers, and the backbiters. They'll go after their tame, indifferent, or naïve fellow residents relentlessly. The affront is usually trivial, but in the long run the consequences can be contempt, derision, and hate. If you don't have anything special to do all day long, a molehill can turn into a mountain. A person's time must be filled with something; one's attention has to have a focus. Nasty character traits need an outlet. In contrast to what you'd expect, narrow-mindedness increases and tolerance lessens with the onset of old age. "Old and wise" is the exception rather than the rule.

I can sometimes feel the tension now. People start coughing into their fists when I approach. Conversations stop. Glances are exchanged.

I mentioned this to Edward and Graeme this morning at coffee; our table remained curiously empty. They too feel the hostility sometimes. It isn't very nice, but we'll just have to put up with it; there's nothing else we can do.

Friday, June 14

The world's most famous old man, Nelson Mandela, is not doing so well. One day he's reported to be a bit better, the next a bit worse. People in here really feel for him. He's probably the least controversial hero of the past twenty years, by far. But even heroes must die. The newspapers can take their time polishing the obituary. The world's leaders are hoping the funeral will fall on a day that's convenient.

Fortunately Mandela has not appeared in public for a long time, so our last image of him will be of a frail but dignified and wise old man. That's where his greatness lay.

Grietje, Eefje, and I have together come up with an Alzheimer's plan of attack. From information provided by Alzheimer Netherlands, it appears that 70 percent of people with dementia live at home. Now, "home" doesn't quite apply in this case, but still, it's encouraging for Grietje to know that it's fairly unlikely she'll be transferred to the dementia unit any time soon. With a little help she should be able to stay in her own room for quite a while longer. The first concrete move we're making is to take turns popping in every afternoon to check that Grietje hasn't left the hamster in the freezer. That was Grietje's suggestion; she doesn't actually have a hamster. Next we made lists, lots of lists. A list of names, roles, and telephone numbers. A list of things that have to be done on a daily basis. A list of things she should never do. A shopping list. A list of where things are and a detailed daily schedule. We'll help where necessary. If she doesn't remember or understand something, she'll jot it down and ask us later. If it's urgent, she'll get us on the phone.

We've also agreed to read a book about dementia, in case our own common sense isn't enough to sort it out.

It felt good to be able to come up with some concrete steps to take. And to consume a pound of smoked eel on old newspaper while we were at it. And a glass of white wine. Grietje is a great hostess. We've promised to warn her if she starts offering us only dry bread and water.

There exists a home for senior dogs where sick, handicapped old mutts live out their days in a homey setting. They are given a great deal of individual attention and, if necessary, hospice care. It's run by an organization called the Djimba Foundation. There's a drawing on the Djimba site of a blind guide dog with a cane and dark sunglasses. I am not making this up.

I wonder if the level of care is dependent on doggy budgets?

We have received an answer to our request to see the regulations, statutes, or other documents that concern us. That's to say, just an acknowledgment of receipt, forwarded to us by Victor.

"The great stalling tactic has begun," our lawyer wrote in an accompanying note, "but by return mail I gave them a deadline of August 1. And threatened them with an interim injunction. I thought, I'll just bring out the big guns at once. I wouldn't want the documents we've requested to be released when we're all senile or dead and gone!"

Good work, Victor.

It's Sunday afternoon, visiting time. The first sons and daughters are already drinking coffee downstairs with their aged parents. The roles are reversed: where the children were once lectured by their elders, the children now reprimand the parents. "We'd appreciate it if you would put on a clean shirt when we visit you, and why don't you ever have anything to offer us but the same old stale cookies?"

Rumors about nursing home closings are swirling around the Conversation Lounge. "That will be the death of me," I have heard several residents stoutly declare. I'm not sure whether you can hold people to that kind of pledge. There are a few I will definitely try to remind of it when the time comes.

According to the consulting firm Berenschot, 870 "elder-care locations" will have to be shut in the coming years. The number of new patrons will start declining precipitously as a result of the new stricter admission requirements. Seniors will have to live independently until they're no longer physically able to, and then go straight into the medical ward, is the idea in a nutshell. Meanwhile the seniors living in care homes now will keep dying. So you don't have to be a math genius to forecast a considerable vacancy rate. The powers that be won't wait for the last resident to die before shutting the place down, naturally; the remaining oldsters will be uprooted and replanted elsewhere.

That's what will be the death of them, some of those potential victims say. Several are even convinced they'll be forced to go back to living independently. Worse still!

The fear of having to move out is great. As a way to keep the discussion pleasant and light, Mr. Bakker likes to call it "deportation." But I'll bet that instead of dying, once they've been transplanted into a spacious new room most of the residents will never want to leave.

To me it doesn't make much difference if I live here or somewhere a few miles from here. As long as my friends move with me, and as long as we get a free trip down the Rhine on moving day.

Tuesday, June 18

Forgive me for writing about the weather, but yesterday was such a lovely summer's day. Not too warm and not too cold. I spent the afternoon in the park with a newspaper and a book. First with Eefje, who left after an hour or so, and then with Evert, who came hobbling along around cocktail hour pushing his new rollator. He had two Thermos flasks in the shopping basket: one filled with whiskey and one with white wine. He pulled two glasses from his coat pocket, neatly wrapped in toilet paper.

"I'm drinking less," he said. "No, really, I'm serious!" And when I kept nodding sympathetically, he added that he'd started splurging on more expensive, therefore more palatable, booze. I told him that was very sensible of him, and the wine he'd brought was indeed excellent, although it did have a bit of a Thermos aftertaste. So we sat on the bench drinking like two respectable winos until it was time to walk home, a bit flushed and unsteady on our feet, the rollator between us, each with one hand on the handlebar. This morning, Edward commented that he'd seen us from his balcony, and it had been a touching sight. Maybe there's an untapped market for a tandem walker, a rollator built for two.

At home I fell fast asleep on the couch and when I woke up it was close to midnight. A nurse had popped her head around the door when I'd failed to make an appearance at supper. She had come to check if I was still alive but did not bother to wake me up.

Wednesday, June 19

Hot weather always brings a spike in the death rate among the elderly. The weatherman is predicting ninety-one degrees. I hope I make it through the day.

I stopped by Anja's desk in the administration office to ask if they are on to us yet. The director was away at a conference on the changes in the elder-care system, so we had the place to ourselves.

She told me there had been an internal memo devoted to finding out who's behind the freedom-of-information request. The director has told the board she suspects that "a small but tight-knit group of discontented residents" is behind it. That's us.

The threat of an interim injunction seems to have alarmed the board, and they asked about the possible motivation. The fact that care-industry bosses have seen their names in the newspapers all too often lately works in our favor: they are terrified of negative publicity. Stelwagen was therefore ordered to do whatever necessary to prevent any exacerbation of the situation. She assured them she would get in touch with the lawyer shortly.

Later Eefje and I debated what we should do with the information Anja has been giving us. We decided to keep the identity of our source from our lawyer as well as from the other club members, in order not to saddle them with incriminating information. We wouldn't want our Anja

Appelboom to be mentioned in the same breath as Julian Assange, Edward Snowden, or Bradley Manning.

I must confess it's making me a bit nervous.

Thursday, June 20

Someone broke into Mrs. Van Gelder's room yesterday. She wandered up and down the hallway sobbing, telling everyone she met that her watch had been stolen from the drawer of her nightstand while she was downstairs having her tea. It was a wedding present from her husband.

The news has shaken everyone up.

The thief must have had a key, since Van Gelder always locks her door.

Residents are required to lock their rooms when they go out. That's been compulsory ever since a befuddled old gent entered the wrong room and got into bed. Later, when the bed's rightful owner pulled back the covers, it gave her such a turn that she fell and broke her wrist.

The missing watch has given rise to vague, almost casual insinuations fingering various housekeepers or attendants. The general view: the browner the skin, the more suspect. And: "It must have been a man, because a woman just wouldn't do that." I wonder if a course teaching logic would be lost on people over seventy?

The theft hasn't improved the atmosphere, anyway.

The director wasn't happy about it. I have it from a trustworthy source that she doesn't so much care about the watch but she does care about the home's reputation.

Friday, June 21

Made it to summer! Even if it feels like autumn.

"Suicide weather!" exclaimed the reliably peevish Bakker at least three times over a cup of tea. After he'd said it the third time, Evert said, "I'll escort you up to the roof if you like." He also offered to look after Bakker's wallet.

The number of suicides among the elderly has increased quite a bit lately, according to the statisticians.

Our institution does not make public the cause of death of residents who pass away. So suicide simply does not exist. Statistically speaking, at least a few must have done away with themselves over the last few years. But any information of that kind would only sow unease and put ideas into people's heads.

I found the sight of my own gaunt nakedness in the doctor's mirror yesterday quite alarming.

Humans really are rather misshapen and ugly animals, I fear. With a few exceptions, people are much nicer looking with clothes than without. Only children are beautiful when they're naked. But the older you are, the more layers of clothes, please. And the looser, or even baggier, the better. The procession of pear-shaped ladies in tight leggings parading through the halls every Monday on their way to the gym is extremely off-putting.

The doctor, by the way, was, all my ailments considered, quite happy with my physical condition. There is nothing that can be done about the dribble. "You'll have to start wearing diapers, Mr. Groen. You'll get used to it soon enough."

Mrs. Van Gelder's watch has resurfaced. One of the cleaning staff found it along with the wet laundry in the washing machine. It's nice and clean, but it no longer works. Mrs. Van Gelder suspects the culprit got cold feet, wanted to be rid of it, and tossed it into the machine. Why the thief would make a special trip to the laundry to dump a watch into the machine was something she couldn't explain. "But crazier things have happened in the world!"

The possibility that she might have dropped her watch into the laundry basket herself by accident was "out of the question."

She gave the honest woman who found it a fifty-cent reward.

My doctor yesterday made me aware of Jan Hoeijmakers, the geriatrics professor whose goal is to have people make it to an advanced old age without suffering from the usual ailments. Hoeijmakers is very optimistic and has already achieved decent results in mice. Something about treating the DNA in some special way. Ten years from now there could be a miracle pill to cure all kinds of old-age problems.

Just a bit too late for me and my friends, then; it makes me sick to think about it. I don't need to get to two hundred, but crossing the finish line in relatively good health, that's a deal I would gladly sign up for.

I forgot again, by the way, to ask my doctor how he feels about euthanasia.

Sunday, June 23

News about the renovation plans. In a letter to the residents, the director has proposed setting up a tenants' committee charged with advising the building committee on "anything to do with well-being and quality of life."

So apparently there's a building committee, and the plans are already far more advanced than we were led to believe. The pretense that we are going to be allowed some input is meant to obscure that fact.

On the one hand, to many residents it comes as reassuring news: if there's to be a major renovation, it means the home won't be shut down in the immediate future. So they won't have to move. On the other hand, a major renovation will almost certainly mean they'll have to move out, even if only temporarily. Just the thought of it makes the average blood pressure in here rise precipitously. Uncertainty and change are two nails in every old person's coffin. Mrs. Pot, a sour doomsayer, could not rule out that the whole point of the renovation is to clear the place out. "That's what they're doing it for. Many in here won't survive it!" There are always some who will nod in agreement, no matter how crazy the remark.

An extensive renovation will be a dust-up, both literally and figuratively, so bring it on. The more action the better. I wouldn't mind being part of the group that's supposed to advise the building committee.

At Eefje's suggestion, I have asked Victor to write another letter specifically asking to be apprised of the renovation plans.

Mrs. Aupers is relatively new here. She has taken to reading aloud the newspaper obituaries at coffee every morning. I am waiting to see who'll be the first to say something to her. Not everyone is keen on being subjected to such a jolly start to the day.

She's not the only one who is fascinated by death. Whenever someone's died, you can just hear some people thinking, *There goes another one, and look, I'm still here.* They also enjoy seeing the black-framed names of people they once knew in the newspaper; that's even more satisfying.

As for me, I am moved only by death notices for children. They make me think of my little girl. Obituaries of big shots with dozens of tributes from all the companies they steered or boards they sat on leave me as cold as their cadavers. Heave-ho, in the ground you go. Now see how important you are.

Our newest club members, Ria and Antoine, have rented the kitchen and dining room in the community center for Friday. I received a very nice card in the mail inviting me to a welcome dinner to celebrate their admission into our club.

The invitation included a request for between-course entertainments in the form of speeches, stories, or songs. You can practically hear my old brain cells creaking.

I took my ancient dinner jacket, which I haven't worn in twenty-five years, to the dry cleaner's, and tomorrow I will buy myself a new dress shirt.

When Mrs. Aupers isn't reading the obituaries, she's whining about her cat, which she's had to put in the animal shelter. She had just spent €3,500 on the creature. Something about a crushed back leg requiring complicated surgery. The vet pocketed Mrs. Aupers's entire nest egg, grinning from ear to ear. I do feel sorry for her, even if she's such a whiner. She loved that cat so dearly. But rules are rules in here: pets are not permitted. That was why she'd wanted to stay in her own home, but her children wouldn't let her. They'd had enough of having to look after her.

The sales lady at C&A wasn't inclined to put herself out for my dress-shirt purchase. The blowsy matron in the too-tight company uniform pointed, bored, to some bins in the distance. "They're over there."

"Thank you kindly for your obliging assistance."

That remark elicited, first, a look of surprise, and then an annoyed glare.

At the next store the service wasn't much better. Clueless old gentlemen aren't very much appreciated as customers. In the end I bought, at random, a light-blue shirt, which turns out to be too big. Which means I have to go back again tomorrow. I bet—it's just a guess—salespeople aren't all that fond of old people returning things, either.

Wednesday, June 26

Evert is not doing well. He went to the hospital this morning for a check-up and they wanted to admit him immediately. Evert insisted on postponing it until Monday, pleading a funeral he had to attend.

"I've invented quite a few funerals in my life," he said. "I can never seem to think of another excuse on the spot. And as long as you don't use the funeral pretext three times on the same person, they'll never have the nerve to accuse you of lying."

Not that a five-day deferment helps him much, even he realizes that, but he needs time to prepare himself mentally for another operation. And he isn't inclined to miss our dinner on Friday night at the community center either.

He did look a bit of a wreck when I stopped by his place. He was holding a mug of tea, which didn't seem very promising. When I mentioned it, he said it had a drop of rum in it. That was a bit more hopeful.

Together we told Mo. When he heard that he would be entrusted to my care again next week, he pricked up an ear and farted.

In the hoopla surrounding the watch theft, the director's plan to install cameras everywhere suddenly gained popularity, but when it turned out that the watch had landed in the laundry by accident, enthusiasm for it waned. I heard from Anja that Stelwagen was almost disappointed nothing was stolen. Such was the report from our woman at the front.

Thursday, June 27

Old people can look so scruffy sometimes, in their stained raincoats with greasy collars. Either they no longer see it, or they don't think it's important. It's a big waste of money to buy a new coat if you don't think you'll be granted the time to wear it out. So they wear threadbare dresses or suits that are forty years old or more, worn-down shoes, and socks full of holes. It's the downhill slide to loss of dignity. If they no longer care very much about their appearance, they needn't worry about piggish table manners, brazen crotch-scratching, or washing their hair only once a month either. "When I'm out of clean undies I just put the least-dirty pair back on," one of my fellow residents announced without blushing.

Fortunately there are some immaculate, fresh-smelling, elegant ladies and gentlemen too: Eefje, Edward, Ria, Antoine, and me included, notwithstanding my dribble problem. Dapper old gents and stylish matrons, pleasantly perfumed and neatly coiffed.

I like to go to the barber's once every two months to have the last few hairs on my skull washed not once but twice.

"So, how do you want it cut today?"

"Smart, please, and a bit modern. And take your time."

"I'm in no rush. Trust me, I'll make you look good."

I've had the same barber for years, and I never get bored with the chitchat.

Friday, June 28

It's June 28, and the stoves are merrily hissing away. In a manner of speaking, since we do have central heating. In most of the rooms the thermostat is set at the maximum allowable, seventy-three degrees, as always, and the first winter coat has been spotted heading outside. Yesterday the outdoor temperature never made it past fifty-seven degrees.

Today I am eating very little or nothing at all in preparation for our dinner tonight at the community center. It isn't hard. The appetite for food diminishes as you get older. Sometimes I have to force myself to get something down. Fortunately they have started offering a liquid breakfast here. A liquid lunch as well, if necessary. It saves quite a bit of chewing. Evert's situation isn't exactly whetting my appetite either.

My old dinner jacket is a bit on the baggy side. But neatly pressed. The new-shirt conundrum was resolved in the end. When I went back to the store to return the one I bought I was helped by a friendly Moroccan sales lady who measured my collar and arm length and then fished the right size out of a bin for me.

All in all I look quite dapper, if I do say so myself.

I also bought myself a new cologne. I had tried out several on my wrist but they soon turned into an unrecognizable potpourri of smells. That isn't what you're supposed to do; you're supposed to spritz a little on a special slip of paper. Finally a saleswoman chose something for me that she said suited me just right. And suited my wallet as well.

Hats off to Antoine and Ria of the pop-up restaurant Chez Travemundi. I haven't eaten so well in years. Six courses! Served in relaxed fashion, modest old-person portions, and the most pleasant company to boot. A wonderful evening. We sat there from five o'clock until ten, we sang while we did the dishes, and then all staggered home. I was sensible about the drink, fortunately, otherwise I'd still be brain-dead now.

After the welcome cocktail, Evert took the floor. He spoke in glowing terms of the pleasures of life and the joys of friendship. He had really put a great deal of thought into his speech. In conclusion he casually mentioned that on Monday he would be taking a holiday in the hospital for a few days, and announced the visiting hours.

"If anyone says one more word about it tonight, I'll personally smear this langoustine carpaccio in their hair."

Silence.

Then Graeme made a toast to Evert, and the spell was broken.

There were other eloquent speeches last night, and songs and funny skits; there was even a food quiz. I'm just sorry I've already forgotten so much of it.

The Tour de France begins this afternoon. You'll find me indoors every afternoon for the next three weeks. I love it: endless live TV. For the first few hours I'll follow the Belgian narration, but toward the end, when it starts to get exciting, I'll turn on Radio Tour de France and listen to the Dutch commentary while watching the television on Mute.

I'm at the midway point of my exposé. At the end of today, the first six months will be behind me. I've only missed five or six days due to illness. Not bad, is it?

It isn't always easy. Material to write about doesn't necessarily present itself spontaneously, and I find myself having to weigh my words carefully. But being obliged to write does sharpen the senses and keep me on my toes. Whenever someone says something noteworthy, I try to remember it, but memory happens to be one of this ramshackle body's many weak links. A small notepad is a solution, but I can't be too conspicuous using it. Beady little prying eyes lurk everywhere.

"What *are* you scribbling all the time, Hendrik? Let me read it!"

"I'm working on my memoir. You can all read it, but not until it's finished."

Then they'll usually want to know if they're in it, and then I'll say they are, no matter who it is. "Only good things!" I'll reassure them. They're usually content with that, even though they do think I'm a bit of a pretentious jerk, slaving away on my *mem-mwahr.*

I have become a rather anxious Tour de France spectator. Last year's race and the one before saw so many pileups of injured cyclists sprawled on the tarmac, with a couple of Dutchmen invariably at the bottom of the heap, that it started to interfere with the pleasure of watching. The opening leg yesterday did not give much hope for improvement. The first one to take a spill was our national fall guy, the unlucky Johnny Hoogerland. Luckily it was a banner he ran into and not barbed wire. There were several other spectacular falls to come.

It's too bad the bus that got itself stuck under the finish-line arch was dislodged just in the nick of time. What a lovely melee that would have been.

Monday, July 1

This morning Evert took a taxi to the hospital. I called him just now. He is waiting for the surgeon who operated on him the last time. "Not my best friend, but you don't have a say in who's going to be your doctor."

No, the free market doesn't work in one's choice of doctors. At least, not if the insurance is paying. If your name is Queen Beatrix, it's a different story, naturally. I wonder if she's on supplementary insurance too?

Yesterday afternoon an unknown Belgian who has never won anything of note before was ten yards out in front of the peloton the whole way to win the second leg of the Tour de France. Even if you don't like bicycle racing, you can cheer when Tom Thumb beats the giant, when David prevails over Goliath. I love underdogs! As long as they're not poor losers, that is.

Grietje has written herself a long letter and pasted it on the kitchen cupboard. In it she explains to herself that she has Alzheimer's, listing the problems she might encounter. She gives herself advice and courage in the face of whatever may come when she starts losing it. She ends with, "Losing it isn't the worst that can happen; winning isn't everything. Love, Grietje." The way she addressed herself moved me greatly. She is handling her illness in her own fresh and unique way.

She wondered aloud how she would react to her own letter later on. By the time I know the answer, it'll probably be too late for her to understand. What a surreal state of affairs.

Tuesday, July 2

Evert is afraid he'll lose at least a couple more toes. The surgeon had looked rather grim.

"Aren't you happy with the result of your own work?" Evert had asked him. Well now, the doctor wouldn't put it that way. He preferred to talk in terms of unforeseeable complications. The doctor who spontaneously admits he's made a mistake has yet to be born. If the baker burns the bread, it isn't the end of the world, but if the surgeon amputates the wrong leg...then it's the fault of the nurse who checked off the wrong box on the form. Tall trees may catch a lot of wind, but they also make sure they have good storm-damage coverage. When a hotshot totters and falls, he'll soon be back on his feet up the road somewhere. On full pay.

Evert's surgery is scheduled for Thursday. They're keeping him under observation until then. He hopes his surgeon is not the vindictive sort and isn't inclined to use a dull scalpel on him.

The phone call left me feeling rather upset. Tomorrow I'll go and visit him. He's asked me to bring him another bottle of that Bols mineral water (*wink, wink*).

I also have to bring him some get-well-soon cards from fellow residents. To save the old skinflints the cost of a postage stamp.

Wednesday, July 3

This morning I paid the sick call. Difficult. You're supposed to radiate hope and cheer, and that's not easy if you regard it as somberly as I do.

I would be a very poor hospital clown.

To make myself feel better, I could say that compared with another visitor there, I was a ray of sunshine. Two beds down, a woman was with her husband who had just come out of surgery. All she talked about for half an hour was herself, especially her own ailments. I did something I'd never have dared to do before. I asked her, "Hadn't you better trade places with him?"

My remark cheered Evert up no end, but the woman just glared at us, as if she had no idea what I was talking about.

"My friend means that your ingrown toenail is far more serious than your husband's open-heart surgery, and so it would make sense for you to lie there instead of him," said Evert, straight-faced.

"Mind your own business!"

As if the bus that got stuck under the finish banner weren't bad enough, the Tour escaped an even greater disaster. In a replay on TV, they showed that at the end of the third stage a little white dog, the spitting image of Tintin's faithful companion, Snowy, started crossing the road just as the peloton came racing up. If the dog had been killed, the Tour would suddenly have become of interest in here, especially among the ladies. Dozens of cyclists have suffered broken bones and concussions, but the death of one cute, little dog would have transcended all. I can tell you they'd have watched *that* slow-motion replay over and over, shuddering with horror.

Thursday, July 4

The expectation is that Evert will wake up in the recovery room at about 7 p.m. this evening. That sounds reassuring: the "recovery" room. He promised to give us a call as soon as he's able. It's going to be a long day.

Maarten van Roozendaal has died. I'd never even heard of him. We exist on a remote edge of society; not everything gets through to us in here. The main thing we're proficient in is recycling old hat.

Grietje let me borrow her van Roozendaal CD. She told me to listen to the track "The Too-Late Ending." It's about a husband taking care of his demented wife.

Never have I heard such a moving song about old age. I told Grietje I didn't know how, as an early-stage Alzheimer's patient, she could bear listening to it. "Maybe it's crazy, but it gives me comfort. Or rather, acceptance. Even so, it's also energizing."

There are several other beautiful songs on this CD. Who will write a song for Maarten—"The Too-Soon Ending"?

Egypt's president, Morsi, has been deposed after a military coup. Well, a coup... "The army has taken it upon itself to guide the transition process," explained our minister of foreign affairs, Frans Timmermans.

"Oh, no, officer, I didn't steal anything. I just guided the transition process to a new owner."

The same goes for our director: she isn't making any cuts, she's just guiding the transition process.

Friday, July 5

Evert called at 9 a.m. His leg has been amputated below the knee.

I can't write today.

Saturday, July 6

I've forced myself to pick up the pen once more. Writing is good for me. Once I have committed something to paper, I can distance myself from it a bit, and then I'm less insufferable. That's a lot nicer for the people around me too.

Yesterday afternoon I paid Evert a rather emotional visit. Evert himself was already over the initial shock. He did admit he had been pretty upset on Thursday night.

"I thought to myself, 'I'll just try to move my foot,' but there was no foot. It's lying somewhere on a heap of offal. I didn't have the heart to call you, Henk. I first had to get used to the idea myself."

I said I quite understood and I'd been afraid of that when I didn't hear from him.

To prove that he was almost his old mischievous self again, Evert wondered aloud if Muslims had to be operated on according to the laws of halal, by which he meant fully conscious.

I worry that one lower leg won't be the end of it, and that my friend will have to say goodbye to a few more affected bits of leg or arm until the inevitable end.

The petty incidents in this home, the chitchat at the coffee table, sail right over my head.

I am leaning a bit on Eefje, who is so strong and level headed, yet at the same time sweet and sympathetic. She cheers me up when we visit each other in our rooms, at least once or twice a day. I'm beginning to grow uncommonly fond of her.

Sunday, July 7

Practically no one in here ever goes on a vacation.

Should I cautiously sound out the others to see if they have any interest in a little wine-tasting trip, for example? (Not to be confused with a Rhine trip, which makes me picture a merry parade of invalids being pushed up the gangplank of the hospital ship *J Henri Dunant* by cheery Red Cross volunteers. Not if you paid me!)

It should be possible to rent a comfortable bus for a small group, to drive down to Champagne, say, and spend a few days there in some nice château. Good food and drink, a few wine tastings, a cathedral or two, and no pathetic or whiny old coots to bother us. It would have to be wheelchair-friendly, of course.

The idea of a vacation occurred to me because after the distress of the past few days, I need something positive to look forward to. I'll find out what Eefje thinks of a short club road trip.

This evening we're discussing what arrangements we can make for Evert. *We* means Grietje, Eefje, Graeme, Edward, and myself. Ria and Antoine had tickets for the theater. They protested they'd rather stay home so as not to miss the meeting, but we were able to persuade them to go. Ria did suggest she drop off some snacks before leaving. For form's sake we protested loudly that there was no need. "But of course it *would* be lovely," Graeme let slip just at the right moment, and then it was a foregone conclusion. Graeme couldn't help looking pleased with himself.

Monday, July 8

"You're making good progress," the doctor told Evert.

"Ha! I'd say having only one leg is rather a setback!" Evert responded.

I went to visit him this morning. Evert will be moved to a rehabilitation clinic in a few days. If all goes well, he'll be sent home after ten days or so.

Last night's discussion was a fruitful one. We came up with a number of practical things we can do.

Edward is taking care of ordering an electric wheelchair. Eefje, who is on good terms with the people in home-care services, will arrange for domestic help. Graeme is going to ask the doctor about the availability of medical assistance. Grietje will do his shopping for the time being. "But you'll have to make me a list! I can't even remember the two little things I have to buy for myself." Ria and Antoine will take care of his food and I'm looking after the dog. Now *that's* what I call a voluntary aid society!

We'll do whatever's necessary the first days he's home, to give him time to work out for himself how to live with one and a half legs. The ultimate goal is to help him to remain in his independent apartment. We all agreed: if Evert were to move into the home proper, we could expect a war between him and a substantial cohort of the other inmates. Clearly a lose–lose situation.

The measures we're taking are not unwarranted. Anja reports that Evert's retirement apartment has been added to the list of residences that will soon become available. Who was behind this move our whistle-blower could not tell us.

Tuesday, July 9

Mrs. Groenteman's Canta was rammed by a motorcycle going twenty-five miles an hour. In defense of the boy on the motorcycle, it must be said that Groenteman had been driving in the road, then suddenly swung around to cross at the crosswalk. It's a miracle no one was hurt. That is, the

Canta is probably a complete write-off. The biker sailed right over it and escaped with just a scratch or two. The way Mrs. Groenteman was carrying on you'd have thought she was dying, but in the end only her hairdo was mussed.

Mr. Ellroy (he of the stuffed moose head) witnessed the incident, and gave rather a juicy account of it at teatime.

Groenteman believes she has an iron-clad defense when it comes to allocating blame for the accident. "Anything on a crosswalk has right of way," she kept insisting. Luckily she has no-fault insurance.

Many of the residents are insured for all eventualities. "Because you never know..." For all the funeral-policy premiums that have been paid in here, we could have bought ourselves a decent-sized cemetery.

Very old people are a hazard at the wheel of any conveyance, even if it goes no faster than three miles an hour. Not just in the street, but also in the supermarket. Even if they're maneuvering their mobility scooter like a tractor-trailer threading its way through Amsterdam's busiest shopping street on a Saturday afternoon. Why all of a sudden the damn machine decides to jump into reverse they have no idea...

However, none of this deters me from wanting to take my own scooter onto the highways and byways very soon, and make them unsafe for everyone else!

Wednesday, July 10

An alderwoman in Hengelo, but it may have been Almelo, is of the opinion that the care of infirm seniors should be given over to the unemployed, who would keep their unemployment benefits in lieu of a salary, putting the professional caregivers out of a job. Then they in turn can go on unemployment.

Instead of a trained person with a diploma, you'll get an out-of-work construction worker to help you into the shower and soap up your bottom. Reaching an all-time low in respect for the elderly. Fortunately a lot of people thought that the woman who said this with a straight face must be out of her mind. But if you're going to allow all 408 local councils in the Netherlands to make their own decisions about elder and invalid care, you're asking for trouble, accidents, and waste. Local dimwits are a dime a dozen.

Bring on the parliamentary investigation.

In Germany, many towns are now entrusting a portion of invalid care, such as running errands, delivering hot meals, or arranging transportation, to other retirees, i.e. seniors who are still fit and able. Their compensation is in the form of time-credit vouchers, which they can trade in later, when they may need help themselves. You do need a reliable stream of new retirees, which could eventually be a problem in light of the alarming graying of the population over there.

However, the trained professionals can keep providing specialized care, and getting paid for it. Obviously!

Thursday, July 11

This morning I took the minibus to the rehab clinic to visit Evert. He seems to like it there. "You do have to slog your guts out. Everyone in here does, in fact—none but the halt and the lame. But to put it in cycling terms: the morale is good."

The doctors and physiotherapists have promised Evert that he should be reasonably independent in a week or so, and then he'll be able to leave. A good goal to work toward, and Evert is doing his very best. He told me he has put himself on a strict ration of just four illicit drinks a day.

He misses Mo. I have the sense that the feeling is mutual, although it's hard to tell from the minimal amount of effort Mo expends to get through the day in hot weather. I have never heard a dog groan as much as he does when he hauls himself to his feet. Once outside, *shuffling* is a word implying more energy than Mo puts into it. That dog has always been a dawdler, but it seems to me that his gait is even more sluggish now. I keep having to wait for him when I take him for a walk, and that's saying something.

Yesterday evening we had a meeting to discuss what's next for our club excursions. Whether to postpone them, against Evert's express wishes, or keep going as planned, was the question. We decided to keep going, despite our dampened enthusiasm. We wouldn't want to incur Evert's wrath.

"Fine, but if we're going ahead with it, it's got to be good," said Graeme solemnly. He is in charge of organizing the next one. He started acting all mysterious, asking if any of us was dirt-phobic, and whether we were all vaccinated against tropical diseases. That did the trick to lighten the mood of the Old But Not Dead Club.

Friday, July 12

I have started cautiously sounding out the others about taking a short summer trip. The first person I asked was, of course, my friend Eefje. If she thinks it's a hopeless quest, I needn't put any more energy into it. But after thinking it over at some length (making me rather nervous), she expressed enthusiasm for the plan.

"It's never occurred to me, but it might be a very good idea," she said thoughtfully. "I'll just let it sit for a while, Hendrik."

I asked her how long "a while" would be.

"I was thinking one day. Can you wait that long?"

We haven't much time left, yet we have all the time in the world.

We should be in a hurry, but have almost nothing left that's worth hurrying for.

The very nasty Slothouwer sisters knocked over a vase of chrysanthemums that landed on Mrs. Van Diemen's lap— "by accident." Edward saw it happen and swears they did it on purpose. The sisters can't stand Van Diemen. Or anyone who has ever made a comment about their antisocial behavior. They mainly target the weaker amongst us. They're both bloodthirsty *and* psycho. There's been a great deal of commotion about wolf packs returning to the Netherlands, but we've had a couple of hyenas prowling about in here for years. The director sees it but turns a blind eye. There isn't much you can do about sadistic behavior. You aren't allowed, for example, to give the

Slothouwer ladies a good kick in the ass. You'd immediately have the press on your doorstep: "AGED SISTERS (87 AND 85) BEATEN UP IN CARE HOME!" Never the headline, "BEATING OF AGED SISTERS (87 AND 85) UTTERLY JUSTIFIED!"

Saturday, July 13

Yesterday afternoon I went and visited my wife. The institution where she lives is located in the province of Brabant. A two-hour trip. Time enough to remember the way we once were.

I'm not sure if she recognizes me, but I think she does. The weather was nice, we strolled together arm in arm through the lovely garden. I was deeply affected, as always. There isn't much to say. Even though there is practically no communication, there is a profound sense of connection. Moving and intensely sad at the same time.

Sunday, July 14

Evert is doing as well as can be expected. He is making a rapid recovery. "I've only fallen down three times."

He is learning to use crutches; a prosthesis is being made for him, but it can't be fitted to his leg until the wound is healed.

If Evert's to be believed, he's almost given up the booze. "I only drink to be social, really."

When I visited him yesterday he asked whether I felt

like accompanying him to Uden for a week. His son has invited him to stay with him the first week of August.

"It's to assuage his conscience, if you ask me," Evert added. "He feels guilty because he's hardly bothered to see me for years."

Evert isn't on such good terms with his extremely proper daughter-in-law, and he thought that if I came with him and could calm the waters a bit, a stay might be quite bearable. I would have my own room and the dog would have his own cage. "She isn't just a fanatic housekeeper, my daughter-in-law; she's also a great cook, and maybe, if we drop a cautious hint or two, they'll even treat us to a day at Efteling amusement park. We can ride the Python together," is how he ended his sales pitch.

I said yes. A week seemed a bit long to me, so we decided to make it five days. A nice little vacation just fell into my lap.

Monday, July 15

"OVER 90 AND GETTING SMARTER," was the headline in the newspaper *Trouw*. Even smarter? Absolutely. According to Danish researchers.

It's a matter of improved mental and cognitive abilities; the brain. The body, sadly, hasn't made any such strides. That's compared to twelve years ago. If the improvement continues at this rate, I'll still have a few marbles left twelve years from now. Hope on the horizon for the over-eighties!

The response to my vacation inquiries has been enthusiastic. Grietje is the only one who doesn't like to commit herself. "It depends—I'll see how it goes," she said, "because I've noticed that I get disoriented more easily in unfamiliar surroundings."

Of course I totally understand. Grietje has been handling her dementia like a graceful tightrope walker so far. She skillfully sidesteps the holes in her memory that crop up from time to time, and she employs a light-hearted irony to conceal her uncertainty. "So far, so good, anyway," she said when I remarked on it.

As far as our trip goes, the preference is for September. Quieter and cheaper. We are Dutch seniors through and through. And not too far away either, if possible. Someone proposed the preeminent holiday resort for old people: Luxembourg. Maastricht was also mentioned.

Tuesday, July 16

"I won't be around to see it" is not such a far-fetched assumption for people in their nineties sitting in their little room waiting for death.

Momentous events pass them by completely. Only trivial annoyances still matter. "If Greece goes bankrupt the bingo prizes will probably get smaller," was Mrs. Schouten's analysis of the eurozone crisis.

To people who have watched every penny their whole life long, something like the U.S. national debt—fifteen hundred trillion pennies!—is quite incomprehensible. As it is to anyone else, in fact. A couple dozen billion euros would end world hunger and provide everyone on earth with clean water. And the Americans are fifteen thousand billion euros in the red and think nothing of borrowing another fifty billion or so.

I have resolved to go to my grave in the red. It isn't that easy to do. I still have about eight thousand euros in my bank account, but of course I have no idea how long it still has to last me. My immediate plan is to do my bit to stimulate the Dutch economy with an additional outlay of a thousand euros per year. If we don't get over this crisis, it won't be because of me.

Wednesday, July 17

Seated downstairs in the lounge, feeling a bit blue, you hear next to you, "And then I go to the bakery but get there late because of my pedicure and I ask for half a loaf of brown bread, and then they tell me all they've got is wholegrain, which I don't like very much, I don't like the crust, but a body's got to eat, and normally I have a bag or two of frozen slices in the freezer but my grandson had eaten it, all six slices, can that boy ever eat—"

"Well, you should see that boy of mine! Eight pancakes slathered in syrup, and it has to be Van Gilse because he doesn't like the other kind very much. My word, it's hot in here!"

"We never had a freezer in the old days; at home we had to eat the old bread first and so we always had stale bread and never fresh because my mother always bought a bit too much bread, since you never know, and it wasn't until it was covered in mold that we were allowed to feed it to the ducks."

Endless torrents of vapid verbiage drowning out everything else like rampant weeds. Thoughtless. Senseless. Relentless. Aired just to let everyone know that the speaker isn't dead yet and still has something to say. Whether there's anyone willing to listen is a question they rarely ask themselves, otherwise they'd keep their mouths shut far more often.

Thursday, July 18

Edward found an old *Consumers' Guide* with an investigation into nursing home hygiene. One hundred and twenty-one homes were asked to participate, out of a total of about three hundred. Half of that number, including ours, refused to cooperate. In the end, thirty-seven homes were inspected. The result: eighteen Fs, eleven Ds, eight Cs, and not a single A. Were they that strict, or were the homes really that filthy? I'm sure the ones that refused to participate wouldn't have come off any better.

I've asked Anja if she can dig up our management's letter to the consumers' union explaining its reasons for not wanting to participate.

Most of the cleaning people in here swab the hallways in silence because they speak little or no Dutch. They do know how to give you a friendly nod. Most of them don't look very lively, however. Let's just say they are good at adapting to the tempo of the residents. I think they do an average job for minimum wage. Every once in a while there's one that stands out above the rest. They're not usually with us long. Lured away by the competition or harassed until they quit, by co-workers who can't stand people who try too hard.

Monday we're having another club outing, organized by Graeme. Evert wants us to send him a postcard. I have already bought a stamp.

Friday, July 19

Mrs. De Koning, my timid next-door neighbor, knocked on my door. Glancing skittishly over her shoulder, as if she were selling me some heroin, she entrusted the cassette player to me. She must have been at her wits' end, because in the two years she has been living next door she has never asked me for anything. "It's a recording of my late husband's voice, you see," she said.

I pried out the tape and then managed to rewind it by twisting a pencil in one of the holes. She must have thanked me at least seven times, walking out of the room backwards, bowing.

I have received a copy of a letter from the board. Victor delivered it by hand. The board greatly regrets that it cannot accede to the request of releasing documents, for vital privacy reasons, and asks if we might like to review the matter further with their legal representative. Victor thinks we should meet to discuss the next step.

Eefje and I have an appointment to see him next Wednesday.

Saturday, July 20

For the first time since I began this diary, I seem to have writer's block.

Sunday, July 21

There are a few residents who have the unpleasant habit of complaining about the condition of their bowels. Preferably on a Sunday, when the greatest number of people come downstairs at teatime. That's when the home offers the residents each a piece of cake. I know from my reliable source that it is a ninety-cent cake from ALDI which, per the unit head's instructions, is cut into at least fifteen slices, so that the gift works out to six cents per person.

And then one of them will make a great fuss about declining the pathetic little slice by announcing, "Only 'cause I haven't had a bowel movement in four days!" Or conversely, "I've been sitting on the toilet all morning, I've got a bad case of the runs."

I DON'T NEED TO KNOW ANY OF THIS!

Have a word with your doctor, or take yourself to the shit clinic (which exists, apparently), but do not come to me with your constipation or diarrhea stories while I'm sitting here trying to enjoy my sliver of cake, because it robs me of my appetite!

The extraordinary lack of shame many old people seem to have! Coupled with the strange assumption that people will be genuinely interested in their complaints and ailments!

Little children are allowed to make a big fuss over their tummy-ache or scraped knee so that their mommy will rush over with a glass of warm milk or a Band-Aid, but in old people, the incessant whining is utterly pointless and quite unbearable.

Tomorrow another outing with the incomparable Old But Not Dead set.

Monday, July 22

The Tour de France has ended. This afternoon the hole it has left in my life will be filled by Graeme. He is the organizer of our day-trippers' outing. Calling us "day-trippers" may be a bit over the top, but if you take into account that the average age of our group is eighty-two and a half, it can be quite a production.

The goal of the biannual outings organized by the Residents' Association, on the other hand, is merely to provide a change of scene for the daily coffee (10:30), lunch (12:30), and afternoon tea (3:30), with a good deal of bus riding in between. No different from the daily routine at home. Any time that's left is spent loading and unloading forty-five elderly people into and out of the bus four times, and allowing for at least three visits each to the service area's restroom for the disabled.

I pleaded sickness for the home's last two outings. The second time I used that excuse it was received with some suspicion. "*Again?* Really, today, of all days?"

Once is bad luck, twice is deliberate churlishness. By the

third time, you're a pariah. I'll have to force myself to go at least twice, or else.

How different are our jovial Old But Not Dead jaunts! Absorbing activities until we drop, interspersed with (for we are only human) coffee breaks, meals, and plenty of wine.

Tuesday, July 23

Fortunately it was loads of fun, if you'll excuse the cliché. I'd been worried that Evert's absence would put a damper on the day, but it turned out better than expected.

It was a day at the zoo, with—an emotional highlight—a baby gorilla landing in his mother's fruit salad while trying to execute a handstand.

Graeme had scoped it out beforehand and had organized a treasure hunt with witty clues. The prizes were handed out at cocktail hour. Ria got the booby prize for being off by six thousand pounds in guessing the elephant's weight. It was a second-hand bathroom scale that was not too meticulous about showing a few pounds more or less.

We called Evert to tell him we missed him. He bought us a round on the phone.

Graeme had also brought along three user-friendly digital cameras, for a photo safari. Edward and I, for example, had to snap a "Great Bottoms" series. Another duo had to photograph animals that looked like members of our club.

Graeme has promised a slick PowerPoint presentation for the next club meeting. Who says we're behind the times?

Departure at eleven and home again at five. I was exhausted. We had arranged for two wheelchairs, so I could sit down once in a while, but it was a lot of walking for me. In the end it was just a shuffle from one bench to the next one. We have just two reliable wheelchair-pushers: Antoine and Graeme. The rest of us are better at getting pushed.

Wednesday, July 24

The heat is taking its toll in here: three deaths within two days. "HEAT WAVE CREATES CARNAGE AMONG THE ELDERLY." Great headline. Thought it up myself.

It seems that geezers like us take advantage of the extreme heat to slip out quietly. Peacefully conking out in one's sleep. A self-fulfilling prophecy.

Eefje and I went to see our lawyer this morning. Victor believes the board's response was meant to win it some time and drive up our costs. To scare us off.

He says he's having more and more fun with it, and in lieu of a fee, he's asking for one bottle of wine from a different country every week. The longer this takes, the further afield we'll have to go in our quest for wine-producing countries. After a year we can start all over again. "Because," said Victor, "it shouldn't come as a surprise if this takes two years at least."

Eefje and I must have looked rather bemused at that point.

"However, in consideration of my clients' advanced age, I'll try to speed it up as much as possible. Taking the lawyer's own age into account as well."

He said he'd immediately write to the board's lawyer and start a judicial procedure.

And all this spoken in that cold, pompous, upper-crust voice straight out of some poorly acted play.

We're starting to like him more and more.

Thursday, July 25

Great brouhaha over the rumor that Mrs. Vergeer pushed Mr. Vergeer down the stairs, wheelchair and all. He's in the hospital with an assortment of broken bones and Mrs. Vergeer has been cross-examined several times by the director herself. Can it still be swept under the rug, or is it too late?

Apparently two witnesses have come forward to say they saw Mrs. Vergeer do it deliberately. Mrs. Vergeer herself claims the wheelchair's handles came off. It seems she was still clutching them in her hands as the rest of the chair lay spinning on its back ten steps below. On the other hand, there was no reason to steer him toward the stairs, unless she wanted to scare him. Which is a reasonable supposition, since Mr. Vergeer is always very mean to his wife. He only communicates by barking out commands. She has nevertheless taken care of him for years with love, patience, and devotion. He should have been pushed down the stairs a long time ago.

I'm curious to see if this can be kept out of the papers. One telephone call to *Het Parool* would do it.

We are earnestly requested "in the interests of all parties concerned" not to talk about it. We may direct any questions to the director.

Since my sympathies are with the alleged culprit, I will say nothing about this unorthodox legal process, but it is of course a scandal that residents can be pushed down the stairs with no repercussions because the director is afraid of negative publicity.

I have decided for the time being to believe it was an accident. But it's always possible Mrs. Vergeer will end up behind bars.

Friday, July 26

Evert came home this morning. It was a joyful occasion, with cake and streamers. To add to the fun, he showed the welcoming committee how to put on and take off his new leg. He took genuine pride in it, but still, a couple of our club members couldn't help looking the other way.

He was most taken with the measures the Old But Not Dead Club had come up with to simplify his life as a new amputee for the first two weeks.

"And at the end of those two weeks you can all take a hike, because by then I'll be ready to take care of my own business again." He opened a good bottle of wine and together we drank a toast to his new leg. With a sufficient quantity of ice cubes, white wine makes a perfectly refreshing soft drink. It wasn't even noon yet, after all.

Mr. Vergeer's tumble down the stairs is still *the* topic of discussion: did his wife or didn't she give him the helpful shove that landed him in the hospital? The official explanation from the director's office is that Mrs. Vergeer, a bit dazed from the heat, did steer the wheelchair in the wrong direction, but that the cause of this unfortunate accident was that the handles came loose. The witnesses who claimed Mrs. Vergeer had done it on purpose now mumble they might have been mistaken.

"Yeah, yeah, a hallucination caused by the heat wave, I suppose," Bakker couldn't help sneering.

I was going to go out and buy a scooter, but with all the commotion I never made it. It will have to wait until tomorrow.

Saturday, July 27

And I wound up buying...the Elegance 4. Stable, comfortable, with a tight turning circle, in a snazzy red color. That's the outcome of my visit to the mobility-scooter store. I tried out three different models, taking each for a test ride. I eliminated the cheap Capri, more like a toy car, and another one whose name I've forgotten, that was too expensive. I told the man in the store that I'd been riding one of these things for years; I thought it better for his peace of mind when he let me take them out for a spin.

Delivery time is two weeks, so I won't be terrorizing the neighborhood with my red monster until after my little vacation with Evert. I still need to find out about insurance. Strange that the salesman never mentioned it—that can't be a good sign.

I'm just going to stop by Mr. Hoogdalen's room; I want him to tell me more about the different accessories his son the garage owner could provide. I am looking forward to regaining my mobility!

As part of her plan of action to combat the dementia, Grietje has composed, with my help, two new notes she is to carry with her at all times: "What to do if I get lost" and "What to do if I don't remember exactly who someone is."

Both notes start with: "Please forgive me, but I'm a bit forgetful."

Sunday, July 28

I propose that during a persistent heat wave the fire brigade be deployed to spray the elderly with water. Not only has the whining about the heat grown as unbearable as the heat itself, but another resident has died, the fourth in one week. It's a record, as far as I know. Fortunately this one too was someone I didn't know very well, involving no funerary obligation on my part.

The building is about forty years old, and besides the window blinds, there are few provisions for keeping the inhabitants cool. "Old people are always cold anyway," the architect must have been thinking. The indoor temperature may soon be over the ninety-degree mark. Portable air conditioners and fans are being provided in order to keep us alive, but it's having little effect on the temperature so far.

My friend in the lion's den informs me that the director is afraid our death toll will make it into the papers if this keeps up. And the temperature is forecast to be over ninety degrees before the end of the week.

The jazz singer Rita Reys, a contemporary of mine, is dead. I just took a survey: everyone knows of her, but nobody ever played any of her records. *Daba-doobi-didoo-dah, dada-diba-doo.*

There's a great deal of complaining about the food. Even more than usual. The new cook has taken it into his head to make everything salt-free, and he also seems to have taken pity on people who have lost their teeth: he cooks everything to mush. You can drink it all through a straw. People tend more and more to shun our soup kitchen for a ready-made microwave meal from the supermarket.

The problem is that no one dares to call for a kitchen revolt, and there's very little chance of seeing any protesters setting themselves on fire, if only because most inmates' hands are too shaky to strike a match.

A few friends from the club and I have contemplated sending in a letter about the abysmal food, but we have decided first to give "the others" a chance to stick their necks out for a change. We'll point out that opportunity to the worst complainers.

We have two residents who play the stock market, Mr. Graftdijk and Mrs. Delporte. It can't be very much money, or they wouldn't be living here, but they always act very self-important about it. They've taken out a joint subscription to the *Financial Times* and pore over it for shares that are about to go through the roof. If they lose, it's just dumb luck, but if they win, it's their superior insight. The news that an ape was once able to secure the same investment returns as an expert stockbroker, with no recourse to insider information, came as a great blow to them. "That ape was simply lucky," Graftdijk said testily.

Tuesday, July 30

Two thousand Emergency Room visits per year are a direct result of mobility-scooter accidents. Eefje came to show me a newspaper report with those hard facts after I proudly told her I had purchased the Elegance 4, the Saab of invalid wheels. Most of the incidents are single-vehicle accidents, unless you count the curb as an opponent. Curbs are responsible for quite a few spills.

Last year the Netherlands had some 350,000 mobility scooters in circulation, so the 2,000 casualty number doesn't sound so bad, considering the embarrassing lack of skill displayed by old people on wheels. To make mistakes is only human, but shouldn't it be possible to learn how to accelerate and how to brake without getting the two confused? I am an advocate of a mandatory driving license for mobility-scooterists. A portion of the exam should be held inside a crowded supermarket.

I am quite a good driver, if I say so myself. I once spent a year driving a forklift. We even held forklift races, my friends and I. It was a long time ago, true, but the instinct's still there. While out on my test drives I did notice that people look down their noses at an electric wheelchair. I can totally sympathize.

A very fat woman—she wasn't even that old—got hers wedged in the checkout lane of a local pharmacy. She could go neither backward nor forward. Of course it wasn't her fault that she'd seen fit to ignore the large sign saying EXTRA-WIDE AISLE a few rows away.

Wednesday, July 31

Some years ago a Belgian couple committed euthanasia together. He (eighty-three) had terminal cancer and she (seventy-eight), suffering from other serious age-related ailments, didn't want to go on living without him. Hand in hand they stepped out of life. There's something very romantic about that.

The public prosecutor had opened an investigation into who might have assisted these two old lovebirds to pass away peacefully. I don't think they ever found out who'd done this Good Samaritan deed.

I was reminded of this when I read that an old couple—again in Belgium—had tumbled down the stairs together. Both died; rather a coincidence, don't you think? And how much better for them, than for one to remain tragically behind with a broken hip and skull fracture. Having to muddle on alone for a few more years, until sweet death finally came for him (or her).

I have occasionally sounded the waters, to learn how one might leave this life simply, and without creating a big mess. Always with the strictest assurance that I myself have no plans in that direction, and that I'm merely interested, "in the unlikely event that..." All I ever get in response are worried glances and few, if any, practical tips. Which reminds me, I must bring it up with my geriatrician.

Thursday, August 1

Evert likes to flaunt his prosthesis, making a big show of attaching his artificial leg and taking it off again.

"It's pinching me a bit, I think I'll give it a little rest," he'll say, and then plonk his plastic half leg down on the table right beside the doughnuts.

After several warnings from the staff, the director came down to tell Evert in person that in the common rooms his leg must remain attached at all times.

"Really, is that mandatory? Is it written down somewhere? In the rules and regulations?"

Stelwagen hesitated, debating whether to respond, then gave him an inscrutable look and walked away. As a tactician, she mustn't be underestimated. She makes few mistakes and her timing is excellent. She never reveals what she's got up her sleeve, she shows little emotion, and she leaves the dirty work to others. I have yet to discover her weak spot.

This morning Anja handed me a stack of papers. Our very own WikiLeaks! I am going to start perusing it this afternoon. I'll take it with me to Uden for further study.

Tonight I was Evert's partner at *Klaverjas*. He has worked up an elaborate system of signals to show which suit should be made trumps. "Only in a case of emergency, and only with certain opponents, mind you," he conceded. My virtuous disposition is opposed to it, but I will allow an exception if we have to play against Mr. Bakker or Mrs. Pot, and it looks like we're losing. Sometimes one has to throw one's principles overboard for the sake of a higher justice.

Friday, August 2

The leaked documents aren't exactly earth-shattering, at least not upon initial review. Alas. However, further study is bound to reveal a few interesting details.

Our spy has delivered to us:

1. The minutes of the last five board meetings
2. The house rules
3. A stack of internal memos
4. The protocol for when a resident dies
5. Staff instructions

I have taken a set of photocopies over to Eefje. As I was using the photocopier in the supermarket I felt everyone was looking at me, and from pure jitters kept dropping papers on the floor. I would make a rather poor spy, I fear.

I don't really know what to do about our lawyer, who has been applying for these documents through the official channels, now that we have illegally obtained them from "a reliable source."

Evert and I wound up losing at *Klaverjas*, which is for the best, really. We are already not all that popular, and you don't win friends by winning *Klaverjas* tournaments.

In some old people, childish jealousy about trivial things can take on almost pathological proportions. People don't like to give you the time of day, let alone grant you the first prize at cards, even if it's only the eternal liver sausage.

The motto of this little group of resentful old coots must be: "How do I make things as hard on myself as possible?" As if being old didn't bring misery enough.

Saturday, August 3

I always get anxious about spending time away from home. I haven't been away on vacation for twelve years.

My weekend bag, from the seventies, had a blackish mold growing inside which probably also dates from the seventies. It's high time I modernized: a brand-new suitcase on wheels now stands packed and ready by the front door.

Jan, Evert's son, is coming to pick us up in an hour and take us to Brabant. According to Evert, Jan has been looking forward to it, and daughter-in-law Ester has been in a tizzy for three days in anticipation of her two elderly guests' arrival. "I reckon it'll take her almost a week to get used to our presence, in other words just about in time for our departure."

I felt some qualms about that, but Evert told me not to worry. "She's always worked up about something; if it isn't us it's the neighbors' cat."

In this case it may be both, us and the neighbors' cat, since Mo is coming too, and he hates cats.

For the last time I'll try to think of what I'm forgetting to bring.

You'll hear from me again on Friday, August 9, barring unforeseen circumstances.

Friday, August 9

Uden—a place to visit! It was fun. A pleasant break from the tedious routine. But I'm also glad to be home again. One's attachment to the peaceful little world of the nursing home is stronger than I'd have expected, although it pains me to admit it. As the years multiply, the ability to go with the flow decreases. I thought I was more flexible. After only five days I started longing for a little room in a house full of old people. I console myself with the thought that I may be a bit less ossified than my average fellow resident.

Jan, Evert's son, is a chip off the old block. He's a riot. But after five days or so there comes a time when you start to think: *one* Evert is exhausting enough. Fortunately that was the time to say goodbye.

We had plenty of laughs; went places every day; and played cards, mini-golf, and Monopoly; and the teenage grandchildren taught us the video-game basics and how to work the Wii. It opened a new world for me. Unfortunately as of today it's closed to me again.

Ester, Jan's wife, had been anticipating a difficult week. Having her uncouth husband and her equally uncouth father-in-law under the same roof in her respectable, proper, and immaculate house was a daunting prospect. My role, as worked out beforehand with Evert, was to thaw her out a bit. It worked. Next to those two unapologetic boors, it wasn't hard for me to play the charming, flattering, well-bred old gentleman.

"Oh, stop it, you old slimeball," Evert hissed at me a couple of times, "you're making me sick!"

Saturday, August 10

I have thought of a good idea for a club outing: a golf clinic. Apparently golf is a sport well suited to the senior citizen, although I do wonder if that applies to extremely old geezers like us. Actually, I don't think it does, but I think mini-golf's a bit beneath our dignity.

This morning I called the local golf course. I explained who we were and what we wanted: an afternoon's activity with just a bit of a challenge. The lady on the other end of the line heard me out sympathetically and said she could arrange something. I did get a bit of a shock when I heard what it would cost: fifty-five euros per person, coffee and cake included, but wine or appetizers would be extra. "Not a problem," I heard myself say nevertheless. I am not very good at negotiating. I never have the nerve to start bargaining.

For that sum we're good for three hours, including a Q&A, a practice session and one round on the beginners' course. It sounds interesting enough to put in some of my own money, in order to keep it affordable for the other members. It's not a bad time to start dipping into my rainy-day fund, which amounts to about five thousand euros.

I am at a bit of a loss over what to do about Evert, but the lady on the phone said that they do sometimes have disabled people playing there. She would reserve two golf carts for us. For thirty euros.

I have booked us for September 13.

Sunday, August 11

Tomorrow I'm picking up my brand-new red scooter. I'm as excited as a little kid.

Yesterday Grietje presented me with a big bunch of flowers and a gift voucher for a book. When I asked what I had done to deserve it she showed me a booklet about dementia, in which she had underlined the following sentence: "The illness will make someone with dementia barely able to appreciate all you are doing for him or her."

"I'm thanking you in advance."

"That's not necessary."

"No, it isn't necessary, but I'm doing it anyway."

I was very touched.

She also gave me the booklet "Caring for Alzheimer's" to keep. I have read it and learned several useful new tips.

I wasn't the only one to receive a gift from Grietje. I found that out when I had tea with Eefje.

Our teatime tête-à-têtes are lovely interludes. Nothing fancy: a cup of tea, a nibble, some pleasant chitchat, and sometimes something a bit deeper. Another time we'll listen to music or discuss a book or DVD. We enjoy each other's company very much.

Monday, August 12

I just picked up my new scooter and rode it home. Excited as a boy with a new bike. It rides beautifully. I tried it out in the park; took my time. Up the curb, off the curb, sharp left, sharp right. Accelerate; brake. I drove on the grass, then through the mud. It was Monday morning, so there wasn't a soul about. It already goes at quite a clip, but I want to get it souped up a little more. According to our scooter expert here, Mr. Hoogdalen, that's a simple thing to do. He and I have made a date to drive over to his son's garage on the East Side next week.

I have started looking up ideas for senior travel in the papers and on the Internet. There are a great many offerings. Tip-Top Elder Travel organizes a twelve-day bus tour to Switzerland for two thousand euros. I presume that *tip-top* refers to the price. Ours will have to be shorter, and cheaper. In the next few weeks I will endeavor to find out what a luxury eight-passenger minibus and driver would cost for a five-day trip. Then all that's left is to dig up an attractively priced hotel in Champagne, and Old But Not Dead's first vacation abroad is a go.

I'll ask Eefje to help me organize it.

Something exciting to look forward to is crucial to keep up one's zest for life.

News from the royal House of Orange, whether happy or sad, always brings out the monarchist ardor in here. Prince Friso's passing has resulted in much sincere sorrow among the residents, although surely relief would be a more reasonable response—he had spent the past two and a half years in a coma. I wouldn't wish that on anyone, to be kept alive for years when you're as good as dead anyway.

This morning I went to the geriatrician. First I asked him what the symptoms of Alzheimer's were, and what was to be done about it. The answer to the second question wasn't very encouraging: almost nothing.

The doctor said that as far as he could tell, I shouldn't worry about it just yet, so I explained that I was asking on behalf of a close friend. The measures he suggested were largely the ones we have already put in place. That's rather satisfying to know.

Then he examined me and concluded that in my case the decline "is progressing at a tolerable pace."

"What's tolerable?" I asked.

"Well, a very gradual downhill slide, meaning that the quality of life will probably be perfectly adequate for a few more years."

Then he again advised me to start wearing diapers.

I asked him for his opinion on the quality of life for a diaper-wearing old coot.

He knew people who wore diapers and were "quite happy in spite of it."

Next he checked the state of various worn joints ("not much to be done about that"), and finally he went over the list of medicines, making some minor adjustments here and there.

I swallowed three times, then asked what he thought about euthanasia.

He said he wasn't against it, but that he wasn't vocal about it.

"But can I count on your cooperation if, after giving it much thought, I decide to put an end to it?" There, the question was out.

He hesitated a moment, nodding thoughtfully.

There was an uncomfortable silence. Then he proposed saving a lengthier discussion about it for my next visit. "These are questions that need more time."

I forgot to ask him how the elderly react to cocaine. I wouldn't mind trying it, once.

Wednesday, August 14

An old man has drowned after driving his mobility scooter right into the Princess Margriet Canal at Kootstertille. Let that be a warning to you, Groen! Don't kid yourself you're Niki Lauda and can just tear about at full throttle all the time.

Yesterday afternoon I toured North Amsterdam on my new Ferrari. Saw parts of my hometown I hadn't been to in years. It feels like such a reprieve, not to be tied down to a limited walking distance, or to be hostage to the bus schedule. I should have done this a couple of years ago. I do have to be on my guard, because danger could come from any direction, but it's mainly motorcycles and bicycles I have to watch out for. Cars, strangely enough, are less of a problem, and pedestrians are easy to avoid. But you have to keep an eye out for those young whippersnappers on their bikes or scooters because they think they're the kings of the bicycle path. Scorn for mobility scooters is etched all too clearly on their impudent mugs.

I do have to go out and buy some rain gear soon. Yesterday I had to take shelter under an overpass for fifteen minutes because I had set out wearing just a summer jacket and got caught in a heavy downpour. The trick is to stay calm and wait until it's over, and not run out of patience after five minutes and get soaked after all.

The same phenomenon applies to crossing the road: first you wait calmly for anything and anyone that comes moseying along, and then, if it's taking too long, you get impatient and step out just when it's most dangerous to do so.

Thursday, August 15

Our home has seen the birth of an Amsterdam Aged Party chapter.

"The old people in this country are about to be victimized by the Cut-baks [*sic*] in all areas of Care overseen by locale [*sic*] authorities. Which is why we have set up a chapter of the Amsterdam Aged Party (AAP) to stand up for our locale [*sic*] rights."

If the number of spelling mistakes is an indication of the caliber of this group, we're in for a rare old time.

Mr. Krol and Mr. Nagel of 50Plus aren't inclined to

put their party forward in the March 2014 local council elections. They can already see it coming: a rabble of opportunistic, incompetent grandpas and grandmas running riot through the country's council chambers. They're not about to let that happen to their party.

Our AAP chapter's number one objective: more benches for the elderly to rest on.

The 50Plus Party could grow into a powerful lobby if it wanted to. It can count on the support of a great multitude of angry, piss-poor seventy-plussers. They're the ones providing the strength in numbers. The party's leaders and organizers, however, come from the political elite, aged from fifty to sixty-five, which is now in charge. Surely there must be some among them who wouldn't mind advocating for the needs of their elderly constituents? Even if only out of sheer boredom?

A nation's level of civilization can be measured by the way it treats its oldest and weakest citizens. The short-sighted and disrespectful way elder care is being slashed in the Netherlands is creating a fertile breeding ground for gray-haired populism. We live in one of the richest countries in the world, but again and again the message is, Your care is unaffordable.

Friday, August 16

My mobility scooter and I have had a close encounter with some bushes.

After supper I went for a little spin in the park. Gazing about, I beheld at least twenty rabbits peacefully feasting on the grass. As I swiveled my eyes back at the path, I spotted a baby rabbit less than three feet from my front wheel. My reflexes must still be pretty good, because a second later I found myself stuck in a tangle of branches. After checking for rabbit remains beneath my wheels, I managed to carefully back my scooter out of the bushes. With the kind assistance of an elegant lady on a bicycle, who was more shaken than I was.

I also had a coffee with Anja in her office yesterday. Staying on top of all the new developments is keeping her on her toes. There have been a great many meetings about the remodeling. The board is considering turning one wing into a medical ward—our growth market, shall we say. Anja also heard something about yet another hefty expense-account raise for our director. Although to my way of thinking she already looks expensive enough in those smart pastel business suits of hers.

Our next club outing is Monday. Departure at 1 p.m. Leisurewear. Group leader: Eefje.

"It's something that's typically *me*," is the brain-teaser she's given us.

It is high time we had some excitement around here.

Saturday, August 17

Sixty-four percent of the elderly believe in the right to end their lives in a humane manner once they've had enough. Fourteen percent think their life has quite run its course. Most important reasons for wanting out: fear of losing one's marbles and fear of intensifying pain and misery. This research courtesy of the MAX Broadcasting Company.

So, statistically speaking, approximately one in seven inhabitants of this home have no problem with having the Grim Reaper come for them. But looking around the circle at coffee hour, I couldn't tell you with any certainty who they might be.

There's a new house rule: residents are no longer allowed to use the stairs unless they've obtained express permission from the staff. Last week Mrs. Stuiver fell down the stairs and broke her collarbone, so that's the reason. (When I heard, I remember thinking: Just her collarbone,? It could have been a lot worse.)

Rules, supposedly, are always for our own good. But of course they're first and foremost a means of avoiding risk and preventing lawsuits.

Perhaps Mrs. Stuiver would have done better to take the elevator, but she'd been walking up and down four flights of stairs every day for the past five years, to keep fit. And as long as Mrs. Stuiver isn't senile or demented, shouldn't it be her own business? The staff should just make sure the staircase isn't strewn with banana peels.

Sunday, August 18

More on that protocol for deceased residents:

One of the provisions is that the cause of death is not to be made public. Employees are to refer any questions to either the attending physician or the management. Who will then refer the question back to one another. If someone continues to insist, he is to be told that for reasons of privacy, the cause of death cannot be made public. Any hint at suicide is strictly *verboten*.

The protocol also says that the family must be tactfully reminded to clear out the room of the departed one as expeditiously as possible.

Management must make sure that nothing is stolen. That's news to me. Apparently belongings have disappeared in the past.

I know that inmates sometimes make promises to caregivers, along the lines of "When I die you can have this or that." That's a sure-fire way to set up a flaming row among your heirs.

I haven't discovered any requirement in the protocol for staff to attend funerals or cremations if these fall within working hours. I thought there was. On the contrary, in fact: staff are not given time off to attend funerals. If they choose to do so, it's in their spare time.

Okay, I think that's quite enough about death for a Sunday morning.

Monday, August 19

I've already taken my scooter out for a run this morning. A quiet run, since one of the nicest aspects of this transportation method is that it makes hardly any noise. Also, it's a comfortable ride. On smooth asphalt it feels as if you were floating. I drove through the Vliegenbos ("Forest of flies"), which owes its name not to a swarm of flies but to a certain Mr. W. H. Vliegen, who was such a big shot that he had a whole forest named after him. It had been ten years since I'd been there. It was well kept, and a good place to practice my steering, because there wasn't a soul to run into—well, except rabbits. I did scratch the paint a little by taking a turn a little too sharply. I've already got plenty of dents and scrapes, so I needn't worry about keeping the chassis pristine. I do have to take it easy a bit; off-road, my mobility scooter isn't looking its best.

I asked Eefje if she'd ever consider riding one.

"No, it's not for me. I'm happy to go out with you, but not on one of those things."

A pity.

But never mind. I have to get dressed for this afternoon's outing. Leisurewear.

We have nothing but leisure, although not all that much leisurewear. Or are the clothes you wear when you have nothing but leisure automatically "leisurewear"?

Tuesday, August 20

Even though I had forgotten to take along an extra incontinence pad, yesterday was a good day.

Eefje had told us that the outing was something close to her heart. In hindsight I should have guessed that our amateur ornithologist would be taking us to the bird park, Avifauna. And although I'm not particularly keen on birds (the way they peer out of their beady little eyes seems a bit shifty and mean to me), I still had a great time. Evert was back in old form, announcing the way he would prepare each species of bird for eating, as well as the best wine to have with it. Antoine would then very earnestly propose a culinary alternative. Antoine and Ria can be a bit gullible, and don't always know when someone's pulling their leg. They're good sports about it, though.

Eefje refused to be put off her stride and was enraptured by her feathered friends.

Grietje got lost only once or twice and didn't seem particularly troubled about it.

Edward stood there beaming when he was given a special glove to put on in order to hold a falcon, and Graeme was just—Graeme.

After the tour guide was finished with us, we had refreshments and a boat ride through the green heartland of Holland, with more drinks on board.

We got home just in time for dinner.

Wednesday, August 21

It still astonishes me how much envy rules the roost in here. Returning from a successful outing, we're given a predominantly cool, even icy, reception by our fellow residents. The thought that others have had more fun than they have is, for many, hard to accept. So today we see lots of pursed lips again.

Our Old But Not Dead Club finds itself growing more and more isolated. Being the common enemy creates an extra-tight bond; but enmity is contagious. If you're not careful it won't be long before you find yourself detesting "the rest of them."

★　　★　　★

The staff deal with dissension like nursery school teachers attempting to keep the peace. "Mr. Duiker, can't you try being a bit nicer to Miss Slothouwer? Come, won't you sit down here? Why don't we all have a nice cup of coffee together?"

I'd rather ram a ginger cookie down her throat and watch her suffocate in drawn-out agony, I can just *hear* Evert thinking. Evert doesn't really belong in the "good-natured" category.

Just so that you don't think this place is a complete snake pit: there are also kind, courteous and compassionate people in here. Although they're not usually the ones you notice.

Thursday, August 22

I wouldn't like to have to play Parcheesi with Mr. Bakker's son. He's even more of a boorish ignoramus than his father.

The Vierstroom care home is telling incoming residents' family members that they are "morally obliged" to perform at least four hours' worth of chores a month. The kind of chores Vierstroom has in mind is taking residents for walks, or playing games or engaging in conversation with them. God save me from perfect strangers who feel obliged to chat with us and so transparently barrage us with feigned interest. Loneliness can sometimes feel even worse when you're with other people.

The compulsory-volunteerism test also demonstrates

that there are some family members who, once invited in, just won't leave. One out of three residents involved in the experiment had a relative who spent more than twenty-eight hours prowling the halls. If one of those volunteers latched on to me, and it was someone I couldn't stand, I'd volunteer to throw myself under a bus.

I don't know why they only ask the new residents to supply the family aides. Maybe they're afraid of being engulfed in a flood of volunteers otherwise.

Our director Mrs. Stelwagen hasn't shown her face down here very much lately. Anja reports she's been called to a lot of meetings with her superiors. Anja hasn't managed to find out why. The reports and memos seem to have stopped coming her way.

Friday, August 23

I got a traffic ticket! For jumping a red light on my scooter. It turned out that I was being tailed by a policeman on a mountain bike. The cop didn't accept my argument that since I was only going four miles an hour and making a right turn, I posed no danger to myself or others. "Red is red!" he said, adding with a touch of pride in his voice, "I think you are the oldest person I have ever stopped and booked." His patrol partner stood there looking a bit uncomfortable. This wasn't a collar he'd be boasting about at parties. "Doesn't your colleague have anything better to do?" I couldn't help asking him. No, he did not.

Evert almost fell out of his chair laughing when I told

him. The entire home knows about it by now. I am either a hero or a hooligan; opinions are divided.

Tuesday is Grietje's outing. She's had Graeme looking over her shoulder, since she's worried about making mistakes. She has been rather muddled about time and place lately, and her judgment does leave something to be desired. Last week, in anticipation of a visit from her sister and niece, she came home with five pounds' worth of assorted cookies. She got mixed up. She did think it was rather a large bag and a bit expensive, but the lady at the bakery had acted as if five pounds of assorted cookies weren't anything out of the ordinary.

She had to laugh about it herself, though not very heartily.

The cookies have been shared among all her friends and acquaintances.

Saturday, August 24

The Arab Spring is no longer going well. I can't think of any other season of the year (autumn?) that would accurately describe the present troubles over there. But the Arabs shouldn't expect too much sympathy from the people here. The general opinion is that if those Islamists are so set on waging a holy war, we're better off if they wage it against one another. It's not keeping anyone in here awake at night.

The cancellation of package tours to the Pyramids has created more consternation than thousands of deaths have.

"My son simply has to kiss all that money goodbye. Two thousand euros down the Nile!" lamented Mrs. Deurloo.

But the photographs of little children asphyxiated by poison gas have persuaded even the safe little world in here that there's something truly horrific going on.

We may complain all the time about our elder-care system, but the health care system in England isn't all fun and games either, with elderly patients complaining of being starved. Probably because feeding them took too much time. Another complaint was that the call bell was left just out of the patients' reach. That must have saved the staff quite a bit of time and effort.

But it isn't all doom and gloom: it's been a gorgeous summer, and yesterday I spent nearly two hours at an outdoor café with Eefje. Lovely company; someone to talk to but also to be silent with. Without its feeling at all awkward. Simply a delightful afternoon. Shuffled our way home slowly. I'd taken my rollator out of mothballs for the occasion, since Eefje says she won't ride on the back of my scooter, not for all the tea in China.

Sunday, August 25

Grietje showed me a photograph of the "Beach Room" at the Happy Days Nursing Home. (A name like that always makes me a bit leery.) It's specially designed for dementia patients, made to look like the seashore. Complete with a fake sun and stuffed seagulls. You hear the crashing waves, and every so often the fans set up a little breeze.

It's meant to make the geriatric patients calm down.

Grietje wondered if she should go out and buy herself a new bikini. Smiling, she said, "Well, Henk, it is what it is. Or rather: what will be, will be. I'll take it as it comes."

My admiration keeps growing for the way she is preparing herself to face her future.

Grietje says that my view of dementia is of a horror show. She's right about that. Today I allowed myself an (illegal) peek into the locked ward, and saw three drooling old ladies vacantly watching *Teletubbies*.

Grietje told me she can well understand anyone's not wanting to have to go through the distressing decline.

Not knowing where you are even in your own home.

No longer understanding the words on the page.

No longer recognizing your loved ones.

Monday, August 26

Anja is being forced into early retirement. I was just on the phone with her. She was on the verge of tears, from disappointment and anger. It was a short conversation, she couldn't speak freely. I'm afraid she may have been unmasked by Stelwagen as the mole. I feel so sorry for her, and guilty too. She took risks, partly on my behalf.

We're having lunch together on Wednesday, then I'll know more.

It's put quite a damper on my mood, which had been elated (for me), since I was so looking forward to the outing Grietje is organizing for us. We are gathering down-stairs at two o'clock.

I think it's best if I don't tell Eefje until tomorrow.

Jetty Paerl has died. I doubt she will be mourned any-where outside the nation's nursing homes. There was much nostalgic reminiscing over tea about Radio Orange and our beloved wartime songbird.

"Ah, yes, those were the days," sighed Mrs. De Ridder, who seemed to have momentarily forgotten that others, the Jews for instance, might think differently.

"You mean the days when you'd also see quite a few German SS around here?" asked Edward wickedly.

Well, okay, but besides those Germans, they were lovely days, she insisted.

The sentiment that everything was better in the old days tends to run rampant in old-age homes and is impossible to eradicate. It's a kind of comfort for old people who find themselves shunted aside.

I'm going to drape myself in sartorial splendor and pol-ish both my shoes *and* my teeth.

Tuesday, August 27

Strange that old people never or hardly ever seem to do normal things anymore, such as go see a movie. We took a survey, and the eight of us in our little club haven't set foot in a movie theater in over a century. And it's a simple and affordable pleasure, after all.

Grietje had chosen a film in 3D for us to see, which was for all of us a new experience: *Cars*, really a children's film, but that was the only one being offered in 3D. There we sat, eight seniors, wearing our special glasses, surrounded by forty or so little kids.

The 3D experience is quite interesting the first time. We kept cringing, panicked, especially the first fifteen minutes or so, as a car came racing out of the screen at us. The sound was three-dimensional as well; there was a loud crunching of popcorn all around us. It did not spoil the fun, however.

The film didn't start until four o'clock; we had an elaborate high tea beforehand. So it didn't matter that we got home just in time for dessert. The cook took it personally. That's his problem, not ours.

Grietje was showered with compliments and thanks. It was moving to see her beaming like a young girl.

I'm worried about Anja. I tried calling her but didn't get through.

I'm taking my scooter out for a drive tomorrow afternoon. The weather is beautiful. I'm going to stop by the garage of Hoogdalen's son, who has promised to soup up my ride. I was going to go last week, but Hoogdalen Jr. was too busy. He said he can do it while I wait.

Wednesday, August 28

It's even worse than I thought. Anja suspects they'd been watching her for a while. She is almost certain that her desk was searched, and she thinks the stack of photocopies of board minutes, reports, and memos she kept in a drawer was the reason for her dismissal. Having those documents in her possession wasn't illegal, of course, but it may have thickened the cloud of suspicion she was already under.

Stelwagen is claiming that Anja's early retirement is a reward for her many years of loyal service.

Her contract is up at the end of October. Since she is still owed twenty vacation days, she can stop coming in as of the first of October. "Is it possible to have her desk cleared out by that date?" Stelwagen asked.

Anja is very upset, and I have little to offer in the way of consolation. I feel so guilty about turning her into a whistle-blower.

Our director still nods at me affably whenever we cross paths in the hallway.

My scooter now runs at a top speed of fifteen miles per hour, I think. Cyclists and even some motorcyclists are startled to see me calmly cruising right past them. I have to say I'm a bit of a threat on the road. I really ought to be wearing a crash helmet. That way I can't be recognized if I'm caught on camera in a speed trap. No, only joking, just let the wind tousle the last four hairs on my pate.

Thursday, August 29

"CASH-STRAPPED SENIORS GO TO JAIL." It would make a great headline.

The prison in the town of Breda stands empty, and now an enterprising contractor has come up with the idea of turning it into cheap housing for the elderly. If the newspaper is to be believed, he thinks a revamped jail cell measuring a hundred square feet is room enough for two oldies. Works out to less than five by ten feet per person.

The oldies barely move anymore, Ouborg must be thinking, and they don't need a lot of stuff either.

Sliding French doors probably not included. A small window for ventilation should be sufficient.

The cheapest room will cost €870. I took that to mean per year, but no, that's the monthly rent. Meals not included, but you do get some kind of "basic care package."

No, it's not a joke.

That is what some people in this wealthy country would like to stick the elderly with: a prison cell with a fresh coat of paint. We're assured that no, it's not meant for people who are already living in nursing homes like us. It's for the "new" seniors, who would otherwise just pine away from loneliness or be forced to sleep under a bridge.

I had lunch yesterday with Anja. "I'm a useless spy," she sighed. I had bought her a big bunch of flowers as consolation; I couldn't think of anything more original.

But she had to admit she was also relieved to escape the chilly atmosphere at work. We drank a toast to her new-found freedom.

Friday, August 30

Our legal counselor is still on the warpath. I spoke to him this morning. Victor, as combative and optimistic as ever, had to admit, however, that we have had a small setback in the form of a letter from the appeals board in regard to our pursuit of the documents. The letter states that our case will be dealt with in mid- to late January 2014, five months from now. That timing takes into account the advanced age of the petitioners.

Victor was still trying to see if there wasn't a way to hurry it up.

"My best advice to you is to stay alive until then," were his parting words.

Sunday morning I'm launching my mobility scooter across the IJ. Having made a number of trips exploring every nook and cranny of North Amsterdam, I think it's time to move the goalposts and take the ferry across the river. I'm looking forward to touring Amsterdam's center at a rare moment of peace and quiet: Sunday morning at 9 a.m. The canals were practically designed for driving laps, up one side and down the other.

Evert is considering getting a mobility scooter of his own. Not surprising, since he has trouble getting about in his wheelchair. Yesterday he came rolling up with difficulty, with Mo on his lap. The poor dog can't walk at the moment because of an infected paw. And he's got one of those lampshade things around his neck to prevent him from licking it. Quite the pair.

Saturday, August 31

The bill before Parliament proposing that citizens have the right to clean diapers has been withdrawn. Just as I'm having to start wearing them! What kind of imbecilic country is this anyway, to need a law to make sure old people don't sit around in their own excrement all day? The reason the bill was scuttled isn't completely clear. The Council of State, the body that issues legal recommendations, claims it's a law that's already on the books. I just couldn't tell you which law a demented old person should appeal to for that extra diaper change. I hope that, long before I find myself having to make do with one diaper a day, I'll be peacefully resting in my grave.

Or... could this report be another hoax? Just like the story about the prison housing for cash-strapped seniors in Breda? (Yes, I did fall for that one.)

There will be an information session about the proposed renovations. The board is not able to rule out that some may have to move out. The underlying motives are unclear. Time suddenly does appear to be of the essence.

Those revelations are probably the last Anja will have managed to smuggle out from behind enemy lines. She's decided to make good use of her last weeks in the office, even though she knows she is being watched. She no longer has to worry about the consequences. The director knows there's no point hanging our whistle-blower out to dry. She is all too well aware that the publicity would almost certainly work in Anja's favor.

Sunday, September 1

In this home people are just called Piet, Kees, Nel, or Ans; not Storm, Butterfly, Perdita, or Sword of Islam.

We were all born before the time when parents began

wanting to show off how original and cool they could be in naming their offspring. With all the dangers lurking therein. You give your daughter the name Butterfly, and damn if she doesn't grow into a lumbering tub of lard. You'd have done better naming her Bertha.

This morning found me and my scooter on the nine o'clock ferry. Took a wonderful drive around a sleeping Amsterdam. It is a privilege to live in one of the most beautiful cities in the world. But you do have to take advantage of that privilege sometimes, or what's the point? So that's what I did, for the first time in years, and I'm going to do it more often, provided I am granted more time on earth. I drove in "turtle" gear the entire way, so that I could calmly gaze about and take in the sights.

But now back to matters of some import: the Residents' Association has proposed a one-time two-euro hike in the membership fee to cover the cost of an attractive package of Christmas bingo prizes. Good governance requires foresight.

Monday, September 2

It is not easy to book an hour-long game of pool on a Sunday afternoon. There is an opaque system for reserving the table. Graeme, Edward, and I, after some insistence and a half-hour wait, were finally given a time slot from 4:40 to 5:20. By then we'd already had a few drinks. Being three sheets to the wind loosened us up considerably; but unfortunately, when it comes to pool, looseness isn't a great advantage. I think that we must have scored fewer than twenty points between the three of us.

Our tongues were loosened, on the other hand, to some effect. Graeme told us some wonderful stories about his childhood. He was the youngest in a family of fourteen boys and girls. All of them dead now. He also has a son in Australia and a daughter in Groningen. Every other year he and his son visit his daughter, and the alternate year his daughter goes with him to visit his son. He's off to Australia for three weeks in January.

"That's what keeps me going, those trips." We nodded. He quickly added, "And your company in here, naturally."

Edward is a bit of a sad sack. He's got a lot to say, but is still practically impossible to understand, unfortunately. It's even worse when he's had a few.

"Why don't you write it down, Ed," suggested Evert, who had joined us for a drink.

Edward said that he would. He has promised to write us a letter once a week. Whether we choose to answer orally or in writing is up to us.

We've decided to play pool more often.

Graeme is going to reserve a permanent hour for us; he is on good terms with the pool club's secretary.

Tuesday, September 3

It's my birthday the day after tomorrow. It's the first time in years that I've had enough friends to make it worth having a party. I have invited the Old But Not Dead members for a drink that night, and have asked Ria and Antoine to provide some savory nibbles, which I will pay for, naturally. I'm doing both them and myself a favor that way. Croquettes are de rigueur, of course—we can't have a drinks party without them—but as far as the rest, they have free rein.

No flowers, no presents: I was adamant about that. I wonder if they'll listen.

Grietje promised to be there, but extracted a promise from me in return: "Once I've gone gaga, will you please refrain from dragging me all over hell and creation?"

"What do you mean?"

She explained that it's a misconception to assume people with Alzheimer's must be entertained no matter what, to prod them out of their apathy. They're taken along on outings, but have no idea where they are, who the people gabbing at them so brightly are, and why they have to climb into some strange little train. On top of that they're given unfamiliar food to eat, and subjected to kisses from total strangers.

"A person with dementia is going to need three days to recover," Grietje sighed. "So when the time comes, just let me sit in my chair by the window."

I promised.

Wednesday, September 4

One of our orderlies is only a few years younger than the inmates. Yet he's always going on about "the oldies" and gives himself airs as if he were the one in charge in here. He isn't strictly an orderly; his job title is "Host/Safety Associate." He likes nothing better than to scold people who ignore the rules.

Evert and I were going out for a stroll. Evert is in the habit of implacably rolling right through the doors as they're sliding shut, so that they close on his wheelchair. They automatically spring open again. This doesn't sit well with orderly Porter (that's his name).

"You should either speed up, or slow down and wait," he told Evert sternly.

Evert looked up at him very slowly, squinted as if trying to see more clearly, and then said, "You have a booger hanging from your nose."

I almost choked laughing.

It caused the Porter some perplexity. Should he ignore that remark? But what if it was true?

We looked back when we got to the door. He was gazing at his finger, which had just gone up for a little inspection.

"A bit to the right," said Evert.

To paraphrase the old saying: "*Porter, c'est mourir un peu.*"

I have bought enough alcohol to supply three birthday parties. Better to have too much than too little. If you have a friend like Evert, it will all get drunk anyhow, sooner or later.

Thursday, September 5

I was born on September 5, 1929. Today is my eighty-fourth birthday. Evert was standing at my door at nine o'clock—or, rather, sitting outside my door in his wheelchair—with an elaborate breakfast tray on his lap. A touching sight. Croissants, biscotti, bread, tea, freshly squeezed orange juice, and prosecco. After an extremely off-key rendition of "Long May He Live," Evert ate and drank most of it himself. I'm not a big breakfast eater.

I've borrowed a few chairs for this evening from housekeeping. I didn't think it would be appropriate at our age for some people to have to stand.

Most residents celebrate their birthday downstairs in the common room. The invited guests sit at the big table and are offered a piece of cake, while the uninvited position themselves as nearby as possible in hopes of some leftover crumbs. A pathetic sight. Not my thing at all.

I prefer squeezing my guests into my cramped, little room; at least we won't have anyone looking over our shoulders.

I've booked a golf clinic for Friday the thirteenth, for eight participants. I hope the weather will be as fine as it is today, since that will increase its chances of success. I'm not all that confident that I've made the right choice. Golf is a good sport for older people, certainly, but not every old person is a good candidate for golf. It's too late to change my mind, however, since I've already paid for it.

Friday, September 6

I had to wheel a very tipsy Evert back to his place at half past midnight. I wasn't too steady on my feet myself. Evert had wanted to stay and spend the night, "So that we can have one last little nip before we go beddy-bye."

I decided it wasn't a good idea. Rolling down the hallway, he launched into "Land of Hope and Glory."

I expect to be told off today for making too much noise.

But the party was great fun. I've got enough leftovers to last me a couple of days, and enough alcohol for two months at least. I'm going to be abstemious for a while in both the eating and drinking department.

The plan for a longer trip has been on the back burner for a while. I'm going to seriously explore the possibilities for next spring.

The main thing is to stay alive until June. I am determined not to let death deter me, at least not other people's deaths. If it turns out that I am dead by then, I want the others to give my urn pride of place on the dashboard.

"He always did like looking out the window." It isn't true but it sounds good.

Saturday, September 7

Old people should take up playing video games. Racing a car on a computer is far better at keeping the aging brain fit than some tedious parlor game. According to the newspapers, research has shown that video games can teach old brains to multitask again.

I am going to try to find out about video games, although the chances of finding someone here to teach me aren't great. Not having grandchildren is a major disadvantage.

I would have loved to have some. I'd have made an adorable grandpa, even if I do say so myself.

If... yes, if only.

Actually, grandkids aren't always fun and games. Edward has a grandson who's addicted to drugs; Graeme has a granddaughter with anorexia. Comes a time when your children finally amount to something, and you're faced with your grandchildren's troubles. Yet another cause of insomnia.

Maybe I should wait on the video games until the next study comes out; I wouldn't be surprised to learn the first was seriously flawed and raises all sorts of scientific question marks.

Sunday, September 8

"Would anyone care for my old pills?" Evert asked. "They're still perfectly good. It does depend on what you need them for, of course."

Evert was just being his provocative self in response to a newspaper story being discussed at coffee hour. A seventy-year-old man was on trial for having prepared a nice pill cocktail for his ninety-nine-year-old stepmother, who'd declared herself done with living. She was in pain and unable to do much for herself, but the nursing home physician didn't consider her suffering unreasonable and would not approve her for euthanasia. The old lady managed to get a bowl of yogurt containing 150 pills down in one try. Quite a feat. Amateur's luck, and a hit-or-miss affair.

Killing yourself isn't against the law. If you succeed, there's nothing they can do to punish you for it. And if you fail, you could always ask for the death penalty, I suppose. But helping someone to commit suicide is a felony.

Evert's offer of pills was greeted with suspicion.

Most of the residents don't need his pills for an overdose anyway; they've got plenty of their own. Almost everyone in here has one of those day-of-the-week pill dispensers. Some old coots take their pillboxes downstairs every morning, plunk them down on the table, shake out huge handfuls of pills, and, with a great deal of huffing and puffing, wash them down with gulps of lukewarm coffee. Sighing about ailments and maladies, misery and death. So if you were hoping to have a good day, best stay out of their way.

Monday, September 9

There's a new resident here, Mr. De Klerk, who is trying to convert his fellow inmates to "the Reformed Church." I don't know which reformed church exactly, but it's one of the more orthodox ones. It's a good thing no one in here still has to be vaccinated against the measles, because "interfering in God's plan for us is stepping into God's shoes, and those shoes don't fit us," says De Klerk.

His attempt to win over Protestant souls is creating rather a furor among the Catholics. I can see an old-time religious war coming. I can't wait for the first heretics to be burned at the stake.

Mr. De Klerk waxed eloquent when I informed him yesterday that I had some doubts about God's good works.

272

"The Lord hath not revealed Himself for us to question Him, but so that we may bow before Him."

Fortunately, eloquent words don't necessarily speak the truth. These weren't De Klerk's own words, in fact, but came from the evangelical magazine *Friend of the Truth*. One of the residents, an erstwhile Communist Party member, mistook it for his old party newspaper, risen from the ashes. Claims to own the truth can come from many quarters.

I left De Klerk with two questions. The first was whether proselytizing was considered work, and if so, if you were allowed to do it on Sundays, and the second, whether his God could create a rock that was so heavy that even He couldn't lift it. (I'd read that somewhere.)

I detected some bafflement.

"Well, you'll let me know, won't you," I said as I walked away.

Tuesday, September 10

This morning I went to the geriatrician. I asked him about the pep pill for the elderly. And also about its polar opposite: Drion's suicide pill.

"Both pills are problematic," said the doctor. "The stimulants you mean are illegal. Their effect on the elderly is not well known. Although it's quite possible cocaine could provide some old people with a nice buzz."

I asked if he had ever tried it himself. Yes, he had.

"Well?"

"*Too* nice. Dangerously nice. I could see myself being unable to do without."

The only thing he could do for me at this time, he said, was to prescribe a mild antidepressant, "although you don't seem depressed to me." The downside was that it might make me a bit groggy.

I said I needed pills to perk me up instead.

He said he would give it some thought.

As for the hypothetical suicide pill, that was a great deal more complicated. The doctor understood that for some people it must be a reassuring idea to have one of those pills in their medicine cabinet "just in case," but the reality was quite another story.

An elderly person who wishes to die has to go to an "End of Life Care Counselor," and will need to convince him or her of a genuine desire to die, to be done with life. You are required to sit through a minimum of two thorough, probing "intake" interviews with the counselor. If the counselor decides to help you, a second qualified provider must be found to agree as well. Next a physician has to prescribe the necessary drugs, to be taken under a doctor's supervision. What a rigmarole—enough to make you wish even more that you were dead.

"However, it seems to me that you are far from being a candidate for that yet."

"You may be right, but I find myself growing a bit unsteady on my feet. Isn't starting to lose your balance often the beginning of the end? Once the balance goes, that's usually the point of no return."

He nodded.

"Can't this conversation be considered the first 'intake'?" I asked.

It could.

Wednesday, September 11

Today most television stations will be showing the airplanes crashing into the Twin Towers over and over and over again: 2,996 dead. The direct catalyst for the War on Terror: at least 200,000 more deaths, including 6,000 American soldiers; over 350,000 injured, and an estimated price tag of $1 trillion and rising.

At teatime yesterday I threw out a few of those numbers (I know them by heart), but the cost of this war didn't seem all that unreasonable to most people there. Several of my friends excepted, luckily.

Just think of all the great things you could have done with those billions! The Americans could have made themselves quite popular in some quarters while they were at it, instead of being hated.

And after Iraq, and after all those Arab revolutions wind up devouring their own children, Islamic fundamentalism will only emerge more powerful than before.

I understand only too well that the Americans have no interest in diving headlong into another adventure in Syria, one that will be of no benefit to them. Other recent ill-advised adventures are still too fresh in their minds.

Overdoing the wise-old-man thing a bit, aren't you, Hendrik? Maybe it's the blustery autumn weather, after such a long, beautiful summer. This afternoon I am going out to buy a roomy rain poncho to wear on my scooter, so that I can clear my head no matter the weather.

Thursday, September 12

I heard that, on the heels of hospital clowns for sick children, special clowns are being deployed to cheer up lonely old folks. I don't know what they're called or where they come from, but I should like to warn them in advance: if any clown arrives to brighten my day, so help me God, I'll use my last ounce of strength to bash his jovial skull in with a frying pan.

A week ago the temperature was still close to eighty-six degrees. Now the central heating is up full blast. It's cold and rainy much of the time. Tomorrow we're off to play golf. It doesn't look like the weather will improve, and I don't have a backup plan. I've been checking the weather report hourly, but it doesn't help. The minibus is coming to pick us up tomorrow at one o'clock.

I'm a nervous wreck.

Friday, September 13

There was a resident who made a habit of staying in bed all day on Friday the thirteenth, just to make sure nothing bad would happen to her. Preparing to have a bite to eat in bed, she poured herself a cup of tea. The handle of the teapot broke, drenching her in boiling-hot liquid, and she had to spend the rest of that Friday the thirteenth in the hospital.

Evert came over yesterday with a belated birthday present: a sheepskin for the seat of my scooter. I should get it washed first, he said, he hadn't had time to take care of it. The poor lamb came from the thrift shop.

"Who knows what the previous owners might have been up to, rolling around on it in front of the fireplace. It's got some funny stains on it," he said with a wicked smirk.

I take no notice of his dirty innuendos. I brought the thing to the laundry and it's already been returned, washed and dried. All clean.

Only: if I do use it on my motorized chair, and it starts to rain when I've parked it outside somewhere, I'll be sitting on a soaking-wet sponge on the way back. As long as I'm still able to hobble, I'll never take my scooter indoors. And I don't really see myself toting a sheepskin around the supermarket when it's raining or snowing outside.

"There's that funny old geezer again lugging his sheepskin," I can already hear them whispering by the grapefruit display.

Saturday, September 14

The golf outing was the first flop of the series.

It started out reasonably well. Coffee and cake in the clubhouse, and a friendly, rather pompous instructor, who explained the rudiments of the game to us. But just as we stepped outside to put into practice what we had just learned, it began to rain. And it was cold. And it was also a bit ambitious for us, to tell the truth; we were barely able to hit the ball. To give you an idea: Eefje whacked her own ankle, and Graeme's club flew out of his hands, missing the instructor's head by a hair. Only Evert, in his wheelchair, was a sensation: he drove a couple of shots at least a hundred yards.

After half an hour we all felt that was enough for a first try, though we'd only used up half of our time.

We tossed back a glass of wine in an otherwise-deserted bar, and then I had the minibus pick us up an hour earlier than we'd planned.

They were all nice about it, assuring me that it had been a great idea, but that the weather and our advanced ages had failed to cooperate. Nonetheless, I am still, a day later, feeling rather let down. I am childishly bad at dealing with disappointment.

Sunday, September 15

I was still fretting about the failed golf outing when Evert stopped by for a visit. After five minutes, he threatened to leave if I didn't stop moping at once.

"I can't stand having to listen to an old fogey whining about a trivial little disappointment."

That snapped me out of it.

Besides, Evert was bringing me a piece of good news: the Happy Birthday Squad for lonely oldies had been disbanded for want of volunteers.

A gang of complete strangers arriving to serenade you and then help themselves to your birthday cake is enough jollity to make you long for a spate of loneliness. I confess: last year I didn't have the guts to tell them not to come in. Evert did. They went ahead with a rendition of "Happy Birthday to You" outside his door anyway.

Mrs. Aupers has taken to walking backward of late, because she thinks it makes her have to pee less often. I am going to nominate her for the Ig Nobel Prize, which this year went to a number of exceptional researchers. To Brian Crandall, for his study of his own excrement after eating a boiled shrew. To a Japanese and Chinese team that investigated the effect of opera on the life expectancy of mice after open-heart surgery. And one more for the road: Gustano Pizzo was given a posthumous award for inventing a cockpit trapdoor to thwart hijackers, dropping them into a capsule the pilots can then jettison by parachute. Some people here thought the parachute was an unnecessary nicety.

Monday, September 16

Mr. Schipper has asked that everyone save their used matches for him. He is planning to use them to build a scale replica of our care home. He's hoping it will make it into *Het Parool*. Stelwagen sits on the paper's advisory board.

Someone once made a replica of St. Peter's with seven million matches. This kind of project always makes me think, *Arson!* Twenty-five years of work going up in smoke within three minutes. I have a destructive trait lurking deep within my soul.

A week and a half ago it was eighty-two degrees outside, and summer. Now it's fifty-seven degrees and autumn. I don't like autumn. Yes of course, the colors are nice, but they're the colors of necrosis. In the late autumn of my life I am already confronted often enough with death and decay, I don't need dying leaf debris to remind me of them.

Autumn smells like a nursing home. Give me spring, a new beginning, to compensate.

I also hate the short, cold days; and Santa Claus and Christmas don't exactly make me jump for joy.

If I sound like an old grump, isn't that what this diary is for? It lets me gripe and moan from time to time, and it doesn't bother anyone.

Tuesday, September 17

Jealousy in old age sometimes goes to ridiculous lengths. Owing to the overabundance of women here, the married ladies do not like to let their husbands out of their sight. Mrs. Daalder never strays more than three feet from Mr. Daalder's side. She growls like a vicious guard dog at any female who dares to pay the slightest attention to her man. Even if the unsuspecting table-mate is just asking him to pass the sugar.

"Can't you reach it yourself? Don't give it to her, Wim."

Wim is thoroughly depressed because he can no longer have a decent conversation with anyone. And no woman wants Wim anyway, because he's ugly as sin; and yet he has to tolerate his jealous wife's watchdog surveillance. I sometimes detect in Wim's eyes a great longing for death.

What put me in mind of this is that about three weeks ago a certain Mr. Timmerman came to live here, and Mr. Timmerman seems to have his eye on Eefje, which I can perfectly well understand. He hasn't got a chance, however; Eefje will have nothing to do with him because he's a big show-off and also because he stinks.

That may sound like jealousy on the part of Hendrik Groen, but jealousy in this case is not necessary. Eefje has already very kindly asked Timmerman several times to please go and sit somewhere else.

That has stoked Timmerman's envy of me, since I always sit next to Eefje, to our mutual contentment.

Wednesday, September 18

Yesterday was Prince's Day, the opening of Parliament.

"Look, that red line, the longest one, that's us, the pensioners," Mr. Ellroy says, trying to explain to Mrs. Blokker the intricacies of the charts showing the cutbacks. "We're the ones having to tighten our belts the most!"

Mrs. Blokker nods.

The anxiety grows. Are they even going to let us have a measly ginger snap with our coffee?

Henk Krol of the 50Plus Party is calling on all seniors to join the fray and come to Sunday's demonstration in Amsterdam. I'm thinking of going, if the weather cooperates. It could be fun. I've never demonstrated in my life, but what's stopping me from marching at the age of eighty-four? Not that I can get all that excited about a possible 2 percent income cut; but I think the wide expanse of Museum Square teeming with rollators, mobility scooters, and Cantas could be a fascinating sight. I hope there'll be shouts of "*Rutte, murderer!*" and scuffles, and the riot police charging a tough gang of over-eighties tossing bricks as if it were a game of boccie.

I predict that in the municipal elections next March, the

local old-age parties will emerge victorious, together with the Socialists and the Freedom Party. The Labor Party will be toast. Its leader will step down. The cabinet will finally collapse. There will be a political deadlock, but in the end, even with the new parties in charge, everything will be the same as before. This is your political commentator Hendrik Groen in the nursing home, signing off.

Thursday, September 19

Two days after the opening of Parliament, the budget is no longer a topic of conversation, but the ladies aren't finished with lambasting the hats on display during the King's Speech. The ladies were not charitable in their appraisal of the female politicians: mousy plain Janes suddenly overcome with the need to wear ridiculous hats. There was one that looked like something torn off a wedding dress, someone said. "Well, that one's not *that* terrible," was just about the most positive assessment.

Our ladies are the last generation of hat-wearers: sensible headgear for the wintry weather, "but also to look nice." They greatly disapprove of the carnival hat procession in the second chamber.

Eefje often wears very fetching hats.

I like walking next to her, proud as a peacock. Preferably arm in arm.

Friday, September 20

There's an announcement on the bulletin board offering a course on preventing falls. All residents are encouraged to sign up.

The people who are most afraid of falling are the ones who fall the most. It's a fact that's been established through biomedical research. People who are afraid think: As long as I don't move, I can't fall down. Their physical condition and motor skills decline rapidly, and so they are bound to fall more often—on their way to the bathroom, for instance. That's the fall paradox for you, in a nutshell.

The course teaches you to "improve your balance" and, no less important, how to get up again if you do fall.

The hard facts and figures: "Falls are the leading cause of injury among people sixty-five and older."

I too have been feeling less steady on my feet...Still, I'm not sure about taking a course...

I asked Eefje what she thought: she won't even *think* of it. Graeme is waiting another year, and then he'll see. Grietje often gets lost but never falls. Evert is the only one who is keen to take part, in his wheelchair. Just to make a nuisance of himself.

Could I ask for a private trial lesson, I wonder?

Antoine and Ria are mourning the passing of their hero, Johannes van Dam, the food critic who used to make chefs quake in their shoes. Toward the end of his life he was giving the eating establishments he visited increasingly high marks. Was it perhaps to support his contention that he was personally responsible for having raised Amsterdam's culinary standards?

Another possible reason for the improved standings was the fact that he could no longer go incognito. He was far too recognizable. So whenever Johannes walked into a restaurant, it was all hands on deck.

Saturday, September 21

A few years ago, Johannes van Dam wrote in *Het Parool* that being unable to live independently was an unbearable torment. I brought this up with eight or so fellow residents over coffee. It set off a lively debate. Evert, the only one of us who lives independently in a retirement apartment, was also the only champion of the late Johannes's view. He was up against a majority expressing outrage at such a negative mentality. It was quite a showdown. Evert was in top form: sharp and blunt.

Stelwagen was watching from a distance. When she noticed me looking at her, she nodded at me and walked away.

Today is World Alzheimer's Day. What are you supposed to do with that? Try to remember it?

It seems silly to me, all those days marking this or that, especially diseases: World Leprosy Day, World AIDS Day, World Diabetes Day, World Diarrhea Day. I must go and see Grietje later, and tell her cheerily, "It's your day today! Actually, it's *doubly* your day, since today is also Good Neighbor Day!" Apparently there aren't enough days in the year, so Alzheimer's has to share its day with the neighbors.

Anyway, Alzheimer's Day is wasted on people with Alzheimer's. They don't even know what day of the week it is.

Sunday, September 22

Even if you're eighty, and you have a big mouth, and your name is Evert, you can still have moments of doubt. Evert asked me for my opinion on his arrangements for next Wednesday's outing. He has booked us into a painting class, and is a bit worried no one will like it. "Isn't it a bit skimpy? Do you think I should add something else?"

I assured him his plan is fine just as it is, that it can hardly go wrong, and will in any case trump my own golfing fiasco.

"That's true," he said with a smirk I really didn't appreciate.

I didn't see any furious fleets of walkers, Cantas, or mobility scooters at the anti-government rallies protesting the fact that the elderly are getting screwed.

Actually, it turns out it isn't as bad as we thought, if I can trust the article in yesterday's *Volkskrant* with the heading, "WHAT DO YOU MEAN, OLD AND PITIFUL?" The conclusion of greatest note: the young people of today will have to work considerably longer and have to pay more for their pension, than all those pensioners who are now screaming bloody murder.

It's a cheering prospect: a Socialist, Communist, and 50Plus coalition going to bat for the poor-beyond-belief oldies. According to the latest poll they stand to have sixty-six seats in Parliament.

Monday, September 23

Yesterday afternoon the sun broke through again, after a week of fall weather. There wasn't an empty spot to be had on the benches outside the front door.

Mrs. Bakel had brought along a bargain-size tube of sun cream, which she generously shared with anyone who asked. A short while later eight senior citizens with gobs of cream on their faces were seen basking in the sun, eyes closed. A pretty picture.

Then Mrs. Bakel, glancing at the tube, exclaimed in horror, "It's out of date!"

"And not even by a little," said Mrs. Van der Ploeg, who had put on her reading glasses.

"August 2009. Do you think it could be harmful?"

The question led to wild speculation.

"Maybe it'll give you the big C, skin C," Mr. Snel suggested.

Upon which eight senior citizens were seen frantically mopping the cream off their faces. Which was easier said than done, because of all the wrinkles.

Tuesday, September 24

Mr. Van der Schaaf was accosted in the street by a young man who asked him if he could exchange a euro for two fifty-cent coins, for a supermarket cart. The kid was very helpful, and offered to hold his wallet for him. When Mr. Van der Schaaf got home, it appeared that he had exchanged a ten and two twenties for the kid's single euro.

And if they do ever catch him...

Unarmed robbery? He's looking at community service at most, with no loss of benefits.

People tend not to get more liberal as they grow older. More right-wing is the norm. What does that say about us?

I believe this was the third obvious scam one of our inmates has fallen for in the last few months. We have all been warned, but when it comes to someone asking us for help in the street, half of us are grimly suspicious, while the other half remain naïvely convinced of the honesty of their fellow man.

Wednesday, September 25

A scientist, I don't remember the name, claims that Alzheimer's disease will be preventable fifteen years from now or thereabouts. That's bitter news for all the old boys and girls who are just starting to lose it. They won't be here to see the breakthrough; not in their right minds anyway. Rotten luck.

On the other hand, Americans have had some dashed lucky escapes over the years. From 1950 to 1968 there were at least seven hundred serious incidents involving nuclear weapons, newly declassified secret documents have revealed. An American bomber once "accidentally lost" two nuclear bombs over the U.S. somewhere—two warheads 260 times more powerful than the ones dropped on Hiroshima. One of them very nearly exploded when three of the four safety devices failed.

There is no reason to assume that such incidents have suddenly stopped happening. Only, they won't be made public until the year 2058. So I won't waste any more time fretting about it, promise.

All things considered, it's through luck rather than wisdom that we still exist.

Mankind hasn't always put the most sensible people in command. Hitler, Stalin, Mao, just to mention a few, are good for a tidy two hundred million dead all together, and that's even discounting any nukes. If there were a prize for the most hare-brained creature on earth, man would certainly be one of the nominees.

Tomorrow I'll go back to reporting on the charming details of daily life. The minibus will soon pull up in front, and eight spry seniors will be on their way to spend a lovely day burying our heads in the sand. We'll only come up for a drink and a nibble.

Thursday, September 26

There's a handsome portrait of me on my dresser, painted by Graeme, who turns out to be endowed with a striking neo-Expressionist style.

After lunch yesterday, the minibus drove us to Bergen aan Zee, the artists' village in North Holland. They were expecting us at an elegant beach pavilion. Evert hadn't taken into account how we were going to get him across the dunes in his wheelchair. It took some effort to push him up the brick path, and once at the top we had to struggle to keep him from hurtling down the other side and landing head-first in the sand. We finally found two strong, young joggers who offered to carry Evert downhill, dragged him a hundred yards through the sand, and delivered him safe and sound to the beach café that was the venue for our painting class.

An artistic lady had set out paints and canvases on eight portable easels. We were divided into pairs and instructed to paint our partner's portrait. The results were hilarious. Every style of the past five hundred years of art history was represented.

Afterwards Eefje and I moseyed down to the water to dip our toes into the North Sea. Arm in arm.

The final evaluation was of a sound culinary and alcoholic nature. Then the beach café's owner gave Evert a lift back up the dune in his tractor, Evert waving at us from his lofty perch like a queen. There was rowdy singing on the bus ride home.

This morning Mrs. Kamerling asked Graeme if he would paint a portrait of her too. Evert advised Graeme to charge her €780, tax not included.

Friday, September 27

"To mark the end of Dementia Week, I'd like to invite the three of you for a glass of wine and a bite to eat at the EYE Café," Grietje said to Eefje, Edward, and me yesterday. When we objected, saying we should share the costs, she just said, "Stuff and nonsense!"

Taxi out, taxi home.

As we sat there basking in the sun, gazing at the waters of the IJ, she explained nonchalantly: "I'm determined to be a big spender in my old age. I want to empty my savings account before I no longer know what a savings account is for."

That's the correct approach to dementia, if you ask me.

But I do think enough is enough. An Alzheimer's Day is one thing, but it seems we now have an entire week devoted to it...! There must have been at least eight shows about dementia on TV recently. Okay, now we know. It isn't *that* complicated: you're diagnosed with dementia, and after a while your mind goes completely blank, and you can't even recognize your own face in the mirror. Then it's time for the locked ward.

There's a big fuss about the prediction that of the female babies born today, half will live to be a hundred. I have yet to hear anyone ask the most pertinent question: is that supposed to be good news or bad? Of the people in this home close to turning a hundred, at least half wish to die as soon as possible.

Saturday, September 28

When the elevator door slid open, there were already two rollators and one mobility scooter inside, but Mrs. Groenteman thought there was still room for herself and her scooter. She revved the engine a little too hard, sweeping the others into a great pileup. It took half an hour to extricate all the dinged metal and trampled oldies. The groaning was deafening, although the injuries were barely perceptible to the naked eye.

The director has let me know—very indirectly—that she believes I'm the one to whom Anja has passed confidential information. Yesterday Stelwagen personally invited me to the farewell cocktail party for Anja on Monday, October 7. I must have looked a bit startled, for she added, "You *are* a friend of Mrs. Appelboom's, aren't you? I mean, I understand you were often seen in the office having a cup of coffee together. I'm just sorry it always happened to be when I wasn't there."

I must have blushed. I stood there and didn't know what to say. I felt a bit checkmated.

"A bit checkmated" is an oxymoron!

Stelwagen smiled, bade me good day, and left.

The fact that the farewell do is on a Monday speaks volumes about the esteem in which Anja is held by her office mates.

In any case, she now seems more relieved than angry about her abrupt dismissal.

Sunday, September 29

As soon as the news got out yesterday about the pileup in the elevator, the hallway turned into a sea of rubberneckers.

"Oh, oh, oh!" Hands up to appalled mouths, heads shaking, and daft speculation as to cause and effect.

"No, it was because the people in the elevator were taking up too much room."

We lose some capacities as we age, but being a busybody isn't one of them.

We're having an Indian summer. Although the weather can be a bit treacherous. Early this morning I took my scooter out for a spin and almost froze my fingers off. I must buy myself some toasty winter gear, or some fine day they'll find me frozen stiff at a traffic light.

They do say that freezing to death, like drowning, is a good way to die. If you can believe those who lived to tell the tale.

I'm not planning to try it just yet, but it may be a useful backup, as an alternative to the suicide pill. All you do is drive to some deserted spot on an icy winter night, fling off your coat, and wait for death. Another plus is that if they don't find you right away, you won't stink.

Monday, September 30

My foot hurts so badly that I can barely walk. I've called Eefje to ask her to get me some aspirin. I think it's gout. I recognize the symptoms—Evert once had it. I've been sitting in my chair with my leg up all morning. I only got up once, to crawl to the bathroom on hands and knees.

Eefje came and sat with me for an hour, and this afternoon Evert's coming for a visit in his wheelchair. The halt and the lame.

I've asked the staff if I can have my supper brought upstairs.

"Sorry, not standard procedure," Mrs. De Roos of housekeeping informed me.

"Standard procedure?"

"Right, we won't do that. You'll have to ask to be moved to the nursing unit."

Stuff your rules and procedures; I'll just ask Graeme to bring me up a plate tonight. Graeme is still ambulatory. They'll probably make a fuss that that isn't "standard procedure" either, but Graeme will ignore them.

The people here are perfectly capable of letting someone die like a dog, as long as it's by the rules.

It's lucky I have friends these days.

Tuesday, October 1

I was right; it's gout. The doctor gave me pills and told me I can't drink while I'm on them, and even when I'm over it I'm to stay away from red wine and try not to eat any strawberries. One can survive without strawberries, especially in October, but the season for red wine has only just begun! Now I'll have to restrict myself to the whites of summer. If that's all it takes to keep the gout away, I can deal with it.

It takes great effort and excruciating pain to hobble to the bathroom. Roaming the premises, so important to my sanity, is out of the question for now. What's left: reading, writing, watching TV, and waiting for visitors.

And leafing through some of my files. I found an old newspaper article in one: "A United States investigative committee has discovered that some 6.6 billion freshly printed dollars that were air-shipped in several planeloads to Baghdad to pay government salaries may have been stolen." The Americans gave Iraq the cash; Iraq simply lost it.

Lost it? Six billion dollars? That's a few trucks stuffed with cash. Lost. Just left it sitting around somewhere.

I know why I kept that article. It's too unbelievable for words. Somewhere, in a Baghdad warehouse perhaps, an Iraqi Scrooge McDuck is diving into a swimming pool full of dollars.

Wednesday, October 2

As consolation I told Grietje that Europe has at least six million dementia sufferers.

Evert: "So you thought, 'Oh well, misery loves company,' didn't you?"

Upon which Grietje said, smiling, "Don't mind him!"

I think I must have gone quite red.

Still, it isn't a very cheering thought, that Europe alone has enough dementia patients to fill 120 soccer stadiums.

Grietje said that when the illness is advanced, you might walk right past a mirror without recognizing it's you. She said she hoped she'd think to herself, "My, what a nice-looking woman!"

Then we went down the list of all the people we know who have dementia. We decided that about half of them are quite unhappy, or very much so. "Therefore the other half can't be that badly off. Not much worse off, anyway, than most of the other residents here. That's the optimistic conclusion," said Grietje, and went on to say that she wouldn't even think of ending her life prematurely.

As if to answer the question I had not dared ask.

The gout is already a bit better. The pills are working. I am even able to hobble about a little.

Thursday, October 3

In our subtropical world of fatuous blabbermouths, you hear at least ten times a morning that everything was better in the old days. Yesterday Mrs. De Vries, in a voice filled with nostalgia, said that there always used to be time for a coffee and a little chat with your neighbors. Evert remarked that in her case, then, nothing had changed.

"How do you mean?"

"For years I've had to listen to your nonstop jabbering, Vera, except when you shut up to take a sip of coffee."

An indignant "Well!" was the answer.

And for the first time since I have known her, Vera was quiet for a full five minutes. When the five minutes were up, she haughtily demanded that Evert address her as "Mrs. De Vries" from now on. Most people in here do call each other by their last names, a relic, presumably, from the time when everything was so much better and people still had respect for one another. Evert's the only one who calls everyone by their first name, no matter who.

I am quite sprightly again today, and feel I can safely have a drop this evening. I find I am more addicted than I thought. You may not realize it as long as you're in the

habit of drinking, but after a few days of imposed absti-
nence, the longing for a nip can take a terrible toll on your
mood.

In defense of my alcohol dependence, I can always tell
myself that at my age it makes no difference anyway. So I
feel justified in pouring myself a little preprandial glass of
wine, the first of the night. Not so long ago I'd also light
up a cigar, but, alas, that pleasure is denied to me now.
Smoking makes me cough my lungs out.

Friday, October 4

On World Animal Day there's no meat or fish on the
menu. We get tofu balls with endive-potato mash instead.
A small gesture. Tomorrow I'll take an extra helping of
meat.

It's not as if the mousetraps were put away on October
4; we don't stop swatting mosquitoes either. There are
animals, and then there are *animals*. The same goes for humans: some get shot or starve to death, and others get to
live in a mansion with a swimming pool.

Mrs. Stelwagen summoned me to her office to ask if I
could think of a nice parting gift for Anja. I could not.

"Cost no object," she insisted. Her conscience must be
troubling her.

"Well then, I suppose an electric bike would be nice."

She thought that was an excellent idea. I had expected
her to stick Anja with a cheap watch or something. I think
I have done Anja a good turn with my inspired suggestion.

★   ★   ★

This afternoon I am off to see my scooter guy. Nice to know that for the first time in my life I have my own "guy" for something. I'm going to ask him to order a windshield for it. The past few days' stiff east wind has been making my excursions bracing, to say the least, even with the autumnal sun shining. A windshield ought to make it more bearable.

Saturday, October 5

Henk Krol, he who scaled the barricades for the sake of our pensions, has had a great fall. It seems he was rather selective in his fight for pension fairness. He didn't think it necessary to pay into a pension fund for his own employees.

It now turns out that at least half the residents always thought Krol was a shifty sort of fellow.

The fact that there was a picture of him in the paper posing with both his ex-wife and ex-husband didn't improve matters. "If you can't even make up your mind if you're queer or straight, how can you look after the interests of three million senior citizens? Screw off, is what I say!" Thus spoke the ever-nuanced Mr. Bakker.

But with Henk Krol's resignation many fellow residents have tumbled into a deep political hole. Whom are they going to vote for now?

A good number of residents, especially the ladies, wish they could vote for Princess Beatrix.

All in all, trying to talk politics in here is not for the faint of heart.

It's not as if anyone had anything interesting or sensible to say anyway. Evert recently asked the assembled, out of the blue, if any of them were still keeping their pubic hair properly trimmed. You should have seen their faces.

Later he explained that it's sometimes necessary to use shock tactics to keep our little table from getting too crowded.

Sunday, October 6

Edward has taped a piece of paper onto one of the tables downstairs that says, "*Please, no ORGAN RECITALS at this table.*" Evert added another restriction underneath: "*And not a word about DEAD SPOUSES (m or f) either.*"

There was puzzlement all around.

"What do you mean, no organ recitals?" asked Mrs. Dirkzwager, who upon taking a seat always slaps down her automatic pill dispenser next to her cup of decaf and proceeds to swallow her daily medicines one by one, announcing with a sigh what each is for. And that happens every day, believe it or not.

Edward laboriously explained that while you are certainly free to bring up your various organs, your troubles, and your dear departed ones, you just can't do it at this table.

"Some people would rather not listen to other people bitching and moaning all the time," Evert clarified.

The room separated uncertainly into two contingents: a small group at the No Organ Recitals table, the rest shuffling off to the other tables, hesitant whether or not to voice their usual health complaints out loud.

By afternoon Edward's notice had disappeared.

The National Senior Song Fest is coming up. The preliminary rounds are being held soon. Let me not fall into the error that was raised a moment ago: namely, bitching and moaning.

Therefore, just one remark: the real winners are the deaf and hard of hearing.

Monday, October 7

There are several ladies in here who are germophobes; there are also several other ladies whose lifestyle, to put it kindly, does not focus on personal hygiene. The two factions are often at loggerheads.

At dinner, Mrs. Aupers, one of those that don't believe in changing their stockings on a monthly basis, tried to persuade two of her table-mates, both great proponents of hygiene, that all that washing and scrubbing made no sense.

"There are at least eighty kinds of fungus on the heel of your foot alone. I read it somewhere. Can you imagine what's living in your crotch?"

"Please! I'm eating!" one of the clean and godly ladies exclaimed.

"I only want to say that I don't see the point of all that lathering and showering. Your hands are covered in germs and mold too, you know."

Well done: the two dirt-phobic ladies called for the nurse. Could Mrs. Aupers please be so kind as to keep her opinions to herself at mealtimes? Mrs. Aupers stood up for her freedom of expression. A row broke out. In the end Aupers, in her grubby dress that showcased what had been on the menu for the past few days, was made to go and sit by herself at another table.

But the harm was done. Most did not care to finish what was left on their plates. Plump Mrs. Zonderland was the only one to take advantage of the situation, making quick work of four custard puddings, which are normally one of the home's most popular desserts. Usually the bowls are scraped or licked clean.

Tuesday, October 8

Do you think a fellow like Henk Krol has been walking around all these years worrying, "Oh, I *do* hope no one starts investigating those pension contributions I refused to make for my employees"? Don't you suppose the suppressed anxiety must have undermined his immoderate self-satisfaction just a little? I hate to think how many other people there must be living with the threat of exposure. The scandals that do come out must be just the tip of the iceberg.

Anja's send-off party was yesterday afternoon. It was better than I'd expected, actually. Some of her colleagues performed a song that wasn't half-bad, and there was a man who gave a nice, respectful speech that even contained a hint of criticism of the corporate culture here. Stelwagen didn't bat an eye. Her smile was firmly pasted on for the duration of the party. I wonder who that fellow was, in fact.

Anja was delighted with her electric bike.

We promised to stay in touch. A sincere declaration of intention. We'll have to see about putting it into practice.

Old people often lose touch with their last remaining friends outside the retirement home; they stop visiting each other or doing things together. They dread having to take any initiative. If you want to be kind, you can attribute it to fear and lack of energy. But I think it's laziness and apathy. Not letting yourself grow lonely costs a great deal of—sometimes fruitless—effort.

Wednesday, October 9

I heard a dull thud in the room next to mine, and then a faint groaning. The walls are thin here. I rushed into the hall and knocked; no answer. The door was locked but one of the cleaning staff just happened to come along, and I prevailed upon him to open it with his skeleton key.

Mrs. Meijer was lying on the floor of her kitchenette, and you didn't have to be a doctor to see that her arm was twisted at a very odd angle. It was a sickening sight. I alerted reception and a short time later Meijer was on her way to the hospital on a stretcher.

That was last night.

It turns out that she broke both her arm and her leg.

She had used a chair to climb up on the counter in order

to dust the tops of the cabinets. "But that's the way I *always* do it," she is said to have groaned. Makes perfect sense.

Myself, I have accidentally sat down on my glasses three times this week. In the end it proved to be too much strain for one of the arms, which promptly gave up the ghost. This was my backup pair, since I sat on my good pair last month. I repaired the arm with some tape borrowed from the handyman, and finally found the time to bring the other pair to the optician.

"I'll see if there's anything I can do about this, Sir."

Thursday, October 10

When the Nobel Committee phoned Ralph Steinman two years ago to congratulate him on winning the Nobel Prize in Medicine, he wasn't able to take the call because he had died three days earlier.

Rotten luck for Ralph, wasn't it? It's not every day you win a prize like that, so you'd want to be alive for it, wouldn't you? On the other hand, as it turned out luck was on his side, even if he didn't know it. You see, the rule is that Nobel Prizes can't be awarded to dead people, so the committee had to scramble to come up with a new rule: you *can* win the prize if you're dead, as long as the committee doesn't *know* you're dead.

It's rumored that someone from the organization now has to speak to the winner personally on the phone before the announcement can be made. Therefore, learned ladies and gentlemen, there's no point in keeping your deaths quiet.

Besides, isn't it the Nobel Committee's own fault?

Awarding a prize ten, twenty, sometimes thirty years after a famous discovery is asking for trouble. Who knows how many dead professors have had to miss the greatest day in their professional lives?

The people here felt very sorry for Ralph Steinman when I told them about it.

"Another thing that's tragic is that Vincent van Gogh never saw one cent of all the millions his paintings were worth later," sighed Mrs. Aupers.

"So it's lucky he's dead, then!" Evert concluded cheerfully.

The Higgs boson isn't likely to come up for discussion in here.

Friday, October 11

Great brouhaha over a Russian diplomat arrested by police in The Hague.

"For a drunk Russian child-abuser, palliative sedation seems more appropriate than diplomatic immunity." Well said, Graeme! Ingenious linkage of two unconnected items currently in the news. The only problem is that hardly anyone understood what you were saying.

"We" aren't very fond of Russians, and aren't inclined to give them the benefit of the doubt; that's evident from the conversation over coffee.

"One look at that Ruskie's vodka mug says it all," opined our Mr. Bakker.

"Some travel brochures make a point of saying that they don't cater to Russians in their hotels," said Mrs. Snijder, who has never in her life ventured farther afield than the Veluwe district.

As far as I'm concerned: thank the Lord that we have Mark Rutte and not Vladimir Putin.

What can explain the fact that we are so bad at remembering names?

"Christ, what's his name again? You know, that singer in that band. There was a blonde girl too. Begins with an A. It's on the tip of my tongue."

You find yourself suddenly unable to pry the name of someone you've known for years from the right brain cell. Then, hours later, the name will pop into your head unbidden.

I have to rack my brain more and more often for a name or a word, only to come up empty. I should just accept it, but it bothers the hell out of me.

Don't let it, Groen.

Saturday, October 12

The director called the fire drill a great success. If the point of a drill is to create as much chaos as possible, I'm in total agreement with her.

They appeared as if out of nowhere up and down the hallways in their fluorescent vests: the "First Responders." The alarm hadn't even gone off, so the emergency personnel had the opportunity to warn us that it wasn't real. "To prevent heart attacks," Stelwagen explained later.

Knowing it was only a drill meant that most inmates took their time finishing their coffees, and then went back upstairs to fetch a sweater, because it was chilly outside. The resulting lines for the elevators deserved a traffic report. As everyone knows, in case of fire, do not take the elevator. Most residents categorically refused to take the stairs, however, which is understandable if you're pushing a rollator. They just stood there waiting for an elevator that never arrived. Finally the emergency-team chief decided that upon further consideration it wasn't a fire, but a bomb scare, which meant the elevators could be used after all. By that time one lady had fallen down the stairs and someone else had had his fingers crushed in the automatic fire doors.

I hope that in the case of a real fire, the flames will take their own sweet time, because it took thirty-five minutes for the last resident to get out, and by that time the first ones had already gone back inside, the staff leading the retreat, because it was freezing outside.

Sunday, October 13

I'm livid just thinking about it.

It was unexpectedly nice out yesterday, and I decided to take my mobility scooter for a little drive. Shortly after I set off, a car, seemingly from nowhere, swerved in front of me. I braked to a stop. A motorcyclist hurtling toward me from the other direction had to screech to a stop in order not to crash into me. The biker, twenty years old or so, shot me a dirty look. "Out of the way, you old coot!"

"*Mr.* Old Coot to you. A little respect, please. Isn't that what you young people are always going on about: respect?" I bumped my fist to my chest and drawled, "No disrespectin', man."

"Back off, old coot!"

I backed up to make room to let him through.

Leaning close, he spat right in my face, then revved his engine and tore off. The gob of spit dripped down my cheek. I wiped it off with my sleeve in disgust.

I drove home seething with impotent fury.

Now I read that "my" mayor, Eberhard van der Laan, has prostate cancer. That piece of news doesn't do my mood any good. Amsterdam's mayor is one of the few people I admire. A nice guy *and* an effective leader—a rare combination.

I glance out the window, where it's been raining cats and dogs for the past three hours, and it occurs to me that unless I go and call on Eefje right now, I might just consider killing myself. And if she isn't in, I'll seek out Evert. If he isn't in either, I'll just have to spend the rest of the day in bed.

Monday, October 14

Luckily Eefje was home yesterday. She has a soothing, cheering influence on me; all she has to do is just *be* there. She listened to my story about the young thug. When I got to the spitting part, her head jerked back in revulsion, as if she felt the disgusting gob hit her own face.

"If you'd had a gun, you'd have blasted him—bang!— right off his motorbike, I imagine."

"That's a thought... But I would have missed because I was shaking so much, and I'd probably have struck an innocent bystander instead. So it's just as well I didn't have one."

Then Eefje suggested we throw all caution to the wind for once, and knock back a "coffee with legs" before lunch. For those not in the know: that's an Irish coffee.

It helped.

At teatime Mrs. Bastiaans gave a report on the *Consumers' Guide* deep-fat fryer tests.

The Moulinex Pro Clean AMC 7 received a "double plus" for its "crumb-sticking performance." Mrs. Bastiaans wondered if that means crumbs will or will not stick to the french fries. She considers herself a french fry expert but isn't sure about the significance of crumb-sticking performance. To make this discussion even more interesting: the report was in a *Consumers' Guide* from five years ago, and the home has a strict prohibition against frying of any sort. And there you sit, more or less forced to listen to that crap.

Tuesday, October 15

There was an announcement on the bulletin board that the annual Residents' Association excursion is canceled because of disagreement among the board members. A new election is to be held in the spring. All current members are putting themselves forward for another term.

The board consists, not coincidentally, of the four most stubborn inhabitants of this institution. With a bit of luck, all four will be reelected and there won't be a field trip next year either.

I did go along on one of their excursions a few years ago. A day-trip to Aachen, in Germany. On the way there, we stopped in Eindhoven for a mattress demonstration; in Aachen we sat through a German version of a Tupperware party; and on the return trip, stopping in Eindhoven again, a man in a white lab coat talked us into buying a vitamin tonic that was supposed to make you live to a hundred. If you died before that, you could ask for your money back.

One hour for pottering about in Aachen, three hours set aside for the obligatory tea breaks, and six hours' bus riding, all at a cost of €22.50 per person. One lady, God rest her soul, bought a thousand euros' worth of stuff that day, including a lovely incontinence mattress. There were ATM machines everywhere for her convenience.

On the way back Mrs. Schaap, who thinks she has a lovely voice, captured the microphone and tormented us with songs from her golden-oldie repertoire for an hour. To be fair, many of our party enthusiastically joined in.

Wednesday, October 16

Eva to the rescue! Since human help is getting too expensive and too scarce (what were those unemployment numbers again?), Eva is to be our tea lady in future. Eva is a robot developed by the engineers at the Delft University of Technology. In the picture she looks more like a cross between a treadmill and an old-fashioned balance scale than an Eva. With a mouth shaped like a mailbox and two black blotches resembling eyes, or rather, eyebrows. Her specialty is light domestic work, and she can even show some emotion, her developers claim. Tinny laughter? Real tears? It doesn't say.

I hope I am dead by the time they've replaced all the nurses with robots to save money. If I'm still alive, I can picture myself removing a screw or two. Evert has vowed to mow down as many robots as he can with his wheelchair "by accident." It would make a great film, wouldn't it?

Old people make less adrenaline and dopamine, the compounds responsible for butterflies in the stomach and heart palpitations. But being in love isn't about the quantity of hormones your body produces as much as the relative upswing in those hormones. In the elderly, that hormone surge can be just as great as in younger people. Says the newspaper. Which might explain why, when Eefje is near, I always find myself starting to stammer and stutter a bit.

Thursday, October 17

"Anything a doctor does for us in here amounts to palliative care, really. Let's not kid ourselves," was Evert's contribution to the discussion about the doctor in the village of Tuitjenhorn who may have been a bit too generous with the morphine.

"Well, at least it's put Tuitjenhorn back on the map," said Graeme.

Opinions about the doctor's treatment by the police

were mixed. Many in here remain staunchly in the straight-and-narrow, Christian mind-set about euthanasia. But everyone did agree that there was no reason to arrest the kind-hearted doctor (which I'll assume he was, until evidence proves otherwise) in the dead of night and interrogate him for hours. Surely it can't have been that urgent.

Incidents such as this, mark my words, will make doctors hesitant to give their patients morphine, no matter how much pain they're in. They'll be too afraid that a patient will die as a result—and of course there's a good chance of that in the case of the very old—and the doctor will be held responsible. But an aspirin tends not to do the trick anymore.

Mr. Bakker, this home's biggest pain in the neck, ran his Canta through the car wash but forgot to close his window. He went to push the window button, but it was too late, he was already sitting inside an aquarium. We split our sides laughing when the orderly told us. He'd seen Bakker come in drenched from head to toe.

Friday, October 18

"I've just about *had* it with all the reports about breakthroughs in Alzheimer's prevention!" said Grietje. "It's after the ship has sailed, for me."

But she remains chipper in spite of everything, gleefully confessing to leaving her slippers under her pillow and her pajamas under the bed. And she often has trouble remembering what she's supposed to be doing or where she's going. "The bathroom isn't a problem yet. The day I forget what I'm doing in there, it'll be time for me to move to the other side."

We're having another Old But Not Dead Club excursion next Monday—it's about time! The organizer: Edward. He is busy sowing confusion with contradictory dress codes and constantly changing departure times. It wasn't really his turn, but he wanted to have this particular date. Expectations are running high.

Yet more good news: our cook, the blandest, most tasteless, no-salt cook in the Netherlands, has been fired. For reasons not made public, but rumor has it that he was too liberal with the wine. Not in the food, you understand.

The Residents' Association board has asked to be included in the search committee for a new cook. All four board members. There's not a chance in hell their request will be granted, but they couldn't agree on a single member to send as their representative.

Saturday, October 19

When the U.S. finds itself in financial difficulties, and the Republicans want to shut down the coffers of the Treasury, we are prepared to offer an impartial opinion on the subject.

"If America's going broke, they'll need a good bailiff," Mrs. Blokker suggested.

"If it comes to that, they may need more than one good bailiff," Graeme muttered, adding theatrically, "Help, we're sitting in a rickety little boat about to pitch over the edge of a waterfall, and nobody's doing a damn thing about it!" Graeme is a great fan of the late, great thespian Ko van Dijk: he likes to lay it on a bit thick. He usually follows it up with a broad wink at Eefje or Grietje, or if they're not available, at me.

"Ah yes, we live in uncertain times," I chip in. "Life is a five-thousand-piece jigsaw puzzle with no picture to follow." Not bad either, even if I say so myself.

There's no point counting on the so-called experts, anyway. They are mainly good at prognosticating in hindsight. Not a single Eastern-bloc specialist ever gave advance warning that the Berlin Wall would be coming down. Not a single economist foresaw the banking crisis. Perhaps mankind is too stupid and too irrational to make accurate predictions. If that is so, then why not get rid of all the so-called experts hogging the airtime on the talk shows?

Be that as it may, every discussion we have here comes down in the end to one incontrovertible truth: we probably won't be around to see it!

Tuesday, October 22

Sometime in the early hours of Sunday, Eefje had a serious stroke, presumably in her sleep. She is almost totally paralyzed and unable to speak.

The nurse who found her on Sunday morning called for an ambulance, and Eefje was rushed to the hospital. She's in intensive care.

Her daughter was with her on Sunday.

Monday afternoon she was allowed to have a very short

visit from nonrelatives. I went to see her with leaden feet. It was dreadful. The only thing she can do is shake her head almost imperceptibly, yes or no. Judging from the way she reacted to my questions, her mind seems to be clear. She is in great pain.

I held her hand until she nodded off into a fitful sleep.

Then the nurse said I had to leave. I asked her to tell Eefje I would come again the next day. That's later today.

Thursday, October 24

Four days since Eefje's stroke, and there's very little improvement. She is able to make some sounds, but it's impossible to tell if it's a yes or a no. She is out of intensive care and is in a regular hospital ward.

She can swallow again, so she's able to sip through a straw, but it clearly takes a lot of effort.

She is visibly losing weight. And she barely weighed more than a hundred pounds even before she had the stroke.

When I visit her she's almost always asleep. If she wakes up, she seems to be happy to see me. Her eyes light up briefly, but after a few seconds they're back to looking so tired and sad that it brings tears to my eyes every time. Then I have to look away, so as not to add to her sadness.

I usually sit and hold her hand for fifteen to twenty minutes, until she dozes off again. There's no need to talk.

Yesterday a few of us spent an hour playing pool, but our hearts weren't in it.

"There's no point," Evert remarked. "If you're just going to stand about with long faces I might as well stay in my room. I'd rather stare at my own crotchety face."

He was right; I said I was sorry. After that we did play a little better.

Friday, October 25

The founding of the Old But Not Dead Club ushered in a period of new-found joy. It now seems that it may have been happiness's last gasp.

Evert disabled, Grietje demented, and Eefje a basket case. That's a blow from which a club with only eight members cannot recover, no matter how many glasses of good wine you enjoy together.

We are all doing our best to be there for one another; it's quite touching. It gives me some strength to carry on.

Two of us go to the hospital every day, one in the morning and one in the afternoon, and we also see to it that Grietje and Evert receive whatever help they need. We're all constantly working on cheering each other up. But it's optimism that goes against our better judgment.

I try to write every day. That keeps me sane to a certain extent. Besides that I read the paper, watch a bit of TV, sit at the window, drink tea. You can't get any more geriatric than that, I know, but I don't know where I would find the energy for anything else just now.

I have always criticized those residents who do nothing but moan and complain. Now it's my turn. Hendrik Groen, do yourself a favor, and the others too while you're at it, and give yourself a good kick up the behind.

The first outcome of that kick: I've asked Edward to arrange, at short notice, another outing to take the place of the one that was canceled last Monday. After thinking it over, he said he would take care of it.

That was the first little step on the way back up.

Our lawyer, Victor, informs us, in writing, that the board of directors has promised to supply the information we request by June 1 of next year at the latest.

Stelwagen is aware that she no longer has much to fear from us. Time is on her side, no matter what.

Finding me in the hallway, she asked solicitously after my lady friend. She had heard there wasn't much improvement. She sincerely hoped Eefje would be able to continue to live independently, but she wasn't very optimistic.

"Her room will soon have to be cleared out, I suppose?" I couldn't help muttering.

Oh no, there was no need for that yet, not at all, the middle of November at the earliest, if that. I do think Stelwagen's sympathy for Eefje and me is genuine. But only as far as it's "in the interests of the organization."

Sunday, October 27

Yesterday I had a "conference" with Eefje and her daughter, Hanneke. I was there at Hanneke's express request; she said her mother wanted me to be there. I had never met Eefje's daughter before. She's sweet, but she lives in Roermond with three children, a husband, and a job, so it's hard for her to get away.

The hospital has informed us that Eefje is to be discharged and will have to be sent elsewhere for rehabilitation. Rehabilitation sounds hopeful, but according to the doctor there's zero chance that she will recover enough to be able to live by herself again.

We sat by her bed. Hanneke asked questions. Eefje nodded yes or shook her head no.

To sum it up succinctly: she doesn't want to go into a nursing home; she wants to die in peace. She has a written declaration somewhere saying she does not want to go on living in a case such as this. She told Hanneke the same thing while still in good health. She just doesn't know where that declaration is.

I have never seen eyes looking as hopeless and miserable as hers.

Tomorrow we have an appointment with the consultant.

I have promised myself I will report on at least one positive or funny thing every day.

This morning seventeen old people sat in church for an hour complaining that the minister was late. They had forgotten to set their clocks back—it's the end of Daylight Saving Time!

The consultant heard us out. We told him life has become an unbearable burden for Eefje. That she possesses a signed declaration stating that should she become totally dependent on others, she does not wish to go on living.

The doctor asked if he could see that declaration.

We had to admit that we hadn't managed to find it yet.

"I don't want to give you any false hope; even *with* a signed living will, in this hospital we will not take any steps to end Mrs. Brand's life. I advise you to consult her regular doctor."

Now *there's* an interesting twist to the ongoing debate in here about that doctor in Tuitjenhorn who first euthanized a patient and then himself!

For the teatime conversation to jump from euthanasia to the controversy over Black Pete is but a small leap. Black Pete enjoys many faithful fans in here. Every year there's great hilarity over which of the ladies Pete will invite to come and sit on his lap. They have been known to fight over the honor. It's always the same Black Pete and Santa Claus that come here. Our Santa Claus is actually more than ready for a rollator himself, but last year he managed to hobble to his festooned chair, propped up by a stout attendant and his bishop's staff as he walked. In real life Black Pete is the head of cleaning services here. He's the only Pete I know who wears pink rubber gloves and carries the goodies in a cleaning bucket. He doesn't strew the sweets on the floor as is customary, out of respect for his cleaning colleagues. That's the controversy. But no one in here can bend down to pick them up without risking a fall anyway.

Tuesday, October 29

Code Red yesterday, wind force 10. Nobody went outside. Every storm inevitably brings up the old story about stubborn old Mrs. Gravenbeek, who was blown into the canal in 1987 and sadly drowned.

"And she'd been expressly warned too!"

I let the scooter stand idle for a day. Flying is easy; the problem is landing safely.

Spent yesterday afternoon searching for Eefje's living will. We didn't find it. Her daughter and I combed through ten folders comprising the sum total of an entire life. I felt awkward having to handle all sorts of private papers and letters. I passed the most private ones to Hanneke at first, but she found them even harder to deal with than I did. So I scanned them as quickly as possible to see if there was anything in them about ending her life.

After two hours I had to stop.

I went over to Evert's for a shoulder to cry on. In a manner of speaking; I didn't mean to literally, but a few tears escaped nonetheless.

Evert brought out a twenty-year-old whiskey that he saved "for special occasions." He also ordered takeout and put on an old comedy DVD for us to watch.

Afterward I did feel a little better.

Wednesday, October 30

"You are born, you die, and the rest is just marking time" (James Joyce).

I must try to draw a few ounces of strength from somewhere so that I may stand by the dearest friend I have in the world, to be of support to her in her terrible plight. That's a sensible way to mark time.

In practice, lending support to Eefje consists of holding her hand every day for half an hour, and trying to think of what is left to say.

She is barely making progress. They are moving her to the medical ward on Friday. We haven't been able to find the living will that says she doesn't want to go on living once she's incapacitated.

We decided the most poignant photograph of the storm damage was the one showing the capsized Fries Ahoy! food truck bobbing in the waves at Lauwersoog.

When it comes to storms, we have front-row seats in here behind the geraniums. Mr. Bakker, sitting at the window in his armchair on the fifth floor, counted six toppled trees, two car crashes, and three near-accidents. What a day!

Over coffee I heard the following rationale: when they introduced the euro, everything suddenly cost twice as much; so conceivably, a return to the guilder will automatically make everything twice as cheap.

I have an even simpler solution to fix the economy: let the banks shift every decimal point one digit to the right. Nothing really changes, but everyone is suddenly ten times richer. Spending goes up, the economy grows exponentially, problem solved.

Thursday, October 31

Mrs. Van Diemen is considering a face-lift.

"What's the plastic surgeon supposed to do with all the extra double chins?" Evert asked straight-faced.

"Maybe he can give them to someone else," said Van Diemen. She seems a bit out of her depth these days, and well on her way to the locked ward.

Another resident, Mr. De Wijs, is changing banks for the third time. He started out at the Postbank, then took his money to ABN AMRO, and finally the Rabobank; and now even that bank's no good. "Can anyone recommend a bank where my money will be safe?" he asked as we were having our coffees. He was met with blank stares. Someone offered to keep his money for him in the meantime. Under the sofa.

An initiative that has been welcomed here by many residents: a last will and testament drawn up for you by the discount store Hema. "It's so reasonable!" Many of the inmates are leery of attorneys—and I can't blame them, considering what the profession charges for just a few pieces of paper—but they have great faith in Hema. Two residents, who had to go to the store anyway because they were out of sausages, decided they might as well pick up a will while they were there. They were greatly disappointed to learn you can only do it on the Internet.

I miss Eefje, who was so good at tactfully helping you

over the hurdles. A single remark from her was enough to make your irritation at all the bellyaching and mindless blather disappear. Giving you the strength to tolerate the sometimes abominable ignorance in here again.

Friday, November 1

Over the course of my lifetime, the number of people on earth has escalated from two billion to seven billion. In one generation the world population has more than tripled. This may possibly be the most drastic change the world has ever seen. More significant than either the industrial or the digital revolution.

When the subject of the population explosion came up over coffee, Mrs. Brom allowed that it was "indeed getting rather crowded."

"I hadn't really noticed," Evert scoffed, "judging by the number of visitors we see here."

"That's because you are not a very nice man," Mrs. Brom replied.

Evert took that as a compliment.

If everyone on earth were allotted the same space, proportionately, as a battery hen—say, five feet by five feet—then all seven billion would easily fit into half of the Netherlands.

If one looks at it that way, there's room for many billions more.

Eefje is coming home this afternoon. That is, she's coming home to the medical ward.

The upshot of her daughter's consultation with the doctor was that euthanasia is out of the question. Even if we were able to find her living will declaring she does not wish to live in a vegetative state, he still wouldn't be able to do anything for her. That's all he would say.

Saturday, November 2

Yesterday late afternoon found five of us club members gathered around Eefje's bed. It looked like a reunion of sorts. Or perhaps a dissolution. The nurse came to tell us only two people were allowed at the same time. "So as not to disturb the other patients."

Eefje is sharing the room with a nonagenarian who is strapped to her bed and can't stop clicking her fingernail against the metal bed rail, and another old woman who keeps up a constant stream of mumbling. The only thing about Eefje that's still in good working order is her hearing. Please God that her mind isn't alert enough for it to bother her.

Three old biddies in one room, no privacy to speak of, no personal belongings. Stark conditions in the year 2013, in one of the richest countries in the world.

I'm even more scatterbrained than usual. I left my toast too long in the toaster three times in succession. Burned to a crisp each time. My mind was elsewhere. I was lucky: there wasn't enough smoke to set off the fire alarm. That would have created a huge ruckus, and my illegal toaster would probably have been confiscated. Making toast is included in the prohibition against baking, frying, and cooking.

Sunday, November 3

Evert and I had a good talk. We were playing chess. That is, I was blindly moving the chess pieces about.

"It's sheer checkmate-suicide, Henk, the way you're playing."

"What?"

"You're doing what you don't have the guts to do in real life," he pointed out. Evert doesn't need much of a pretext to get to the heart of the matter.

Naturally I began by beating about the bush, but with Evert you can't get away with that. First he let me stutter on a bit, until I fell silent. Then came the advice.

"Henk, if you're sick of life, just put an end to it, why don't you? Don't mess about with assisted-suicide counselors or doctors, just go out and buy yourself a sturdy rope. As long as you're still able to get up on a chair and step off, you don't need anyone else. And if you don't have the nerve, which is normal, then stop whining and just try to make the best of it."

There was no arguing with his logic.

I tried protesting that some people don't kill themselves because they don't want to cause their loved ones grief or saddle them with guilt.

Well, as far as he could tell, there wasn't much need for me to worry about that. He was willing to give me a helping hand in tying the noose. Not that he wanted to be rid of me, certainly not, but true friends are there to help you in your hour of need. Without thinking of themselves.

"And you can trust me to explain it to the other club members, although I don't think they'd have any trouble understanding. After all, we're all in the same sinking ship. And now, back to chess!"

Monday, November 4

At lunch Graeme announced that he hears a strange click every time he picks up the phone. "I've got the feeling someone's tapping my phone," he said gravely. A few hours later, at teatime, five other residents announced that they too could hear a strange click when they answered their phones.

"Now I understand how Mrs. Merkel must feel," said Mrs. Schenk, without a grain of irony.

Graeme later confided to me that his phone has been sitting in a drawer, unused, for weeks. "I never get any calls. If the phone does ring, it's always for Neonatal Care over at the IJ hospital. Their number is practically the same as mine."

Our Prime Minister Rutte has lodged a sharp protest with the NSA: how come they've been spying on Merkel and the pope, and not on him?

We haven't heard anything further about the building's renovation, which is supposedly imminent. No news is often bad news here. I miss having Anja as my mole in the administration. Our retired whistle-blower is doing fine, by the way. She's enjoying her life. We see each other for coffee on a regular basis.

Nothing new on the Eefje front.

Tuesday, November 5

I decided that Eefje might like it if I read to her. She always was a big reader. I found three books in her room that looked as if they hadn't been cracked yet. But it wasn't easy. The manager wouldn't allow me into Eefje's room at first. So I marched straight to Stelwagen, explained the situation, and asked if I could collect a few of her books. That turned out to be the right tactic; from now on I have access to Eefje's room whenever I want. I was even given a key, which I believe is against the rules.

Our director mentioned in passing that Eefje's room would have to be surrendered on January 1, unless there was a marked improvement in her condition of course.

"That's so flexible of you."

"If there's a need, I'll use any space I have."

Eefje nodded when I asked if she'd like me to read to her. I let her choose from Simone van der Vlugt's *Jacoba*, Paolo Giordano's *The Solitude of Prime Numbers*, and *Sarah's Key* by Tatiana de Rosnay. She nodded when I showed her the last. I hope it isn't too gloomy. In hindsight I am glad she didn't choose *Jacoba*, which is about Jacoba van Beieren, the fifteenth-century countess of Holland. Chapter One begins: "Death drifted into the room." That would have been a tough way to start.

I read seventeen pages in half an hour. The book is 331

pages long. So there are enough words there for twenty reading sessions.

When I stopped I asked her if she'd enjoyed it. She nodded.

Wednesday, November 6

"Right, girlies, I've spiked your coffee with a couple of pills, and I'll be seeing you in my room shortly." Evert could already picture it. He was hoping it wasn't too late to have a shot at the new female-libido-enhancing pill.

"You old blowhard," Graeme grunted.

"I have a lot of catching up to do," said Evert, "because I was married for thirty years to a very sweet woman, but she was as cold as a chest freezer and as dry as a cookie."

"That pill makes ladies grow a mustache," Edward warned.

"Most of the ladies in here already have one," Evert said, putting the problem in perspective.

"Right, Evert, enough now," said Grietje, giving him a withering glance.

The Old But Not Dead Club was assembled for the first time in weeks, and it felt good. We drank wine and snacked on croquettes and the mood was serious and cheerful by turns. Ria and Antoine are inviting us to dinner on Sunday in the restaurant of old friends of theirs. Everyone's going. Well, except one. I'm going to read to her again this afternoon. I don't know if I'll have the heart to tell her about our dinner out on Sunday.

In Norway they're watching a TV show that's just twelve hours of nonstop knitting: "from sheep to sweater." To promote the notion of "Slow TV." For the Dutch version, I propose a twelve-hour broadcast of people shuffling in and out of our elevators. Now *that's* slow television. The threshold alone, a minuscule ridge, causes tremendous delays.

One day one of the elevators was out of order because of a technical hitch. It gave rise to a line stretching as far as the eye could see. Having to wait their turn does not bring out the best in our residents: there's a great deal of pushing, shoving, ankle bashing, and cursing.

Bakker: "Goddamned crap elevator!" Not exactly a good title for the latest *Hello Kitty* book. There were shocked, indignant glares and some *ooh*ing and *tsk-tsk*ing.

I read to Eefje for the third time. It feels good, except that the woman in the next bed won't stop muttering. I asked the nurse if she ever shuts up. "Only when she's asleep, but then she snores a bit," was the alarming answer.

I asked Eefje if she'd like me to bring her some earplugs. She nodded yes. I told her I would take care of it. It shouldn't be a problem; ears appear to be a booming business these days, because within a short space of time two new hearing-aid outlets have opened in the shopping center. I'm sure they must stock earplugs as well.

Friday, November 8

The financial problems of the publishing industry have caught our attention. That is to say: there is great alarm about the impending demise of the women's weeklies *Margriet* and *Libelle*, two cornerstones of our civilization. The consternation is felt largely by the ladies, but there's even a gentleman or two who will miss those magazines dearly.

They were offended at my suggestion that once those exalted magazines have ceased publication, there's always the option of going back and rereading the old issues.

"Most of the people in here have such bad memories, they wouldn't even notice," Graeme said to back me up, but that only made it worse. Furious glares! We had to save ourselves by assuring them we were only joking.

"I enjoy reading *Margriet* myself from time to time," I even added.

I'm offended that nobody realized it was meant as a joke.

I am not underestimating the importance of magazines like *Libelle* and *Margriet*. For many of the residents they are their windows into the world. Few people here read the newspaper, and they rarely watch current-events shows. As the years add up, the world of the elderly shrinks. They venture outside the four walls of this home less and less often. Friends and old acquaintances die. They haven't worked in many years. Nothing and no one to cater to or care for. What remains is *Margriet*. And plenty of time to keep a nosy eye on everyone else.

Grietje was wondering if it made sense for her to hurry up and try to become bilingual.

I must have looked surprised, because she added, "It's a joke, but I read that it takes four years longer on average for bilingual people to lose their minds. Wouldn't that be nice?"

"No, Grietje, it's too late for you. The only difference would be that you'd be unintelligible in two languages instead of one."

Thank you, Evert, for your helpful and positive comments.

Sarah's Key, the book I've been reading to Eefje, is heavy going. I don't sense there will be a happy ending. I've asked Eefje twice if she wouldn't prefer me to read something more uplifting, but she shook her head both times.

Reading to her gives my days structure. The afternoon, or the occasional morning, finds me ambling to the medical unit to read to her for a half hour. Then I'll hold her hand for a while. She often falls asleep after fifteen minutes or so.

A small slate that Grietje bought for her at the toy store hangs at the foot of her bed. I always write a little message on it, and when I'll be there next. After that I usually pop in at Evert's for a drink. I have yet to thank him for the kick in the behind he gave me last week. Don't whine; *do* something. I think I'll buy him two big bunches of gladioli. I'm sure he doesn't have a vase to put them in.

There was Evert, with ten pounds of flowers in one hand, and two crutches in the other.

"Well, I'll be going, then."

"Don't you dare leave, you jackass!"

I pretended to close the door.

"Henkie...please..." He sounded helpless.

I had a good laugh at his expense, and then went to the rescue.

I had guessed right, Evert didn't have any flower containers. The two gigantic bunches of gladioli are now arranged in two vases that somehow found their way into his backpack after a lightning visit to Eefje's ward. He's been carrying a backpack ever since losing his leg. The medical ward has a cupboard full of vases, but they don't allow flowers in the rooms. Apparently flowers are bad for something. In hospitals they used to put all the flowers out in the hall at night.

We sat and had a coffee. He said he was delighted with the flowers and very pleased that I was no longer whining but doing something. "Even if it's only reading to Eefje." I am also quite pleased with myself again.

The restaurant outing is this evening. I have been fasting all day, because it certainly won't be fried potatoes and cabbage or nasty stewed endive. If there aren't at least five courses, I'll eat my hat for dessert. Mr. Hendrik is going to dress for dinner in a natty suit.

I didn't have it in me to tell Eefje about our dinner. I thought it would be too painful.

I must have gained three pounds last night. Seven courses and six different wines. A personal record. For someone who for the first fifty years of his life never had more than two courses and a glass of water, it was definitely a step up.

Well, some of it was just a mouthful or two, of course. But delicious mouthfuls. The waiter's explanation took at least two minutes for each dish. I'd never even heard of many of the ingredients. So don't ask me what I ate.

At least as important was the fact that they weren't too stuck-up in there. Nobody seemed to mind the occasional burp. Not an uncouth belch, mind you, like the one Evert let out, but a discreet burp of satisfaction made no one turn a hair.

We were all in absolute agreement: it was the best meal we'd ever had. Ria and Antoine, the organizers, were beaming as I had never seen them beam before.

We raised a glass to Eefje, our dear absent friend. We missed her, but didn't let it spoil the mood.

After yesterday's poached quail's eggs on a bed of lamb's ear (or whatever it was), today I am digging into a big bag of St. Martin's Day candy. I'm already on my third mini Mars bar.

We never had children come around to our rooms trick or treating on St. Martin's Day until last year. That's when a few kids discovered the advantage of roaming warm, indoor hallways. (I suspect the receptionist must have been dozing.) Last year, of course, nobody was prepared. People had to ransack their rooms for cookies or candy. Boxes of expensive chocolates were sacrificed and a number of piggy banks raided.

This year we were better prepared. You'll see that not a single child shows up and we'll wind up having to eat it all ourselves.

Tuesday, November 12

I've been to the Better Hearing store. I wonder if they deal with "worse hearing" as well? I explained the problem to the man behind the counter: a sick old lady who is bothered by the noise of her roommates. The best thing to do, said the man, was to have earplugs made to order; that would come to about ninety euros. The cost is no object, but for Eefje the measuring could prove difficult. I bought a pair of good standard plugs and tried them on Eefje. That was an unexpectedly intimate operation. How would you feel, poking about in someone else's ear? My hands tend to tremble anyway, and it took a while to maneuver them more or less into place.

For just a moment I thought I heard her laugh, but it was wishful thinking. But her eyes definitely did twinkle.

The nurse came along and started raising objections. Patients weren't usually given earplugs. She would have to discuss it with her supervisor. "No, you can't come along to ask her." She demanded that I remove them.

I had to do some quick talking to get her to let Eefje keep them in whenever she doesn't have visitors, for as long as her neighbors keep up their clicking and mumbling.

Eefje had to nod a few times to the nurse's questions to confirm that it was what she wanted.

* ★ ★

When Miss Slothouwer was made to see that a couple of trees felled by the wind in the Netherlands two weeks ago really did not compare to the current devastation in the Philippines, she brought up the North Sea floods of 1953, which in her opinion were worse than any measly typhoon. Put your own disasters first, that's her motto.

Wednesday, November 13

Some good old-fashioned bellyaching again at coffee time: it seems that supplemental insurance policies are for the most part dropping physical therapy. Mrs. Van Vliet, who goes to the physical therapist at least a hundred times a year for God only knows what imaginary ailments, has calculated that she'll have to start coughing up five thousand euros a year. "Then I just won't go. That's much too much money."

"What about your aches and pains then?" someone asked.

Van Vliet ignored the question. The story goes that she's sometimes had trouble remembering which ailment she needed the physical therapy for. "Just do something for something," she once told the therapist.

Our in-house physical therapist didn't mind. He was quite happy to fill out the insurance forms. He's in for some hard times now. He's been driving a BMW thanks to Mrs. Van Vliet alone.

Graeme summed it up as follows: people will go to the physical therapist for the time it takes for the ailment to heal by itself in the first place. Yes, yes, sorry, I suppose there *are* lots of old people who benefit from various treatments, of course.

Thursday, November 14

This morning in a moment of clarity it suddenly occurred to me that bedridden patients might like to listen to music. The body may be shackled to the bed, but the ears can still travel. It could be a welcome distraction to hear music once in a while. Or to listen to the radio. To make the suffering a bit more bearable. I'll ask Eefje about it this afternoon. I know she has an extensive collection of CDs, mostly classical music, that she liked to listen to.

I took a spin through the misty meadows of Waterland yesterday in the late afternoon. It's rarely busy there. From time to time a car will come zipping along the narrow roads at fifty miles an hour, but then it's back to the sound of the cows, sheep, and birds. I felt at peace. That may sound a bit cliché, but I can't describe it any other way. I even started feeling a bit *too* peaceful and almost landed in a ditch.

A farmer on a tractor stared at me in surprise and silently held up a hand in greeting; he must have been wondering what this old geezer was doing so far from home.

It started to get dark. It drizzled a bit, but I didn't care.

It was the first time I ever drove with my lights on.

Mr. Bakker's analysis of the disaster in the Philippines: "It's lucky they're so poor over there, the damage would have been even worse otherwise." The residents aren't usually all that interested in what's happening in the world, but they do make an exception for natural disasters. It would be surprising indeed if at least one person didn't remark on man's insignificance against the forces of nature.

They do pray for the victims, but that has not yet led to any results. To some people, prayer is a substitute for contributing to a disaster fund. Instead of taking out their wallets, they leave it all up to that great Director in the sky.

A bit of a damper: the nursing unit is not prepared to take on fitting earplugs or playing music as part of the standard care package. Not enough time, too much work. "No will" wasn't said in so many words but was obviously a factor.

On the other hand, there is no outright prohibition against headphones or earplugs. If family or friends wish to provide these, and as long as it doesn't bother the other patients, it will be permitted on an experimental basis. The hemming and hawing is courtesy of Mrs. Duchamps, head of nursing, a small, snippy woman who always seems to know best. She's French; she should have stayed in France. Arrogant and unsympathetic, but she does have a cute French accent.

Saturday, November 16

Evert has discovered a suspicious black spot on his remaining big toe. "I hope they don't have to lop off another piece, because this is my last foot," he said, joking. I did detect some hoarseness in his voice, however, and a pearl of sweat on his brow. Then he showed me. I scrubbed his toe with a scouring pad, and it came out white as snow. I have never seen him look so relieved. He promptly poured himself a whiskey, for he'd been so nervous that he hadn't had a drink in two days, the first time that had happened in twenty years. I laughed and laughed; I couldn't help it. It took awhile, but then Evert couldn't help laughing too.

I have purchased an iPod. I had never even seen one of those gadgets before, but an intern who works on my floor told me exactly what to buy. Tonight she'll load it for me with a couple of CDs I found in Eefje's room. A lovely girl. Her name is Meta and she's from Badhoevedorp. She is glad to help me.

Will human rights ever improve all over the world? I've grown a bit more optimistic, actually, since reading a small item in the newspaper, namely, that Russia, Cuba, China, and Saudi Arabia have all been elected to the United Nations Human Rights Council. Each brings a wealth of experience to the table pertaining to human-rights violations.

Meta returned the iPod to me this morning. It now holds nine classical CDs.

"Did you like the music?" I asked.

"Not really," she said, after some hesitation. "Not really" means "*Really* not."

"That's too bad."

"To upload it you don't have to listen to the whole thing, you know," she said consolingly.

She didn't mind Beethoven, actually. Was he still alive?

Meta doesn't have any grandpas. One is dead and the other one is on the other side in a family feud. She never sees him now. She thinks I make a rather good substitute. I'm quite willing to be her grandpa once in a while. Not for long, alas, since her internship is almost over and then she'll have to go back to Badhoevedorp.

I immediately took the iPod to Eefje. I'd wrapped it in pretty paper, which I ripped off as she watched. Carefully I put the headphones on her head and pushed play. The opening bars of a Mozart symphony.

She was very happy.

I promised to be her DJ for half an hour every morning, and to read to her for half an hour every afternoon. And if I can't do it, I'll arrange for a replacement.

Thirty minutes is long enough. She usually falls asleep after that. As she did this morning. I slowly turned the volume all the way down, then carefully removed the headphones. I wrote on the slate at her feet, "You looked so peaceful sleeping, I didn't like to wake you. See you this afternoon."

"I suddenly had no idea how to turn on my television! I sat there staring at the buttons on the remote control. Couldn't for the life of me fathom how it was supposed to work. So I just listened to the radio instead."

I made Grietje promise to call and ask me next time.

She's definitely going downhill. She has noticed it herself. I pop in every day for a chat and to see how she is doing.

Within a very short space of time I seem to have built up a busy home-care practice. That leaves me little time for all the coffee klatches and tea cliques and their depressing bellyaching. So much the better. I do have to make sure not to neglect the healthy members of the club, Graeme, Edward, Ria, and Antoine.

Our congenial lawyer called me to keep me apprised of where we stand. I had to tell him that we have lost our motivation in our battle with management. When I explained that my most important partner-in-arms is now in a quasi-vegetative state, he quite understood.

He was very sorry and asked if he might continue pursuing it on our behalf.

"Of course you may. And if I can find the time and the energy, I'll do what I can to help."

"I am sure Eefje will appreciate it if you do."

Tuesday, November 19

Graeme said that it's exactly seventy years ago to the day that he lost his little dog. He was twelve. He had let it run off the leash in the park when four German police officers grabbed it. The date is etched in his memory like a rusty nail. He never felt as powerless as he did that day. Later he heard that confiscated dogs like his were used as land-mine detectors.

My all-consuming caregiver tasks provide me with an anchor in my daily life. It gives me a sense of peace and of being useful. My three patients, Evert, Grietje, and Eefje, are grateful clients. As far as reading to Eefje, I'm not sure *Sarah's Key* was the right choice—it's not very uplifting. But Eefje likes it. She is also very pleased with her music.

I got up the courage to ask her if she still wished to die. Yes, she still wanted to die, but less desperately than before. I gathered this from the way she nodded her head.

Good news for most of the residents: the renovations have been postponed a year. Several ladies wondered if they should leave the moving boxes stacked in their rooms for another year or lug them back to the supermarket one by one. A conundrum. Then the conversation turned to fibroids. Lacking the moral fiber to stay and listen, I decided to go out for a stroll.

Wednesday, November 20

Grietje and I decided to go and have a look at the dementia unit. Getting in wasn't difficult. We just followed a nurse through the door, telling her we were visiting Grietje's sister-in-law. We'd looked up the name of a patient at random, but as it turned out it wasn't necessary. No one asked any questions. We wandered through various common rooms and saw a number of old acquaintances. We didn't have to worry about being recognized.

It was lunchtime. A nurse was feeding a short woman with a bib around her neck. "Toot, toot, here comes the train... and...in we go!" They call it senility or dementia nowadays, but they used to say you were in your second childhood.

Another lady sitting in a chair asked me if I wanted to see her pussy and promptly spread her legs. I won't give you a description. Some of the patients stared listlessly straight ahead, but there were others who nodded and smiled at us amiably. Grietje has the enviable ability to take things in calmly as they come.

"So this is where I'll be in a year or so," she said. "I hope I'll still have some good times first. By the way, I don't want you to visit me, Hendrik, unless I specifically ask for you. Agreed?"

Yes, that was agreed.

Thursday, November 21

In a care home called High Time, in Den Bosch, some of the residents had to pay for their own toilet paper. That was the case two years ago, anyway. There was great indignation about it at the time. Now there's a rumor that a similar economy measure is being considered for our own institution. I don't think that's such a good idea. Some residents here are such penny-pinchers that if they had to pay for their own toilet paper, they'd probably just not wipe themselves; they'd wait and scrub it off later in the shower.

Unless we're going to have to cough up money for taking a shower too.

It doesn't smell all that fresh in here anyway. I sometimes get the sense that the toilet paper is already being rationed.

What intrigued me about that newspaper article was that only "some" residents had to pay for their toilet paper. Why not all of them? Were the residents given an allowance of a certain number of pieces and had to pay extra once they'd used them up?

Not exactly a subject for polite conversation, Hendrik! Whereas I am, in fact, a reasonably respectable gent. "Inconspicuously respectable" is how I would describe myself. Not tall, not short, not fat, not skinny. Gray or navy trousers, neat blazer. Plenty of wrinkles and just a few gray hairs, which the barber trims for sixteen euros—in less than ten minutes. And at least five of those minutes are time wasted. Going to the barber's will soon cost me more than one euro per hair.

Friday, November 22

Eefje's room is to be cleared out by December 1 at the latest. The director had been rather rash in giving us a deadline of January 1. She really wishes she could give us a little more time, but upon further reflection, the regulations won't permit it.

"You mean the regulations we aren't allowed to see? Those?"

Yes, those were the ones she meant. I thought I saw a flicker of shame steal across her face.

I was summoned to Stelwagen's office with Eefje's daughter, Hanneke, to "discuss the situation," but it turned out there wasn't much to discuss. Hanneke asked me if I would go with her to tell her mother.

I didn't want to, but I thought that I should.

We decided to take the news to her right away. Eefje did not seem surprised that she'd have to move out of her room. She has made some progress. She can say something that sounds like yes, or is at least easy to distinguish from no. She can move her right hand and right leg a little, and is able to swallow with less difficulty.

We'll ask her which of her things she'd like put into storage and which personal effects she'd like by her bed, where she has a wardrobe, a chair, and a nightstand. In the medical ward, personal belongings are reduced to the sheer minimum.

Then I let Eefje listen to some music for half an hour; it relaxes her and brings her peace. I already know my way around the iPod quite well. I've bought another one for myself. (Someone said I was "so hip"!) Only, I don't know how to load it up myself.

Saturday, November 23

The orderly has refused entry to one blue and one green Black Pete. The only Pete he allowed in was a black one, but Mrs. De Roos said he couldn't strew his goodies all over the floor, as is the custom, because they'll get trampled into the carpets.

Rumor has it that the blue and green Petes have lodged a complaint, saying it's discrimination. The management has issued a statement that the orderly acted on his own authority. They're terrified of a brawl. No one knows who sent those Petes here.

As a favor to Evert, I took part in the *Klaverjas* tournament again yesterday. No one else will play with him. They'd also rather not play against him. Some of the old coots have developed an unhealthy aversion to my friend, which he doesn't deserve, even if he can be rather annoying.

Unlike my usual habit of just slapping down some cards, I really did my best, resulting in a splendid third prize: two chocolates.

Mr. Pot, as sour as they come, said, "I don't like chocolate anyway, at least not that kind."

"Well, I do love chocolate, but I'm giving my prize to the tournament's sweetest player, Mrs. Aaltje, who can use the calories," said Evert, offering his chocolate to Aaltje, the skinny little mouse who came in last, and was now beaming from ear to ear. Evert isn't allowed any chocolate because of his diabetes.

Sunday, November 24

Nobody knows who sent us those three Petes.

The green and blue ones, as I said, were barred entry by the orderly, and the black one left after just three minutes, uttering all kinds of incomprehensible sounds. Various conspiracy theories are circulating:

1. They were thieves in disguise. ("I could hear metal objects rattling in the sack.")

2. A rival old-age home tried to play a trick on us. ("That one Pete, you know, was the spitting image of that Surinamese nurse from nursing home X.")

3. It was supposed to be a surprise set up by our own Residents' Association, which, when the joke fizzled, pretends it had nothing to do with it. ("I even heard him say, *Surprise!*")

The residents in here don't have a shred of imagination, except when it comes to back-biting and baseless accusations.

Ria and Antoine consider it an honor to adopt Eefje's houseplants. They have been to see her, to tell her the plants are in good hands.

In my own room there isn't a speck of green. I can't even keep a sansevieria alive. Potted bulbs, I can handle those. They bloom and then get tossed in the garbage. The only place plants stand even less of a chance is at Evert's. His dog, Mo, devours anything that grows and blooms. Only to spew it all up again.

Monday, November 25

In the hall I bumped into that sweet little social worker who was once sent to ask me about my suicide plans. She asked if I was still trying to see the sunny side of life.

"Well, to tell the truth, the skies are rather gray these days," I said.

"But behind the clouds...?"

I answered truthfully that I did not expect to see many

sunny days anymore, and that when I'd finally had enough of this bad weather, I would let her know prior to taking my own life.

Hanneke and I spent a couple of hours yesterday sorting through Eefje's effects. We stacked the stuff that can go to the thrift shop on the right side of the room. On the left are a few pieces Hanneke is going to try to sell online. In the middle of the room are two boxes containing personal items: photos, paintings, a few statuettes, jewelry, books, and CDs. An entire life in just two boxes. No need for a moving van; it will fit on the tea cart.

The thrift shop van is coming on Friday to pick up what's left.

The director, in a gesture of goodwill, says the home will cover the costs of removing the nails and screws from the walls. "How very generous," I couldn't help muttering.

The living will still hasn't turned up. We've given up hope of finding it.

Tuesday, November 26

"With a little luck, next year I'll believe in Santa Claus again!" said Grietje gaily.

"Yes, just keep going the way you're going, and you'll get there soon enough," Evert egged her on.

She liked the prospect of trustingly leaving her shoe by the hearth again. "Santa Claus could leave me an arch-support insole!"

"Made of marzipan."

Anja came to see me yesterday. Being forced to take early retirement seems to have done her a world of good. She does say she is sorry she wasn't given the time or opportunity to smuggle out all the documents the board wants to keep Top Secret. "I failed as a spy."

"But as a human, you're a success."

"Sweet of you to say so, Hendrik."

We decided to go to Museum Amsterdam Noord, she on her electric bike and I on my scooter. I could barely keep up with her. Museum Noord is the only museum in this part of Amsterdam. It turns out it's closed on Mondays.

Wednesday, November 27

One advantage of living here is that there's little chance you might be lying dead in your room for ten years before you're found. The residents are all able to agree on this. "But that's only an advantage for the living, isn't it; the stench won't be as bad. It makes no difference to you once you're dead," Mr. Krauwel pointed out. Mr. Krauwel is our latest prize addition: negative as a nematode, always complaining. He and Mr. Bakker together are a fine pair of crotchety old coots.

The ladies think Krauwel is handsome on account of his leonine gray hair. Every new gentleman is welcomed with secret excitement because of the great surplus of women. It's embarrassing to see some of the old girls trying to attract the new guy's attention. They daub their thin lips with lipstick, hike up their deflated breasts, squirt themselves with overpowering perfume, talk too loudly, and laugh too readily.

The one that hooks Krauwel will live to regret it. She's getting a hyena for a mate.

I feel a bit under the weather. I can't afford to be sick now. The caregiver must keep giving.

I happen to have an appointment with the geriatrician the day after tomorrow, so he can take a gander at this stubborn little cough while he's at it.

Thursday, November 28

I had a dream that I put a pillow on Eefje's face and then sat on it. I woke up in a sweat, panicked. It took me thirty minutes and two cups of tea to calm down.

Sitting by her bed, seeing her sadness and pain, I have from time to time wished her a peaceful death. But to make it happen by my own hand—I could never. The very thought of it makes me ill.

We have finished the first book. Thank God. To be continued with something lighter, I hope. *The Solitude of Prime Numbers.* The title doesn't give much away. Of the remaining candidates, Eefje chose that one.

I have the sense it doesn't make that much difference what I read to her, as long as I read to her. I see myself as a tranquilizing, babbling brook.

The choice of music for her daily iPod session doesn't matter much either, although I would never put on a heavy-metal band, or one of those rappers raging about fuckin' this and fuckin' that. With that genius trio of Bach, Mozart, and Beethoven, a disk jockey can't go wrong. It usually puts her right to sleep.

Friday, November 29

I have just ambled through the supermarket in my first diaper. It felt fine.

So that barrier has been broken. It may have something to do with the fact that there's a new lady resident who is often seen walking around with a big wet spot on the back of her dress. It's always pointed out to her discreetly, although loud enough for all to hear.

"Oh, did I leak again?" she'll say, in surprise and dismay, as if it weren't something that happens several times a week.

Just to rub it in, someone will then exclaim that her chair is also soaking wet.

I want at all cost to prevent people from pointing out that I've wet my pants. So I decided to try out the pack of incontinence diapers (mini) the geriatrician gave me this morning.

Aside from that, the doctor told me nothing new. No new ailments ("Status quo equals progress," said the doctor, satisfied), and no fresh hope for Eefje either.

"Since the lady did not make her wishes known beforehand that she did not want to end up in a medical ward, the living will can't be found, and she is now unable to express herself clearly, euthanasia is not in the cards, I'm afraid. There's no doctor who would risk it."

I read that Bernard and Georgette Cazes, married sixty years, departed this life hand in hand. Bravo!

They chose a luxury Paris hotel as the scene of their final deed. I am sorry that they had to resort to putting plastic bags over their heads. They'd ordered breakfast in bed, so that it wouldn't be long before they were found. The poor chambermaid.

On a more positive note: I had dinner last night with Ria and Antoine in a little Indonesian restaurant. Delicious meal, except that at one point I had such a coughing fit that the *kroepoek* were blown off the table. But nobody seemed to mind.

The conversation was not only about food this time: it seems they want to go on a wine tour next spring, and asked if I'd like to join them. They were very disappointed to see me look rather dubious at first, but I thought they said "Rhine tour." The thought of a boat trip down the Rhine with several hundred old people, and being unable to get off, doesn't appeal to me; that's a living hell.

When we'd cleared up that little misunderstanding, I told them I had been chewing over a similar idea. "Let's join forces," I proposed. I do have some reservations about lugging Evert in his wheelchair from château to château. He tends to fall off his chair from time to time, especially when he's had a few.

We might ask Stelwagen to look after his dog.

Just one month to go, then the year's out and the diary is full. Last night I reread some of it, and, I'm sorry, it does sound rather down in the dumps a lot of the time, doesn't it? When one of the reasons for writing was to poke fun at the reigning glumness in here.

But it is what it is: my daily rounds take me from amputated Evert to demented Grietje to vegetative Eefje.

Our Old But Not Dead Club, which flourished but shortly, is in dire straits. Its misfortunes were greeted by Mr. Pot as follows: "They had it coming, didn't they? We weren't good enough for them. So now they can just stick it up their asses."

"What did they ever do to you? Did it bother you, then?" asked Mrs. Aupers, surprised.

Fortunately there are also plenty of residents and staff members who have expressed sympathy for our club's tribulations.

Would I care to come for a ride? Mr. Hoogdalen, he of the Antelope mobility-scooter club that never got off the ground, was just the person I needed to shake me out of my gloom. Absolutely! I said. He on his pimped-up scooter deluxe, I on my quite respectable Elegance.

He knew of a nice route: "Follow me, and just call me Bert." After an hour we stopped at a café for a cup of soup. Bert is a man of few words. He doesn't like to speak in complete sentences.

"Nice ride," about the ride.

"Good soup," about the soup.

"Shall we?" on resuming our journey.

And upon parting: "Chin up. And, uh...give 'em hell."
My mind is pleasantly emptied out.

Monday, December 2

I don't often receive mail, but when I do it's usually a letter advising me to cash a check for €8,990 without delay. A stamped request form enclosed. And, as a further condition, I am to order six pairs of overpriced thermal insoles.

The implication is that I've already won that money. It's only upon reading the fine print that you understand you just have a *chance* to win it. The whole thing is "supervised by a neutral third party," so that's reassuring.

I once casually asked how many people here receive this kind of unsolicited prize letter. Most of them do. And many are unable to resist the temptation. They have not won any prizes, but they are now the proud owners of very expensive horse-chestnut extract for varicose veins, or have paid through the nose for bamboo health socks or energy hair balsam. I am not making this up! You'll find such items stowed away in the bottom of a wardrobe in many a resident's room.

Most of them don't like to talk about it. But occasionally there's one who'll make a great fuss about how he's been swindled.

The elderly are easy marks.

I don't bother to cancel these solicitations when I get them, in order to drive up the enemy's costs.

Tuesday, December 3

I had to attend yesterday's Christmas Claus party. Evert had promised to make a nuisance of himself for a couple of hours, and I felt obliged to step in and save him from himself. It wasn't easy.

He began by joining in the Santa Claus sing-along much too stridently and off-key, to glares of annoyance. Next he insisted that Santa Claus should invite Mrs. Van Til to sit on his lap, which the jolly old elf refused to do, and for which I can't blame him. Van Til weighs over two hundred pounds.

Within half an hour my friend had managed to swig four mugs of hot cocoa, generously spiked with the rum he had brought along, and slurped down big chunks of almond pastry he first dunked into the cocoa.

It would definitely have ended in a brawl if Mrs. Zonnevanck hadn't created a diversion by tripping over Black Pete's big sack and fracturing her arm.

It took half an hour for Mrs. Zonnevanck to be removed by ambulance and for the crowd to calm down again. Evert, sated after six cocoas, had nodded off in his wheelchair, and I was able to trundle him to his apartment. There I left him, wheelchair and all, securely wedged between his wardrobe and his bed so that he couldn't fall out, before heading back to my own room. There are limits to the caregiving mission.

The Christmas party in the lounge downstairs never really took off again. The question of whether or not Black Pete should be held responsible for the accident because he left his sack lying around put a damper on the festivities.

We don't have any Chinese residents in our nursing home, unfortunately, otherwise Evert would surely have cracked a few politically incorrect jokes in sympathy with Gordon, the judge on *Holland's Got Talent*, who really put his foot in it the other day when he told an Asian contestant his singing was "the best Chinese I've had in weeks—and I'm not talking about chow mein." We don't see much in the way of discrimination in here, since all the minorities living here are such nice people that no one has the nerve to say anything even slightly inappropriate.

A nation whose biggest gaffes are a joke about a Chinese singer and the desire to keep Black Pete looking black isn't half as odious as some people here maintain. Do I take offense when a brown, yellow, or black person calls me pale-face, cheese-head, or skinflint? No. Would I be offended if Santa Claus were black and all his Petes were foolish, thin-lipped white helpers with exaggerated Amsterdam accents? No. Is that because my great-grandfather was never a slave but a factory worker slogging away sixty hours a week for a pittance? No.

I've decided to be Santa Claus this year, and have bought some gifts for my friends. Namely: perfume for Eefje, gloves for Evert, a book about champagne for Ria and Antoine, a tear-off calendar for Grietje, a pool-instruction video for Edward, and a fold-out Nativity scene for Graeme.

I bought a pullover for myself. The sales lady thought it looked very hip on me.

This evening I'll wrap the presents in Christmas paper

and tomorrow I'll tiptoe from door to door spreading comfort and joy.

Thursday, December 5

The friendly cashier at the local supermarket didn't know what to do with a tip.

"That'll be twenty-four ten."

"Make it twenty-five even," Graeme said, handing over a fifty.

No, sorry, she couldn't do it. Her register wouldn't balance tonight.

Graeme patiently explained in that case she should have a tip jar next to her register. He was delighted with his own off-the-cuff joke. The grumpy man behind him was not. "Oh come *on*, I haven't got all day."

When he heard Graeme's story, Evert immediately came up with another idea: haggling.

"That'll be twenty-four ten."

"I'll give you eighteen euros for it."

"Huh?"

"Well then, fine, twenty, but I won't go any higher."

"Sir, you have to pay twenty-four ten."

"No, that's too much. Just forget it, then."

Upon which, Evert proposed, you should walk away, leaving the groceries on the conveyor belt. He's going to try it tomorrow. He hopes it will start a fad.

The first snow is on the way, says the weatherman. I don't like the winter. I wish I could hibernate and not wake up until the first days of March. It's a pity I'm such a light sleeper. I have enough trouble staying asleep for a full six hours. I would make a useless bear.

It's getting too cold to take the mobility scooter out for a ride. It means sitting still, so you're forced to wear so many layers you can hardly move. Still, the prospect of three whole months parked in a chair at the window waiting for the first crocuses to emerge doesn't thrill me either.

Friday, December 6

Nelson Mandela is dead. One of my last heroes. The man who never tumbled off his pedestal. All the world's leaders will gather to show their respect for Mandela, but few of them have learned anything from him.

My friends were pleasantly surprised yesterday, delighted with their presents. I had some difficulty convincing them I didn't expect anything in return. We live in much too much of a quid pro quo sort of world.

I told Eefje I had a present for her and then, after unwrapping it before her eyes, let her smell it. At the same time I realized that I didn't know if her sense of smell was still intact. But she nodded when I asked if she liked it. I dabbed a drop on her neck and one on her wrist, and rubbed it in. It was an intimate moment, and I'm not very good at intimate moments. I get clumsy. Most of the perfume went wide of the mark.

Luckily I could quickly pull out *The Solitude of Prime Numbers* and start reading to her. I've already asked her three times if this book is too sad for her. Her answer is always no.

Half an hour later I left her sleeping like an angel.

I went downstairs for a cup of pea soup. It went down great, but I had to listen to at least ten stories about mothers and grandmothers whose pea soup was *so* much better. The past, they're always going on about the past. Live in the present day for a change, you mummified nitwits!

Saturday, December 7

Emotions are running high about the goose population, and whether the nuisance they present justifies their being shot.

We have our own mother goose, who for the past ten years has been in the habit of trudging out to the store three times a week for half a loaf of white bread (she claims that geese don't like whole wheat). She has two slices for her own lunch, freezes two for the next day, and takes the remainder to feed the geese that have been dropping their poop in a nearby field all this time.

"If every Dutch province is to be allowed to decide for itself on a goose-shooting policy, isn't that terribly unfair to the geese? A goose has no idea what's in store for it, or in which part of the country it can or cannot be shot," says our goose woman.

After the insulted Chinese and endangered Black Pete, now we have the outlawed goose. How many major crises can this country be expected to withstand?

The inhabitants have been informed in a short letter that it is now official: the extensive renovations to this building are to begin in September. Not a word on the former pledge that the residents would have a say in the matter. The letter doesn't explain what exactly is involved either. You could not create more anxiety if you tried.

"I hope I'll be dead by then," said Mrs. Vergeer, and she meant it too.

"You should never repot an old plant," said Mr. Apotheker. He must have repeated it at least five times. What an old whiner. If they're thinking of repotting him, let them plant him head down.

Sunday, December 8

I had left the book in my room and asked Eefje, in jest really, if she'd like me to read from the newspaper for a change. She just nodded, the way she always nods when I ask a question.

I suddenly wondered if there was far less going on inside her head than I have been assuming. Who knows, maybe she is in a sedated stupor, calm and serene. Or maybe she is silently screaming. I have no idea.

I read to her, I put on music for her, and tell myself she appreciates it. It can't do any harm, anyway, and at least it makes me feel good.

Talking about the newspaper: "Could someone pass me the paper?" Mr. Bakker demanded last week in the Conversation Lounge. Evert, rummaging in the rack, pulled out one that was a week old. Bakker never noticed! When Evert casually asked half an hour later if the news didn't seem a bit familiar to him, Bakker blew a gasket. Not at himself, which I suppose would have been reasonable, but at Evert. Which delighted my friend, of course. We do enjoy seeing Bakker fly into a rage.

Monday, December 9

Grietje and I went online and perused the website Alzheimer Experience. It's an interactive site that shows the progress of the disease in an old woman and an old man in a few short videos. You can switch from the patient's point of view to that of the caregiver. You can also click on a doctor in a reassuring white coat who'll give you a professional explanation.

It gave me the heebie-jeebies to watch those videos with Grietje sitting next to me, but Grietje herself was quite relaxed. She sat there looking with interest at what was going to happen to her in six months to a year.

The last video was about the funeral.

I didn't know what to say.

"Come on, Henk, don't look so gloomy. You should be thinking, If she doesn't mind, why should I? Anyway, Alzheimer's is very hip these days. You can't open a magazine without stumbling across a mention of it. Adelheid Roosen has written a play about her mother's dementia, Jan Pronk talks about his demented mother on YouTube,

Maria van der Hoeven described her husband's decline in *de Volkskrant*. If you don't have anyone close to you with Alzheimer's, you're just not with it. You ought to be grateful you have me!"

I gave her a round of applause.

Tonight she's taking me out to dinner.

Tuesday, December 10

It seems that *Old Sore* is already taken as a book title. It's a book by Ellen Pasman about the *Willem Oltmans v. the Netherlands* court case. If my diary is ever published, it can't be called *Old Sore*.

I have come up with the following alternatives:

1. Down the Drain
2. The Living End
3. Over and Out
4. Not the Bee's Knees
5. The Last Hurrah
6. Smoke Signals in a Hurricane (Sounds good but doesn't really apply here)
7. Flies on the Caviar (ditto)

Yesterday Grietje and I had dinner at Stork, a hip fish restaurant on the banks of the IJ. The trend of using old factory buildings as restaurants is something I have yet to get used to, but the food was good and the people were nice.

We took the minibus out and a taxi home. Grietje insisted on paying for all of it. "I have seven thousand euros left to spend before I no longer know what money is for."

In just a few months, Grietje has grown far more open and direct. As if Alzheimer's were having a liberating effect on her. She hopes to be able to come along on the wine trip in the spring without being too much of a nuisance for the rest of us. At first glance she seems to have everything under control, but if you pay close attention you notice the regression. She had trouble finding her way back to our table from the bathroom, for example. And when we went out to the taxi she tried to get into the driver's seat—the driver was having a cigarette on the sidewalk. The man thought she was criticizing him.

Wednesday, December 11

Eefje is slowly fading away. She is losing more and more weight and sleeps practically the entire day. Every so often she'll wake up for a bit. I still read to her and let her listen to music, but her nods of approval are getting fainter and fainter. She seems to be sinking slowly into death.

I sit next to her and hold her hand. Sometimes I'll caress her old cheeks. Very occasionally she'll look at me as if recognizing something.

The doctor says it could still take a week or a month, two months even.

In a fit of rebellion I have put up a Christmas tree in my room, which is against the rules. Even though my Christmas tree is only eighteen inches tall, angel at the top included, it isn't allowed—a fire hazard. I smuggled it inside on my scooter, in a trash bag.

I am curious to see if anyone will give me away, and if so, who.

Thursday, December 12

This morning Mrs. Tan accosted me in the Conversation Lounge. "Are these the right pills?" she asked, waving a little bottle in my face. I said I was sorry but that I couldn't tell one pill from another.

"I can't either," she said, "but my other pills are finished and these are the same color."

I called for a nurse, which sent Mrs. Tan into a huff.

In order to prevent squabbles, a weekly TV schedule is sent down from on high telling the residents which channel is to be watched on what day. Soccer receives precedence over all other programs. When the national team or Ajax are playing, you can count on finding a big group assembled in front of the TV. They're not necessarily all soccer fans; there are people who watch the TV downstairs no matter what's on, so there are some who are completely ignorant about the game.

Mrs. Sluys, for example, only comments whenever a player spits on the ground. "Why do they have to spit so much?" she says every time, baffled.

"Yes, now, with pool there's far less of that," said Evert.

Friday, December 13

Friday the thirteenth, a good day to buy a lottery ticket. One always has to have something to hope for. If I win the jackpot, I'm buying a small, private, old-age home for myself and my friends. It won't have a director, an orderly, or a board of directors. No human-resources manager, accountant, or head of housekeeping. No rules, regulations, or interdictions. That will save buckets of money and a lot of red tape. What there will be room for is common sense, friendly staff, and a good cook who's always on call, in case we don't feel like preparing our own meals in our well-equipped kitchen. A home with spacious, light-filled rooms where you can keep your cat, dog, or Christmas tree if you are so inclined.

How simple is that?

Keep dreaming, Hendrik.

Today I received by express mail a letter of "nontransferable original documents," plus a secure envelope for cashing in my €7,450 check and placing my papaya capsule order.

Saturday, December 14

The fish in the fourth-floor aquarium are all dead. This time there was no tell-tale sign of crumbs. I stopped in at Evert's just to double-check, and asked if perhaps he had poured some Drano in this time, but he swore he knew nothing about it.

It may just have been some kind of fatal fish epidemic, although nobody will believe that, given the previous two aquarium genocides.

We are informed that "Management is conducting a thorough investigation, and is awaiting the report from the veterinarian." I suppose performing an autopsy on a neon tetra is easier said than done.

This time the police were left out of it. That does show a learning curve on the director's part.

I found an invitation that had been slipped under my door. It is for a Christmas dinner *chez* Evert, organized by Ria and Antoine. Our whole club is invited, minus Eefje. It's going to be a bit of a squeeze in Evert's cramped apartment, and Mo will have to be put outside so that his farts won't spoil our appetites, but it's something to look forward to. Evert's place was chosen because it's a retirement apartment, where cooking is allowed. The feast is scheduled for Christmas Day, coinciding, not really by accident, with the home's traditional Christmas dinner. It gives us a good excuse not to attend.

Sunday, December 15

Our proposed truancy from the official Christmas dinner has not been received kindly. Last night the cook came out while we were eating our puddings to demand, in front of all the other residents, if his cooking wasn't good enough for us or something. I was rather dumbfounded.

"What do you mean?"

"Well, because you prefer not to join us for dinner."

"We are having dinner *en petit comité*," said Antoine.

"On petit comitay?"

"That means in intimate company."

"What's wrong with *our* company?" Mr. Bakker yelled immediately.

"Nothing."

"Well then!"

This new cook takes everything rather personally. If someone leaves so much as one potato on their plate, he likes to storm into the dining room to chew the miscreant out. He has pride in his profession; he just can't cook, which is a distinct disadvantage for a cook. Perhaps, in my drive for complete candor, I should have told him that, but it didn't feel like the right moment. I could have had a knife plunged into my ribs. And, in the immortal words of Karel van het Reve: "I hate being stabbed to death." The atmosphere is hostile enough already. People were muttering darkly about the fact that they weren't considered fun to be with. I didn't think it was the right moment to tell them to look in the mirror.

Monday, December 16

People were giving me pitying glances; ah, look at the old man on his little buggy in the pouring rain. But I was having a grand old time. I had been waiting for a good downpour to try out my new rain gear. It isn't as waterproof as promised on the package—it leaks a bit at the seams. But fine, no whining, just keep your eyes on the road.

After about an hour I wheeled into the lobby, drenched to the skin. The orderly looked furious because of the trail of mud behind me, and he's the one who has to keep the entrance hall clean. I gave him an extra-friendly nod.

In this weather you mustn't forget to load up your battery before setting off. If you run out of power on the way, and nobody shows up to rescue you in time, you'll die of hypothermia. On a Sunday afternoon in December, many parts of North Amsterdam are completely deserted. And if anyone does come along, the question is whether he'll stop for an old man on a mobility scooter desperately signaling to him, or just give a friendly wave and continue on his way. I always take my cell phone, just in case. I don't know if the AAA comes out for a motorized chair.

After my rain-soaked ride I stopped at Evert's for a glass of brandy. It wound up being three. Then we ordered a pizza. The pizza *quattro stagioni* had been sitting in its cardboard box for a pretty long time. Even Mo found it tough to chew.

Back in my own room I had just enough energy left to fall asleep in front of the TV.

Tuesday, December 17

"You may as well stop reading to her. I don't think Mrs. Brand can hear you anymore."

Eefje rarely opens her eyes now and barely reacts, so the nurse may be right. But viscerally, I think, she might draw some vague solace from the voice at her bedside. And as long as I'm sitting there twice a day, I might as well read a good book to her or let her listen to some music. If it doesn't give her any comfort or peace, then at least it consoles me a bit. You can't read aloud and fret at the same time.

I have also just started reading a new book: *Your Money or Your Life*. It's about five old geezers in a nursing home who decide to rob a bank. So far I think it's a good book, with recognizable protagonists.

Old is in. At least, there seem to be films, books, documentaries, and newspaper articles galore about old people. We don't notice all the extra attention having very much effect on our daily lives; on the contrary, there is less money for us and less care than there were a few years ago.

The next generation of pensioners is starting to get nervous, now that they see their fathers and mothers growing lonely and isolated or already in their graves. The rich and influential sixty-year-olds of today certainly don't see themselves wasting away in a place like this.

Wednesday, December 18

Mr. Tolhuizen took the minibus to visit his son in Geuzenveld. Quite an undertaking for a man of ninety-three. On the way back the thoughtful driver helped him climb into the bus. He found a seat in the back, since there were already six old folks sitting in the front seats.

It was a long trip, via Bijlmer and South Amsterdam, and Mr. Tolhuizen grew a bit sleepy because the driver had turned up the heat to seventy-three degrees for the sake of the old people. Mr. Tolhuizen must have nodded off at some point.

When he woke up, he was slumped low in his seat. It

took awhile for him to realize where he was. It was silent and dark. The engine wasn't running, and he was alone. The minibus was parked in a quiet lane in Koog aan de Zaan, and the doors were locked.

It took half an hour for Tolhuizen to catch the attention of a passer-by, and then another fifteen minutes before the police breezed along. Within thirty seconds they jimmied open the door.

It took twenty minutes for the driver to be located. He came running over, terribly upset, in his slippers. He kept saying again and again how sorry he was, all the way home.

"I started to feel sorry for him," said Tolhuizen, a man who had never been the object of so much attention.

Thursday, December 19

Mrs. Trock ("I'm ever such an *eggsellent* speller") thought she'd give the televised national spelling bee, *The Grand Dictation of the Dutch Language*, a try. She had thirty-seven errors. And that was just in the first sentence. Then she urgently needed to go to the bathroom. She was about to take her sheet with her, but Graeme stopped her. "I'll keep it here for you, if you like." The other four participants gave up after the first read-through.

I myself am too chicken to give it a try.

Mr. Tolhuizen was informed over the phone by the Connexxion minibus representative that the driver who left him on the bus had been fired on the spot.

Tolhuizen protested that it was his own fault, he'd ducked out of sight and had then fallen asleep. He said he wanted to speak to the driver, but Connexxion refused to give him his phone number.

"He was such a nice fellow. He couldn't count, that's all, but is that a reason to fire someone?"

In the end he did manage to find out the man's phone number, and called to tell him he was prepared to declare under oath that he'd hidden himself on purpose.

"People are so ready to jump to conclusions, when sometimes it's just an unfortunate set of circumstances."

Hats off to Tolhuizen.

Friday, December 20

Eefje is slowly, gently, slipping into death. She no longer opens her eyes. And the only sign of life is that she's still breathing. I have stopped reading to her. I visit every day to say hello and hold her hand.

We've had so little time together.

I never told her I am crazy about her.

Saturday, December 21

"If there's anyone in here who's against diarrhea, it's me," said Mr. Bakker. "I have the trots at least three times a week. But I certainly don't need anyone to start a fundraiser for me."

Some residents thought the week-long campaign on the

radio against world childhood diarrhea was pure nonsense.

"Why can't they just send a few truckloads of Imodium over there? It doesn't have to cost ten million, surely?" opined Mrs. Pot, who on an annual basis swallows at least a thousand euros' worth of pills herself.

Today I visited Grietje in her room. She had a nice Nativity display on the table, but I couldn't help noticing that the baby Jesus was swarming with flies.

"Yes, I'd noticed that too," she said.

The fruit-fly trail led to two rotten bananas hidden behind the crib.

"Oh, I've been looking for those everywhere!"

She had spent days trying to find the bananas, because she'd checked them off on her shopping list, but had finally given up hope of locating them before they spoiled. We had a good laugh about it, and she cleaned up the mess. Hopefully the flies will leave of their own accord. Now Jesus knows what it's like to be a poor African baby.

Grietje is slowly and almost imperceptibly going downhill. But: "Every fine day is one more day," she says.

Sunday, December 22

Preparations for the Old But Not Dead Christmas Day dinner are in full swing. On Boxing Day we'll join the other residents down in the dining room. Although even that was far from simple.

"So I assumed that you wouldn't come on Boxing Day either," said the cook, waving the meal-plan form I'd filled out.

"On what do you base that *So*?" I asked.

He needed some time to think about that. "What do you mean?"

"Well, you said 'So' we wouldn't come for Boxing Day either."

"Oh, that."

"Yes, and so?"

He was completely confused. "So...you *are* coming, then?"

As the scribe in charge of writing the Christmas Day menus, I'm the only one who knows what we're having to eat.

I am looking forward to my first stuffed turkey. It's *the* Christmas dish they always have in movies and books, but I have never seen one of those giant chickens carried to the table myself. With Ria and Antoine as chefs, you can be sure *that* turkey won't have died in vain.

I am also struck by the come-back of the fondue. A few years ago it was definitely passé, but these past weeks the supermarket shelves have been groaning with ready-to-cook meat-fondue packages. (Won't they spoil?)

We had fondue bourguignonne in here once, a couple of years ago. The damage: several first- and second-degree burns, a number of dresses and suits to the cleaner's, one singed wig, charred meat, and two staff members who finally blew their tops. A complete shambles!

It must be the devil's work: our most obese resident, who loved to eat—nay, to stuff herself silly—just passed away, two days before the culinary high point of the year. She weighed 350 pounds, a bit on the heavy side for some-one her height (four foot nine), wouldn't you think? She couldn't help it; she had Prader-Willi syndrome. She did nonetheless reach the surprisingly ripe old age of seventy-eight. Permanently parked in her custom-sized wheelchair for almost ten years, she occupied herself with just a single activity: gorging herself. Besides that, there was nothing very human about her. She had no friends. It must have been quite a job for the nursing staff to keep that huge tub of lard, with all her rolls and creases, reasonably clean. The undertaker will have to have a coffin specially made for her, in the shape of a cube, I imagine.

Forgive me, I'm being a bit crude and rude about this, but I can't make the reality prettier than it is: sad, grim, and funny all at once.

I had a surprise visit from the head of housekeeping. She had been informed that I have a real Christmas tree in my room, which is against the rules. She was prepared to turn a blind eye this year, however. Hmm, how very tolerant of her!

She wouldn't tell me who had "informed" her of it.

Tuesday, December 24

I am fasting today so that tomorrow I'll have a good appetite.

My best suit is hanging next to a freshly ironed shirt and the gold bow tie I once bought in a party store long ago. My shoes have been polished.

I'm still quite dashing for my age, if I may say so myself. Vanity is forever.

All the menu cards have to be rewritten on account of one or two unfortunate mistakes in the French names. Antoine tactfully pointed them out to me. I must also polish up my after-dinner speech a bit. Busy, busy, busy. I won't have time for my daily drive.

At teatime yesterday I asked around and found out that some of the residents have not set foot outside since October. They remain indoors for most of the autumn and the entire winter, unless there's an urgent reason to venture out. And then it's usually limited to shuffling to the minibus or an offspring's car and back again.

I like to get good and drenched sometimes, and to let the wind tousle my few remaining hairs. I've had more than enough occasion to do so these past few weeks. No sign yet of the severe winter they've been predicting.

Wednesday, December 25

This morning I popped in to see Eefje and to wish her a merry Christmas. Standing at her bedside, it occurred to me there wasn't much left to wish for. A pleasant voyage, perhaps.

She looked so peaceful lying there, thin and pale, yet dignified and lovely.

The nurse said it probably won't be long now.

Then I felt compelled to go to Evert's, to take my mind off Eefje. Before I had a chance to open my mouth, he said, "Ah, your pretty old sweetheart—it's close, is it? Let her have her peace."

Then he poured me a cup of coffee, offered me a chocolate, and glanced at the clock. It was twenty-past twelve.

"Now that's good timing," he said. "On holidays I don't drink before twelve o'clock." He poured us each a small extra-special Christmas brandy.

"Cheers to you, my very dear friend."

Then I went back to my room to get my feelings off my chest by writing this down. I'll try to take a little nap, then get changed and plaster down my hair, and at four I am expected back at Evert's for Christmas dinner. I can't wait.

Thursday, December 26

The Christmas dinner was splendid. Ria and Antoine shuffling into the darkened room bearing an enormous turkey with three sparklers in its bottom, Evert helping his own lap to a big slice of tiramisu when dessert was served, and, if I may say so myself, my after-dinner speech wasn't bad either. It was about friendship as the essential ingredient for a good life. It may have been a bit on the sentimental side (Antoine dabbed away a tear) but it came straight from the heart. We raised a glass to Eefje, "the silent heart of our club, tragically *too* silent now." Then we drank to friendship, until death do us part. Not an abstract concept for any of us.

After dinner the chefs were given a standing ovation.

Our Boxing Day dinner is at one o'clock today, when we'll join those residents whose children haven't picked them up to spend the day with them. The timing gave rise to some sighs from people who hate to be put off their schedule, not even for the birth of their Savior.

We'll have to listen to at least a few grumbles in the order of, "I'm not that fond of a hot dinner at lunch," or some variant thereof.

In an hour or so I'll go downstairs, determined not to let myself be irritated. By anybody.

Friday, December 27

Christmas dinner number two did not disappoint. The staff had put out place cards, because last year there was a bit of a skirmish over who should sit where, a number of residents having staked out a place for themselves early in the day by leaving a purse on "their" chair. At least they hadn't taped it off with a NO TRESPASSING sign.

I discovered that I'd been seated next to Evert. I bet they didn't dare put anyone else next to him. Grietje and Edward were also at our table, and the Eversen sisters, who find everything delicious, lovely, wonderful, and fantastic, so you can't go wrong.

The cook had outdone himself and instead of the old pork tenderloin in cream sauce, he served up a wild game ragout over rice. Quite a daring move. In order not to shock us too much, it was shrimp cocktail for the appetizer and vanilla ice cream with hot chocolate sauce for dessert.

It was delicious and quite convivial.

Even Mrs. Stelwagen's speech was excellent—that is, mercifully brief. If you aren't a gifted speaker, the least you can do is follow one rule: keep it short.

It's a rule that is often forgotten, especially at funerals. "I'll never forget the first time I met Piet, it was at a meeting of the Flying Rats, the pigeon-fanciers' club, and he said to me, 'Jan,' he said, 'won't you...' " Whenever someone starts off that way, you know you're in for a snooze, and that it's going to be mainly about the speaker himself.

Saturday, December 28

At Evert's suggestion, we are moving New Year's Eve forward by two hours, because he says he'll never make it to midnight. Nobody raised any objection. We'll simply set the clock ahead two hours. We're celebrating it at Ria and Antoine's.

On New Year's Eve old people are just like dogs: they're too scared to go outside because they're terrified of the fireworks. Not wholly without cause. There are quite a few hooligans in this neighborhood who have it in for dogs and old people. One Canta had a firecracker tossed under the wheels; the blast caused it to veer off the road and plough into a fence. Luckily the damage was limited to a dent or two. For the rest of his life the owner never dared to take his vehicle out on the road again in December. The intrepid delinquents immediately took to their heels. The police took firm action: they made one extra round of the neighborhood. That should teach those miscreants a lesson.

Although the victim wasn't one of ours, there was great indignation about it in here.

The newspaper has published a list of famous Dutch citizens who died in 2013. There were a couple that I had missed.

The deceased are a favorite subject of discussion among the elderly. Perhaps it's to remind themselves that they are still alive.

Sunday, December 29

Eefje is dead.

At eleven o'clock last night I kissed her on her wrinkled forehead and whispered, "See you in the morning."

She drifted off peacefully an hour later.

I just went to look at her. She still looked so beautiful.

I wish I could be happy for her, but I'm too sad for that right now.

We are starting 2014 with a funeral. Unhappy new year.

We're not canceling our club's New Year's Eve party, although it will be a lot less fun than we had anticipated. The sanctioned festivities for the residents here are never called off either; with so many extremely old patrons, management can't afford to cancel everything every time someone dies. There would be nothing but cancellations.

Ria and Antoine were just frying up a batch of New Year's doughnuts when they heard that Eefje had died. They thought doughnuts would be inappropriate, and decided to donate them to the Salvation Army. Later they regretted their decision, and now they've made another batch for tomorrow night.

"It was best for her."

You can say it a hundred times, but it doesn't make a dent in the grief.

We have ordered red roses for Eefje. The funeral is Thursday afternoon. I hope the sun shines for it.

Eefje was a night person, and would have loved an evening burial, with Chinese lanterns and torches and everything. Apparently that can't be arranged.

Afterward we'll gather at Evert's for a glass of white wine and croquettes. Eefje hated cake; or the cake served at funerals, anyway. Or tossed into fish tanks, presumably. I never did get up the nerve to tell her the story of the cake in the aquarium.

Tuesday, December 31

This is the last time I'll write in this diary. Funny idea. It has grown to be part of the daily routine, like dinner. Sometimes you look forward to it, sometimes you don't have any appetite, but you wouldn't ever dream of skipping it altogether.

Without Eefje and without the diary, I will have time on my hands. Maybe I'll have to write a novel.

It could have been a very good year, and for part of it, it was. But what happens last skews the final verdict. I met someone I wish I had met half a century ago. Now I'll just have to make do with nine wonderful months followed by two very sad ones. I must try to be thankful for every happy day, as Grietje is, and I *am* trying with all my might, but sometimes I'm just not mighty enough.

I won't let the new year slip through my fingers. On to spring! And then: on to the wine country! Trembling with fear and trepidation to see if we'll make it. We have the trembling part covered, at any rate.

The Old But Not Dead Club must stand by its name, or else it's a club of nothing.

And after that trip, I'll have to come up with another plan. As long as there are plans, there's life.

This afternoon I will go out and buy a new diary.